A Little Blue Jacket

A Little Blue Jacket

LUCY ANN WHITE

L
LIBERTY
BOOKS

First published 2005
This paperback edition published 2007 by Liberty Books

ISBN 978 0 9551000 4 8

Typeset in Galliard by M Rules
Printed and bound in Great Britain by
Cox & Wyman Ltd, Reading, Berks

Liberty Books
8 Cromwell Road
Hove, East Sussex BN3 3EA

www.alittlebluejacket.com

To my daughter

Contents

Author's note

After I was born my father went to register my birth. He recorded the name my parents had chosen for me, as he had my brothers' before me. When my elderly grandmother was informed that she finally had a grand-daughter she was overjoyed. She subsequently arrived and, holding me in her arms for the first time, announced that she would have liked me to have been given one of her names.

Consequently, at my christening my grandmother stood as my godmother and I was given the baptismal name of Lucy. She died one year later. Throughout my childhood I cherished the special bond that I felt had existed between my grandmother and myself. She was an extraordinary woman and was my inspiration for the character Ursula. Whilst the narrative and the characters in *A Little Blue Jacket* are a product of my imagination, the essence of the main events that occur in it happened to my grandmother.

Lucy Ann White is a landscape architect and writer. She is married with two children and now lives in Kent, England.

Although based on true events, this is a work of fiction and the characters portrayed in it are solely the creation of the author. Any resemblance to actual persons with the exception of historical figures mentioned by name is entirely coincidental. Some dates of actual events have been manipulated or adjusted to serve fictional purposes.

PART I

The nursery
Johannesburg, February 3rd, 1912

It was hot. Although screens covered the open windows flies still flew about the hushed room, settling only for seconds on the dark furniture before resuming their wandering drone through the heavy air. The light that filtered through the ornate wooden screens traced filigree patterns on the highly polished floor and doilies of lace on the smooth, silken wood of the table. Like a mute *corps de ballet*, dust motes skittered in the shafts of sunlight and fell obliquely across the foot of the cot and the baby that lay so still in it, as silent as they.

Beside the cot a small truckle bed was set up and on the table next to it stood a white china jug covered with a crocheted cotton square, its corners weighted with green glass beads, to keep the dust and flies off. Ursula, swinging her legs over the side of the bed, lifted the cloth and poured a small glass of lemonade. The liquid was tepid but nevertheless refreshed her and she sipped it slowly, thoughtfully, as she sat at her vigil. Her eyes never left the cot.

Did the baby stir?
Ursula was at once alert – watchful and tense. But it was no more than a change so slight that after a minute she wondered if she had imagined it. Inching forward to the very edge of the bed, hampered by her long straight skirt, she bent her head over the

lowered side of the cot. Her knees pressed into the iron spindles. She welcomed the discomfort for it helped her concentration. The baby was so quiet that she could not be sure he was breathing. Not for the first time that morning she rose, hung over the cot and, holding her hair out of the way, turned her head on one side and placed her ear as close as she was able to the baby's face. She could hear nothing and held her breath. Raising her head, she extended her index finger under the baby's nose and felt the slightest warmth spread along it. Her neck muscles lost their rigidity, her shoulders dropped and the pain in her chest eased.

A dozen times in her head Ursula had gone over the events of the previous day – it seemed like days ago to her now – in case she had missed something crucial. The grizzling, the sudden temperature, the rash spreading over his skin and the vomiting that followed it had all been so quick. She had examined every inch of Edward to see if there was any sign of a bite; had a spider, a snake, a scorpion caused it perhaps? No tell-tale marks could be found. Or was it water? Endless diseases were caused by polluted water. Joseph had been called from the garden and, trusting to fast Zulu feet, sent to fetch the doctor. But the doctor was not at home. Within two hours the baby was a rag doll in her arms. She had kept him cool with wet lawn cloths but there was no improvement.

The unexpected and violent symptoms had been confusing and her inability to bring about any improvement agonizing. Distraught – but aware that she had to remain calm for the baby's sake – Ursula held on to her sanity during those first few hours by clenching every muscle and locking every joint in her body. When the doctor finally arrived he gave her little hope. The baby had cerebrospinal meningitis; he might wake from his coma but it was a slim chance. Shocked, Ursula vowed to stay as close as she could, never to leave Edward's side – she would will him to live with every mental force at her command.

But it had been twenty-four hours now and she was so tired. Soon she would have to ask Lizzie to leave her jobs in the kitchen and watch over the baby whilst she went to bathe. Ursula looked down at the baby and finally let her tears fall unchecked. He was lying unusually still, lips pouting, long lashes resting on rounded cheeks. Dimpled limbs, tiny fingers curved like petals, soft feet with their perfect toes – all reminded her of the flawless beauty of a little white alabaster putti that stood on her dressing chest. Suddenly scared by her image of him as a cold lifeless figure and desperate for her baby to recover, she closed her eyes and prayed for the first time in two years.

Oh God, I can't survive another calamity but it's not for myself that I ask.

Please God, he's an innocent baby and his life's so precious. Please God, please, make him better. If it's because of something I've done in the past, I'll make amends, I promise. I'll forgive Jessie – anything. Just help him get well again.

One

Alas! they had been friends in youth;
But whispering tongues can poison truth;
And constancy lives in realms above;
And life is thorny; and youth is vain;
And to be wroth with one we love
Doth work like madness in the brain.

Christabel (1797)
Samuel Taylor Coleridge 1772–1834

It was through Jessie that Ursula first met David. On a fine Saturday morning in late May, when the autumn sun shone and there was no sign of rain, Ursula and Jessie called into the tobacconist off Greenmarket Square. When they first opened the shop door a man was lounging with his elbow on the counter – one hand in his trouser pocket and his feet crossed – talking to the lady behind it. The woman, who had been leaning towards him, immediately straightened up and, flustered, smoothed her apron as she turned towards them. Directing a final remark to her – a remark that turned her pretty face pink – the man also turned his head towards the door. His features were lively but as Jessie and Ursula walked through the dimly lit shop towards the counter his expression became more thoughtful and he slowly straightened up.

"Good morning, Frau Hofmeyr," said Jessie, fixing the woman with a direct look. "No news of your husband yet?"

"*Ne,*" the young shopkeeper replied quietly, her face turning a deeper pink.

"I'm sorry to hear that," replied Jessie with a sugary smile.

"Just my usual then please, Frau Hofmeyr," she continued, nodding at the young man as she spoke.

As the shopkeeper turned to find the cigarettes the young man inclined his head in return, "Good morning Jessie, how are you?"

"Very well, thank you David," she replied, touching her hat and then her collar in an unconscious gesture.

"Are you and your friend on your way somewhere?" he asked with interest, glancing past her towards Ursula.

"No – nowhere special that is – we're working this afternoon."

"At the theatre?"

"It's the matinée of a new show," said Jessie leaning towards him confidentially. "You must come one night in the week, it should be good."

Ursula wondered who he was; a new face in Cape Town was always a matter of speculation but to young women that of a young man was especially interesting. Left out of the conversation, she looked as casually as she could at the gleaming glass jars and tins painted with gilded numerals that were lined up on the shelves covering the dark walls, until such time as Jessie might introduce them. But looking at David from the corner of her eye, she sized him up: average height, slim, dark haired, fair skinned; a *rooineck* – the English accent confirmed it.

"You work together do you?" he asked Jessie.

"Only some of the time," she replied dismissively. "I usually hold the fort there on my own, as you know."

"And your friend," he asked slowly, more softly "where does she usually work?"

Ursula, expecting Jessie to introduce him now, looked up. David was looking directly at her and held her gaze – brown eyes deep enough to swim in.

"She works as a clerk in town – she's only a cloakroom assistant when we're busy," replied Jessie with a perceptibly impatient tone.

7

As no introduction by Jessie was forthcoming Ursula looked away.

"Which explains why we haven't met before," David persisted.

It was obvious to Ursula that he too hoped Jessie would introduce him but as she did not want to be embarrassed again, she studiedly looked down into the glass-topped counters filled with cigars and cigarillos, pipes and tobacco pouches.

"No, that's right," said Jessie shortly, as she rifled through her purse and placed several coins on the counter.

"There we are, Frau Hofmeyr," she continued, picking up her neatly wrapped purchase and her gloves, "good-day to you. I do hope your husband returns soon," she finished, pointedly.

"Please forgive me," said David, looking at Jessie and putting his hand to his heart in an attitude of sincerity, "but perhaps you'd be kind . . ."

"I'm afraid we must be off David," interrupted Jessie, briskly. "Love to natter but the *Baas* is a stickler for time. Still, perhaps I'll see you at the theatre next week? Don't forget," she said smiling at him encouragingly. Placing her hand in the small of Ursula's back Jessie steered her toward the door, "Come on Ursula, we haven't time to waste."

Behind her Ursula heard David wish the tobacconist good-day.

"One moment, I've finished too, let me get the door for you," he said, nimbly passing them.

He held the door open for them and followed them through. They turned to thank him, he bowed and smiled; the girls turned to the right and he to the left.

As soon as they were out of earshot Ursula said, "You didn't introduce him when I was expecting you to, Jess. It would have been civil because I couldn't avoid hearing your conversation and I felt a real gooseberry."

"Oh, did you," replied Jessie, offhandedly. "Well, you might not meet again and, still, it wasn't really the time or place was it."

Ursula was about to reply but stopped; it was pointless remonstrating further. Criticism rarely bothered Jessie, nor did it ever seem to temper her behaviour. The identity and details of the young man were far more intriguing.

"Who is he anyway?" she asked instead.

"He comes into the theatre every few days," replied Jessie airily, "sees Abe about things. Then he comes to see me. I've had some interesting conversations with him."

However, apart from first name terms, it had not seemed to Ursula that David and Jessie were quite as well acquainted as she inferred. Ursula glanced over her shoulder across the square towards the Old City Hall to see if she could get another glimpse of the young man Jessie was trying to keep to herself, but she immediately turned back again. Taking Jessie's arm Ursula warned her not to look round and hurried her along without speaking, away from the square and around the next corner.

"Jessie, he was watching us!" she said, pulling Jessie to a halt as soon as they were out of sight. "He was holding his hat in front of him – look, like this, against his waistcoat with both hands – and walking backwards watching us. People had to dodge around him; he could have bumped into anyone, fallen over things."

Ursula's annoyance was wholly dispelled by seeing David act in such an unusual way. Jessie snorted at the information.

"Bit of a skirt-lover that one," she warned as they walked on at a more leisurely pace, adding matter-of-factly. "I expect he was just sizing us up."

"But what could he see from the back of us," asked Ursula at a loss, "only our hats surely."

Jessie laughed, "More likely looking at our behinds," she said audaciously.

"Jessie you are awful!" retorted Ursula, digging Jessie with her elbow, but hiding a smile.

Jessie sometimes said shocking things – and often said things that infuriated her – but Ursula knew that, for her, Jessie's irreverent attitude added a piquancy to their friendship. With other more reasonable friends (those with less spark to their character), Ursula occasionally found herself teasing them into a reaction; with Jessie the opposite was required.

That evening – just before the end of the show – Ursula had to retrieve several articles of lost property from under the coat stands at the rear of the cloakroom. When she returned she saw David talking to Jessie. Noticing Ursula he whispered in Jessie's ear before turning towards her, smiling broadly. Jessie shot her a withering look and introduced him, unenthusiastically.

"It feels as if we've already been introduced," said David, bowing slightly and extending his hand.

"Indeed," replied Ursula, inclining her head. She had no choice but to take the surprisingly proferred hand – she liked it, it was warm and dry with a very firm clasp.

"But here in a Cape Town theatre we shouldn't be bound by British conventions," he said, smiling. "Please call me David too."

She thought his informality refreshing, "And my name's Ursula."

"Have you worked in the exciting world of the stage for long?" he asked, still holding her hand.

"No," interjected Jessie, impatiently, "she only started a few months ago."

Ursula gently pulled her hand away; there had been no need for them to shake hands and her cheeks were beginning to warm because he had held it for an embarrassingly long time.

"And I've not long arrived from England," he said, still looking at Ursula, "so we've both made a new start."

"But yours is a much more *dramatic* one than mine," Ursula replied, smiling.

He laughed and Jessie tapped him on the arm, "We had a *really* funny lot over here from London last month – Music Hall – you would have loved them. You might even have seen them there."

"I didn't go to the theatre much in England."

"Still, you can come as often as you like here, it's not all music and plays you know," said Jessie, animatedly adding, "we've got all sorts of things lined up – performing monkeys, snake charmers, escape artists – you name it, we've got it. Abe's sure to let you have a ticket any night of the week it's not too busy; Tuesdays and Thursdays are the best – they're fairly quiet."

Whilst Jessie was talking a man came up holding out a ticket for his hat and Ursula went to collect it; as soon as she returned with the hat another man came to collect an overcoat. Have to get that too, thought Ursula, and this next one; Jessie's putting on her act and is never going to stop talking – hooked on those magnetic, dark eyes.

There was a crush of people as the show finished and Ursula, looking for Jessie to help her, received a wide smile from David and saw Jessie reluctantly rise and take a proffered ticket.

When the crowd thinned Ursula noticed that David had gone; the last coat was finally collected and Jessie flopped down on the stool.

"*Ag* man, I thought this afternoon was bad enough but this was even more of a rush. It's just as well you're here to help, before you worked here I hardly had time to sit down, let alone stop and chat to anyone."

"Still, you and David managed to have a pretty long conversation tonight," replied Ursula, remembering how long Jessie had actually sat down.

"Well, he's usually even chattier, but to tell you the truth he seemed a bit preoccupied tonight. I suppose it was you going backwards and forwards – makes it difficult for anyone to concentrate."

11

"All the same, you seemed to be getting along splendidly," Ursula said, angling to see if Jessie was smitten or if David had asked her out.

"*Ag* well, after your little flurry with those coats he disappeared. I expect he knew we'd get busy and he wouldn't be able to chat to me."

"Did he mention me?"

"He said you seemed . . . nice," said Jessie, grudgingly.

"He never spoke to me again, so he can't think I'm that nice," laughed Ursula.

"You never know with men," replied Jessie in a resigned voice "they can be very contrary creatures."

Ursula deduced from this remark that Jessie did not expect to make an easy conquest.

On the evenings that Ursula helped at the theatre (when it was impossible for her to travel home) she would stay with Jessie who lived on her own in some rooms on the top floor of a terrace of shops in Long Street. Every nationality traded in Long Street – amongst them a Greek grocer, a Portuguese ironmonger, a Polish draper – their shops lining the pavements; fresh vegetables, enamel buckets and rolls of material displayed outside on the cast-iron *stoeps*. The floors above with their tiers of decorative cast-iron balconies housed a variety of photographers' studios, architects' and lawyers' offices, various clubs and rooms for rent. And squeezed between the shops and commercial buildings, and the many hotels and boarding houses that existed in Long Street, were an eclectic mix of houses of worship: a mosque with its minaret, a plain fronted synagogue, a Lutheran church with a steeple. All existed amicably together against the impressive natural backdrop of Signal Hill and Lion's Head.

Jessie, who knew every tradesman by name, liked to recount the gossip of their daily lives to Ursula as they walked home.

Jessie's rooms were reached through the *boekwinkel* below – the dark shop walls lined with a wide variety of books on subjects of limited interest – up some steep and narrow stairs. The rooms were neither large nor smart but the view from her small high window – a church tower and the silhouette of Lion's Head against the sky – was as impressive as any from the most prestigious dwelling. Jessie had made the best of the rooms and the décor she had chosen was influenced by the theatrical milieu in which she had always worked.

The most unattractive pieces of furniture were draped with Indian shawls, their deep woollen fringes brushing the floor. A large throw thickly embroidered with flowers in lurid colours covered the bed and old ostrich feathers were tucked into the gaps around the wooden bedhead. An opened fan was mounted on the wall to disguise a large crack and the light from the lamps was softened by the addition of coloured chiffon scarves; the effect was very cheering and warm. A little room (more like a large walk-in cupboard) opened off the bedroom and in this was a deep stone sink and a wide shelf on which sat a small Primus stove; this scullery also served as Jessie's washroom. For more thorough ablutions Jessie relied on the Turkish baths and steam rooms around the corner.

On Saturdays the girls would buy little packets of foodstuffs – Fry's cocoa powder and *soet koekies* were favourites – and at the end of the evening they would dunk their cookies in their hot cocoa as they dissected the events of the day. That evening, after they had eaten their supper and brushed each other's hair, Jessie lay on the bed and Ursula curled up in the large armchair.

"I love your room, Jess, it's so cosy. But, tell me, don't you ever get lonely here all on your own?"

"If I get lonely I can always go home to Ma's."

"Why don't you live there anyway – I would if I had a family like you."

"*Ag* no man, you wouldn't," replied Jessie with feeling. "It's

13

not like the homes of our snooty school friends. And it's worse than when you used to visit in holidays; even though we have help Ma's always tired – too busy shouting at the young ones and trying to clean up and cook at the same time. The house is in chaos – laundry hanging everywhere, children crying and quarrelling – and sometimes worse. *Ne,*" she shook her head, "you'd prefer to live here alone like me if you had all that – even if you never saw a soul."

"Jessie, you're one of the most gregarious people I know. You'd go barmy if you never saw a soul," laughed Ursula.

"Still, you know what I mean."

"I don't know what you mean by 'sometimes worse'," said Ursula, remembering the remark with concern. "It sounds very mysterious, almost threatening. Have you trouble at home now?"

"Sometimes," admitted Jessie, unusually spare with her words.

"Is it too terrible to talk about?" asked Ursula gently.

"Not really, I suppose. I'm used to it. Most of our neighbours are in the same boat anyway," said Jessie in a long-suffering tone of voice. "Mrs Burger's husband was a *trekboer* – great brute of a man – but they ran into difficulties so they had to come back; after the war he could only get work as a *smous* here, trading anything he could get his hands on. Can't stand the shame of it and takes it out on her – every Saturday night."

"Oh!" gasped Ursula.

"And when my Pa's had a few drinks he gets very quarrelsome," said Jessie matter-of-factly. "When he goes over the top Ma and I have to hide the little ones; as the biggest left at home now he can't miss me and I have to make a run for it to avoid his fist."

Ursula was aghast, "That's horrid. Can't anyone reason with him."

"Not when he's that way."

"Poor Jessie, I can see why you prefer an independent life."

"Don't get me wrong," added Jessie stoutly, "I love my Ma and I'm very fond of the little ones but living with them is very wearing. I never get a minute's peace – always having to do something for someone else. They make much more fuss of me when they don't see me so often. So here I am, the only one I know who's her own mistress," she finished, smiling proudly at her unconventional status. "Bit of a black sheep don't you think?"

"No, a real Bohemian," said Ursula in admiration. "You even look like a gypsy; the mysterious way you narrow those hazel eyes of yours and all that curly black hair. It all makes my own life and home seem very tame and provincial."

Jessie did not disagree but raised her eyebrows pityingly and began to undo the string of her parcel and unwrap her purchase. Ursula lay back in the chair and closed her eyes.

She is handed out of the hansom cab by a young man with dark eyes – 'you were wonderful tonight' – her buff ostrich feather fan brushes against her cheek as she waves it in acknowledgement. A group of drunken gypsies clad in lurid colours, gesticulate from across the road and she hurries away up the steps to the front door. Her brother opens it and shouts to them to go away, to leave her alone. Inside all is neat and tidy and her sister is helping a tall dark haired woman with brows like the outstretched wings of a bird – her mother – with the mending. Her father, sitting on the stoep, reads his newspaper and calls to her – 'Ursula, take my shoes and fetch me my pipe, what a good girl you are.' And now mother, an Indian shawl around her shoulders, calls – 'Ursula, dearest, whilst I finish my sewing will you recite one of the poems you performed this evening.' The applause rings in her ears, encore, encore! The little ones come tumbling into the room and press into her – 'Ursula, sing to us . . .'

Ursula was jolted awake by Jessie prodding her with her foot, "Ursula! I've called you three times; you've been like a zombie."

"Sorry, I must have dozed off," she said, rubbing her eyelids with her fingertips.

"I wanted to know if you'd like to try my cigarette, it's another advantage of living on my own – no disapproving parents."

Ursula thought Jessie looked very worldly as she held the thin coloured cigarette between her fingers and – with head tipped back so that her curls billowed down to the mattress – exhaled a slim line of smoke up towards the ceiling.

"Come on, have a puff," continued Jessie, holding the pastel wand out.

Taking it carefully, Ursula put the gold paper tip to her lips and took a hesitant puff. Not knowing how to inhale, her mouth filled with smoke and she started to cough. Jessie laughed and retrieved the cigarette.

"Look, like this," she said, and drawing on it again she blew a perfect circle of smoke above her and smiled smugly at Ursula.

After all the years we've known each other, thought Ursula without surprise, Jessie never misses an opportunity to gloat. However, she would not let Jessie get the better of her again; I'll get the hang of it first, she thought.

"Perhaps another time," she replied, in an uninterested and even tone to convey that she was not bothered.

Sunday was Jessie's day off at the theatre and she and Ursula woke late and breakfasted on tea and toast in bed. After dressing – and spending too long doing each other's hair in some new style – they hurried along the cast iron *stoeps* of Long Street and cut across the Company's Gardens to attend the morning service at St Mary's Cathedral. Following the service they agreed that, as the weather was so pleasant, they would walk to the bay before deciding what they would do with the afternoon, and they turned towards *Groote Kerk* to walk down the wide expanse of

Adderley Street, hansom cabs lined up like skittles along its centre.

Cautiously, they walked out along the old central jetty that served the harbour of fishing boats – peering down into the sea between the wooden slats as they went – laughing as the wind blew their skirts out like open umbrellas. However, too blown by the wind to linger, the girls retraced their steps to Adderley Street and studied the advertisements that were displayed in the windows for something to do that afternoon. Most of what was on offer was discounted as tedious or unsuitable but a poster advertising a boxing match caught their attention,

"Danny Buchanan of Durban will fight David Lewis from London"

and there were two murky photographs.

"David's a boxer," said Jessie, pointing to one of the photographs, "that must be him."

"I thought you told me he did something else?" said Ursula peering closer.

"Well, he did in England but here he boxes for fun."

"For fun?" asked Ursula in disbelief.

"Well, not fun really," admitted Jessie "he says he loves it and wants to be a champion."

"I've always thought boxers were very big and beefy," said Ursula with a look of distaste.

"Only if they're heavyweights'" replied Jessie, knowledgeably.

"Oh. Well, that could be him," agreed Ursula tapping the picture of the slimmer of the two men with her finger.

"It *is* me," said a voice from behind them.

The girls started and turning round found David standing there, dressed in a tweed suit and looking very unlike the picture on the poster.

"Oh!" they both exclaimed in surprise, their eyes wide and

17

their hands flying up to their mouths as if their remarks had escaped in error, shamefaced at having been caught discussing him. David smiled.

"Please, come and have some tea with me," he said, and taking both their arms he swung them round and began walking across the road between them. "I know it's a little early but I need to eat and I can't leave it any later. The tea rooms over the shops may be closed, but I'm sure we'll find some here."

In their surprise and embarrassment Jessie and Ursula allowed themselves to be swept along and installed in the lounge of the Adderley Hotel without demur.

Two

He that wrestles with us strengthens our nerves,
and sharpens our skill. Our antagonist is our helper.
Reflections on the Revolution in France (1790)
Edmund Burke 1729–1797

David ordered a pot of tea and several portions of bread, butter and *konfyt*, and asked them where they had been.

"We've been for a walk," replied Jessie. "Just deciding what to do next when we saw your poster."

"And it says you're from London," added Ursula, "it must be such an exciting place, why did you come here?"

"London born and bred, but I wanted to travel. My uncle came to the Cape and my grandfather visited before him, so I thought I'd come and see for myself. They said this was the most beautiful country. Then I saw an advertisement for boxers to come out here and that settled it."

"And is it as you expected?" Ursula asked.

"Yes. Everything looks so green and fresh here that I'm not disappointed and I don't think I'll miss home too much," replied David with a smile. "If things don't work out as I've planned, I'm willing to try my hand at something else – farming, mining, anything."

"The Boers call it 'God's own country' because it's so beautiful and fertile," said Ursula, "and there's plenty to remind you of home, this part of the Cape's mostly British."

"Ah, but I don't want it to be too much like home," said

19

David, shaking his head. "The smog in London's choking and the opportunities for advancement are few and far between. I want something better."

"Don't get too carried away, we might not have smog but we've plenty of dust in the colonies," said Ursula rather dispiritedly. "And as for advancement – everyone's struggling to make their own way here too, what with droughts and strikes."

"But you also have gold prospecting and diamond mines and we don't have opportunities like that at home," David replied, with real enthusiasm in his voice. "And I've made a start."

"Boxing, you mean," volunteered Jessie.

"Yes, after all, it's my excuse for coming and it's what I'm best at. I've been in steady training since I got here and Abe's backing me. My trainer at the gymnasium has lined up a fight – we're not really matched but it's only three rounds – with more suitable things in the offing if that goes well."

"But you told me that your mother wasn't keen on all that," said Jessie suspiciously.

"Well I'm not in England now and she only had my interests at heart – she thought I should have some trade or qualification to fall back on, that's all," said David loyally, liberally spreading a slice of bread and butter with the watermelon jam. "But I love boxing, more than my other sports. I hate being stuck at a desk."

Frowning slightly, Jessie compressed her thin lips until they were barely visible, and started playing with a stray curl of her hair. Ursula knew well that this was the sign that Jessie had tired of a subject but Ursula knew nothing about boxing and was curious.

"Is boxing a proper sport or just something you do unofficially?" she asked.

"It's beginning to be recognized as a proper sport. It's been accepted now in the new Olympic Games."

Ursula was unimpressed. "Instead of hitting people for fun

you could put your fighting to serious use here," she suggested. "English men used to queue up to fight the Boers. The army's still looking for people like you."

David didn't answer immediately and then in a clipped voice said, "I don't hit people for fun, I compete with an equal. And they had 'people like me' – my uncle fought in the Cape many years ago. I've come here to make my way, not make war. Fighting to protect your homeland is understandable, but fighting over control of someone else's land . . ."

"But I was born here," interjected Ursula, sensing the criticism: no recent colonial she.

"Does that make it right?" challenged David. "There were people here before the Boers, before the British. They have a prior claim you know, this is their homeland."

Ursula was taken aback and felt uncomfortable. Living in Cape Town – far from the sieges of the North-west and the fighting in Natal – the war with the Afrikaners had not had a huge effect on her life. In a household without men, politics and war had not been chosen subjects for discussion. She had never questioned the reasons for the war but simply accepted it as something that was unavoidable, the unassailable right of the British.

"I've never thought about it," she said in defence, and immediately realized the weakness of her admission.

"You mean to say that you've never questioned the rightness of it?" asked David with a look of disbelief.

Ursula looked at David blankly then, as the import of his questions sank in, with embarrassment. She had always thought herself well educated; was she really woolly minded, she wondered. She firmly believed that the British Empire was great, and had done great things, but should she have questioned some of the actions taken in the name of British Imperialism; did it show a lack of enquiry, an absence of philosophical investigation that she hadn't? Did he think her a fool, did he think her a colonial without a conscience?

"I didn't know anyone fighting," she replied, stalling for time. "We couldn't miss all the soldiers arriving on the ships from England, of course, and obviously we saw them riding through town on the way to the Front . . . and naturally we knitted for the soldiers, and did volunteer work at the hospitals but . . ." Ursula faltered again and, as if to justify herself, added stoutly, "I mean, no one here ever wrote at the time that we shouldn't be fighting the Boers."

"Well I knew someone in the war – my uncle – he fought," interjected Jessie, "not that we ever had a letter from him, so I never thought about it too much. I was like you at the time, wasn't I, Ursula, we preferred to concentrate on pleasant things like the ladies' fashion pages and social news."

Ursula groaned inwardly and thought – now he will think us totally shallow. Perhaps she could draw a line under the subject.

"It's not an issue now anyway," she said firmly, "officially it was over a few years ago."

"And I suppose you thought it was a great victory?" said David, with a very stony expression. "In fact the war here was no picnic by all accounts, not in the slightest bit glorious – even women and children in concentration camps, some of them dying like the men – nothing like Mr Kipling chose to make out."

He held Ursula's gaze until she dropped her eyes – defeated, feeling foolish, unable to respond. Of course keeping the Boer women and children in camps had been brutal; she had read the outrage of some in England, she had sympathized. But it had been war. Now she felt she had accepted the glib reasons for the war and the unpalatable aspects of it all too readily. Ursula particularly disliked David's criticism because she instinctively felt the superiority of his views; here was someone who questioned the morality of the war – she had never heard anyone voice such radical ideas.

Jessie took advantage of the lull in their conversation.

"No, you're so right, David, it wasn't a picnic, absolutely not," she said heartily. "Mr Kipling and his rhymes and ballads and things! *Two Kopjes* and *Stellenbosh* for a start. They were everywhere – the lads sang them, and the Music Hall stars spouted them, and all the papers printed them. But when my Uncle Patrick was blown to pieces by Boer shellfire my Pa had plenty to say about the fighting and it was *definitely* not poetic."

She accompanied this observation with such an amusing shaking of her head and rolling of her eyes that it made them all smile – Ursula rather ruefully – and David visibly relaxed.

"I'm afraid it's all rather a sore subject with me," he said. "I'd rather talk about sport."

Ursula tried to remember what they had been discussing before her ill-advised remark – she did not enjoy feeling belittled and hoped to reassert herself.

"Even if boxing is a sport," she ventured, "it *is* still violent, isn't it?"

"Not if you're skilled," David replied in a reasonable tone. "The whole idea is to use a combination of speed and style to hit your opponent – an opponent as evenly matched as possible – but avoid getting hit yourself."

"But you must get hit sometimes. Why do you do something that hurts?" She hated pain herself and could not imagine anyone willingly subjecting themself to pain or choosing to inflict it.

"I don't think of that, I just love the thrill of it, the sheer physical action of it and if I'm hit hard enough to hurt I'm so involved I hardly notice."

He looked between them, his hands open and his shoulders lifted, as if inviting them to wonder at the magic of such a thing. Jessie raised her eyebrows, Ursula knit hers.

"Can you earn a living at it?" she asked, doubtfully.

"If you're really good, get some well-known opponents, have a proper manager and all that. Then you can turn professional and there's prize money," replied David, smiling encouragingly.

"But there can't be many famous boxers in the Cape."

"There have been," said David, looking at her steadily. "There was Barney Barnato – he was a successful boxer in England and then here before he made a fortune mining. Owned most of the mines at one time. I wouldn't mind being as successful as him, following in his footsteps."

But Ursula – still stung by David's criticism – spoke thoughtlessly.

"Well, you don't want much!" she said, the mockery of her words unmistakable.

David sighed loudly and his shoulders fell. But almost immediately he sat up very straight.

"There's nothing wrong with ambition is there. Have you no ambitions?" he replied staunchly. "Do you only think about trivial things – do you never consider larger issues? Don't you ever strive to make a worthwhile difference to someone else's life?"

"I, I . . ." Ursula stammered, unprepared for his questions and surprised at his forceful reaction.

"And then you work in a theatre – do you mean to say you've no desire to be a star of the stage?" he continued, fixing her with a very direct look. "No plans to make a success of your life, no dreams of being famous?"

Ursula, the heat rising in her face, did not reply. I shouldn't have laughed at his ambitions, she admonished herself. It came out all wrong – what a fool I am. And do I have ambitions – no, not ambitions as he has, not worthwhile, attainable ambitions. Not ideals. But I do have dreams.

Like many young women not admired for great beauty, Ursula was proud of the features she possessed that were noteworthy. Her graceful bearing and heavy amber-coloured hair, her long tapering fingers with their perfect almond-shaped nails, and her ability to dance well were such. And these attributes figured prominently in her dreams, the favourite versions of which now flashed before her. Silly, impossible dreams – she admitted to herself in those intense minutes of introspection – dreams that have no chance of coming true. Trivial dreams. With depressing clarity she realized that her aspirations as well as her views were quite lacking in substance, and it was a bitter blow to her pride.

Jessie had taken advantage of Ursula's silence and regaled David with her family's sporting activities, both the successes and the disasters. David was laughing, helping himself to bread and butter, obviously now quite at ease.

"And of course," said Jessie, "Ursula's never seen any boxing. She's led a very sheltered life."

Ursula heard her name mentioned, "But I'd like to," she said impulsively, hoping to appear bold and quash Jessie's remark.

"Come along tonight then," David said encouragingly, moving forward in his chair. "Ladies have been known to come and you can leave before it gets gory – we don't want maidens fainting all over the place," and he leant back and laughed wholeheartedly.

Ursula was tired of being ridiculed.

"All right, we will," she said unequivocally and gave Jessie a sharp kick under the table to make sure she did not disagree.

"Good," said David with approval as he rose to leave.

He bade them goodbye, saying he would leave tickets for them at the hall and, having eaten all the bread and jam, he left them to finish what tea remained in the pot.

"Oh dear, Jess," said Ursula with a sigh as soon as he was out of the door, "all I do is quiz some people. I don't mean to. I just want to know everything about them and I like to get to the point. And then it comes out wrong and people think I'm being critical and they don't react as I expect."

"Sparks," said Jessie very bluntly.

"Sparks – what do you mean?"

"My Ma says that if you put something sharp next to

something rough – just like a knife grinder does – you get sparks, that's what," replied Jessie pursing her lips.

Ursula was feeling crushed and wished that for once Jessie could be sympathetic, "Thank you Jessie, which one am I supposed to be, the rough one or the sharp one?"

"Frankly, you're just as bad as each other – neither of you would give up – put you together and sparks are sure to fly."

"I certainly caused some friction today," admitted Ursula despondently, "and he seems to be quite able to make his point. Perhaps we should be getting back."

Ursula was anxious to leave the hotel; the memory of her rash promise to go to the fight was beginning to make her feel uneasy. Why did I open my big mouth before I thought, she chided herself, now I shall have to go through with it. And it's my own stupid fault.

The Drill Hall, a building of some architectural merit, did not however look very promising to Ursula that night; there were too many men hanging about the doorway – hands in their pockets, cigarettes in their mouths and caps pushed to the back of their heads – to make her feel comfortable. Several of them were placing bets with a scrawny man near the door; he put the money they held out into his jacket pocket and then, after licking the tip of his pencil, wrote in a little notebook. Ursula gingerly pushed between them all and looked inside the hall from the doorway.

"There aren't any women in there," she said to Jessie who had followed her. "Perhaps we'd better not stay."

"But we're here now; it's a shame to go home."

"Are you the young ladies from the theatre?" asked an elderly man with rheumy eyes from inside the door. "'Cause I been asked to see you seated all right and give you these."

He held out two tickets at arm's length and Ursula was

obliged to take them. Without waiting for a response he said, "'Ere, follow me," his tortoise-like neck disappearing into his oversized jacket as he turned and led them to two chairs near the ring.

"Thank you, but this isn't really our sort of place," Ursula tried to explain as they followed him, "I mean, what if it gets rowdy. Jessie, do you really think we should?"

The old man stopped, the girls stopped; Jessie raised her eyebrows and shrugged. "Perhaps we could sit a bit nearer the door?" she suggested, looking at the old man, who stuck his bottom lip out and scowled. Shuffling away he motioned them to take two seats on the aisle near the door. When Jessie and Ursula had settled themselves Jessie turned to look about – quite unabashed by the stares that they encountered – and said to Ursula, "That's better, isn't it. The hall looks a bit different from how I remember it – I've only seen it full of raw recruits."

"I know this sounds unbelievable but I've not been in here before," said Ursula, resigned now to staying. "It's very plain – I thought it would look a bit more prepossessing for a boxing match than it does. The ring's only a little off the ground and the floor doesn't look very stable only supported by trestles like that. And those posts and ropes round it don't look very strong either, do they?"

"Just as well we aren't near it any more then. I must say that is rather motheaten bunting hanging around the walls and that banner," Jessie pointed to a large swathe of limp material with 'Isaacs Boxing Club' embroidered on it, "looks a bit sad, doesn't it?"

"Sssh, don't talk too loud. Those men over there reading their papers might hear us."

"You don't have to worry about them, they're marking the racing pages, the only thing they're interested in is form."

"Well I'm very glad there are one or two other women here now," said Ursula with relief.

"They look a bit rough though," said Jessie with disdain.

"But at least it doesn't make us look quite so conspicuous."

Just at that moment, the men from outside the hall rushed in and started jostling for seats. A large man in a waistcoat and shirtsleeves came through the door off to the side of the hall, followed by several others, and climbed into the ring.

"Good evening, gentlemen," the referee in the waistcoat boomed, his large moustache appearing to move quite independently from his mouth. "Beg pardon, *ladies* and gentlemen – I have much pleasure in introducing tonight that well-known boxing champion, and favourite of ours, Mr Danny Buchanan, who has come all the way from Durban."

Amidst loud applause Danny Buchanan stepped forward and raised his arm. The applause was then accompanied by much stamping of feet.

"And his opponent tonight will be young Mr David Lewis from London," continued the referee.

A rather thin round of polite applause greeted this announcement. Ursula looked hard at the men. Danny Buchanan was of indistinct age, stocky and very wide shouldered; his face was ruddy and his features battered. David was taller, but slimmer, and looked unblemished beside such an opponent.

The gong sounded and the men came into the centre of the ring. Ursula noticed that David's expressive face was now as fixed and immobile as a mask carved in mahogany. Whenever Danny made a jab at David the audience cheered, but if David ducked or deftly moved aside, they snorted. The body shots David inflicted on Danny seemed to have little effect on the larger man. David took several glancing blows to his arm and body himself but, as he was very fast on his feet, appeared to move back just enough to reduce their impact. Ursula was transfixed by David's physique – how his vest stretched taut as his chest expanded, the way the smooth skin of his biceps shone in the lamplight like highly buffed ironwood. When time was called she realized that she had inched forward to the edge of her seat and self-consciously rearranged herself.

"Well, what d'you think?" asked Jessie looking at Ursula closely.

"I don't know. It doesn't seem too bad. No one's crippled yet," said Ursula, trying to sound offhand. She did not admit that it was more exciting than she had expected.

"No, I mean what do you think of David?"

"Oh . . . it seems he can move fast enough."

Ursula did not want Jessie to know how impressed she was with David's appearance and to guess how his physique had affected her; Jessie would rib her unmercifully.

"Ursula, I mean what do you think of his, you know, looks."

"Ah, yes; Roman nose, lean build – classical." I hope that sounds like a clinical enough description to put Jessie off, she thought, and then added for good measure, "Looks like that statue of Mercury that's in the museum – but bigger of course."

Jessie raised her eyebrows, looked up to the ceiling and shrugged, "That's not quite what I meant, but never mind."

The gong sounded for the next round. David was out of his corner first and began immediately taking jabbing shots at Danny. Every time Danny took a hefty swing at David he neatly sidestepped it; then unexpectedly Danny managed to land a hook and David winced. He was no longer sprightly and within moments took a blow under the ear; he tottered, grimacing with pain, and grasped the rope for support. Falling on one knee, his chin sank to his chest and he stayed in that position whilst the referee counted. The crowd cheered but the girls gasped. Then Jessie began to giggle.

"Jessie!"

"Sorry, just nerves – gets me that way."

At the count of six David shook his head violently and rose to his feet. By moving quickly out of range, he managed to avoid any further shots until the gong sounded.

"That's what it's all about," said Jessie excitedly. "Are you enjoying it?"

"What do you mean Jessie? That crowd of men who just went out of here are positively bloodthirsty," said Ursula, no longer as detached or as able to control her feelings as before, "and David was in terrible trouble when he was punched."

"Buchanan would have pulverized him if it hadn't been for the referee," said Jessie with eyes open wide and an expectant look. "He's obviously not the same class."

"Oh dear. He's certainly not looking too well now, is he? He's not moved off his stool."

David sat slumped on the stool with his head bowed and his elbows resting on his knees. Every few seconds he lifted an arm and wiped his face with his forearm, but still he did not look up. All the while his trainer wiped the back of his neck with a sponge. Ursula, unaware of everything else around her, studied him intently, worried that he was in great pain.

Ursula felt Jessie poke her, "Ursula, you're in a bit of a *dwaal*. I said, he's probably just winded."

"Sorry, I didn't hear you. But he must be in pain, look at him. Why does he do this to himself?"

"He's a lot tougher than you think, or he wouldn't keep boxing."

"Why didn't he pick a lighter opponent, a less experienced one?"

"He must have known all about him when his trainer booked the fight" replied Jessie matter-of-factly.

"He's going to get really hurt," said Ursula anxiously, "I don't think we should stay, Jessie. Everyone's coming back in. Let's go now. I don't want to see grown men beating the brains out of each other."

"Too late, there's the gong, we've got no choice," said Jessie, grinning. "Remember, it was your idea to come."

"Oh, Jessie, don't," wailed Ursula.

Ursula was straining forward in her seat from the very start. David was slower to begin this time and Danny was very confident. He goaded David and swaggered about the ring; one, two, three jabs. The crowd was delighted, some of them stood up and called 'Come on, Danny'. *Come on David, come on David*, said Ursula in her head – she would champion him even if no-one else would. Then something happened. It was so quick that it was difficult to follow. David was punching very fast and suddenly Danny was staggering backwards: another punch, this time hard on the point of his chin, sent Danny reeling. Losing his foothold, he crashed to the floor – his head hitting it with great force. Much to everyone's amazement, he stayed there. The referee seemed as baffled as the audience and started counting without conviction.

"One, a-two, a-three, a-four, a-five . . ."

Danny groaned but did not move. After the count of ten the referee pronounced David the winner and the girls both let out their breath. Jessie started giggling again.

There was a hullabaloo in the hall, men were shouting abuse and swearing at each other and the atmosphere was getting very heated.

"Come on," said Jessie, "it's best if we get out of here now," and they made their way outside.

"Where did David go?" asked Ursula, wanting now to congratulate him.

"Gone to ground," said Jessie with a knowing air. "I suppose we could try and get round the back and leave a message."

"Look there's that old chap who saw us in."

"Well ladies, what d'yer think of the fight?" the old man asked, his chin stuck out in anticipation.

"Bit of a turn-up," said Jessie, raising her eyebrows and smirking.

"It was a cracker," he replied, pulling his neck back into his jacket and beaming.

"He's not badly hurt is he?" asked Ursula, concerned.

"Nothing to worry about, miss. Now, Mister David asked me to see you home. He says sorry but he can't possibly see you home his'self 'cause if Danny's supporters see 'im they'll probably lynch 'im."

"*Ag* no man!" exclaimed Jessie.

"Lynch him?" asked Ursula, in disbelief.

"Yes, you chump," replied Jessie. "It's probably because they've lost a fair bit of money betting on Danny winning. Probably didn't know David's won things before."

"He don't mean the lynching thing seriously, miss," the man added, looking at Ursula through watery pools.

"I see," replied Ursula, not really listening to the man. "Has he won things before, Jessie; is he better than we thought?"

"He's had quite a lot of experience in England and he got invited out here, so he must be pretty good. And he's probably learned to be a bit of a showman, too."

Doubts seeped into Ursula's mind, puzzled, she put her hand on Jessie's wrist to keep her attention, "Do you think it was all play acting then; that he only pretended to have been hurt when he fell down?"

"Wouldn't be surprised. And maybe David let them all think he was inexperienced to improve the odds."

"A fix – is that it – you think that's what happened;" asked Ursula with a frown, "would he do that?"

"If he did, he may have put money on Buchanan losing and himself winning and really cleaned up."

Ursula was shocked and, as she absorbed the news, she remembered her feelings during the fight. Throughout the evening, quite unconsciously, she had worked herself up to a pitch of emotional excitement quite new to her. Now she was annoyed with herself for admiring David's physique and being touched by his pain.

"No. I can't believe it! That is the most despicable thing I've ever heard and to think I was foolish enough to worry about him," she said, completely ignoring the old man who was shaking his head and trying to speak. "I'm not staying here a moment longer."

And as she turned and walked briskly in the direction of Jessie's rooms she expunged the picture of David's upright muscular torso and head bowed in defeat from her mind.

"Don't let it upset you; it's nothing," said Jessie as she followed Ursula, her tone placatory now.

"Wish I'd never come," said Ursula, forcefully, "I didn't want to. It wasn't a very nice place – all those raucous men – my sister Meg would never have let me come. I knew I shouldn't have. If I'd known what a thoroughly unprincipled person David was I would never have come."

"Oh, they all get up to that sort of thing, Ursula – fiddling and fixing – you just haven't come across it before," said Jessie, in an off-hand manner.

"No, I haven't first hand – living in a house of women means we've been spared that – but I have heard of it. And just because it is more common than I thought doesn't mean that I have to condone it," she replied. Odd snippets of her conversation with David in the hotel were now coming back to her and adopting a lofty attitude helped her ignore them. "So he told you he'd won things before, did he?"

"Abe mentioned he'd won some cup or other in England. I forgot all about it till we got to the fight."

"I wish I'd known," said Ursula. Jessie keeps things to herself when it suits her, she thought. Annoyed now with Jessie she increased her pace and added angrily, "You should have told me Jessie."

"Calm down, Ursula," said Jessie firmly, taking little running steps to keep up with her, "it's not the end of the world – a little bit of rigging's not so very bad."

Ursula suddenly remembered with clarity the worst of the conversation in the tearoom; David had questioned her critical faculties and moral integrity. Resentful now that it was he who sought to open her eyes to better motives, she was glad to replace his observations with her own righteous indignation and new found moral superiority.

"Isn't it?" she said, adding sententiously. "If a man can't behave honourably in a matter of sport then he can't behave honourably in any aspect of his life."

And they hurried on through the cold evening without speaking. I knew he was bad the first time I saw him in that shop, Ursula told herself. Talking like that to a married woman; not someone I want to be associated with. When I next see him I'll ignore him, cut him dead. And those first impressions of David as a libertine were to come back and haunt her again.

Three

O body swayed to music, O brightening glance,
How can we know the dancer from the dance?

Among School Children', VIII
W.B. Yeats 1865–1939

It was the day of the ball. Ursula and Jessie had arranged to attend the charity event with Bernard, a young man from Ursula's office, and his friend Ralph. It was an event they had all been looking forward to for some time. Most public dances were held in venues with little glamour but as it was the quiet season the ball was being held at the Grand, one of the most luxurious hotels in Cape Town.

Ursula had not seen David at the theatre during the week following the fight and Jessie said he had not been in – 'probably still lying low' was her observation. Ursula nurtured the opinion that David's conduct at the fight was contemptible. She had effectively managed to deny all the more tender and admiring feelings she had for him during the fight, replacing them with a cool contempt. She was now prepared to snub him if she saw him alone; she had even practiced some cutting repartee in the event that she saw him in company. Having divested themselves of their wraps and coats, Ursula and Jessie preceded Bernard and Ralph through the double glass doors of the ballroom. As the doors were closed behind them a man detached himself from a small group and walked towards them: it was David.

"Good evening Jessie, good evening Ursula," he said, bowing and looking directly at Ursula.

Ursula gave him an icy stare, inclined her head in a perfunctory way and, turning, slipped her arm in Bernard's. In the coolest tone she could affect, she proceeded to introduce them.

The men smiled at each other warmly and bowed graciously. This was too civil for Ursula, she had wanted to snub David, and if she were not careful he would soon be deep in fraternal conversation with Bernard. Adopting a very waspish tone, she said, "Bernard, you'll be interested to hear that Mr Lewis is not what he appears, he's a pugilist that . . ."

David did not wait for her to finish but interrupted, "A what?" he asked abruptly, his eyebrows meeting in a dark line.

Ursula was taken off guard: she had intended to be in command when she met David, to be cool and dismissive. She had thought that calling him a pugilist would be scornful enough to convey her contempt for him. She had only ever seen the word in print, perhaps he too did not use it; now she would obviously have to convey her opinion of him more fully.

"A pugilist, I'm not sure of course, but is that perhaps an unprincipled fighter?" she asked, looking at him with a challenging air.

"If you mean a pugilist," he said coldly, condescendingly (he pronounced it with a soft 'J' unlike Ursula had) "no, I am not. A pugilist fights with bare fists; I am a boxer. I may be pugnacious though, but then, as you've come out of your corner fighting, so are you," he finished, in an equally challenging tone. With a sardonic look, he nodded abruptly to her, and turning bowed more graciously to Bernard, who was looking confused. Then he turned on his heel and walked away without another word. Jessie gave Ursula a pitying look and talked to Ralph.

Corrected and admonished so unexpectedly, Ursula felt her

cheeks burning and stood with her mouth slightly open, watching David's retreating figure.

She started when somebody touched her on her arm: it was Bernard.

"Will you have this dance with me, Ursula?" he asked, looking at her uncertainly.

"I shall be very happy to, Bernard." Feeling upset, Ursula was grateful for the diversion. She liked Bernard; he was very tall with a loose limbed gait and flaxen hair that fell over his eyes and had a simple character incapable of malice. She decided immediately that men like him with a total absence of combative spirit were to be preferred.

"I say, I do like your dress," he complimented her as soon as they began to dance.

"Thank you. I cribbed the design from the ladies' page of a *Tatler* that I borrowed, so it's the latest London fashion," she said, feeling a little more sure of herself.

"Oops, sorry, was that your foot?"

"Yes," she said grimacing.

"I've always been keen to dance well but somehow I can't get the hang if it," said Bernard with a wide-eyed expression.

"Ouch!" blurted out Ursula involuntarily, when Bernard trod hard on her toe trying to get out of the way of another couple.

"I didn't see that chap, sorry," said Bernard, with a shake of his head, his hair flopping left and right over his forehead as he spoke. "That's the trouble with dancing – you need to have eyes in the back of your head."

"And preferably all your limbs connected to your brain."

"Quite. Can't do it without putting a bit of thought into it," replied Bernard, artlessly.

"Quite," agreed Ursula.

Temporarily, these barbed remarks went some way to making her feel better about her clumsy partner and the brush with

David that had hopelessly backfired. They danced on for a few minutes without too many mishaps and the music stopped.

"Oh, that's it then," said Bernard. "That didn't last too long did it?"

"Oh I don't know," said Ursula, drily.

"I think waltzes are probably my best – but I'll have a shot at this one if you like. Polka is it?"

"It may be just a little fast for us, Bernard, lots of high stepping. Perhaps we should just sit down for a spell."

After a while Ursula began to feel thoroughly ashamed of her remarks to Bernard and had one more attempt at dancing with him in an effort to be kinder. But his ineptitude was hard to bear and she felt herself becoming impatient again. I mustn't take it out on Bernard, she told herself, it's not fair. He tries so hard to please, and so easily manages to fail. She diplomatically refused his further invitations to dance but danced instead with Ralph or with anyone she knew who asked her. But her evening was blighted – her partners either held her too close or did not lead well – and Ursula knew that it was her *contretemps* with David that caused her to be more put out by events than she should have been. She was relieved when the band broke off for the supper break: a cold table of hams and salads was provided, with punch, beer or lemonade to drink. Stronger alcohol was available in the bar off the billiards room but Ursula and her friends could not afford the inflated prices there. The four of them sat at a small supper table and spent the time passing idle remarks about everyone else in the room.

The band began to play and, as the others talked on, Ursula sat tapping her feet, rocking her shoulders and swaying her head in time with the music. She had decided not to dance but, as the music played, her frustration increased and she began to feel cheated. She would have to do something to stop her mood deteriorating again. She suddenly stood up and, taking her evening purse, excused herself.

In the ladies rest room she tidied her hair. David has spoilt my evening, he really has, she told herself in the mirror (conveniently forgetting that she was the instigator of the ill-fated exchange); and as a result I've not enjoyed myself and been horrid to my friends. But all the epithets she chose to apply to David, all the accusations she aimed at him, would not wipe from her mind the humiliation of being corrected so publicly.

She decided to take the lift down to the foyer where she pored over the jewellery in the glass display cases ranged around the walls and examined the magazines and journals in the news store. Passing the reception desk she was dismayed to see David, hands in his pockets, nonchalantly chatting to the clerk. Had he been watching her; she hoped not. Ursula looked past him, pretending not to see him, and quickened her pace. She sighed with relief when the lift doors were closed and she reached the ballroom.

Nearing the edge of the dance floor someone took her hand from behind. She turned around and was face to face with David. He slipped his other arm round her waist and, steering her onto the floor, started to dance with her. She cursed under her breath; remembering how nimble he was she realized he must have run up the stairs after her.

"Dancing together might be more fun than fighting, don't you think?" he said, raising his eyebrows and smiling.

Still smarting from their earlier confrontation, she was unable to answer him as if nothing had happened. I definitely don't want to talk with him, she thought as he expertly turned her around on the floor, and I really don't want to dance with him either; perhaps I should just stand still. However, as she planned her response it increasingly became obvious that he had an excellent sense of rhythm. She decided that it would be too embarrassing to struggle out of such a firm hold with everyone looking; she would force herself to be polite and finish the dance.

They danced in silence and the waltz finished but David's

hand remained on her waist. Ursula had so enjoyed dancing well that she did not repel him as she had intended and, without asking her, David began the next dance.

"I'm not unprincipled," he said quietly, his mouth so close to her neck that she could feel the warmth of his breath. "Abe simply didn't advertise my previous success and Buchanan's supporters didn't bother to find out, they just assumed I was green. I suppose you did too?" he drew the upper part of his body back from her, whilst still holding her firmly round the waist, so that he could see her face. She did not look him in the eye. It was true, she had thought him an inexperienced boxer but Jessie had not enlightened her. She said nothing.

"And I didn't bet," he continued firmly, still looking at her, "as an amateur I'm not allowed to. I trained hard for the fight and I won. I was paid half the gate money; if you need money, and you don't have regular work, you have to use what skills you do have. It's as simple as that."

He spoke with authority and, obviously thinking his explanation was enough and the subject therefore closed, he looked over her shoulder once more, his cheek inches away from hers. Somebody's been talking to him, Ursula thought, it must have been the old man. She remembered their conversation in the hotel and had relived the events at the fight in her mind so often (and unconsciously been disposed to feel better about herself by thinking the worse of him) that she had convinced herself that David was guilty of misleading the crowd. She remembered that Jessie, who knew about such things, had taken it for granted. But surprisingly David seemed uncowed by her accusations. Had Jessie misled her – why should she do such a thing – but no, surely she herself could not be so mistaken. She would give him one last chance to own up to it. With her high heels on they were nearly at eye level, and by turning her head slightly to one side Ursula could see his face obliquely from under her slightly lowered eyelids. Softly, calculatingly, she asked, "Is trickery one of them?"

David's face took on a thunderous look and his arm tightened around her.

"Are you suggesting that I was feigning – or worse? You've a lot to learn about me if you think I'd ever do that," he said through clenched teeth. "I won fairly and squarely."

Ursula could feel David's breath come out in violent bursts as he spoke the last words. His affront at her implied slur, and his repudiation of it, was quite obviously genuine and she wondered how she could have been so wrong about him. Chastened by the strength of his denial, Ursula unconsciously adopted a more compliant attitude – her head leant a little closer to his, her body softened and her movements melded with his. She regretted accusing him of being underhand and the unfairness of her accusations now weighed heavily on her. How could she excuse herself, what should she say; best not to say a word till he does, she decided, can't be sure of his temper. He danced on without talking and slowly his grip loosened. Grateful that he continued to dance with her at all, she wondered if he had forgiven her without her having spoken. She shut her eyes and felt as if she was floating. She hoped he would not stop dancing, but continue round and round: it felt heavenly.

When the music finished he escorted her to her table – his palm resting lightly on the small of her back. At the table he kissed her hand in a chivalrous way and, looking at them all and making a small bow, said, "Goodnight everyone," then turned and left.

Ursula watched as he walked across the ballroom without a backward glance, went through the doors and disappeared. She wished he had stayed: she wished she had apologized.

"Shall we be off then?" asked Bernard, in his usual open and hopeful manner.

"Might as well now Cinderella is back," replied Jessie, drily.

*

"See you had a few dances with David," said Jessie as soon as the girls were in bed and the gas light extinguished.

"Yes," replied Ursula concisely. She did not want to discuss her less than successful conversation with David.

"How was he?"

"We didn't say much," replied Ursula, her cheeks burning at the thought of her false accusations.

"Did he mention the fight?" asked Jessie, cautiously.

"Only that it was all above board."

"He didn't mention the betting then."

"He said he hadn't bet. What made you think he would?" asked Ursula, wishing she could see Jessie's face. She might have been able to guess if Jessie was being truthful.

"Must have been something he said, gave me the wrong idea. We have these little chats when he pops into the theatre and they go on for so long sometimes I forget all the details."

"It's a pity you didn't tell me about the conversation before you forgot the details, then I might have known he didn't bet."

"How did you two get on anyway, after your rocky start?"

Ursula thought that Jessie probably wanted to hear that they did not get on well, but she would not give her the satisfaction, "Like I said, we didn't really say much, we just danced."

"Well, he talks non-stop when he comes into the theatre of an evening; he's probably more relaxed then," replied Jessie in a smug tone. "Perhaps he finds you a bit sharp. Was he friendly?"

"Well he was dancing and not wrestling with me so I think we can assume that he wasn't totally opposed to me." Here Ursula mentally paused – and was glad Jessie could not see *her* face – when David clasped her very tight it had been rather like punishment.

"But did he say he'd talk to you again?" persisted Jessie.

"In spite of my sharp tongue you mean."

"Come on Ursula, you know you were in a stinking mood. What do you think of him now then?"

Not sure of Jessie, Ursula was guarded in her reply, "He dances wonderfully of course. But he has so many sides to his character it's difficult to say; he's unusual, different – not like most of the men there tonight."

"That is the most wishy-washy answer I've heard yet. What a complicated thing you are – all words and no action or all action and no words. Me, I like both at the same time. You should try getting to know Ralph – he can be very amusing and he's not a bad dancer," said Jessie as she turned on her side away from Ursula, "you might find him easier to understand than David."

"I don't find anyone easy to understand at the moment," answered Ursula, obliquely.

Now David's good opinion was important to Ursula, her ill-judged remarks an embarrassment she would like to forget. The shoe is firmly on the other foot now, she admitted ruefully to herself. She spent nights fretting about her high-handed stance and wanted to know for certain that David did not resent her accusations of trickery. By Wednesday, when she was due at the theatre, she had convinced herself that if David came in he must surely have forgiven her. But he did not come – which ruined her theory – and by the following Saturday Ursula was not at all certain how he would greet her when they met. He had left the dance without speaking to her, which was unsettling.

However, Saturday at the theatre proved to be so chaotic – a catalogue of disasters occurred – that she had no time to dwell on how David would act when he saw her. Paula, the fiery red-headed leading lady, had fainted at rehearsals that morning and Ronnie, the leading man, had flapped around saying, 'Paula, Paula, it will be all right, trust me'. When Paula came round she called him some very rude names – Boris, one of the stagehands, told Ursula all this – and went off to her dressing room where she was heard retching and swearing by turns – this related by the chorus girls in the dressing room next door. The understudy, Emma, was asked to do the rehearsal instead but she was unfamiliar with the scenery and tripped as she ran across the stage, twisting her ankle. The matinée was cancelled.

When Ursula arrived the stagehands were changing the scenery back for the first scene. As they did so one of the ropes holding the hanging props snapped and a hitherto resplendent twinkling star crashed to the ground.

"Not the first one today," muttered Joe the caretaker to Ursula when they were both standing looking up at the damage, "and 'twon't be the last," he added philosophically.

Ronnie spent the afternoon making a great fuss of Paula so that she would agree to perform that evening. Everyone was affected by the drama – all were pressed into helping. Ursula had to sew a young understudy called Ellie into the nymph costume because she was too big for the fastenings to meet. Then, whilst the stagehands tried to reconstruct the celestial scenery, she had to deal with more down-to-earth tasks such as brushing the stage and dusting the table and props for the first act. By the time the evening performance started Ursula had forgotten about the possibility of David coming to the theatre.

The dramas of the day gave everyone but the strained actors a fillip and the girls plenty to talk about when they resumed their normal tasks. Jessie and Ursula spent the show in speculation that, at times, bordered on recrimination.

"What do you think was wrong with Paula?" Ursula asked Jessie as soon as they were alone. "She really was awfully upset and not at all well."

"She was certainly unwell and very brassed off with her amour Ronnie," said Jessie, lowering her eyelids. Ursula knew this as the sign that some mystery or intrigue was going to be disclosed. "And it's not the first morning she's been dickie," Jessie added.

"Oh!" said Ursula in shocked surprise. "Are they going to get married then?"

"Bit difficult that one," replied Jessie, tightly pursing her lips, "I don't think his wife would like it."

Ursula was taken aback, "I didn't know he was married," she said in disbelief. She realized how little she knew about the actors and how unaware she was of their way of life; she tried not to think of the dire consequences of Paula's condition.

"He is. Happens all the time here," nodded Jessie, eyebrows raised, "away from the wife – too many evenings rehearsing alone with a voluptuous leading lady willing to give you more than tea and sympathy."

"I think that's awful, I don't think men who are married should have liaisons. It's not right."

"You are a moral old thing aren't you. Where I live they're always cheating on their nearest and dearest. And I tell you, it's just the same if you're top drawer – difference is, money helps you out of fixes."

"It's not because I'm moral, I don't think I am particularly," said Ursula, unwilling to appear naïve, "it's just that we've always been spoon fed the sanctity of marriage. Perhaps I've just got a romantic view of things. I mean – I've no example to go by of course – but I do rather think that married people should be faithful to each other. Surely marriage vows don't mean anything otherwise."

Jessie had listened to the little speech with a dubious expression and lowered eyelids.

"What will Paula do?" continued Ursula, when Jessie did not respond.

"She's probably tried all the tricks and if they don't work she'll have to disappear for a while, I suppose."

"Oh dear, what a disastrous position to be in. Poor Paula, she must be beside herself thinking of the shame she'll bring on her family."

"Don't suppose they'll even know about it, she'll keep well away."

Ursula did not want to hear details, "Oh no! I've forgotten Ellie," she said suddenly. "I'll lose my job if I don't go and release her from the confines of her costume," and she was glad of the excuse to leave the cloakroom.

After the interval Ursula – carefully side-stepping the morally sensitive subject of Paula and Ronnie – returned to the fiasco of the day.

"Poor Emma is out of action for a while too."

"Doing in her ankle is going to affect her dancing," said Jessie, savouring the misfortune, "ankles never mend properly you know."

"Somebody must have forgotten to say 'break a leg' to her," said Ursula wryly. "When I went backstage her ankle was strapped up and she was using a stick so I don't think it's too bad. She says she's getting a cab back to her digs. It's bad luck that she's missed her chance to shine, though."

"Emma's lucky to have a Pa who's rich enough to bankroll her and keep her in cabs. I told you money helps you out of fixes, didn't I."

"I know. We'd probably have had to go hobbledehoy all the way home. But Emma's not the only injured thespian, I think poor Ellie's stuck full of holes. I had such trouble trying to squeeze her into Emma's nymph costume, by the time I'd tacked and pinned she was a positive sieve."

"She's fat that girl, like most of her *volk*," said Jessie contemptuously, narrowing her eyes and compressing her lips. "Don't know how she ever got a part in the chorus."

Ursula could guess the reason; Abe, who owned the theatre, might have a small pocket but he had a large heart. It was true that Ellie never stopped eating but as an Afrikaner child during the war she had been interned in one of the concentration camps. Like most there she had come out malnourished but – unlike

46

many – did not come out full of enmity. Ellie was a simple character but a willing worker; Ursula did not like to hear her criticized unfairly. However, Ursula reminded herself that Jessie's uncle had fought for the British at *Spion Kop* and died: killed in action. Perhaps Jessie had reason to be bitter.

"She's not fat, more solid, plump maybe, but I have to agree she doesn't suit Emma's part; she's very sweet but just a bit slow."

"Bit slow? Dead slow and stop that girl – both upstairs and downstairs," said Jessie scornfully. "I thought nymphs are meant to be beautiful little things that are 'fleet of foot', or whatever the phrase is."

Ursula realized that Jessie's dislike of the young Afrikaner was deeper than she had thought and she could not maintain her even-handedness.

"Like lovely little Emma you mean?"

"Yes, I suppose so," replied Jessie grudgingly.

"Then it would seem that slow is safer."

"I suppose you think you're clever. Joe would agree with you though, he was muttering about fast women being bad luck."

"It was red hair that Joe said was bad luck," replied Ursula, correcting her.

"Hmm," grunted Jessie.

It was clear that Jessie was now thoroughly disgruntled and, as Ursula could not bring herself to agree with her either, they were heading for an argument. To avoid an altercation and a resulting sulk from Jessie, but to continue to enjoy her lively tone and outrageous observations, Ursula sought to appease her at no real cost to her own pride or her principles. She would change the topic of the conversation to one of Jessie's favourite subjects and indulge her with undivided attention. Ursula had used this conciliatory approach many times; Jessie rarely noticed the re-direction and was happy to hold forth on a fresh topic whilst she had neither to concede defeat nor argue to the bitter end.

"As a matter of fact, it's more likely to be bad luck for us, Jess," she said in a conspiratorial tone, "because we'll be tremendously busy over the next few matinées – you especially – unless everyone gets their money back."

"Yes, me especially," said Jessie, emphatically.

"You'll have to cope with Wednesday afternoon on your own – you'll be run off your feet."

"Abe doesn't realize how busy it gets. I'm back and forth, in and out, up and down: exhausting it is."

"You're a Jack of all trades."

"Yes, I am. I'm expected to do the lost property, and the first aid, and now I've got to check off all the laundry when it comes back. It's not everyone can turn their hand to so many different things."

"And the laundry?"

"Yes," said Jessie looking put-upon. "All the theatre clothes that are cotton or linen – anything that can be laundered; bags of it. You can't imagine how much stuff the cast gets through: shirts and cravats and skirts and petties and . . . I don't know what." Then, unexpectedly, she smiled broadly and asked with relish, "But did I tell you what I found in the bag last week?"

"No, what?"

"You'll die laughing, you really will," said Jessie. With a loud guffaw she slapped her thigh and threw her head back, "Don't know how they got in there: a pair of silk – silk – knickers and an enormous pair of long johns – eenormous – all the buttons popped off . . ."

Ursula burst out laughing; Jessie was back on form.

Gossip was the currency of the theatre. When Ursula's days seemed boring and uneventful, when her office duties were onerous and she had had little opportunity for light-hearted conversation, she craved a glimpse into lives more interesting, of actions more exciting: gossip fitted the bill. Speculating about the lives of people they knew, or had heard of, was an amusing and cathartic exercise to indulge in with Jessie; Jessie was the actor, Ursula the audience. And when Jessie became too extreme or volatile (for instance when there was the risk that she might perpetuate false rumours or initiate hysteria among the chorus), the restraining and calming influence Ursula exerted on her justified the occupation in her own mind. However, when the conversation transcended light-hearted gossip and hearsay to become criticism and harsh judgement, she thought Jessie's views nothing short of vitriolic – and her own quite reasonable of course – and she withdrew her patronage. But now the gossip was as light as it was harmless; there were still safe avenues for them to go down and – at least backstage – the second act was a very enjoyable affair.

Ursula and Jessie were late leaving that night and were still in a state of suppressed excitement after the unusual events of the day. Abe always arranged for one of the stagehands to escort them home at night and this evening they had the company of a dark-haired young Welshman called Alf. The girls were glad of his company when a man stepped out of the shadows on the opposite side of the road. They instinctively slowed down and Alf took a step in front of them; Ursula was very touched by his gallantry because he was half a head shorter than she. The stranger threw his cigarette to the ground, removed his hat and hailed them.

With relief they now saw it was David. Ursula was surprised – with the melodramas of the day she had forgotten about David – and realized he must have been waiting some time as they were later than usual.

"Good evening ladies," he said coming up to them and giving a nod to Alf, "would you like to join me for a nightcap?" They were in front of a smart hotel – the porch sheltered a doorman in uniform and they could hear the hum of voices from within. The girls looked at each other and they both nodded at David who immediately landed a friendly slap on the stagehand's back, "It's all right Alf lad, I'll see them safely home."

"Righto," said Alf, "I'll be off to have a few then. Goodnight girls," and he disappeared into the gloom to join his drinking companions without any second bidding.

Four

Unlearn'd, he knew no schoolman's subtle art,
No language, but the language of the heart.
By nature honest, by experience wise,
Healthy by temp'rance, and by exercise.

Epistle to Dr Arbuthnot (1735)
Alexander Pope 1688–1744

David coaxed them into the hotel where they cursorily checked in the large mirrors that their hats and general appearance were respectable before he guided them, in a rather proprietorial manner Ursula thought, through the reception hall.

David kept up a steady stream of small talk – Ursula deduced that he must have been to the hotel on several previous occasions because he was very much at his ease – pointing things out to them and exchanging niceties with the staff.

He ushered them into the main lounge bar where he pulled out a chair for Jessie. She sat down with exaggerated care, arranging her skirts about her, as if she were a duchess. As David helped Ursula to a seat a waiter dressed in a smart gold-buttoned outfit came up. Without consulting the girls, David ordered sherry for them both and a whisky for himself. Brought up by two women Ursula was not used to a man taking charge so high-handedly.

"Ooh, its lovely here," enthused Jessie, forgetting her aristocratic role and stroking the plush covered arm of the chair.

"I'm glad you like it," replied David, "and do you like it?" he asked Ursula.

Before replying Ursula looked about her. Burnished brass, a thick Indian carpet, gleaming surfaces on heavy pieces of furniture and swagged curtains of expensive looking stuff gave the impression of dependable luxury. Mirrors. Mirrors everywhere reflected the interior and multiplied the illusion of wealth and comfort. On the one hand, she felt reassured that her insults at the dance had been forgiven because David was seeking her company and good opinion but, on the other hand, she was now piqued that she had spent nights worrying about insulting him. Consequently – perversely – she was less inclined to be magnanimous; his previous criticisms and corrections still stung her pride, his constantly getting the upper hand niggled. In addition, keeping Jessie in a good humour throughout the evening had taken its toll on Ursula's patience and she was no longer in the mood for rapprochement.

"It seems pleasant," she said with reserve. "Not quite as smart as the Grand."

"Good, good," he replied affably, not appearing to notice her ungracious remark.

Ursula thought he did so on purpose, which was galling. The waiter brought the drinks over and he also brought a second whisky for David – compliment of the bar he was told.

"Do you like the sherry, Jessie?" David asked.

Jessie wrinkled up her nose and took a sip, "Rather. It's much better than the Cape one we get at home for Christmas."

"And how about you Ursula?"

"No, I don't like it I'm afraid," she said bluntly, and placed the glass of viscous golden liquid on the other side of the table.

However, David looked so concerned that she immediately regretted her words. Oh, I wish I hadn't been grudging before, she thought, after that remark he'll think me thoroughly peevish.

"Is there something wrong with it?" he asked leaning forward, solicitous.

"No, no, it's just that it's not to my taste," she said apologetically, "rather sweet."

"Well, we'll just have to think of something else, how about a brandy and water?"

"Thank you, I'd prefer something else. What are you drinking?"

"Me? Whisky. Women don't usually like it."

"We're not all alike you know," Ursula replied trenchantly, "and I always prefer to choose for myself."

"Yes, by all means," replied David wholeheartedly. "What would you like?"

"Could I try a whisky please?"

David looked mildly surprised. "Of course, of course you can, please have this one," he said and passed her the second glass of whisky that had not yet been touched. "Soda?"

She nodded and when he had added the soda she took a tentative sip. David lounged back, one elbow on the arm of his chair, a hand under his chin; his eyebrows were raised rather superciliously she thought. Jessie pushed her head forward and knitted her brows, "You won't like it Ursula, have something else."

Ursula took a larger sip; she looked at David who now smiled slightly – she did like it – she would enjoy confounding them.

"It's very good, I do like it, thank you," she said and putting the glass down on the table in front of her she sat back in her seat.

"Splendid," replied David, sounding genuinely pleased.

"Always one to be different," Jessie said petulantly.

David's appreciative tone mollified Ursula – perhaps he considers me more of an equal now, she concluded, so I don't need to make the point. She assumed once again her usual open manner, and keen to satisfy her natural curiosity, asked, "You seem to know everyone here, is this where you're staying?"

"No such luck; when I first arrived I was staying in the YMCA whilst I looked for somewhere more permanent. Then I was introduced to this ginger nut – Scottish chap – who's interested in the same sort of things as me and it turns out his family had a free room so I'm lodging there now. A hotel would be far too expensive, I'm afraid, and this one would be quite out of the question."

"So how do you know everyone here?"

"She's always like this David – needs to know all the ins and outs," said Jessie in a weary, apologetic voice.

"I'm interested that's all Jessie."

"I come in here for a nightcap sometimes," he explained, "usually on my own. People tend to chat to someone on their own in a bar, and I've often heard of opportunities that way."

"Are you looking to find work between your boxing bouts then?"

"There she goes again – questions, questions, questions. Ursula would make a good detective but I don't think there are such things as women detectives," said Jessie rolling her eyes upwards. "She keeps it all to herself though, I often think her head must get clogged up with all the answers that are in there now."

"Well you can't learn things if you don't ask questions," Ursula replied. "It's interesting finding out about people, what they do, where they go and so on. What can you think about when you're on your own if you haven't got something inside your head to work on?"

"Well I manage pretty well," said Jessie, looking at Ursula from lowered eyelids. "I think about what happened to Auntie Vi when she went up to the hospital and they found a cockroach in her hair – don't laugh, they did really. Or I wonder if that good looking chap down the road has asked to walk out with my cousin Maisie yet. And then I think about beautiful clothes, and hats, and the latest fashions and all sorts of *dinges*."

"I certainly don't understand some of the things my Scots

friend Duggie says," David said rapidly. "I've had to ask him to explain quite a few, but then he says he can't understand some of the things I come up with."

Ursula recognized David's attempt at keeping the peace. She did not want to have a disagreement with Jessie again.

"What sort of things?" she asked, looking expectantly at Jessie. "We could try and guess their meaning."

But Jessie was twiddling with a stray curl and purposely looking elsewhere.

"Let's see," said David thoughtfully. "I know – cockney slang – how about, 'apples and pears' or 'porky pie'?"

"I know the first one because a man in my office is always using it – it's stairs. And something that rhymes with 'porky pie' is . . . sky, dry, fly? Come on Jessie, have a guess."

"Die?" volunteered Jessie, caustically.

Ursula and David smiled at each other – although Jessie was obviously not enthralled with the conversation she was still droll.

"No, you'll have to put it in a sentence for us," said Ursula, not giving up.

"I'll give you a clue – it's wrong to tell one – especially in court."

"Lie!"

"Bravo."

"Listen here you two," interrupted Jessie in bored voice, "I've got a question now. Are we going soon? I'm really tired."

They finished their drinks and left the hotel. David, walking between the girls, linked both their arms through his. Ursula noticed that he held her arm very tight but yet he chatted almost exclusively to Jessie. By the time they reached her rooms Jessie was in good spirits again. Addressing neither of them in particular David asked, "Would you like to come climbing with me tomorrow and . . ."

"Thank you," said Jessie, interrupting bluntly, "scaling mountains is hardly our idea of fun."

"What do you think, Ursula?" he asked.

"I can walk uphill well enough but I'm not sure about climbing."

"Walking will do," David said quickly.

"What time are you thinking of?"

"Twelve noon, or I could call for you at half past eleven."

"I thought you said you didn't want to be late home tomorrow?" Jessie said accusingly as she turned and unlocked the door to the shop. "If you go with him you will be."

Jessie's remark annoyed Ursula, "Well, I could go home shortly afterwards," and turning towards David she said, "Yes, that would be lovely."

The next day the weather was perfect. The sun shone, there was no wind nor was there the tablecloth of cloud that so often lay on the mountain.

"I need exercise and fresh air," David said as soon as they had gone through the usual polite exchanges, "you don't mind walking do you?"

"Not at all. As long as it's not a marathon."

"Don't worry, we'll work up to that," he replied, smiling broadly. Indicating with his head he asked, "This way?" Ursula nodded agreement and as they walked together he continued, "Is it always warm like this in autumn?"

"Sometimes; it's never very cold but the wind and the mountains around about cause a lot of rain."

"In London it's summer now and it won't be very much warmer than this. But I suppose it's very hot in the summer here," he said, nodding as if he expected the answer to be in the affirmative.

"Oh no, it's never that hot. In fact we often have fierce winds and rain even in the summer. It's not hot like in Kimberley."

"Oh. Have you been there?"

"When I was young we lived there." Whenever she mentioned it every colourful, noisy, dusty memory came back to her in a great rush and her brother, Jimmy, was there; she could see him now standing in the red water of the stream, still twelve years old, making little clay oxen for her. She tried to distill the picture, to keep it safe.

"When did you leave?"

"We stayed there until I needed school. My sister hated it and she brought me here as soon as she could. Do you have brothers and sisters?" she asked quickly, before he asked more questions about Kimberley; not wanting to share her precious memories, in case it spread them too thin.

"A brother, George, and four sisters. Two of my sisters still live with my mother."

"And your father?" Ursula asked, interested as always in other's parents.

"He was never healthy – he was a refugee from Poland – died several years ago."

"A refugee? But your name sounds so English."

"Father anglicized it; he said he was fed up that no-one could pronounce the Polish name but I think he liked the anonymity of the English version. People who fear persecution, or suffer intolerance, feel safer if they blend into their new surroundings."

David turned to look at her, unsurely Ursula thought. She wondered if he thought he had said something too revealing, or perhaps he was only gauging her reaction. She was on the verge of asking him what he meant by persecution, when he promptly asked, "What about your parents?" in a voice that clearly meant the previous subject was closed.

"They were from Ireland but they couldn't live there together – my mother was Roman Catholic, my father was Protestant. Thinking about it, I suppose they were escaping intolerance. But they're both dead, I never knew them," said

Ursula evenly. "My father was killed at the Battle of *Isandhlwana*, and my mother died a few months afterwards."

David did not reply and, turning to look at him, she quickly looked away; he was looking at her intently. Remembering their previous conversation about the morality of war Ursula wondered if he was about to criticize the British campaign; she was hoping he would say something to that effect. Since the dance she had visited the library and read every foreign newspaper clip she could find on the Anglo-Boer wars. Whilst they continued walking she formulated a knowledgeable response to impress him but when David did not speak she glanced at him again.

Now his face wore a kindly expression, and he smiled at her and asked softly, "So who looked after you?"

Ursula was surprised at the gentleness of his tone.

"My childhood nurse and my sister," she paused, and added in a low tone "but my sister's gone now too." It had been a difficult and painful time and still caused her sadness. There was rarely a week when Ursula did not think of Meg, did not miss her, did not wonder if she was at fault; Meg's loss was another regret she tried not to dwell on and so she quickly added, "It must be so nice to have a big family around you. Do you miss yours?"

"I don't miss them but I think about them a great deal. I'd like to make a success of it here, be able to help them out," he said solemnly.

"Make them proud of you?"

"I suppose so," he shrugged.

"So why did you think of leaving them? Apart from the boxing opportunity of course," she asked, thinking how she would never leave a family if she had one.

"You've no idea how stifling it is in a job you don't like – adding up figures all day long – in an airless fog-filled city, leaving for work in the dark or getting home in the dark, or both. And knowing that with father gone the family expect things of you . . ." he trailed off.

"What sort of things?" she asked innocently, when he did not continue.

"To be the main breadwinner, to . . ." he paused and looked at her.

She smiled at him and he continued, "To marry as they want you to, that sort of thing – knowing that sooner or later you'll be trapped by it all."

Ursula thought he looked dejected, sounded worried – she would help, "So you thought you'd escape," she said simply, cheerfully.

"I'd never been anywhere; done anything different," he explained. "And I want to be free to make my own choices; live my own life, by my own rules. So, yes, that's about it," he finished, sounding positive again.

They walked on for a while lost in their own thoughts. Do I live my own life . . . wondered Ursula, I think so, but by my own rules, I don't know. Surely no-one can make up their own rules – there are things one has to do, niceties and conventions to be observed. Certainly there were for her, a woman. It's easier for men, she decided, they can take off into the interior, be their own master, leave towns and society behind.

"Where are we now?" David interrupted her thoughts.

"Ah, *Schotsche Kloof*, I was going to suggest that we walked up the first little bit of the Lion's rump – it's a good place to start from."

"Righto."

They branched off the road and started up the lower slopes of *fynbos*, crossing the occasional small rivulet, the water copper brown with the soil of the hillside. Ursula warned David to keep his eyes on the ground to avoid the snakes that were always concealed in the natural heaths and scrub.

"Sometimes I walk at Camps Bay," she said, after they had

been climbing for five minutes, "and when I look up at the Table – on a day like today when it's gloriously clear – I think that the scenery's like a painting, it's too beautiful to be real. It's the wild flowers," she paused for a moment and looking round pointed "look, look there, the *baviantjes* on that slope, the first I've seen this year, just a sheet of blue."

David nodded appreciatively, "If you go in the woods around London when the bluebells flower it's the same – beautiful"

Ursula smiled at him, "So what do you do to enjoy yourself?"

"Boxing, of course, and I enjoy playing cricket enormously," he replied eagerly. "My friends and I play billiards or cards together – sometimes for money – or I go to the races. In a new country like this I'm hoping there might be some opportunities in the horse racing line, what do you think?"

"I don't know anything about horse racing," she said, bluntly.

"It's very exciting; it's like cards, you never know what the outcome will be but if you know the odds you can do all right. If boxing doesn't work out for me, horse racing would be just the ticket, it's all action and thrill," said David with enthusiasm. "Like I said, that's the reason I came here, to do something different – avoid being stuck in a straitjacket all of my life."

"The race course is open again now, at Green Point Common, where the prisoner of war camp was. I've seen the large crowds on race day but I've never actually been. You could try going to the next meeting there."

"I may do that – I've won money on the horses many a time," said David confidently.

Realizing that the subject of betting might not be a good one – and anxious to avoid anything contentious – Ursula quickly changed the subject. "David, I think we'd better stop climbing now. The scrub is much thicker than I remember and it's making the hem of my skirt very wet."

"We'll go down then."

They turned and started down the slope.

"With these wide skirts it's almost more difficult to go down than up somehow, they drag so," she grumbled. "I do so wish women didn't have to wear such long skirts."

She was also wishing that women could dispense with corsets that were even more of a hindrance to exercise, but she could not say so.

"Skirts don't have to restrict you," David said, enthusiastically, "we can get down in no time – we'll run down."

"I can't run, I'll fall over"

"No you won't," David replied confidently, holding his hand out to her, "here, take my hand, hold the hem of your skirt up." Ursula wrinkled her nose in disbelief and David laughed, "Come on, you'll be all right," he urged her.

She hesitated for a moment longer, then impulsively gathered the hem of her skirt up onto her arm. David needed no further encouragement, he took off his hat, grasped her hand tightly in his and they ran down, across the slope for several hundred yards until, feeling her face tingle and short of breath, she called, "Stop, stop: I can't run any more."

Gasping for breath but exhilarated Ursula halted. Suddenly shy she let her skirt fall free and, taking her hand out of his, looked around to see if anyone was watching. He smiled at her; he showed no sign of exertion but his face was so full of unalloyed pleasure that she smiled too.

"Shall we go towards Green Point?" she said, still trying to get her breath back. "I can catch a bus that last stretch home from there."

"Yes, and I can buy us a cup of tea."

They had a cup of tea and a bun at a stall near the sea and threw crumbs to the gulls. Soon Ursula told David that if she was to catch the bus she would have to leave; her old nurse would be worried if she was not on it. David offered to accompany her and, as they had passed such a pleasant time together, she agreed, warning him that the return transport on a Sunday was unreliable.

Ursula lived in a small *dorp* that was reached by bus from town. The bus was old and rickety, the wooden seats ridged and uncomfortable, but it managed to make the return journey twice a day, every working day, along the uneven roads to Sea Point stopping en route as required. The area she lived in had once been unpopulated and quiet, reached only by well worn tracks up the lower slopes of Signal Hill; the shrubs on it buffeted by the wind, the buildings scattered and scarce. The houses themselves – built of sun dried bricks – were low with strong corrugated roofs to cope with the south-east gales and howling north winds that caught the area summer and winter. But increasingly large and smart villas had been built on the level areas by the sea – from Green Point to Sea Point, and lately on the cliffs at Clifton – for wealthy residents who wanted houses with wide views of the Atlantic set off by the imposing backdrop of Lion's Head. And now further houses were encroaching up the slopes, roads coursing like contour lines, towards the once isolated *dorp*.

After the bus dropped them off Ursula and David climbed the slope of Signal Hill, between sugarbush protea (startling the long tailed sugarbirds away from their honey) and ordinary pink heaths, until they finally reached the *dorp*. Some children were playing cricket on an almost level area of grass, and a few elderly people sat nearby under a Cape Beech tree that had defied the wind and survived to attain a stature large enough to give shelter. David said he missed playing cricket, in a rather melancholic tone. Ursula was about to remark that Bernard watched cricket matches at Newlands and she was sure would be delighted to take David, when a cricket ball came bouncing across the grass towards them. David immediately brightened and, lobbing it back, shouted words of encouragement.

She smiled, "I'll go in, if you don't mind," she said, glad to be spared an awkward farewell on the *stoep* and grateful that she would not have to explain there and then to her old nurse,

Hannah, who David was. "Will you be all right getting back? You know the bus might have gone already."

"Definitely, all in a days training," he said, with a smile.

"Sorry we didn't scale the heights."

"Don't worry, we will one day, I have high hopes for you," he said seriously.

She smiled in a non-committal way; surely he meant climb the Table, and she would never do that.

"Ursula?"

He's got that intent look again, she thought, I hope he's not going to take ages saying goodbye.

"Yes?" she replied, trying not to sound impatient – she was now very tired and looking forward to going inside and sitting down.

"Will you have a drink with me on Wednesday – after the theatre, at the hotel?" Ursula nodded. "I'll meet you at the theatre then, when you finish," he said.

"Certainly," she replied. "Thank you for the cup of tea, and I enjoyed the walk. Goodbye."

"Goodbye," he replied, not moving.

But as she turned to go he impulsively took hold of her hand and squeezed it; she guessed it meant he had enjoyed the day and smiled at him. From the *stoep* she could see him showing one of the boys how to hold the bat; looking up he saw her and holding the bat high above his head, he waved it.

Most of Ursula's neighbours were white but some successful Indian merchants owned property nearby and although the area was affordable it was nevertheless respectable. Hannah accepted that she would have to live out of the town away from her *volk* although occasionally she went to Hanover Street to sit around and have tea with those of her friends who lived in that district.

And whenever there was a major Malay ceremony or celebration Hannah would eagerly attend. She would put on the bright clothes she saved for these occasions and make her way to the Malay Quarter to join in the festivities. Here her friends – flower sellers and washerwomen, sweetmeat sellers and seamstresses – welcomed her into the terraces of flat-roofed, painted houses in the streets leading up *Bo Kaap* whilst their men attended the ceremony at the mosque. But generally Hannah stayed close to the area they lived in and, since they no longer had Meg's income, she took in sewing and did some cooking to help finances: she was a loving mother substitute who rarely castigated Ursula. Nevertheless, Ursula could feel even mild disapproval if she did something of which Hannah – or Nana as she still called her – did not approve.

"Nana, I'm back," she called from the door as she took off her hat.

Hannah came immediately, "Hello, *kleintjie*. Goodness, what you been doing? Your cheeks all pink, hair all over the show."

"I went for a walk with David – he's a *protégé* of Abe's – and it probably came loose in the wind."

Hannah was looking at Ursula with a faint frown.

"He's very polite, he brought me home," explained Ursula.

"*Is it*? Where is he?"

"He's . . ." Ursula hesitated and looking out of the window said, "gone. Must have gone back to town."

"*Passop!*" warned Hannah, smoothing her spotless *voorskootje*, "What Meg say?"

"You always mention Meg when you want to make me feel guilty."

"*Ne*. Meg got standards to live up to," replied Hannah, her normally smiling face serious.

"Nana, we only went for a walk," Ursula replied in defence.

Meg's not here now, Ursula thought, and I'm free to make my own choices. However, Ursula felt Hannah's mild rebuke – more

64

effective than any lecture – might be justified although she considered that her sister's standards were difficult to maintain and rather old-fashioned. She knew that Meg would not approve of most of the players in the theatre and certainly would never have agreed to her working there.

"Still, I may not see him again, Nana," Ursula said to appease Hannah. "I know Meg would be sure to disapprove of going out unchaperoned."

"*Ja.*"

For a second Ursula could see Meg; sitting on the *stoep*, thimble on her finger, letting the hem of one of Ursula's frocks down, complaining that she was growing too fast.

"I'll help you with the mending now," she said, almost without thinking, as if she were talking to Meg, trying to please her.

"Do mending *just now*," said Hannah, "*rather* Hannah do that hair," and putting her arm around Ursula's waist she guided her to a chair.

Ursula let Hannah take the pins out of the hair that was still partially in coils on the back of her head.

"When I take this hair down Meg say 'like thick stream of honey pouring out of a honeycomb'. *Ne*, never forget that," said Hannah, starting to brush Ursula's hair with long rythmic sweeps. "*Ag shame*. It catch the light like gold when I brush."

"That feels lovely Nana, thank you."

Ursula had not expected to be out so long and was tired; the stroke of the hairbrush lulled her and brought to mind past times when, upset or over-excited, Hannah had soothed her by such methods.

"And, Nana, I'll make the candles with you next Sunday," offered Ursula, thinking again of Meg, and how they had all made the candles together on Saturday afternoons, "how about that?"

"*Ja,* thank you, *kleintjie.*"

Ursula closed her eyes whilst Hannah brushed her hair; it

65

would shine when Hannah had finished. Comfortable and safe in her own tiny home, surrounded by familiar and well-loved objects, Ursula's fondness for everything she knew glowed bright. And as it did so, her subtle impressions of David that day, the nuances of look and touch – the magnetism of his eyes, the firmness of his clasp – faded slowly with the evening light.

Five

Could swell the soul to rage, or kindle soft desire.
Alexander's Feast
John Dryden 1631–1700

Ursula had made up her mind not to encourage David. When she arrived at the theatre late on Wednesday afternoon she went straight to Joe, who was leaning over the half-door of his compartment.

"Good evening, Joe. May I leave a message with you?"

"You can, Miss, but I got summat for you first," he replied, reaching into a pigeonhole.

"Oh, really?"

"Here, young David left this for you, sent his apologies, said he wouldn't be able to come after the show tonight," and he passed her a small bunch of violets.

Ursula was taken aback, and mumbled her thanks. The violets were very pretty – it was the nicest apology she had ever had. The flowers made Ursula feel very special and she was pleased with his thoughtfulness. But they also had the unfortunate effect of making her feel guilty – she was going to decline his offer of a drink: now she regretted their not meeting.

"What's the message then, Miss?" asked Joe.

"Oh nothing, never mind. Thank you Joe".

Joe looked up at the ceiling, "Gawd," he muttered.

"Coo, who's the beau?" asked Jessie when Ursula came in holding the violets.

67

"Oh no, it's nothing like that," replied Ursula. David was not her beau.

"Well, who are they from?"

"David."

"David? Why is he sending you violets?" asked Jessie, frowning.

"Only to apologize because he can't come this evening when he said he would," Ursula said in a low tone of voice.

She hoped that she sounded very matter-of-fact and that Jessie would not be too inquisitive; she did not want to arouse her curiosity about the previous Sunday and be quizzed about the outing and the reason for the violets. The violets, and the warm feelings they kindled, brought all the pleasant aspects of their afternoon fresh to her mind. She had dismissed their outing but now she would think about everything she and David had said and done; later, when she had more time.

"*Ag*, he's probably been buttering up that Lydia who does the flowers outside, just like him. He's quite generous though, brought me some grapes one time. Mind you, he stood here so long talking to me that he ate most of them – said they're very expensive in England."

"I'll put these violets in that little glass that's next to your stool then. If he does turn up he can have them for an *hors d'oeuvre*," said Ursula with a smile, her dry humour an attempt at masking her pleasure.

"Very funny," said Jessie dismissively. "Still, we won't have time for anything tonight: we've got a full house and we're going to be run off our feet."

"Why is it going to be so busy?"

"Some of the people who couldn't make the matinée when Paula was, you know, *ill*, are coming tonight. Emma's doing the part."

"Her ankle's quite better then?"

"Seems so. She's not got quite so much stage presence as

Paula though," said Jessie disparagingly, turning up her nose.

"Do you mind if I just pop down for a minute and wish her luck?"

"What for? She did it at this afternoon's matinee. Abe dressed the theatre . . ."

"Excuse me," interrupted Ursula, "*dressed* the theatre, what's that mean?"

"Gave away tickets, you know, sent some for the nurses at Somerset Hospital and to the barracks, otherwise the audience would be very thin on the ground. I mean, who wants to come and see a nobody."

Ursula had struck up a friendship with Emma over the weeks and wished her well, "In the theatre everybody's a nobody until they're a somebody," she said solemnly, "she needs our encouragement. I'll only be a minute," and she scurried off before Jessie could disagree.

The Tivoli was a lavishly built and decorated theatre. However, it was all for show – that which could not be seen was very poor quality. Ursula clattered down the narrow wooden stairs and found the rooms that were used as dressing rooms; there were only two, one for the male cast, one for the female.

Off the end of each was a cubbyhole called The Star's Dressing Room. Emma had declined the use of this and was sharing with the rest of the female cast as usual when Ursula entered the crowded and cluttered room. A strong smell of greasepaint and cold cream greeted her, and the stifling warmth of too many nervous bodies confined in too small a space.

"Emma, I've just come to say 'break a leg' this time."

"Thank you Ursula," said Emma with a sweet smile. "I did the show this afternoon but I pretended it was just a rehearsal – not disastrous like the last one of course – but it feels like the real thing this evening and I'm very nervous."

"You'll be wonderful, really," said Ursula, positively.

"No, I know I'll forget my words," replied Emma as she finished brushing out her pale blonde hair.

"Balderdash. But if you do, just smile – the audience will be so overcome with how pretty you look that they won't even notice."

Emma's skin was as translucent as the most delicate china, her large eyes a startling light blue, her hair like silk from unripe corn. But Ursula felt no envy; Emma was a fairytale figure – beautiful, naïve, kind – but hardly real.

"You are sweet," said Emma. "I only hope I don't let everyone down."

"Emma you're the star. Stars don't let anyone down – they're supreme. Why aren't you in your rightful place in your own dressing room anyway?"

"Have you been in there?" She leaned close to Ursula to whisper, "'Don't tell anyone but my wardrobe at home is larger than that thing – it gives me claustrophobia. No, I'm much happier out here with the girls – it's friendlier anyway."

Ursula smiled, "Well, I best be off," she said, giving Emma a kiss on the cheek. Emma responded by giving her a little wave and a thin smile.

It was a very busy evening but Ursula enjoyed it in spite of her continuing disappointment – with the violets as a reminder – that she would not see David. That it was Emma's first lead part added a certain frisson to the air; even some of the visiting actors came to the wings to watch her. After the show, whilst Ursula and Jessie were sweeping up under the coat stands, Emma came in wrapped in a large velvet cloak.

"Ursula, I did it!" she said, throwing up her arms theatrically, uncharacteristically confident.

"Well done. How do you think it went?" asked Ursula leaning on her brush; not waiting for the reply she added, "I popped in for a bit and you appeared to be doing splendidly."

"You are kind; it went off without a hitch thank goodness," said Emma, looking relieved. "I was terribly nervous before I went on; I really thought I was going to be ill but someone gave me a push and I just had to get on with it. To tell you the truth I'm still feeling a bit wobbly inside."

"We were all crossing our fingers for you – everyone here wanted to see you and those that did were very impressed. You're a real star now."

"Well, I don't know about that but Ronnie is taking me for a drink to celebrate – that is, to celebrate me not forgetting anything I think – and I wondered if you and Jessie would care to join us?"

"Thank you Emma but Jessie must decide, I'm staying with her."

"We'd love to come," said Jessie with alacrity, "we don't get enough invitations to refuse any. But are we smart enough?" she asked eyeing Emma's cloak.

"Gracious me, yes, we're only going to the lounge bar in the Royal."

Ursula and Jessie exchanged glances with eyebrows raised – it was where David had taken them and they had thought it a rather elevated place.

"Well, perhaps we'll just pop downstairs and borrow some jewels and a boa or two," said Jessie storing their brushes away.

"That's a good idea, Jessie, something modest like that, nothing pretentious," said Ursula, digging her in her ribs with an elbow as they hurried downstairs giggling. They reappeared five minutes later: Ursula had put on a short moleskin cape over her dress and Jessie had substituted an enormous mauve hat with an oversized bow and a feather in place of her normal black felt one.

"My goodness," said Emma with wide eyes, "that is certainly quite a hat."

"And I restrained her," whispered Ursula loudly, "you know how she loves gaudy things."

71

"I heard that," said Jessie holding the brim steady with both hands. "*I* think it suits my large and colourful personality."

Emma and Ursula snorted with laughter at her studied pose. Ursula took the bunch of violets from the little vase on the counter and, shaking them to get rid of the excess water, took a pin from under the counter and pinned them onto her cape.

"How does that look?" she asked, pulling her shoulders back and smiling in anticipation.

Jessie raised her eyebrows and looked doubtful.

"Very pretty," replied Emma, smiling.

"Shall we go?" asked Jessie.

Ursula and Emma walked side by side through the passage to the foyer, with Jessie and her hat following behind. When they met Ronnie there, he said that he had arranged to meet a friend at the hotel and so it would be quite a party. Jessie and Ursula looked at each other and smiled – this was going to be fun. Arriving at the hotel they were greeted very courteously by the doorman who recognized Emma and greeted her by name.

"You must come here often," said Jessie when the girls were rearranging their dress in the powder room. "You obviously don't have to act for a living; don't you find us lot at the theatre rather below par."

"Not in the least. I made up my mind to be an actress and I love everybody and everything about it," said Emma, sincerely. "I would rather live in a garret and be an actress than live like this all the time."

"*Ag* well, you can change places with me then – anytime," replied Jessie, ungraciously. "I've got a very little garret that you are most welcome to."

Emma looked embarrassed.

"Take no notice of Jessie," said Ursula, "she's not got your aspirations but she does have illusions of grandeur – take that hat for example."

They looked in the mirror at Jessie's hat; it was so wide that

Emma on one side and Ursula on the other had to duck to see their reflection. They all burst out laughing.

The girls came out to find Ronnie talking to a tall, thin man wearing a cloak rather dashingly thrown over one shoulder; he held his hat in one hand and with the other played with a thin cane. He was introduced to them as Webster – Ursula assumed it was his last name as that was how English men seemed to refer to each other – and Ronnie explained that in the past he had played with him in popular theatre. Webster was now stopping over in Cape Town en route back to England. Ronnie suggested that they went into the lounge bar for a drink. Ursula was glad that they had been before and that she could concentrate on her friends and not the surroundings.

They chose the table and banquettes in the corner furthest from the bar and when the waiter reached the table Ronnie asked what Emma would like to drink.

"No Ronnie," replied Emma, "this treat is on me. I promised myself there would be champagne the first time I did anything special on the stage. Won't you order it for me please?"

"Dearest, I can't possibly let you do such a thing," said Ronnie in a voice full of sham outrage.

"No Ronnie do, I can afford it this month. Be a sweet, please," urged Emma.

"If you really, really must," Ronnie replied immediately, throwing up his hands in an attitude of surrender. Without delay he turned to the waiter and gave the order. "Mustn't argue with a lady," he added as an aside to Webster giving him a large wink.

"Just like my Uncle Joe," Jessie confided to Ursula who nodded in agreement, "out for everything he can get."

Ursula disliked Ronnie; he had shown no remorse whatever for the fact that Paula had to leave the troupe and stay far from friends and family in Port Elizabeth. His hair was long and, brushed back from his face, it rippled over his collar; he kept it slicked with pomade and as he passed a mirror he would reaffirm, with a sweep of his bony long-nailed hand, that his *coiffure* was still as he wanted it. The pomade smelled like the heady scent of a dying lily. Ursula looked away from him in contempt. She had seated herself on a chair facing the banquette with her back to the bar and could see the barman preparing their glasses on a tray in the reflection of the large mirror that covered the entire rear wall of the lounge bar. She saw the waiter come around the bar with a wine cooler, the bottle of champagne nestling in it covered by a large white linen table napkin.

"This is a real treat Emma," she said. "I've only ever had champagne once."

"Well this is a special occasion," replied Emma, "even if it's not what I really want to achieve. I may never get to play the main character in a classical production so I shall celebrate all my little successes just in case; sooner or later Father will pull the plug. It's a shame that we don't have just one more to make up the party," she added looking around in a half-hearted manner to see if she recognized anyone.

Jessie readily joined the quest. "Well that looks like David over there by the bar," she said in a loud voice.

"No, it can't be," said Ursula trying to see in the mirror whom Jessie was pointing out at the bar. "He couldn't come to the theatre tonight; he can't possibly be here."

"Yes, I'm sure it is, at the end, talking to someone," added Jessie craning her neck to see around the tables.

At that moment the champagne cork popped loudly and the waiter apologized; everyone in the lounge bar turned towards them. Ursula looked in the mirror, her eyes drawn to the bar. She was amazed to see David turn to face them and a young woman at his side glanced around too. Ursula's face froze and her throat constricted; what was he doing here with someone else when he couldn't meet her. She could see David moving to one side to try and get a view of them and now Ursula was grateful for Jessie's huge hat as it hid her from his view. She sunk a little lower in her seat; in the mirror she could see the girl at David's side tug his sleeve. Ursula was relieved that her friends were all pre-occupied with the ritual of the champagne being poured.

"Oooh! The bubbles went straight up my nose," laughed Jessie, "just like sherbet, it is."

"A toast to Emma," said Ronnie with a flourish, holding up his glass. "Here's to a glittering career on the stage."

They all raised their glasses and said 'To Emma' and Ursula hoped that their voices did not travel as far as the bar. I hope Jessie doesn't draw everyone's attention to David again, she thought, and let the cat out of the bag; if they know he was meant to meet me it will be mortifying and if he comes over here it will be embarrassing. She would try and steer the conversation in another direction; turning to Webster she asked, "Have you ever played here with anyone famous, Webster?"

"I was in Variety at the Old Pekin Music Hall when Mark Twain performed his *At Home* at the Opera House," he replied, leaning towards her.

"Is that so," Ursula replied, half-heartedly – it was obvious from the oblique reply that he had not played with anyone famous.

"Webster's career here was cut sorely short or he may have been up there with the best of them," Ronnie said in his defence.

"What happened?" demanded Jessie.

"With the war the theatres came to a standstill and I had to go back home," said Webster resignedly, crossing his arms.

"Oh I see," said Jessie, sounding unimpressed.

Ursula looked in the mirror and her eyes were drawn involuntarily to the bar; David had his back towards her now and was introducing the smiling girl to someone. Ursula was wishing it was she who was standing next to him, enjoying his attention, laughing with him.

"It's only a little better now – look what Ronnie has to do," said Webster, flinging one arm in his direction. On cue Ronnie sighed and his expression turned to one of self-pity. Pursing his lips Webster continued, "Of course, if theatre was up to the mark again, I don't suppose your amateur company would get a look-in," and he sat back and admired his nails.

There was a hush around the table; Emma looked crestfallen, Jessie looked ready to burst. Ursula searched for some subject of interest to rescue the conversation (pleased to have something to occupy her thoughts) and steer it onto a more friendly footing.

"I've read about Miss Fortescue – whom I think was with D'Oyley Carte in London – and Genevieve Ward," she said, "does anyone know about them?"

"I do," said Webster immediately. "Miss Fortescue was young and rather delicate but she was much better known for her beauty than her acting and singing, you know."

"Well, I read that Miss Fortescue was very clever," Jessie added. "She must be because she had the sense to marry a Lord."

Ursula could see David and the young woman talking, their heads close. The small hat worn by the woman could not conceal her abundant, auburn hair. Of course it doesn't matter that he cancelled our meeting, Ursula sensibly told herself. Nevertheless, she was surprised at how upset she felt to see him with another young woman.

"And Genevieve Ward married a Count," Webster continued, looking round to check that he was the centre of attention. "She was dressed totally in black at her wedding – which says quite a lot about her state of mind don't you think – and she chose never to see him again after the ceremony." He paused momentarily to check that his statement had the effect of capping Jessie's remark, before continuing in a low condescending tone, "But she really was the most wonderful opera singer you know, *wonderful* – until she suddenly lost her voice that is."

Ursula was amazed to see Emma suddenly sit up in her chair and, opening her eyes very wide, chime in enthusiastically, "Then she became one of England's great Shakespearian actresses, didn't she? My parents saw her here in several plays. Mother said she did twenty-six plays in the nine months she was in the Cape, isn't that marvellous?"

"Perhaps we could do a spot of Shakespeare?" said Ronnie with a theatrical gesture. "The majority of the cast might only be amateurs but one has to start somewhere. You could emulate the glorious Genevieve to your hearts content, Emma, and I could be your leading man – our chance to reach the pinnacle of serious theatre. What do you think?"

"Oh Ronnie, yes. I shall swot up on my Shakespeare just in case. It's what I told Father I was studying for. It's the only reason he let me join you – so I must give it a go if I have the chance," Emma enthused. "I do so want to be a classical actress."

Ursula sighed, the effort of concentrating on the conversation, whilst trying to keep detached from her emotions, was enervating. She glanced again in the mirror: David and the young woman were preparing to leave. Ursula held her breath hoping that he would not see them. David held the lounge bar door open for his companion but, just before he went through himself, he turned and looked straight at their table: he frowned and then, lifting his head a little, stared straight into the mirror. The expression on his face changed from one of mild interest to one of recognition and then set into a scowl: he took a step back into the room. Her cheeks burning, Ursula dropped her gaze to her hands that now lay clasped tightly together in her lap. He's annoyed I've found him out, she thought, and he's going to come over with some lame excuse. She braced herself – the seconds seemed interminable. Around her the conversation continued unabated and then, with relief, she heard the lounge door swing shut with a bang. Thank goodness he's gone, she thought with great relief, and lifted her head to check. And thank goodness Jessie didn't see.

"Thank you for coming everyone," Emma was saying, "but I think I must be going, I'm suddenly very weary, it's been such an exciting day."

They collected their wraps and coats and everyone thanked Emma for the champagne and congratulated her again.

"Of course I shall see you safely home, Emma. We'll take a cab naturally," said Ronnie when they were outside the hotel. "Can you do the honours with the girls, Webster?"

"Delighted of course," Webster acknowledged in an apathetic voice. "Can we walk – I mean to say, do you live nearby, is it safe to do so?"

"It's too close to do anything else – it's only a ten minute stroll," said Jessie, looking at Ursula and rolling her eyes.

Ursula nodded in agreement, she thought him a skinflint and a coward too.

"Just our luck to be saddled with the *windgat*," Jessie whispered to Ursula, as she tied the ribbon over her hat to keep the brim down.

"Jessie!" expostulated Ursula, shocked but secretly thrilled by Jessie's language, she couldn't help but agree.

"Still, he is one," Jessie concluded.

They turned to walk three abreast along the road. Webster's boasting had annoyed Ursula too, and his effete manner and histrionics had grated on her all evening. She had had enough of men getting the upper hand and was in the mood for making mischief.

"I've heard that some of the actresses in the Durban and Johannesburg theatres carry a little pistol at night if they have to go home alone," she said, teasingly. "I hope you have a gun to protect us, Webster."

"Never touched a gun in my life – nasty smelly things," he replied disdainfully. "I leave the theatricals for the stage."

Ursula nudged Jessie, and Jessie nudged her back to indicate she understood.

"My Pa carries the most enormous club-headed stick you ever saw," she said with expansive gesticulations. "And he's had occasion to use it more than a few times here on an evening out drinking."

Webster shuddered and walked faster.

"And we have an old army pistol at home, just in case, but we've never had the need to resort to it – yet," said Ursula ominously.

"But if there is trouble," Jessie added, clenching her hand into a fist and winking at Ursula, "fists are the quickest and most effective weapon my uncle always says."

Webster visibly flinched. Ursula slipped her arm through Jessie's.

"I'd be safer with my umbrella as a weapon than with Webster as a guardian," she muttered. "Come on, Jess, let's show him," and without another word they marched ahead of him – Ursula brandishing her umbrella like a baton – their heads held high, their breath like dragons in the cold night air.

As they strode on Ursula thought about David. Along with Webster and Ronnie – she told herself – he's simply another useless and unreliable man that I should happily see take it on the nose tonight. Violets! She pulled them roughly off her cape and dropped them in the road – apology my foot!

However, Ursula could not stop thinking about David and the evening in the bar. I don't care a fig that he spent the evening with someone else, she told herself a hundred times. She convinced herself that she felt nothing for him. She reasoned that as David knew the days she worked at the theatre he would avoid her. Arriving on Saturday afternoon she was therefore surprised, and more perturbed than she expected, to see David waiting outside the theatre. Walking very fast and keeping her eyes straight ahead she started towards the main door; David moved quickly in front of her. She tried to move to one side and then the other but he always managed to stand between her and the door. She gave up trying to outmanoeuvre him and, with a shrug of her shoulders and a big sigh, stood still.

"Ursula, I need to talk to you," he said urgently.

"Why?" She did not want to speak to him.

"I need to explain."

"I don't need any explanation, please let me by," she said, clutching her handbag close to her chest and moving to one side to get to the door. She did not want to see him, she did not want to talk to him. She wanted to escape from the hurt feelings he was stirring in her.

David dodged the same way so that he was in front of her again, "You don't understand. You need to know why I couldn't make it here on Wednesday."

"I don't care," she said, but she knew this was not true. Now that she saw him she cared very much.

"Please, Ursula."

"Just go away. Go and see your other friend," said Ursula shortly, unable to control her pique.

"I won't go away until you let me explain. I'll badger you all evening. Be reasonable," he said sternly.

"Reasonable? I am reasonable, was reasonable." How dare he accuse her; she was not at fault.

"Look here, if you just let me explain I promise I will go away and leave you in peace. That's fair isn't it?" David stood before her with his arms outstretched, his hands palm upwards.

She stood quite still now and looked at him full in the face. Dropping his arms he took off his hat and ran his fingers through his hair; she noticed his nails were short and neat and how his thick black hair sprang back naturally. It struck her how wholesome he was compared to Ronnie.

"Maybe," she said slowly.

"I'll get out of your way now if you'll meet me half an hour

80

before this evening's performance and let me explain to you – on your own – what happened on Wednesday. Is that fair?"

Ursula thought about it. At any moment one of the front-of-theatre staff might arrive and see her arguing with David on the doorstep – it might be quicker to agree. And she began to hope that there was an innocent explanation.

"I suppose so," she said, resigned.

"Good. I'll be outside the office at six o'clock," he said looking at her closely. "You will come won't you?"

"Yes."

"If you don't, I'll come and look for you," he warned.

"No, don't do that," Ursula shook her head vehemently. She had an awful vision of David recreating this scene in front of Jessie and anyone else who might be present. "I'll come, but just for five minutes."

"Good, see you at six then." David opened the door for her, stood aside and let her pass.

Half an hour before Ursula had to be ready for the evening performance she told Jessie that she had to go to the office to sort out a small problem. She was glad that Jessie was not interested. The office was where the theatre clerk – an inoffensive young Afrikaner called Petrus – dealt with any wage matters. Ursula went down to the dressing rooms, along the passage and up the back stairs to the little office on the first floor. David was not outside but she could hear the murmur of voices from inside the room. Annoyed that after all his protestations he was not waiting for her, and not wanting to be discovered herself waiting outside, she decided to leave when the door suddenly opened and a fair-haired young man with stooping shoulders came out.

"You want David, *Ja*?" Petrus asked.

"No. It doesn't matter," replied Ursula turning away, her pride pricked by the suggestion.

"*Ne*, wait – he's in the office here – please go in," Petrus stood holding the door open for her with a long thin arm – she had no alternative but to enter.

81

Six

It is not in the storm nor in the strife
We feel benumb'd, and wish to be no more,
But in the after-silence on the shore,
When all is lost, except a little life.

On Hearing Lady Byron was Ill
Lord Byron 1788–1824

Petrus closed the door firmly behind her and she could hear him going downstairs. David stood before her in the small room.

"Thank you for coming," he said quietly.

"I said I would," she answered, dispassionately.

"I really want to apologize for not coming here on Wednesday as I'd arranged, but it was unavoidable," he explained earnestly.

"Oh," was the most indifferent response she could make. She did not want hear lame excuses; it would make it worse.

"Did you get the violets?" he asked tentatively.

"Yes. Thank you," said Ursula with a small polite smile. Did he think that a bunch of violets excused him?

"They were just a little thing, I would much rather have come here and seen you," his tone was lighter now and he took a step nearer her.

"Really," she said in a studiedly flat voice, taking a step backwards. She was not that gullible; she had seen him talking to that redhead, had seen him leave with her.

"Yes, really. Don't you believe me?" he took another step towards her.

If he preferred to see someone else at least he could be honest about it, she thought, I'll show him I don't care two hoots.

"I don't know why you couldn't come and it doesn't matter," she said as calmly as she could, sounding as unconcerned as she could.

She moved back a little more – he was uncomfortably close.

"Yes it does matter. I don't make arrangements to see people willy-nilly and then not turn up. There was a good reason," he said, looking serious again, an edge to his voice.

Ursula said nothing. Yes, he was right, it did matter. She knew in her heart that she was fooling herself, she minded much more than she had admitted; she liked him, she really liked him, and she had thought he liked her.

"Look, I was hoping you would just believe me but you are obviously a harder woman than I thought," he said frowning and, seeming embarrassed, he tapped the leg of the desk with the toe of his shoe. "I shall have to explain further."

Ursula felt misjudged, she knew herself to be kind, and although she did not think he had been quite honest when he cancelled their meeting, she did not want him to think ill of her. Perhaps, just perhaps, there was a good reason. This doubt, and the sight of his discomfort, brought out her more tender feelings and her attitude towards him softened.

"There's no need, really," she said quietly. But she did want him to explain; she wanted to believe.

"Yes there is, I want you to know now," he said with feeling. "It was Duggie's sister you saw me with – you did see me didn't you?"

Ursula nodded. Duggie's sister, of course. David had said that Duggie had red hair.

"I thought so. You see, she's in the most awful fix: her husband's an Afrikaner, he had an accident and can't work and so she needs a job. They have a little son. She refuses to ask her family to help because they didn't approve of her marriage to a

Boer and they broke off all contact; only Duggie is sympathetic, but she won't involve him either, and he asked me to talk to her. Her husband would be furious if he knew she was asking anyone for help. The only time she can slip away is when her husband and baby are asleep. She really is at her wit's end. So I said I would take her to meet the boys in the bars – near the end of their shift they're less busy. Some of them have sisters or wives who work there who would put in a good word if a vacancy comes up. I had to help. Do you understand now?" he asked, leaning towards her.

Ursula felt humbled. But secretly glad that there was a good reason.

"I'm sorry, I didn't know," she said in a soft voice, her head slightly bowed.

"That's why I had to explain. I was worried when I saw you at the hotel that you'd misunderstand and not talk to me again."

Ursula did not reply; she knew that was indeed what had happened.

"Am I forgiven now?" He took another step towards her.

"Yes, of course you are."

"Good," said David and took yet another step towards her.

They were almost touching now but Ursula stood her ground. She glanced over her shoulder to see how close she was to the wall.

"This is what's called being 'backed into a corner' isn't it?" she said with an ironic smile.

"Nearly," he laughed. "You look even prettier when you smile, you know," he said and put his arms around her, clasping his hands together behind her back.

"Well, I'd better stop smiling if this is the effect it has," she laughed, "one more smile and . . ."

"And I'll kiss you," interrupted David and he bent his head and kissed her tenderly on the mouth. She only half-heartedly tried to push him away.

"I'm not smiling at that," she said as firmly as she could, and emphasized her words with a frown. The kiss was very nice, being held was very nice, but she must not appear to encourage him.

"And funny when you frown," and this time he pulled her closer to him and starting at the corner of her mouth gave her several small, soft kisses.

She wanted to tell him to stop but she could not find the will. She closed her eyes and, as the pressure of his kisses increased, she returned them with equal enthusiasm. Her mind held nothing now – not a thought, nor a picture, nor a word – only a soft deep brown darkness; all she was aware of was David, his arms and his chest, and his mouth on her mouth.

A door banged somewhere and Ursula abruptly opened her eyes. Moving her hands to his chest, she managed to push him away from her.

"No, we must stop, please, somebody might come in," she said, agitated.

"But that was so good; I could hold you all day," he said with his arms still round her.

"Don't be daft," she laughed, putting his arms away from her.

"You thought that was nice too, didn't you?" he sought her agreement with a teasing smile.

"You get much too sure of yourself much too fast," she said in her school mistress voice, trying to regain her composure. "I don't know what I'm thinking of, I've got to go, I've got work to do."

Ursula took hold of the doorknob but David put his hand against the door to delay her, "I've got something on this evening but you will see me again next Wednesday won't you – outside the theatre at five o'clock? We could have tea together."

"I'll think about it," she smiled.

"Say yes, or I'll come down and keep asking you when you should be working and wear you down with my ardour," he said with a mischievous grin.

Ursula suspected that this was all too likely. "All right," she laughed, "you win," and David let her open the door and escape.

She ran back downstairs and onto where Jessie was already taking coats and hats.

"Where have you been?" asked Jessie. "You've been ages and you look very flushed."

"Sorry Jess, I've been running, I didn't mean to be so long. Here let me take those, you sit down for a bit."

Ursula took the coats away, and, with them still on her arm, inspected her face in the mirror by the coat hooks for any tell-tale signs. Her lips felt swollen and tingled pleasantly but she was relieved that she looked quite normal. Throughout the evening Ursula was cheerful and volunteered to do most of the work; she greeted the patrons with a broader smile and more warmth in her voice than her usual polite tone expressed.

"What a happy little *dassie* you are tonight," Jessie said to her, "anyone would think you had a secret love."

The clerks in Ursula's office worked on a Wednesday afternoon and had Saturday morning free instead but occasionally they were allowed to leave a little earlier than usual. Ursula was pleased to take advantage of this the following Wednesday and was at the theatre five minutes before five o'clock to meet David. Couples, taking advantage of their half-day to stroll out together at leisure, smiled at her as she waited by the theatre door and she smiled in return. *Prettier when you smile*. She looked her watch, it was a quarter past five. Where was he? She had arrived in plenty of time and was sure that he had said five o'clock.

She recalled how wonderful she had felt with David's arms around her; he had held her as if he would never let her go. Feeling conspicuous waiting in the same spot on the street, she crossed the road until she was opposite the theatre where she walked up and down in front of the Opera House. How dizzying those kisses had been; she had experienced their embrace over and over again – in bed at night, on the bus to work, during her lunchtime breaks. The memory of their kiss caused her to shut her eyes momentarily, and then, suddenly opening them, she felt her cheeks redden as if people could read her thoughts.

It was now nearly half past five; where was he, she was so looking forward to their meeting, to seeing him smile, perhaps he had said half past. Impatiently she banged her handbag against her leg and looked about; a tram trundled past, faces turned towards her, wondering; a well-dressed lady carrying neatly wrapped purchases viewed her critically as she passed by. As she wondered where David was the glances and smiles she received gradually began to take on a more sinister aspect. A soldier walked towards her and winked at her as he passed. The driver of a horse and cart drove close to her and raised his cap, an unpleasant smirk on his face. What did people think of her standing around on the street; she felt her cheeks warm as the realization of this dawned on her and her feeling of well-being vanished. And as it did so she simultaneously knew that David was not coming. He had amused himself and was now making a fool of her; perhaps he was at this very moment with another girl. Smarting with indignation and muttering to herself through clenched teeth she stormed across the road and into the theatre.

In the privacy of the rows of coat stands, Ursula kicked the wall hard until her toe hurt – *I hate him, I hate him, I hate him*. Tears of anger ran down her cheeks; they stung her eyes and she wiped them fiercely away. How could he put me in such an embarrassing situation, standing around on the street; he's probably seeing that redhead again, probably kissing her now. She had a drink of water and washed her face to calm herself – it had always worked when she was upset as a child – but her anger was still simmering. When Jessie appeared after her break Ursula was sitting on the stool behind the counter.

"What's up with you?" asked Jessie as soon as she saw her.

"What do you mean? Nothing's up with me," Ursula said firmly.

"Well you're sitting there with a face like a plum duff and a mouth like a prune. You look in a real mood."

"Well I'm not. I'm perfectly fine, just let me be."

"See what I mean, you're in a bad mood."

"Jessie," warned Ursula, "now you're making me in a bad mood."

"*Ag* no man, don't blame me because someone else has upset you," said Jessie with her hands on her hips, not antagonized in the least by Ursula's tone. "It's not some beau that I don't know about is it?"

"No, it's not any beau. I think men are absolute beasts, they lead you on, then they let you down. You just can't rely on them."

"Steady on, now. So this is what it's all about. Come on, you'd better tell *Tannie* what's happened."

"Nothing, nothing's happened. Well . . . that is . . ." Ursula hesitated, she wanted to get it out of her system, she would tell Jessie. Not all of it – not the kiss, not the lie – it was too humiliating; too hurtful. "David said he would meet me – it's happened twice now – and he hasn't turned up. And I had thought . . . well, anyway, he just left me waiting for hours and hours. It was very embarrassing. Upsetting."

"I must say, it was quite obvious right from the very start that you two weren't going to hit it off. I told you I didn't think he was trustworthy didn't I?"

"Hmmm," grunted Ursula, "I don't remember you saying that."

"Still, it *was* him I saw last Wednesday with some woman at the hotel," said Jessie nodding knowingly at Ursula. "Of course,

I didn't know you were that interested in him or else I would have told you sooner. No one likes to be made a fool of."

This was too close to the truth for Ursula in her fraught state and, overcome by her emotions, she stormed off.

"You look awful," said Jessie when Ursula returned.

"I know, and I feel awful. Would you mind telling them I'm not well, I think I'd better go home. I couldn't be civil to anyone if I stayed, especially David, I'm just too angry."

"I'm not surprised. You simply can't trust him. After all he used to chat me up quite a bit didn't he?"

Ursula ignored this remark and went for her coat. She came back with it on.

"I'm going home then and I won't come to work on Saturday; I don't want to bump into David. In fact I don't want anything to do with him and if you see him you just tell him that if he ever comes near me again I shall . . . I shall . . ." she could feel her anger rising again.

"Off you go then, you'll still be in time for your bus," said Jessie authoritatively. "And don't you worry, I'll soon tell David to sling his hook if I see him. And I'll leave word at your office or write you a note when I know the coast is clear."

"All right Jessie, goodbye for now."

Ursula walked for a long way at a rapid pace, breathing unevenly, and as she did so her injured feelings and anger metamorphosed; she now blamed herself. I'm an idiot that's what I am, she said to herself, believing in such a man, letting him cajole me into embraces, looking forward to meeting him. But this merely masked her disappointment; her disenchantment was deep. By the time she waved the bus down she had talked herself numb and slowed to a normal speed. Reaching home she surprised Hannah.

"*Kleintjie*, you not look well," Hannah said as soon as she saw Ursula.

"I don't feel very good, Nana."

"Take off those things, man, *rather* put on your old *tabbertje*. You eat?"

Ursula shook her head.

"You get comfy. Hannah make something to eat."

"I don't think I could eat," she said. She would choke.

"*Ja*, I know best, man. Eat something light. You feel much better."

Ursula was too tired to disagree and went into her bedroom to put on her old dressing gown. As she changed and undid her hair, she could hear the back door swing to and, a little later, swing shut again. Nana must be lighting the stove and collecting eggs from the yard, she thought, as she re-arranged her loosened hair into a long plait that hung down her back. Ursula went into the sitting room and propped open the door to the lean-to where Hannah was cooking.

"Just make *seammelt* eggs," explained Hannah. "Those fowl not laying good; the pot for them soon . . ."

Hannah chattered on and Ursula sat down by the table and watched the small plump figure – coal black hair pulled into a bun, skin glowing the colour of crushed coriander, spotless apron and feet creeping out of sagging slippers – as she adjusted the flame of the primus stove and poured the eggs into the pan. Bending down, she broke off some of the leafy herbs that grew in the large tin cans, rusty now, that had once held tinned meat from England.

"Nana?"

"*Ja*?" replied Hannah, as she stripped the leaves into the eggs and stirred them around in the pan.

"Am I like mother or father?" Perhaps one of them became angry and upset like her self.

"I never meet your *Pappa*; you got *Mamma*'s grey eyes."

"I know, and Meg has her dark hair, but I meant my nature. Mother was a bit bookish like Meg, wasn't she?"

"*Ne*, not so serious, man. Meg read the bible over and over.

Ja, most when your Mamma gone," said Hannah shaking her head, "she miss her very much."

"Meg accepted every hardship as God's will – I can't be that meek."

"Meg say they go to church a lot when she a little one. Not like you. You and Meg different, man."

"Yes, perhaps I do take after my father. It seems I come out of my corner fighting . . ."

"*Is it*? Here, eat these eggs up. I make a pot of *tee*," said Hannah, scraping the eggs onto a plate. "Sound like your mind working too much, man."

"Thank you Nana. Home is definitely my best medicine."

As Ursula ate her scrambled eggs she looked around the familiar room, off which the only other room – her own bedroom – opened. Hannah had not been expecting her back and so the curtain that hung over her little bed in the alcove was pulled aside, displaying all that Hannah could call her own. Elsewhere in the room rustic furnishings and home-made rag rugs contrasted oddly with the few fine possessions of her parents that were left: a handsome pair of upholstered easy chairs faced each other like husband and wife; a portrait of her mother in an oval frame – her hair dark, black eyebrows like outstretched wings of a bird – hung on the wall and china figurines stood on the shelf that Hannah now dusted daily in Meg's memory. The tiny ivory box with her father's golden lock of hair in it and other small boxes – with various little curls of blonde, black and brown hair – clustered together on a neat hanging shelf surmounted by a small brass cross.

Ursula thought of these belongings – of the mother and father she had never known – with a sentimentalism that Meg had fostered. In addition, for Ursula brought up from babyhood by Hannah, they were the proof that her mother had existed; had been a real person. She liked the watch that she wore, suspended from a small bow of gold, because it had been her mother's. But

Lucy Ann White

she was particularly attached to the silver brush and comb set that stood on her dressing chest – not because they had belonged to her mother – but because her beloved Meg had cherished them and brushed Ursula's hair with them and finally left them for her to keep and use.

When Ursula had finished her eggs Hannah put a cup of bush tea down before her.

"Better is it? Better now something inside. You look more like my *kleintjie*."

"Yes, Nana. I feel much better." It was reassuring to be home; she had let herself get too worked up.

"Now, what *is* this all about?" Hannah asked pulling out a chair.

"It was nothing really – it was just that someone that I had arranged to meet didn't turn up, that's all. I waited for ages. I don't know why I got so agitated, I was just tired I expect, and annoyed."

She would play it down – she did not want Hannah to get any hint that there was more to it than that.

"*Is it*? That not so bad. Drink your *tee*, *kleintjie*. Who is it?"

"Don't be put out Nana – you can say it's my own fault – it was David, whom I came home with the other week. I was going to tell you all about him. I am very, very silly, that's all," said Ursula, remembering their embrace with chagrin now.

"*Ne*, it not the last time you get let down, lose respect. Things fade with time, man," said Hannah patting Ursula's hand. "Believe me, things fade with time."

"I'm sorry Nana, here I am making a fuss about a man who didn't turn up to meet me for something as unimportant as having tea together and you . . ."

"*Ne, ne*. My story's very old, man," interrupted Hannah, smiling good-naturedly. "My man good, kind. Something terrible happen or he come for me. I lose my baby when I come to Natal, look for him. But I am only glad I get you for my *kleintjie*."

92

Dear Nana, thought Ursula with affection. She got up and, walking around the table, bent to kiss the warm cheek.

"Nana, I'm going to clear this all up and help you tidy the yard and then I'm going to read to you while you do your sewing – would you like that?"

"*Ag shame.*"

Ursula did not expect to sleep well that night but Hannah gave her herbal tea before bedtime and she did not stir till the morning. Waking refreshed she went to work as usual. Mulling over what had happened she convinced herself that she had merely over-reacted to things and become too emotional. She had been like it as a child – it really was time she learnt to control her emotions.

By Friday evening Ursula felt sure that she could cope with seeing David and, whatever his excuse, could quite dispassionately tell him not to bother her again. However, on Saturday morning she received a scribbled note from Jessie.

Thursday

Dear Ursula,

I hope you are feeling better now. I promised to write if anything happened.

I saw that Duggie chap today as he came out of Abe's office (can't make head nor tail of what he says) and I told him to tell David that you didn't like him, and you didn't care about him and that you did not want to see him again under any circumstances. Now it should be quite all right for you to come to work this Saturday.

I'll see you then.

Love, Jessie

It was raining as Ursula left the house and the sky was gloomy. Jessie's letter had not reassured her and she wished that she had not bared her soul quite so passionately. She could not rid herself of a strange sense of foreboding. Entering the foyer Ursula noticed Joe talking to a stocky, red-headed young man, who was turning his flat cap round and round in his hands like a wheel; the regular theatre staff did not come in through the main doors so she knew he was not a stangehand. As she shook out her umbrella she heard the young man ask Joe something although she could not make out the words. Just as she was about to pass them he turned towards her, "You're nae David's friend are ye, Miss?"

"I know him if that's what you mean," Ursula answered guardedly.

"Aye, I thought ye'd likely be," he said nodding, "he said ye're a bonny lass."

"Really, and who are you may I ask?" Ursula was now sure that this must be David's red-headed friend, Duggie, as he had a lilting Scottish accent.

"I'm Duggie McNair."

"How do you do," nodded Ursula politely.

"I'm fine but I'll be awa noo," he said. "I just wanted to see what sort of a woman wad gie a decent lad the push when he's doon," and giving her a quick and dismissive look up and down he turned towards the door.

Ursula, disturbed by his tone as well as his words, turned around and put her hand on his arm to stop him.

He half turned towards her, "Aye?"

"What do you mean, when he's down?"

"Did ye nae hear of it? I told yon friend of yours, Jessie, all aboot it" replied Duggie, putting his cap under his arm, and his hands in his pockets.

"Hear of what?"

"David's wee brush wi' the criminal element at the races on Wednesday," he said, looking at her with a frown.

"I really don't know what you are talking about. Please stop scowling at me like that and tell me what's happened," she said in an authoritative voice.

"Weel," he drew the word out so that it was several syllables longer than normal, "if ye care, if ye're really interested . . ."

"Of course I do, I am, what happened?" Duggie raised his eyebrows as if to question her attitude and softly she added, "Please tell me."

"Aye, right ye are then" he nodded. "Weel, David tried to find ma sister a job – ye ken aboot that?" Ursula nodded. "Aye," he continued, "but he could'ne get her one richt awa, so he gae her his savings, he just kept a wee bit to try his luck on the horses, see if he could'ne mak a bit tae fill his coffers agane.'

Ursula had to listen intently and checked that she had understood, "He gave her his savings and kept a bit to bet with, is that right?" Duggie nodded. "And?"

"An' he won a fair bit, aye, he's rare gambler as well as a braw laddie, yon David."

"Ah, so that's it," she said, not surprised. "And is that all?"

"Nae, nae. The chappie he won it aff wasnae so happy, nae happy at all; he was a richt skellum. David canna prove it was him ye ken, but he woke up in a ditch, drookit, wi a bloody face an a sair heed: bump there the size of his fist," said Duggie, holding his own clenched fist up to his face. "An' nae a penny left in his trousies," he finished, dramatically pulling the inside of his trouser pocket out with his other hand and twitching it.

Ursula had not expected such a story and her tenderest feelings were roused. Her hand clasped Duggie's forearm tightly.

"Beaten up and robbed!" she said, shocked. "But he's all right now isn't he? He's not seriously hurt?"

"Och aye, he's fine the noo, dinna fash yessel. You look fair worrit, sorry lass, I dinna expect ye tae be upset," said Duggie, his broad Scottish accent flattening now and his tone becoming less strident.

"I'm glad he's all right," Ursula said, slightly relieved.

"Och he's fine – nae so fine when I gae him yon message frae Jessie – but he's made up his mind to mak the best of it."

"What do you mean? What message?"

"I've just been telling this chappie, he's awa tae Durban. He reckons he'll get more work there, he'd only been staying here on account of a lassie he was awfie sweet on."

Ursula closed her eyes and bent her head, "Oh dear . . . oh dear." So Jessie must have passed on her message word for word.

"Ye're nae feeling unwell are ye?" asked Duggie.

He took a step forward and turned his head to one side so that he could see her face. She lifted her head then and he did too. His face was broad with high cheekbones and pale blue eyes, the skin that was visible between his freckles had a bluish tinge and seemed strangely delicate for such a burly man. The general impression was a pleasant one. It had not been her first opinion of him, but now his features had softened he struck her as well meaning.

"I didn't expect such news," she explained, "when does he go?"

"He's awa tae the docks this morning looking for a passage; he's missed the mail boat but he's fair got the gift of the gab and likely talked his way steerage on anither vessel. He'll nae bide his time here longer than he needs the noo," said Duggie shaking his head. "Onie way, if ye're all richt, I'd best be aff. Can I gie him onie message?" he asked.

She bit her lip, Duggie was looking at her in expectation.

"No, that is, not really. I can't think. Can you tell him that I, that I, I wish him well and, um . . ."

"Aye, richt ye are then. Fare thee well," and, giving her one last long and searching look, he put on his cap and went out of the theatre into the rain.

Ursula stood quite still. David had gone; what had she done. Shortly she rushed to the door and, putting her head round it, called after Duggie's fast retreating figure, "And please tell him I'm so sorry."

But Duggie had crossed the road and was turning the corner towards the sea and never looked back. Ursula felt at a loss – she did not want to see Jessie – and she needed more time to think about what Duggie had told her. Creeping into the auditorium she sank down into one of the velvet seats and went over the story again; her thoughts and emotions were in complete turmoil. Soon the sounds of the bars being opened meant that she could hide there no longer. Ursula decided to find Emma – she was always a sympathetic ear – to help her make sense of it.

Down in the dressing rooms Emma was in with all the other girls and Ursula, putting her hand on Emma's shoulder, spoke quietly, "Emma, please come with me, I need to talk to you."

"What's wrong Ursula? You don't look yourself."

"I just need to talk to you alone, that's all."

Emma got up immediately, threw a shawl around her shoulders, and took Ursula's hand, "Come in here, no one uses it, we'll get a little peace."

They squeezed themselves in the tiny room off the end of the dressing area and Emma let the curtain fall behind them. It was very dark but Ursula preferred it that way. Emma sat on a box and made Ursula sit on the only chair, "There now, you can tell me all about it. I've never seen you look so worried."

"I'm not worried Emma, I think I'm just confused, and upset" explained Ursula. "You see, I've got to know David – you know David? Jessie and I met him for a drink – then he and I went out together for an afternoon, then we arranged to meet and he cancelled it because . . . anyway, we did meet and we, we . . . arranged to meet again and he didn't turn up when he said he would and I got very upset because I had come to trust him I suppose – but it turns out that it wasn't his fault. In fact he did someone a good turn and then got beaten up and I told

97

Jessie to tell him I never wanted to see him ever again and his friend says he truly likes me but now he's going away to Durban – going away today – and he still thinks I don't like him but," Ursula paused, she had not expected her explanation to come out in such a stream, "but I do, I really do Emma, very much and now I don't want him to go."

Emma leant forward and put her arm around Ursula's shoulder, "You look thoroughly miserable my poor sweet. If you don't want him to go why haven't you gone to tell him so?"

"Go to the ship you mean?" Ursula was surprised at herself, why had she thought it too late.

"If that's where he is, go and tell him," said Emma. "It's very simple."

"But what if he goes anyway?" What if he now rejected her, it would serve her right but oh, it would be so awful.

"What if you don't tell him and you never see him again? Remember, 'Nothing will come of nothing'."

Ursula sat very still; her ideas and feelings were beginning to take shape. She began to rationalize and distill what hitherto had been panic and confusion. Emma is quite right, she thought, if I don't tell him I'll regret it – if I do tell him but he still leaves, then I will have done all I can. She had never met anyone like David before and she might never again; someone with ideals to admire, someone with character, someone who made her laugh. And – remembering his muscular torso and his head bowed in pain, how it had felt when he held her as they danced, when they ran down the hill together, and how wonderfully strange it was when they kissed – she knew that she always wanted to be with him.

"You're right Emma, I'm going to try and find him," she said with sudden conviction. "I couldn't bear it if he left."

"And 'If thou dost love, pronounce it faithfully'."

"I suppose that's Shakespeare too?"

Emma nodded and smiled.

"Will you make my excuses upstairs," said Ursula, "say I've had an urgent message or something. Thank you Emma, you are an absolute angel," and giving Emma a kiss on the cheek she ran out of the room, up the stairs and out of the theatre in the direction of the docks.

A thick mist hung above the streets and the air felt heavy although the rain had finally stopped. As Ursula hurried along towards the docks, avoiding the puddles as best she could, she tried not to think what she would say when she saw David. She would concentrate on getting to the docks on time, not until she was there would she know how to put it. But fast as she walked her mind ran ahead of her; he had done a tremendous favour and been beaten up by a *schelm;* he had ended up in a ditch with his head bleeding – and she had cursed him for not turning up! A ship's horn sounded; can't be far, she told herself, walk faster. She imagined Duggie telling him – don't like him, don't care about him, don't want to see him again – he must have thought her the meanest person ever. And he had stayed because of her; could it really be true, she asked herself, did he really like her that much, could it be that he loved her too? Durban was so far away!

Reaching the dockland area, she walked briskly past the warehouses and timber yards, shops and stalls. The area was full of Malay workers; blowing horns – strings of *snoek* hanging from their fishing carts – on ladders repairing timber shutters, broadcasting newspapers from their corner pitches. A ship's horn sounded again and she hurried on. Through the open doorways of boarding houses and saloons Ursula could see men propping up the bar, playing cards, smoking. Unemployed *volkies* from the Cape winelands and poor white *uitlanders* loitered on the corners hoping to acquire spoiled foodstuffs. Don't look them in the eye and I shall be safe, she told herself, remember that they're only hungry. She must hurry – she was nearly there, it was just around this corner. A little further. At last, she sighed, I've got here, and there is the ship! Thank goodness.

Ursula finds her way around the produce that lies stacked along the wharf ready to be loaded for shipping abroad: crate upon crate of fresh and dried fruits; boxes of flowers from the neighbouring farming districts; wine from the nearby vineyards; piles of maize and bales of wool from outlying areas. Keeping her eyes fixed on the ground to avoid tripping over the cables and pulleys, she carries on. The dock is busier and noisier, now that she is in amongst it, than could have been imagined from her more distant impressions.

What a crush at this gate, she frets, better push through. Don't want to be stopped, "So sorry – please let me through – oh dear, excuse me."

She picks her way around wicker hampers and cabin trunks that lie in her path. She can still see the ship; nearly there now, she assures herself, then I can tell him. Tell him how I feel, tell him I'm sorry. Squeezing past a red-faced stevedore – his breath smelling strongly of ale – and several Malay stevedores and wiry Indian labourers doing the lion's share of the work, Ursula is getting uncomfortably hot. She is almost at the ship and keeps up her mantra – nearly there now, nearly there. At the bottom of the gangway stands a large man with his sleeves rolled above his elbows, a hat pushed to the back of his head and a clipboard in his hand. He does not look quite as Ursula has imagined – expecting someone smarter to be in charge – but as he is the only vaguely official looking person she decides that he must be the one to ask.

"Excuse me?"

"Yes Miss, what can I do for you?" replies the man, looking at her with surprise.

"I'm looking for someone who's going to Durban."

"Well Miss, that could apply to a hundred people hereabouts. What sort of someone would this be and when would this someone be going?"

"He's a, a gentleman, who wants to go to Durban today," she says, feeling a little foolish that she cannot be more exact.

"Well he won't be getting there on this ship, Miss. We're loading passenger supplies bound for Lisbon. Youse be wanting another ship that goes from the other dock."

"Oh dear, where's that?"

The man points to a large empty area over to his right, "Right there, Miss."

Ursula is perplexed, "But there isn't a ship there?"

"No Miss, that's because it left not fifteen minutes ago."

"It can't have, it can't have gone," she says in horror.

"You just walk this way a bit Miss and – just a bit further so we can see round the stern – and there youse can see it clear as day, that cargo ship, only one leaving for Durban today, just about to turn south, see?"

She experiences her breath leaving her body. Feeling faint, she sways, her hand to her head.

"I say Miss, you look like youse about to faint," and the man, his jocular tone gone, takes hold of her arm and walks her off to a squat bollard. "Sit on this Miss 'til youse feeling a bit better. How's that now?"

"You're very kind I'm sure. I'm just rather hot and it's making me queasy. I'll be all right now."

"Well you better just rest there awhile till youse quite up to it."

"Thank you, I will."

I cannot bear it, she thought, if I hadn't told Jessie all would be well. David has gone and it's all my fault; now I will be here and he'll be there. I shall never see him again, I know I won't. When people leave they never come back.

And, as the nauseous feeling subsides, and her disappointment

101

increases, a heaviness settles on her. Unable to stir from her seat, the thought of walking back through the tangled mass of the dock becomes a dread. She has not felt so sad since they left Jimmy in Kimberley; she has not felt so deserted since the day that Meg entered the convent. Putting her elbows on her knees, she covers her face with her hands, and sobs.

PART II

The nursery
Johannesburg, February 7th, 1912

Tuk, Tuk, Tuk, Tuk; had it not been for the regular tick of the clock Ursula would have said that time stood still. Nothing had changed; the baby lay exactly as he had for days now. The only other sound in the room was the occasional plash of water as it landed on the china basin. She watched as the water ran around the rim of the tap to produce a promising bud, enlarging as if by some magical force until – suspended like a swollen fig – it fell suddenly, breaking onto the hard surface: shattered, scattered; expected, but unexpected.

Ursula looked at the clock; the doctor would probably call by at two o'clock. She would have to explain again that she had been unable to contact her husband; that he was up country and unlikely to return for another few days. It was tedious and trying. The doctor seemed to have no conception of how much she wanted her husband's support; how much she felt his absence at yet another time of crisis. The ringing of the doorbell rent the hush of the house.

The doctor feels Edward's forehead and cheeks with the back of his hand. His temperature is reduced but there is no other improvement, the doctor says. She must have a nurse to help with looking after the sick child and allow herself to rest.

"But doctor I can manage."

No. The doctor does not want two sick patients. He knows

her husband would approve of the arrangement. He will organize it. The woman he has in mind is highly qualified, very efficient, has 'dealt' with this 'sort of thing' before.

"Doctor, what can we give Edward? Are there no medicines, no antidotes, nothing?"

"Only give sugar water, nothing more, on no account anything more; there is no cure. Good day."

I don't want a nurse! I don't want anyone to look after my baby but myself. But I have to agree. It's hateful. If I refuse the doctor's advice Edward's father may never forgive me.

The nurse arrived the next morning. She looked forbidding with a crisp cap and starched apron, stiff collar and cuffs. *Ja*, her name was Mrs Van Der Ploeg; she was to be addressed as 'Nurse'. Her hours would be two o'clock until eight o'clock; it would allow Madam to rest. Nurse would wash and bathe the child, change his linen, make him comfortable, give him sugar water. And do her knitting. A small sandwich and a cup of tea around five o'clock would be all she required.

I hate her. She looks like one of those cardboard cut-out dolls I hung paper clothes on as a child. She's straight and flat and got sharp corners. Her cuffs will scratch Edward, her apron will crackle. He's thinner, losing his dimples – she will eat in front of him – and Edward poor lamb with nothing but water!

Surely Madam should still be resting? Two hours is not sufficient to renew the body or the mind. Now if you don't mind Madam I have everything under control. *Ja*, I have tucked him in quite securely myself Madam. And I shall sponge him down to cool him. If you please, I do need to tidy the room.

But he needs a little touch – he needs to hear me, feel me here – I know him best.

She's insensitive, cold, she's going to freeze my little baby's heart.

Madam must not keep popping in; it is not going to do Madam or the child any good. Madam must rest in this heat and conserve her energy. And if it is possible to have ham instead of cheese tomorrow in the sandwiches she would be obliged; ham is more digestible. *Ne* Madam, only sugar water is allowed.

But it's been days now, how can he exist on water? How many of their patients have – he won't have the strength to survive. And with only the odd dribble of water he will dehydrate. There must be something we can do; I'll find out from someone. My lovely Edward.

Ne, it is not yet time for me to leave Madam. If Madam is looking for her 'bits' she will find them in the top drawers of the chest. And please note, flowers should never be left in the room of an invalid.

She moved all my things – the photographs, the note cards, my books for Edward, and the flowers – he can't smell the flowers. And his play things, Edward has none of his favourite toys!

Goodnight Madam. *Ne*, there was no change in him; none at all. And perhaps tomorrow we can keep to our regime. If Madam rests she will be less anxious. Better for Madam, better for Baby.

She may be efficient but she's only a nurse – I know what's best for my baby. Yes, I shall rest tomorrow, but I shall rest easier in the knowledge that I've helped Edward. I shall feed him, I shall boil a fowl with vegetables and barley. The stock should be as nutritious as anything solid. I know I'm right. I know I am. No one can live on water. And now I will read to him and stroke his little arms and legs. And with food and love I pray my baby will live.

Seven

When green buds hang in the elm like dust
And sprinkle the lime like rain,
Forth I wander, forth I must,
And drink of life again.

More Poems (1936)
A E Housman 1859–1936

June turned to July, the skies were leaden, the weather worsened – a ship broke from its anchor and mountainous seas cast a wreck on the coast. The grey rain clouds that lay heavy on the mountain threatened worse to come. Life for Ursula resumed its previous pattern although an aura of disappointment cast a pall over her days; her office work seemed more monotonous, the theatre less exciting. Small kindnesses that Bernard and Emma showed her did not lift her despondency; Jessie's inability to understand it depressed her. Jessie now saw Ralph several times a week, including Saturday evenings when Ursula stayed with Emma instead. After evenings out with Ralph, Jessie regaled Ursula with every detail of their conversations and activities together: where they went, what they saw, whom they spoke to; his protestations of love, attempts at passion – her choice of dress, intended outfits. Bored by this onslaught, and excluded, Ursula felt a lack of companionship and lost hope in a brighter future.

At night, in the large iron bed that she had shared with her sister, under the cotton quilted coverlet Hannah had made from scraps of every dress they had grown out of, she read herself to sleep. And then Ursula's dreams were vivid – every sensation heightened: movements dynamic, colours intense, sounds amplified.

David whirls her around a cavernous ballroom, music surrounds them, chandeliers glisten in candlelight, taffeta trains brush against silk skirts, but nothing impinges on her consciousness – nothing except the warm words softly spoken in her ear. Holding her hand he smiles at her as they run side by side down a slope, a sward greener than green, damper than the dew.

Unexpectedly next to his half-clothed muscular body in the boxing ring – so close to him that she can feel the heat of his breath on her neck, see the pinpricks of sweat on his skin – the bones in her body feel as if they dissolve. She sees the naked Hercules in Lord Leighton's powerful painting, Watts' Orpheus caress Eurydice, Waterstone's water nymphs seduce Hylas. Sensual image after sensual image crowd in upon her.

Such dreams would disturb and awaken her. To banish the reality of them she performed the little rituals she normally practised in order to settle down for the night. She straightened her nightdress, tucked her hair behind her ears, pummelled her pillow (making sure her handkerchief was beneath it) and smoothed the sheet beneath her chin until she lay quiet and calm again; concentrated on the repetitious tap of the rain on the metal roof until she slept. After a night of such dreams she would not have been surprised to see David as she travelled to work, entered her office, looked up from her books. How wonderful that would be. But on such mornings expectation inevitably turned to disappointment, and desire to ennui, as the day progressed.

Ursula pushed herself to her physical limit in an attempt to rid herself of the regret that clung to her. With her felt hat pulled well down over her eyes, her thick waterproof shoes on, she walked home each Sunday via the sea wall at Green Point and along the coast towards Sea Point. The windier – the stormier – the weather was, the more Ursula felt that she was being purged. Buffeted by the westerly wind, her face lashed with the rain, she would stand looking out to sea, listening to the rasping cries of the seagulls, in tune with every heroine of the sad romantic novels she consumed. Reading in bed each night by the light of her small oil lamp she sympathized with the shattered hopes of *Jane Eyre*, the trials of *Mary Barton*, the tragic fate of *Anna Karenina*

July turned to August, the wind and gales lessened but the soft showers that replaced them lasted for hours without let up. Under the gaze of the mountain Ursula walked the slopes of *Schotsche Kloof* and Signal Hill where she trod with little care on the snow of white daisies and the brick and yellow *kalkoentjes;* ignored the striking proteas, the pretty hooded *moeder kappitjes*. The flowering sea of yellow that was now Point Common usually filled her with pleasure but even this sight did not elicit a smile. However, Ursula had a character too positive to accept defeat or court failure. Replete with self-pity, tired of mourning over lost opportunities and weary of the unfulfilled expectation of seeing David, she finally gave up the solitary walks. She would not give up hope, but she determined to look forward.

One Wednesday – a day golden and bright, a promise of days to come, with no mist on the mountain and no wet mud on the road – Ursula left her office early to buy fruit from the market at Grand Parade before going to the theatre. Her spirits rose with each step she took – spring was not too far away and the flower market was full of early sweet-smelling blooms, collected by the flower sellers, and happy-faced pansies, raised by more enterprising souls. Walking along she recognized the figure of Duggie sauntering in the same direction; when she stopped to buy fruit he stopped at a stall opposite. She lingered over the purchase and noticed him looking her way although he showed no signs of recognizing her. Unsure of his response if she approached him, she carried on with her purchases.

That evening at the theatre a dance troupe was due to perform the Highland Fling – among other things – as soon as the preceding dog act had finished. An impressive bearded Scottish piper strode onto the stage ready to accompany the dancer. Unfortunately, when his bagpipe wheezed into action the star of the dog act, a snappy little terrier, returned to the stage and attacked his ankles. Having silenced the monster the dog ran off and the Scot left the stage, amidst roars and howls of laughter, brandishing his *skean-dhu* ready to thrash or, worse, murder the offending mutt. When the dog was finally apprehended and the red-faced Scot calmed, Jessie was asked to minister to the bites the piper incurred.

"That's the most difficult job I've been given yet," Jessie said when she returned to the cloakroom. "A furious Scot is bad enough but getting his laces undone and his stockings down is more dangerous than stealing a fish from a seal. Especially when you can't comprehend a word he's saying. Ten times worse than Duggie to understand."

"Have you seen him lately, Jessie?" asked Ursula, with interest.

"Who?"

"Duggie."

"I've seen him hanging around Abe's office now and then," said Jessie with a non-committal air.

"Have you spoken to him?"

"A little," said Jessie, guardedly.

"And did he mention anyone?" asked Ursula, brightening.

She hoped she might learn that David was coming back. Jessie looked blank. "David perhaps?" she prompted.

"Come to think of it he did," replied Jessie, enthusiastic now, "said that David was doing very well in Johannesburg. And did even better in Durban. A popular success is how he put it, I think."

"Oh. So, there's no chance that he'll be coming back here then, is there?" said Ursula, her voice flattening.

"Shouldn't think so," said Jessie shaking her head. "Once they get out there into the bold new towns there's no stopping them. I've seen it all before; too many exciting things going on – too much to tempt them. Especially cockerels like David! Who in their right mind would want to come back here to us country chicks?"

Ursula did not reply – there was nothing to add. David would never come back. In her disappointment she had no wish to hear more about the fracas off-stage and she went to brush the floor around the coat hooks.

As Ursula left her office the next day she again saw Duggie; he was sitting on a bench under the spread of a tree whittling away at a stick. The next evening he was standing at the bus stop opposite to hers. On neither occasion did he show any wish to acknowledge her; she felt sure now that he recognized her but decided that he probably still thought ill of her. Her bus came, but by the time she had pushed her way on and sat down, she could not see him through the window: he had gone. She wondered where he was living that he now had to catch a bus.

On Saturday afternoon Ursula arrived at the theatre as usual to find that there was a special, and unexpected, evening performance of the play *The Royal Divorce,* with a famous actor playing the part of Napoleon. Many of the supporting actors were already booked at the Opera House and so one or two of the Tivoli amateurs were required; Emma would have the chance to perform with a professional group and gain valuable experience. Jessie and Ursula were nearly as excited as Emma by the unexpected and delightful change of programme. The advertised matinée was cancelled to give the actors a chance to rehearse and time for alterations to be made to the costumes.

"Emma looks a bit pale and English for the part you know," said Jessie critically, as the girls tidied the lost property cupboard.

"So you think a more colourful character would be better?"

"Definitely – put those gloves on that shelf with the rest – yes."

"Just remember what happened when we had a red-headed leading lady," warned Ursula. "Life backstage is a great deal calmer with an amateur actress like Emma."

"*Ag* man, that reminds me – I haven't told you about my evening at the Royal on Thursday," said Jessie, leaning against the cupboard for support, as if she intended to be some time in the telling. "Ralph did take me for a drink there. I told him it was the place for celebrations and it was his birthday so he fell for it! I think he was impressed. I could get used to it you know, the rich life. There was a lady there with the loveliest gown, plum colour, she was too old for it but I shall look out for a dress length that colour at the market. Maybe Mrs Naipul – you know, who makes the costumes downstairs – will cut it out for me. It had a sort of cummerbund that . . ."

But Ursula had not been concentrating – she had been thinking of David and wanted to know if Duggie's sister did get a job at the Royal – and she interrupted, "Were the same people working there?"

"Excuse me?"

"You were talking about the hotel. Did you recognize anyone there?"

"I did actually – when you said 'red-headed lady' you reminded me of the scarlet woman – the woman who was with David that night, when we went with Emma, she was working

114

there; helping a doddery old dear into that clanky brass lift. Funny hours if you ask me; suppose they need people all hours in a place like that. Couldn't mistake her – all that red hair, poor girl."

The answer annoyed Ursula – Jessie never misses the opportunity to get a dig in, she thought, she likes to imply that David's meeting with Duggie's sister was not above board.

"She's not a scarlet woman, she's Duggie's sister." Now Jessie would know why David had been with her.

"How do you know?" asked Jessie accusingly. "You haven't spoken to Duggie have you?"

"It wasn't Duggie who told me."

They were interrupted by one of the stagehands putting his head around the door, "Jessie, your first aid skills are needed again. There was a nail sticking out of one of the screens."

"Righto," Jessie called in reply. "Can you finish this while I'm upstairs?" she asked Ursula.

Ursula nodded. Jessie took a small box from under the counter, and as she made her way out she shook her head and added, "Well she was definitely the one I saw canoodling with David. She may be Duggie's sister or she may not, but I wouldn't believe everything you hear, Ursula."

"I don't, Jess," replied Ursula tersely, too furious to say more.

The following Monday evening Duggie was again waiting opposite Ursula's bus stop but this time he stared at her, nodded, and smiled. Ursula hesitated, her regret at not giving him a message for David before he left, returned to her. Duggie had acknowledged her now and she would not miss this chance to correct her omission; Jessie's remarks about David not wanting to come back and her doubts about Duggie's sister were fresh in her mind. She would clarify things if she could, she would show Jessie how wrong she was about David. She crossed the road and smiling said, "Hello Duggie, remember me? I'm . . . I was, a friend of David's."

"Aye Miss, I remember ye weel enough," he replied, politely lifting his cap.

"How are you Duggie? And how is your sister getting on?"

"I'm fine Miss, an mae sister's got a braw job the noo. Yeself?"

"Oh, I'm . . . I'm well thank you," replied Ursula, involuntarily giving a negative shake of her head.

Duggie looked closely at her and nodded but did not respond. Ursula filled the awkward silence by looking around to see if her bus was coming: there was no sign of it. Still Duggie said nothing.

"Duggie?" Ursula began, kneading her gloves nervously.

"Aye?"

"Do you know . . . can you tell me . . . I mean, have you heard from David?"

"Aye," he replied, with a nod.

Duggie's not making this easy for me, thought Ursula. She would try once more, "Is he all right? Doing well?"

"Aye."

"He'll be staying in the east then, I expect," said Ursula, no hope in her voice. She was wasting her time.

"Nae doot. Have ye onie message for him?"

"Yes, yes I have," said Ursula regaining her resolve, "can you get a message to him?"

Duggie nodded.

"Will you tell him please that I'm very sorry," said Ursula and hung her head, it was embarrassing saying such things to a virtual stranger. She took a deep breath, forced herself to stifle her pride, ignore her burning cheeks and start again, "Please tell him that I'm very sorry that he left. And that I wish he'd come back."

"Aye, I'll tell him. Ye fair took yer time to get that oot. Ye best be aff, that's yer bus the noo," he finished, not unkindly.

"Thank you Duggie, goodbye," she muttered quickly, before she boarded her bus and found a seat.

That was awful, she thought, admitting to another man that I want David to come back. But Duggie was quite nice, not annoyed with me after all. But I haven't clarified things at all, I should have asked further questions about David, said more – but how could I to Duggie? Hope he remembers the message – hope he can write! If David doesn't get the message he might think I still don't care. Maybe find a sweetheart in Durban or Johannesburg – probably already has – she concluded depressingly.

At the theatre on Wednesday evening Ursula was given several errands to run whilst the first act was on. Passing Joe's cubbyhole she was hailed, "Hey Missy, got a message for you from the Scotch fixer feller."

"Who?"

"Well, I dunno what he does but he does it a lot round here – that ginger Scotch chap."

"His name's Duggie; he works for Abe. Petrus says he travels, arranges things for Abe's business interests."

"That's what I thought I said. Anyways, he asked if you 'could meet by the sundial in the Company's Gardens, one o'clock, Friday'. Says he'll be back tomorrer for the answer."

Ursula was surprised, "Did he say he had some news then?" she asked.

"Didn't say nothing to me Miss, 'cept the message. I memorized it for him, he didn't write nothing and he didn't say nothing 'cept . . ."

"Yes, thank you Joe. I understand," interrupted Ursula.

"Well what's the verdict?" demanded Joe.

"Excuse me?"

"Is he to be a lucky man or not?"

"Oh you don't think . . . oh dear me. It's nothing like that Joe," said Ursula shaking both her head and her forefinger in the air, appalled that Joe might think she and Duggie were more than acquaintances.

"And it's nothing to me, Miss, how many sweethearts you 'ave," said Joe with feeling. "I'm just the geezer who delivers these billy dux. Is you, or isn't you, going?"

"I would, but . . . he didn't say I had to come on my own did he?" she asked, trying to get more information out of Joe.

"No, I said what he said. Make up your mind Miss, I haven't got all day."

"Yes, all right then, one o'clock in the Gardens," agreed Ursula. "Please tell him, yes Joe."

"Wimmen – at last!" expostulated Joe, slapping his palm down on the counter. "Thank Gawd for that."

Ursula went straight down to the dressing rooms to see if Emma was there and found her changing her costume for the second act.

"Hello Ursula, this is a nice surprise," said Emma. "Can you do this up for me?"

She turned her back for Ursula to do up the buttons on the back of her frock.

"Emma, listen," began Ursula. "I told you I'd seen Duggie didn't I?"

"Yes."

"Well, I've seen him nearly every day now and on Monday I finally plucked up the courage to give him a message to pass onto David. He's in Durban – Johannesburg – I don't know which. Anyway, now Duggie wants to meet me at lunchtime on Friday. I said I would go but do you think someone should come with me?"

Emma turned round and looked at her.

"Are you worried he's sweet on you then?" she asked, wide-eyed.

118

"Not really, it's just something Joe said. After all he can't be can he? It's me who approached him not the other way round."

"Perhaps he feared a rebuff," said Emma smiling encouragingly at Ursula. "Some chaps are awfully shy about that sort of thing."

"No, no, it's too silly," replied Ursula shaking her head. What was she thinking – she wasn't the weak and wilting type, was she – this sort of attitude would not pass muster. "I'm sure Duggie has the most innocent reason. Don't worry; it will be perfectly safe for me to see Duggie alone. I'll have to get back to my office by two anyway. And now I better get on and complete my errands or I shan't get finished. Can I stay with you on Saturday?"

"Of course, I love having you."

"Good. I'll tell you what Duggie wanted then. Bye."

But Ursula did not tell Jessie about her arrangement to meet Duggie. She was annoyed that Jessie continued to refer to the days leading up to David's departure as the 'David fiasco'. If someone as uncomplicated as Emma isn't sure of Duggie's motives, she decided, then I definitely don't want Jessie with her over-active imagination jumping to any wrong conclusions. I'm sure she's keen on Duggie and she's all too likely to get involved and put a spanner in the works. Then I won't hear anything of David. Wouldn't it be wonderful if he came back, she thought, even if it isn't for some time. On Friday Ursula dressed with care – she chose a crisp white blouse that had a plain round neck and large flat collar to go with her customary black skirt and wide belt – she wanted to give Duggie the impression of primness, just in case.

Ursula told her office colleagues that she would take an hour for lunch and was in no hurry to get to the Company's Gardens. She had a slight butterfly feeling in her stomach; she did not feel wholly at ease with Duggie and planned to make the meeting as brief as possible. Hear his news, good news with luck, she thought, then make the excuse that she had to go. If it wasn't the news that she wanted, or if Duggie made any suggestions that they should meet again, then she would leave immediately. Either way, she would still have plenty of time to eat her lunch and buy a cup of tea. As she walked up St George's Street she stopped to admire the fashionable clothes in the windows, unconsciously delaying meeting Duggie.

She finally reached Wale Street and turned into Government Avenue. A large group of office workers, chattering loudly, were strolling into the Gardens by the library gate and Ursula followed them. Unable to see far ahead of her she admired the exotic shrubs and banana trees that grew on each side of the central path, as she walked along. Soon the young men and women turned right off the path, and when they did so she was at the intersection where the sundial stood. And there he was with his back to her, reading the time on the brass dial; one hand in his trouser pocket, his hat in his other. She turned about and stared back down the path she had taken, unbelieving. What cruel joke was this; her mind was playing tricks on her, re-creating her dreams.

"Ursula."

She cocked her head to one side – that voice!

"Ursula, I'm here."

Spinning around she gasped.

"You're not supposed to be here!" she blurted out.

"That's not quite the reaction I'd hoped for but I suppose it will have to do," said David smiling broadly as he walked up close to her.

Ursula looked up at him – his familiar eyes, his mouth, his touchable hair. Her emotions overtook her.

"I thought I'd never see you again," she said tremulously.

David took her hand and put it to his lips.

"Come," he said softly, leading her towards a cast-iron bench nearby, "sit next to me here. I've got something I want you to see."

They sat side by side and David removed a flat, claret-coloured box from his pocket. Ursula felt her heart had expanded to fill her chest, as if that was how it should be, that at last everything was right. Did he feel the same she wondered as she watched him carefully opening the box. He passed it to Ursula. On a piece of padded red silk lay a medal beautifully crafted in silver, a miniature figure of a boxer on the domed vermilion and azure enamelled surface; a rich blue grosgrain ribbon and an inscribed pin held it firm. Ursula rubbed the shiny surface with her finger, "It's beautiful," she said admiringly. "Congratulations."

"Thank you. It's quite something. I didn't expect to do this well quite so soon."

Ursula, looking at his smiling face, could feel the pride he had in his achievement suffusing her too.

"I'm sure you deserve it," she said warmly. "I'm very pleased for you," she smiled and returned the open box to his hand.

David sat for several minutes looking hard at the medal. Suddenly he shut the box and offered it to her, "I'd like you to have it," he said decisively.

"Oh I couldn't. I couldn't possibly. You must keep it, cherish it."

David took her hand and, putting the box in it, held his other hand over it, "I want you to look after it for me. You were the reason I left here and the reason I've come back. The medal's a reminder of that."

"But what if you want to leave again?" she asked hesitantly.

"If I leave again," he said, looking at her steadily, "I'll take what's precious with me."

Ursula held his gaze, her heart full. No gift of priceless jewellery, no flowery speeches could have pleased her half so well. Hardly able to contain her feeling of elation, she slipped her hand with the box out of his.

"I shall keep it very close to me then," she replied.

Raising her arms she undid her silver necklace that held a small crucifix and, opening the box, took the medal from its ribbon and threaded it onto the chain where it lay side by side with the silver cross.

"There," she said, holding it up in front of her. "What do you think?"

"Perfect," David replied, looking at it admiringly. "Shall I do it up for you?"

"Yes, please." Ursula turned around on the bench and, bending her head forward, allowed David to secure the clasp. She felt his fingers fumble with the clasp and then the warmth of his breath as he planted a soft kiss on the nape of her neck: his touch was exquisite, her joy intense. She savoured the moment and was slow to straighten up and turn around.

"Do you ever take that off?" David asked lifting the chain with his finger, concern in his voice.

"No. And I shall never take it off now. It will lie here with my cross until God forsakes me: until my heart is plucked out of me; until the sky falls down."

"Forever then."

"Forever."

"You will be all right won't you Nana? I mean, you will be able to manage without my wage?"

"*Ja*. I can manage, man. I got plenty jobs."

"You know we're having a civil ceremony don't you Nana?"

"Meg . . ."

"Meg's not here and David's not Roman Catholic. He hasn't asked me to change my religion and I shan't ask him to convert to mine; it's immaterial to us. But it means we shan't marry in a church. I don't care what he is or where we marry, I love him and that's all there is to it – and it means you can come. You will come won't you Nana? We only have to get the licence and make a few other arrangements, then there's nothing to stop us. We're free to make our own choices, live our own lives. After all, we're both over twenty-one aren't we?"

"*Ja.*"

"There won't be any sticky British there to disapprove. Only Jessie and Duggie, and Abe and his wife Rhoda, are coming to the ceremony – Emma and Bernard can only come to the breakfast. So you will be there won't you, Nana?"

"*Ag* no man, I feel a bit *skaam* there on my own."

"Nana, you must come – you're the only family I've got left. Bring Mrs Hendricks from next door."

"*Ne, ne. Rather* I like to bring Mr Essop. He is very quiet, respectable. So lonely since his wife die. When I cook for him he ask – stay and eat with me – but I say *ne*. I feel more comfortable with Mr Essop along, *ja*? We can stay way back and come home on the bus together. Then you can celebrate, man."

"We're having the wedding breakfast at the Savoy."

"*Ag shame*! The Savoy!"

"Yes, and Abe is giving us a few days in Muizenberg as a wedding present. We only have to pay for the train."

"Holiday too!"

"And he's giving me a full-time job in the theatre."

"*Is it?*"

"So, that's settled then. You are coming. And Mr Essop."

Eight

Then nature rul'd, and love, devoid of art,
Spoke the consenting language of the heart.

Dione, prologue
John Gay 1685–1732

"What do you think Jessie – the mauve at the back of the window or the blue at the front?"

"They're all wearing white when you see them in the Tatler and the illustrated weeklies now."

"I can't run to that. It will have to be something I can wear afterwards. A smart walking dress like those – perhaps one like that with the new panelled skirt. That mauve one has a very useful waistcoat. And it would match my amethyst brooch."

"Looks a bit dull. The blue's brighter."

"Something blue – that's it. That lawn blouse underneath is so pretty with the blue embroidery. David's promised me a little pearl pin with a dove and it would look lovely on the blue bolero."

"Still, the mauve might be more serviceable."

"We'll try them both on then. And I have to find a hat to match. How about one of those little toques, or that jaunty tricorne?"

"You can only wear those if your *coiffure* is perfect. Without a lady's maid I don't think you're going to manage that."

ropriate

"No, you're right. I could wear a larger one with my usual hair style, just knotted in the nape of my neck. That blue and black one with the bunches of flowers and enormous black feather would look wonderful, wouldn't it?"

"Mmm . . . *Ag* well, I suppose it would do. Still, pity it's not summer, a white rice straw with bunches of wild flowers would be perfect."

"Can't help that. Shall we go in? I've never bought anything in such a smart shop before – just fancy me shopping in St George's Street!"

"Emma, we've found a cottage!"

"That's excellent news. Where is it?"

"Go up Breedestraat and it's just off Buitengracht. It's inexpensive because it's close to *Bo Kaap* but the bonus is that it's easy to walk to the theatre from there."

"Near Hottentot Square?"

"No, nearer the *Tamboers Kloof* end."

"And does it suit your needs?"

"Quite. It's terraced with a lovely honeysuckle growing over the *stoep* – two rooms deep as usual – tiny garden."

"And furniture?"

"There's some there but we need more. I don't want to take everything from home, not just yet anyway, it'll be such a shock for Nana. So I thought I might bid for a few pieces at a house sale advertised up the road. Will you come with me? I've never bid before and I'm afraid of buying something I don't mean to!"

"I shall be delighted."

"Sorry I've been so long Bernard. It took us ages deciding on a menu."

"Never, mind. We're very quiet this week. Tell me what you chose for the breakfast."

"You'll find out on the day Bernard. I shall bring your invitation tomorrow."

"How kind. How many courses are there to be?"

"Now, Bernard."

"Fish? Will there be fish?"

"You're the only man I know who ever shows this much interest in food."

"David must be interested in food. Don't know a chap who isn't."

"Yes he is but I sometimes think quantity is more important than quality with David."

"Probably is if he's training; quantity's an important element. Chap can't exist on air."

"There should be quantity and quality at the Savoy. David said that whatever I decided on would be perfect with him, with a few provisos – the full works, and it should include chicken and an apple pudding."

"How sensible. And what are we going to start with – a little soup?"

"If you promise not to tell . . ."

"Of course not; not a word. Start right at the beginning."

"Mulligatawny soup served with sherry followed by trout, with hock I think David said. Then the entrée and the second course – um . . . fricasseed chicken followed by boiled tongue with beets, claret with that I think – David said he would have preferred Brussel sprouts rather than beets but I pointed out that we haven't got those – then . . ."

"Stop. Let me think about this . . . mm, yes, that sounds excellent. Go on."

"Then custards in glasses and ices – that's for me because I don't think I could eat anything else heavy."

"Is there something else in the pudding line then?"

"Oh yes, apple fritters, especially for David."

"A true trencherman after my own heart."

"What a wonderful day! Wasn't it David? And the restaurant – so smart – a sea of napery and shining flatware and sparkling crystal. Such pretty flowers. And those enormous entrée dishes! Oh I do love you David; don't squeeze too tight – mind my hat; no, no, not in a cab! Jessie and Duggie were getting on like a house on fire weren't they? The champagne Abe bought went straight to my head too. Ah, here we are."

"Mind the step, take my hand." said David. "You go on in," he added, as he paid the grinning Malay driver.

"Our own front door. Oh look David . . . Nana must have come here after the ceremony; freesias on the table, mmm, they smell wonderful, one of my favourites. They always make me think of the mountain walks I had with Meg. Could you just pull this hat pin out for me it's stuck – yes, that's the one – ah, that's better. Thank you. I'll just put my hat away . . . David, in here. Look. My silver brushes have been polished bright and . . . oh! that linen coverlet was my mother's! All bright white and starched; I wondered what was in that big bag Mr Essop was carrying. And there's . . ."

"Ursula."

"Yes."

"Stop talking."

"Oh."

"And come here."

Dappled sunlight, flickering tongues of sunlight. Flickering through bright green leaves. And rocks, rocks covered in moss. Hard. No! Warm shaft of sunlight: deep in the moss; deep. A stream; flowing over the soft moist earth. No! Slow.

Carry me along, carry me forever. Bubbling stream. Bright, clear, moving, moving. Follow it, follow it now – let it take me. Faster. Until it cascades; breaks out. Into the bright golden burning sun!

More vivid than any dream she ever had.

To Ursula, Muizenberg was as ideal as any seaside spot could be. At Sea Point the beach was narrow and strewn with seaweed and detritus brought by the unforgiving Atlantic waves. The tall, pommel peak of Lion's Head dwarfed the low houses dotted among the trees along the exposed coastline below. But at Muizenberg the solid, squat mountain slopes protected and enclosed the western end of the beach – houses nestled comfortably at its feet – and an old wood and iron cottage, gaily painted in stripes and advertising refreshments in the season, stood on the clean, sheltered sands. A haphazard collection of timber shacks and tin bathing boxes stood in untidy rows further along the beach and tussocks of grass sprouted defiantly from the soft dunes that relaxed onto the gently sloping sand. The beach ran eastwards in a large uninterrupted sweep as far as the eye could see, until the sea disappeared around the farther edge of the bay, distant mountains silhouetted against the sky. Gentle waves, like scalloped edges of lace, arrived in orderly procession to break gently on the sand.

Ursula and David strolled along, hand in hand, on the firmer sand near the shore. So early in the season they shared the beach with only a few solitary figures – throwing driftwood for their dogs, walking briskly for their health – and several fearless seagulls. Every now and then Ursula would stop and pick up a small shell from the myriad of mussel shells that littered the shore; if the shell was unusual in colour or shape she slipped it into David's pocket. She would take these home with them and use them to decorate a card or make a collage. The sea air was sharp and the sun shone thinly through the clouds as they turned and walked back the way they had come.

"David, I'm tired. That was a long walk. Can we just sit on this bench for a while and look at the sea?" asked Ursula, adding encouragingly. "If we're lucky we might see a whale."

David smiled, "If you want."

"Gosh, you've quite worn me out!" said Ursula leaning back on the bench.

"One way or another?" said David grinning. "You look dead beat. Do you want to go back and rest?"

"David this is the first time we've been out of the hotel since we got here! We can't spend all day in bed."

"Why not?"

"Because," said Ursula with a mock frown.

"Because, Funny Face?"

"Because I can hardly walk; because Mrs Farthing will think we're degenerate; because . . ." Ursula paused, thinking up some more reasons, "I want to paddle in the lovely warm sea here; because I want to see some of the place before we go back. Because," she finished, out of ideas.

"I love you, Mrs Lewis," said David, stroking her cheek and smiling.

"That's no excuse," replied Ursula, with a coquettish sideways look at him.

"Oh, is that so?" said David as he stretched his arms around her.

"Don't, don't. Help!" she screamed. "I was joking. I love you too, I do. I was only joking."

"Don't help?"

"No, no. You'll tickle me to death! Stop, stop. Please stop."

*

The following day they walked south along the wooden walkway that skirted the bay, over the rocks to St James. The beach at St James was only small with tiny rock pools and so they walked across the road and peeped in at the windows of the small thatched cottage where Cecil Rhodes had died, not believing that such a famous man could have chosen so modest a house to end his days in. They walked on and climbed up to the tiny church on the hill. Ursula asked David to wait for five minutes whilst she went in to give a quick thanksgiving prayer for her blessings. And she did feel blessed: overflowing with love, satiated with lovemaking. Yellowwoods grew on the far wooded slopes, *rooi els* and wild olive trees near *spruits,* but the slopes nearer the coast were dotted with Cape May trees that glowed with white blossom, their citrus scent drifting over the air. In the *fynbos* pink Cape heaths continued to bloom, their honey smell mingling with the sweet perfume of the *keurtjies.* Ursula, sitting on some large boulders arm-in-arm with David, brushed the flowers with her hand and knew she would always associate the fragrance of them with their holiday there.

"David, when did you realize you loved me," Ursula asked, leaning across to kiss his ear lobe. She still could not believe that someone could love her as much as David said he did, and she wanted to hear him say it over and over again.

"The very first time I saw you," he said earnestly, without hesitation.

"No, when did you know you really loved me?" she urged.

"I see. You mean when I really knew. Not the first time I realized?"

"Don't tease. Tell me."

"When you said you liked whisky."

"No!"

"I thought 'this is my kind of girl'!"

"Tell me the truth," she said, petulantly.

"Ah! The truth. That's different. Let me see . . . yes, when you

130

pulled your funny, frowning face in the office the first time I kissed you."

"You are horrid."

He laughed, "Since then you'll forever be Funny Face to me. Ow!"

The next day was very warm and David talked Ursula into hiring bicycles. They wobbled and laughed their way along the rough road and, in Ursula's case, into ditches. David, weak with laughter at Ursula's spills and inability to master her bicycle – and aware that they would be unable to cycle anywhere – promised her a drive in the bus to Fish Hoek. They left their bicycles in the safe-keeping of a homely woman who lived in one of the few fishermen's houses overlooking the harbour at Kalk Bay. When the bus stopped for them there at noon they waited whilst a passenger bought fish and bread out of the door of the bus from the fish carts and baskets loaded ready for deliveries.

Fish Hoek Bay had fewer houses still. David and Ursula sat on boulders there overlooking the sea as they ate the *padkos* of bread and cheese they had brought – taking it in turns to drink ginger beer from the bottle – and watched with delight as seals stole from the fishermen's nets and wrestled together in the bay. Cormorants, like beggarly old men, stooped on the rocks and waited for their luck to change whilst dolphins appeared to perform a watery ring dance. Later, in the gas light of their bedroom, David was shocked to see bruises on Ursula's buttocks and he applied a vaseline rub of *buchu-boegoe* from Ursula's dressing-case, as tenderly as any nurse, kissing each bruise as he finished.

On their last day Ursula and David took their *padkos* in a rucksack and – starting from behind the Park Hotel where they were staying – trekked up the shallow depression of Farmer Peck's Valley. Sweetpea bushes clambered over the slope, their pink flowers still in bloom, and the scent of mauve *afrikanders* filled the air as they climbed. Finally they went over the top space and reached the seclusion of Silvermine Plateau. Tired, Ursula sat on a rock to admire some elegant painted ladies – the pure white petals marked with red streaks – and suddenly a robin flew up, revealing three soft-blue eggs in the neatest of nests.

David inspected the grass to be sure there were no snakes and spread his jacket down. They ate their fruit and sandwiches and afterwards, reclining on one arm, lay together on their sides in the bright sunshine – David's hand gently stroking Ursula's hip – amongst the sweet-smelling flowers. Close by they could see the dark purple-blue petals of a *bobbejaantjie* curved elegantly back to reveal delicate stamens, while dark magenta and vibrant orange daisies opened wider in the warmth of the sun. They watched, mesmerized, as an orange-breasted sunbird with metallic green plumage collected nectar from the richly coloured proteas, darting in and out, thrusting its long beak deep, deep into the flowers. The three-noted call of a *piet-my-vrou* cut through the air, heralding summer as only a cuckoo does, whilst an eagle floated effortlessly in circles above their heads.

As they made love in bed that night – their last night in Muizenberg – the images of exquisite nature at Silvermine returned to Ursula in intense recurring waves of heightening richness – the boundary between pleasure and pain finally indistinct, when memories of the screech of the gulls and the sound of the waves breaking onto the sea wall at Sea Point, reached a crescendo.

"So, how is the young bride; how was Muizenberg?" asked Jessie, the first day Ursula worked at the theatre.

A Little Blue Jacket

"It was wonderful thank you Jessie."

"*Ag* well, down to earth now; back to a new job," said Jessie, joylessly.

"I'm afraid so," replied Ursula, "but I mustn't complain, it'll be a nice change from the office."

"So what's your official title?"

"I'm stock-room assistant; so I'll be mostly in the bars."

"But you're still helping me?" asserted Jessie.

"Only as before."

"Huh," Jessie grunted, not impressed. "I could do with a change myself. Wouldn't mind working behind one of the bars for a bit."

"You'd like that Jessie, it would be more sociable than this."

"That's what I think. I reckon I'd be good at it – give that lot in the auditorium a run for their money – and keep those promenaders in order."

"Yes, I'm sure you would. But tell me, how is Ralph?" asked Ursula, changing the subject and quite happy now to be entertained with someone else's romance.

"I'm not seeing him anymore," said Jessie bluntly.

"But I thought you and he were getting along so well."

"We were but he started to get a bit too intense. Said I was the most lovely girl he'd ever known. Saturday, he said he wanted to marry me!"

"But that's wonderful Jess," said Ursula enthusiastically.

"*Ag* no man! There is no way I'm ever getting married."

"Everyone wants to get married eventually Jessie."

"Oh no they don't," replied Jessie forcefully. "I have no intention of ever getting hitched. Just look at my Ma: screaming babies, loads of laundry, drunken husband. No thank you. That's not for me."

"And you told Ralph that?" asked Ursula with disbelief.

"Absolutely. I said 'think again'."

"Was he very upset?"

"Desperate. Cried. I mean, cried!" said Jessie rolling her eyes up to the ceiling. "How could I stay with a man who cried?"

"He's obviously very much in love with you. Couldn't you have let him down gently?"

"There's no such thing. They never let you down gently; don't think twice about scarpering if they have a mind to."

"But I'm sure Ralph wasn't like that, he seemed very serious, very sincere. He must be broken-hearted."

"I told you, you should have had him then," replied Jessie, flicking her hand in the air. "He's too boring for me, too serious. I need a little excitement!"

"Jessie – you are incorrigible!" remonstrated Ursula.

"Not really. I simply mean to get the best out of life. And if that means picking men who are not going to pester me to get married, well, so be it."

"Does Duggie fall into that category?" asked Ursula astutely.

"Maybe."

"But David says he has a fiancée."

"Has he?" replied Jessie, with a raise of her brows and a smirk.

Ursula enjoyed her new job – it required organization and logic and after only two weeks Abe, always with economy in mind, saw to it that it encompassed much more than he had intimated. Every morning she had to count the bottles of spirits and liqueurs and restock the shelves. She then checked the ale, ensured that enough ice was delivered, that the champagne was padlocked securely in its cage, that the figures tallied, and the float in the tills was correct. Delivery and storage of the steak and kidney pies had to be overseen – they were needed as much as anything to absorb the vast quantity of alcohol consumed by the promenaders – and she had to check that the washer woman left sufficient clean cloths to dry the glasses. Ursula was quite content behind the bars on her own, yet her days were sociable enough to help them go quickly. She saw a side of the theatre that she had hitherto not been involved in as the bars opened directly onto the auditorium and the orchestra pit.

She was often the sole spectator as illusionists practised their tricks, soubrettes their scales, tenors their repetoire, actors and actresses their recitations, chorus girls their routines, masters of ceremonies their introductions. Meeting David for lunch, she would entertain him with every detail as he consumed whatever was put in front of him; anything except fat and beer which his trainer had banned. He was in training again for a fight and had warned Ursula that it might be in Durban, although nothing was agreed yet.

When Ursula worked in the evening David met her to walk her home and on Saturday nights they sometimes had a nightcap at one of the smaller hotels. When Jessie's birthday fell on a Saturday they invited her to have a drink with them at The White House Hotel after the show. When they arrived Duggie was at the bar in the lounge; Ursula was not expecting him but neither Jessie nor David seemed surprised so she assumed that one of them had asked him. They found a table and settled into the comfortable leather chairs. Ursula asked David for a whisky and soda. Duggie came over to join them with his glass of beer from the bar and Jessie asked if she could have a half of beer. Ursula was intrigued,."I didn't know you liked beer Jessie?"

"I'm full of surprises," said Jessie, seeming very pleased with herself.

"Don't you find it very bitter?"

"My Pa usually stopped for a beer at the Irish pub on the way home. Ma sent me to meet him – she thought that would stop him – but he still had a few. And he'd give me a few sips just to keep me on his side," she said, looking at Duggie who had sat down beside her.

Lucy Ann White

"We certainly sell a great deal of ale at the theatre," acknowledged Ursula.

'Well, I seem to have discovered a taste for it, don't I Duggie?' Duggie did not respond. Unruffled Jessie continued, "I intend to try all the drinks now so that I know what I'm doing behind a bar."

"Are you going to work behind the bar then Jessie?" asked David.

"I'm thinking about it," she replied, lowering her eyelids mysteriously.

"You'll be very good at it Jess," said Ursula. "Still, you do rule your own little world here."

"*Ag* no man, I'm fed up doing this same old job. I need a change of scenery. And the tips should be just as good – if not better."

"Abe will have to find someone to do your job," said Ursula, ever practical.

"We may be able to think of someone who wants evening work," replied Jessie smirking. "What do you think Duggie?"

Duggie still did not reply but merely raised his eyebrows and took a deeper draught of his beer. David tapped him on the shoulder, "Do you want to come for a cigarette Duggie? We'll order from the bar at the same time."

"Aye."

"Duggie doesn't talk much in mixed company does he," said Ursula once he was out of earshot.

"It depends what you're talking about," replied Jessie. "If it's David he seems to have enough to say and we seem to get along quite adequately even when he doesn't say much."

"Does he talk about David?"

"Oh, I hear all the news. And I've been able to piece together a fair amount about Abe's business interests now. He has quite an empire. You'd never guess it to look at him would you?" said Jessie. Leaning forward confidentially she added, "Apart from his boxing interests he has racing interests too. And as well as the

Tivoli he's got a theatre in Durban and a share in one in Johannesburg. Did you know all that?"

"No, I didn't. But you're not usually this interested in business Jessie," said Ursula, surprised. "Is there a reason?"

"I'm thinking about the bar work. I'm toying with the idea of doing it in Durban."

"Durban! Good gracious, what about your family? Won't it be rather a wrench for you, so far from your mother." Ursula could not imagine going to such lengths for a job in a bar.

"I'm only thinking of going. And it would only be for a couple of months. I told you I need a change. Quiet now, here come the chaps," she said, adding in a whisper, "We'll talk about it another time."

"I've brought you a Madeira, Jessie," said David, indicating the waiter behind him holding the tray. "It's something else to add to your repertoire and more fitting for a birthday girl."

"Aye," said Duggie, "an it mebbe mak ye a wee bit more ladylike an stop ye blathering."

Jessie scowled at Duggie but David did not appear to notice and, raising his glass, he proposed a toast.

Ursula did not want David to go to Durban – Jessie's remark had reminded her of the impending trip – and she was not looking forward to being on her own. She knew how much she would miss him. The evening following their drink, after they had finished their supper, she broached the subject of the fights he had planned. She would find out what it was like there and how long he was likely to be away.

"David?"

"Mmm."

"Your fights; when do you have to go to Durban?"

"Not just yet."

David was not as forthcoming as she wished, and trying to draw him out she asked, "Tell me what it's like there, is it very much hotter, is it very British, like here?"

"It is and it isn't."

"David, please, talk to me." Sometimes she felt that he shut her out: he doesn't volunteer the sort of information that helps me imagine a scene, she thought.

"Sorry," he said smiling at her apologetically. "Yes, it's hotter. And the humidity in the summer is appalling so it will be quite a problem for me; I'll have to get there some time before the fight to get used to it. And no, it's not so British; there are lots of Xhosa, and Indians, and now Chinese."

"Chinese?" The picture in her mind now was rather more exotic than she had expected.

"They were coming in by boat when I was there; I think they were mostly being sent on to work in the Johannesburg gold mines to make up for labour shortages."

"Oh, I see. Fancy bringing workers so far."

"That's how the majority of Indians originally came, as labour for the sugar plantations," he explained.

"I thought most of them came as traders. One of Nana's friends came from India – she's just gone to her family in Durban, hoping to go into service."

"She'll regret leaving the Cape."

"Why?"

"Surely you know they have to have passes there; not allowed to travel about without one and only at certain times."

"Of course I know about the pass laws," replied Ursula shortly, feeling that he was being critical, that he thought her uninformed. "Because we don't have them here one tends not to consider the consequences elsewhere, that's all."

"It's a problem all right," continued David, calmly. "I met an Indian chap whilst I was waiting for a cab there one day – very cultivated, smart suit – seemed surprised that I was willing to talk to him, said most whites wouldn't. I said my family had suffered from prejudice and I didn't care for bigotry. He says he knows the area I come from in London, so he's well travelled too. Told me that he's trying to organize a self-help scheme for the Indians. Apparently all the better educated Indians – including those wealthy traders you know about – are complaining about their lack of civil rights."

"Before I joined the theatre they had a large meeting of that sort in the International Winter Gardens," said Ursula, pleased to demonstrate some knowledge of political events. "They were protesting against not having the vote in the Transvaal and Orange River Colony."

"According to this chap, his scheme will take a very long time to have any effect. In the meantime he's started an Indian newspaper to try and generate interest."

"Did you meet up again?" asked Ursula, trying to gauge how involved David was in Durban events.

"No, it was a chance meeting, that's all. He was a bit of a political fellow – lawyer I think – hoping to open an office there. What he said was thought-provoking but I was there to box and I had to concentrate all my energies on that."

She had assembled a good enough picture now and said, "So, if I'm right, the climate there is less pleasant and it's not such a friendly place as Cape Town?"

"That sums it up, I suppose."

"Then you wouldn't choose to stay there longer than you needed, would you?" asked Ursula, hopefully.

"Not any longer than I had to," David reassured her.

She was relieved to hear him say this but was not altogether resigned to his eventual tour.

"I do hope you don't have to go there too soon then," she said despondently. "In fact I wish you didn't have to go at all."

"Come here, Funny Face," David said smiling at her. "Sit on my lap. There. Now, tell me, would my wife miss me?"

Whenever David was affectionate it cheered Ursula. Pleased with his attention she responded with the mischievous banter they both enjoyed.

"She might," she replied with a coquettish air.

"Would she?"

"Ooh! Don't bite my ear – it's not edible you know!"

"What bit can I eat?"

"It would be difficult to eat any of me in this outfit!" laughed Ursula.

"But if I undid these buttons . . . there we are . . . and maybe a few more down here . . ."

Nine

*The woman's cause is man's: they rise or sink
Together.*

The Princess; A Medley (1847)
Alfred Lord Tennyson 1809–1892

Married life had, to date, agreed with Ursula. She helped Jessie in the cloakroom whenever she was needed or if David was busy. But on other evenings she looked forward to leaving work on time in order to prepare a meal for him.

"Can you cook something really English for a change?" asked David one evening.

"I can only cook what I learnt from Nana and Meg," answered Ursula, chopping a peeled pumpkin, "don't you like what I cook?"

"It's good but everything else here either smacks of palm-oil chop or it's curried fowl of some sort" he replied dispiritedly. "And if I never see another *snoek* in my life . . ."

"Still, you wolf down the *bobotie* and the *tamatiebredie* I make readily enough," interrupted Ursula. "So, tell me, what's a very English dish then?"

"Boiled beef and dumplings; very plain, nothing spicy."

"We never cooked that. The plainest thing I can think of would be boiled mutton. But I could make *kluitjes*, they're like dumplings, to put in with the mutton if you want."

"What about that cookery book you bought?"

"*Diary of a Cape Housekeeper*? Some of the meals take too

141

long to make after work and most of the meats are jolly expensive."

"I'll buy the meat," said David decisively.

"But this week we barely had enough for the rent, I know it's my fault; I shouldn't have talked you out of going to Durban."

"No, it's not, the first one scheduled was a mismatch. The other bouts they suggested weren't with suitable opponents or they were twenty rounders; I want to fight properly or not at all. And anyway, I wasn't in condition. Abe and Duggie are working on something else and in the meantime I'll get into top condition."

"So we have to economize."

"Not on meat; a man's stomach comes first," said David putting his arms around Ursula's waist.

"Ha! Not that I've noticed," she said, laughing.

"No, you're right, Funny Face. You look very fetching in that pinny; leave that pumpkin and come with me."

How well David and Ursula got along depended to a great extent on whether there was enough paid work for David between his training sessions. Ursula realized that David was very adaptable and willing to do whatever was necessary to pay the bills but he was constrained, like most workers, by the state of the economy. He had even agreed on several occasions to evict drunken promenaders for Abe, who paid well for the service of 'chucker-out'. But it was a role that was alien to David's nature and one Ursula knew he disliked. Generally, David was sanguine about their finances but Ursula worried about their lack of funds and she thought of ways to improve their financial position.

"David, perhaps I could work a few more evenings," ventured Ursula one night, noticing his glum looks at their supper of curried vegetables and rice.

"No. I like you here. The butcher I got that beef from last week has invited me to a poker game."

"But we haven't any money!"

"Duggie is game; he'll put up the stake," replied David.

"But what if you lose?" said Ursula horrified. "It would be much safer if I did more hours at the theatre."

"Look here, Funny Face, I've been playing cards since I was knee-high to a grasshopper. And if I can't win playing the honest burghers of Cape Town I don't know how I ever won from the sharks in the East End of London."

"But David . . ."

"Ursula, just leave it to me," he said firmly, "I know what I'm doing."

Ursula looked doubtful; she had discovered that David was inclined to be over-optimistic when something exciting was in the air.

"When is this game?" she asked without enthusiasm.

"The day after tomorrow."

Ursula prepared an enormous plate of sweet potatoes, onions and *boerewors* on the evening of the card game.

"This is good," said David eating with relish, "they're better than the sausages at home."

"I thought they'd absorb anything you might drink," Ursula said looking concerned, "you don't want to cloud your judgement."

"I don't drink if I'm playing for money."

"Oh, I see. What time will you finish?"

"When the game's over."

"But when will that be?" she asked in need of facts, of reassurance.

"I can't say. You go to bed as usual. Just leave the door on the latch."

"David, you won't do anything rash will you?"

"Gambling is gambling; you have to speculate to accumulate," said David matter-of-factly.

"Still, if you lose everything . . ."

"Not another word. I'm doing what I can," he said shortly, with finality. "Now, give me a kiss . . . and a smile. That's better. I'll see you later."

Ursula went to bed at her usual hour but lay awake for a long time imagining the worst – what if he lost the game, how would they pay Duggie back? They'd be in a terrible fix. We have little enough to pay for food at present, she thought, we'll only be able to afford mealie-meal to eat. The memory of such food during the straightened years after Meg had left stuck in her memory as intractably as the meal had in her throat. She finally drifted into a shallow slumber.

David had lost his way and been drawn to a house with blinds half lowered, warm lights glowing on green cloths. But it was the wrong venue, the game in progress was new to him, and he took several whiskys to give him courage. The stakes were high: he lost badly. Distraught and destitute, he staggered out of the house and wandered the streets, unable to find his way

Ursula woke in a panic, where was he, what time was it? She lit her candle – it was after midnight; the door was unlocked – anyone might be about. She lay for a while listening, watching the molten tallow of the candle build craggy fountains. Calmed by the hypnotic process – the candle burning down, the tallow building up – she became practical; she was wasting precious wax. She snuffed the candle out and, tired, drifted back to sleep. Some time later she woke to the sound of the front door closing.

Sitting up in bed she called out, "David, is that you?"

There was no reply; Ursula waited for a few minutes, listening.

"David?" she called again, softly, unsurely.

Fearful that a stranger was in the house, she remained quite still. She knew that was what she should do – stay in bed and pretend to be asleep; that was the sensible, the safe, thing to do. But Ursula could not resist the urge to interfere. Very carefully, quietly, she got out of bed and tiptoed to the bedroom door. A light was spreading along the floor and she could hear a clinking sound, as if someone was going through their drawers. She had an old army pistol in her drawer, but she had no ammunition. Feeling around in the gloom for something heavy to protect herself with she stumbled on one of David's heavy leather boots and taking it firmly in her hand, she lifted the door latch as gently as she could, and peered through the slit. Shadows were cast across the room. Someone was moving – she opened the door a little more: the movements stopped.

"Guess what?" A man's voice.

Ursula opened the door wide. The boot she held fell to the floor with a thud: David was standing in the middle of the room with his arms open wide. Ursula looked at him in disbelief; bank notes were sticking out of his breast pocket, his jacket pockets, the tongue of his shoes, his cuffs, between his fingers, his shirt collar, his hatband. On the sideboard beside him were neat piles of coins in differing denominations.

"David!"

"What do you think then?" he asked, beaming.

"You won! You won all that?" said Ursula in wonder, her worries instantly dispelled.

"Every single pound, every single penny. Roll up, roll up, come and see the money man!"

"How much is it?" she asked in amazement.

"I don't know. Just thought I'd give you an eyeful first!"

"You daft egg. Let's count it!"

"Not so fast. Let's have a little appreciation first," he replied, tapping his cheek.

"You're a clever, clever, lucky, lucky thing!" she said giving him a noisy kiss on the cheek.

"That's better. Now you can pull out all these notes I've spent ages arranging for your benefit and put them on the side."

"How did you do it?" asked Ursula incredulous, as she carefully pulled notes out of David's clothes. "Who played – did Duggie, did the butcher?"

"One thing at a time," he said, laughing. "First you can have a glass of that whisky with me and then I might give you the benefit of my experience and then, if you are lucky, you can seduce a rich man."

"That will be novel," she laughed.

"Cheeky hussy," said David, as he poured them out two small tots of whisky. He passed a glass to Ursula and raised his, "Cheers."

Ursula raised her glass too, "To my hero!"

"Quite right", he said smiling at her, adding more seriously, "but I don't think everyone there viewed me quite in that light tonight. Not when I left anyway."

"Tell me all about it," she said, pulling him towards the couch. "Who was playing? What happened?"

"When Duggie and I got there – it was in the back room of a shop in Strand Street – we had to ring the bell and Duggie gave the card of the chap who had invited us. All very discreet. I'd expected there to be just a few of us but they had three tables set up. Middle-aged businessmen: big money."

"How much did you start with?"

"Not much, only the stake Duggie leant me. But Duggie bowed out after the first game – gave me his stake to add to mine – just watched, and insisted on walking back with me when it was over. It took me a very long time to build up a big enough reserve. By then we were down to the serious players and there was a lot in the pot to play for. I just played a percentage game; didn't take any risks, didn't give anything away. Just steadily won for the last couple of hours."

"It is absolutely amazing," said Ursula patting the pile of notes. "We only need one of those evenings every few weeks and you wouldn't have to fight again."

"This is the woman who didn't want me to play!" said David incredulously, looking up at the ceiling.

"No, I don't really mean it," she said shaking her head, "I'm just overwhelmed – you might lose another time. Have they asked you to play again?"

"Somehow I don't think they'll be extending an invitation for me to join their little school again."

"That's probably just as well."

"Probably. But now, Funny Face, I think it's time for bed. We have to be up in a few hours."

David and Ursula were happy and relaxed now their financial worries were allayed; Ursula no longer dreamed of having nothing but *pap* to eat and David gave up looking for work, concentrating instead on his training. There was talk of a boxing competition in the old Vaudeville Theatre and a tournament in Good Hope Hall. He walked ten miles in the morning and bicycled for ten more in the afternoon; in between he practised ball-punching or skipping in the gymnasium. Ursula bought and prepared for David the best produce she could find, he gave her some money to buy whatever took her fancy and they spent several evenings out each week in the local hotel lounges.

Ursula had not seen Hannah since their windfall and now she asked David if he would mind if she spent the following Sunday with her. He encouraged Ursula to go and walked her to the bus stop, carrying the parcels and presents that she was taking. He said he would take the opportunity to have a long discussion with Abe about his boxing regime. Ursula had a dull worry that Nana was lonely and might have difficulty managing financially. She wondered how to help as she travelled the familiar route by bus towards Sea Point. Spring was turning to summer; by the roadside the shiny leaves of the silver trees reflected the bright sunlight and clusters of pink flowers stood out like jewels in the crowns of the wild chestnut trees. Climbing the hill Ursula noticed that a man in a fez sat on the *stoep* with Hannah – he looked familiar – but before she could be sure who it was he stood up and left along the side of the house.

Whilst still a little way off Ursula called, "Nana, Nana, it's me!"

Hannah raised her head and shaded her eyes against the bright sun with her hand. Then, dropping her sewing, she hurried down the small wooden steps and over the grass to greet Ursula, waving her arms, "*Kleintjie!* So good to see you."

"I've come to spend the day with you," said Ursula giving her a hug.

"*Ag shame!* But I got no *kos*, man," said Hannah raising her hands in an attitude of helplessness.

"You don't have to worry about that. I've brought your favourite *frikadel* and a *spanspek* – and I've got all sorts of other nice things."

They went inside and Ursula looked around the familiar room with satisfaction, noting that everything was much the same.

"Who was that I saw with you on the *stoep*?" she asked.

"Mr Essop. He make himself scarce if he see anyone coming," said Hannah, nodding seriously. "He is a very shy person."

They spent the day pleasantly exchanging their news; Hannah told Ursula all the local news and Ursula explained her new tasks at the theatre and related the most interesting details of the acts that she saw rehearse. She recounted the story of the card game and what a difference it had made to their finances whilst Hannah prepared the savouries and fruits that she had brought with her. They ate on the *stoep* and Ursula helped Hannah to clear everything away and wash the dishes.

"Now tell me what you've been doing Nana," asked Ursula as soon as they were seated.

"*Ag* well, nothing so different," said Hannah, shrugging. "I been hemming linen for Mrs Rowling; *just now* she ask me to sew a trousseau for her daughter. *Nou nou* I make pickles for Mrs Wagram shop. Often I cook and clean for Mr Essop."

"Do you make enough Nana?"

"*Ja,* man, more than enough," said Hannah, firmly.

"And how is Mr Essop?" asked Ursula wondering why he had been visiting.

"He is very lonely," said Hannah not looking at her.

"Is that why he visited you?"

"*Ja* . . . because . . ."

"Because what Nana?"

"He is so lonely, man. He say his house is too big for him on his own. He need some company in it. He come here for a few hours in the evening time *rather.*"

"Oh, I see. And is that quite . . . are you sure that's quite the thing?"

"Mr Essop is a polite man. Very respectful," replied Hannah, sitting a little straighter in her chair.

"I'm sure he is Nana but you live alone now. You don't want anyone to think that there is any impropriety," said Ursula unable to conceal the hint of disapproval in her voice.

"*Ja,* this trouble Mr Essop too. Mr Essop he . . ." she looked unsurely at Ursula, and taking a large breath continued more confidently, "*ja,* Mr Essop like me to marry him."

Ursula looked at Hannah with disbelief, "But, Nana, that's, that's . . . I mean . . . do you want to?"

"*Ja,* why not? Mr Essop lot older than me but, still, I think I make him happy."

"But Nana, what about you?"

"*Ag* well, I have no-one to look after nowadays. And Mr Essop is very kind. He want me to marry him for a long, long time. *Ja*," nodded Hannah, as she spread her work worn hands out on her lap and sighed, "*just now* maybe I not able to work so hard, *rather* I think it good to rely on someone."

Ursula, a little over her surprise, and filled with gratitude and love for Hannah, took one of Hannah's hands in hers, "You are the very best at looking after someone, Nana. If you decide to marry Mr Essop he will be very lucky and I hope you'll be happy."

Hannah beamed at Ursula, "*Ag shame*! Thank you, *kleintjie*. I am very happy you like the idea."

Ursula felt a fraud; she did not like the idea, she was disturbed by it. After Meg, Hannah had been her only family – she had always been there for her, a still point, a solid rock in a rushing stream. She needed time to absorb the news.

They spent the remaining hour before her bus was due turning out her bedroom cupboard and sorting the clothes and books into piles; some would be delivered to Ursula, some sold and the rest were to be distributed to the needy. Hannah walked to the bus stop with Ursula and they parted affectionately; she waved until Hannah was out of sight. As she travelled home she chided herself for her selfishness. No doubt Mr Essop asked Nana before and she refused him because of me, Ursula thought, because there was no one else to look after me! But now I have David to love and look after me and Nana will have Mr Essop. She considered him a fortunate man to have Hannah as a housekeeper and hoped that he would be kind to her in return. But Hannah married! Ursula knew it would be difficult adjusting to the idea, for both of them possibly.

David's winnings lasted a month. Ursula, used to David now, was not surprised that he was not perturbed about how they would manage now. He seemed to accept turns of fate – good and bad –

with an equanimity she found incomprehensible; if he had money he spent it, if he had none he could not. Ursula preferred to know there was always a penny in her purse. She was concerned and mentioned her financial worries to Jessie.

"That's the trouble with relying on men and their luck," said Jessie whilst they were waiting in the cloakroom for the final curtain. "What will you do now?"

"We shall draw in our belts again," she replied matter-of-factly, taking umbrage at Jessie's criticism of David and wishing she had not mentioned the subject, "until David gets some work or the tour comes off."

"But I thought that was all sorted?"

"What was all sorted?"

"His tour next month."

Ursula stiffened; David had not mentioned the tour was arranged. But Jessie knew. *Jessie* knew. Embarrassed and hurt – too proud to admit she did not know anything about the arrangements – and anxious that Jessie should not suspect her ignorance, Ursula shrugged and pretended to look for something under the counter.

"Oh that," she said, in as off-hand a manner as she could. "Still, we need to manage till then."

"Talent and charm are all very well, but they don't pay the rent do they?" said Jessie with a self-satisfied look.

"No," replied Ursula, walking off.

When David came to meet Ursula after the show she was subdued; she had repressed her hurt feelings and drawn strength from her anger, in order to get through the last half hour of the evening without Jessie noticing that anything was wrong. She ignored the arm he held out for her to take. David said nothing and they walked in silence for a while.

"You're very quiet," said David, after a while. "Did something happen this evening?"

Ursula did not reply.

"Ursula, what's wrong?" asked David stopping.

Ursula turned to face him. "You are," she said accusingly.

"And what's that supposed to mean?"

"It means that Jessie seems to know more about your arrangements than I do." How it hurt her to even utter those words.

"What arrangements?"

"Your tour next month."

"Oh that: I see. Let's get home. Hurry up," said David taking her arm, "I'll explain then."

Aware that they could not discuss it in the street, Ursula allowed herself to be guided home but she would not look at David.

When they reached the house David poured the last tot of whisky into his glass while Ursula took off her hat and, sitting down, removed her shoes. He seemed in no hurry to explain and she was still too angry with him to speak. David downed his tot of whisky and looked at the glass wryly, "That's that for a while then," he said.

Ursula did not reply.

"Are you going to stay silent all night or are you going to talk to me?" he asked, looking annoyed.

"It's not up to me", she replied coldly. "I think it's you who should talk."

"If it's about the tour I was going to tell you tonight. I didn't tell you before because I knew you'd be upset that I was going."

"I'm much more upset hearing it from someone else. How could you tell someone else before me, David?" And Jessie of all people, she thought. Jessie who criticized you while I defended you.

"That was unfortunate," replied David, looking down.

Ursula felt a combination of emotions that were beyond her experience – whichever was uppermost altered by the minute; she wanted to beat her fists against his chest, she wanted to shout, she wanted to cry. But at the moment anger still held sway. Strengthened by this she was able to remain calm enough, for long enough, to determine the facts – taking several deep breaths she asked in a clipped voice, "And when, precisely, are you going?"

"Immediately after Christmas," he replied without emotion.

"For how long?"

"I'm not exactly sure. It depends if any more bouts are arranged. Of course Duggie and I have discussed it. He's off next week to settle things."

The remnants of Ursula's fury enabled her to speak haughtily, "When you know perhaps you would be kind enough to tell me."

But it had been a supreme effort; she had controlled her conflicting emotions for some time. Now that she could no longer; she stood up and rushed to the bedroom. Slamming the door behind her, she threw herself on the bed and, beating her feet and fists against the counterpane – jealous, embarrassed, hurt – she let the hot tears come.

Ursula fell into a fitful sleep and at some stage removed her skirt and blouse and crawled under the covers. She woke when David came to bed, but he seemed oblivious to her mood because, ignoring her stiffened body, he put his arms around her, his head on her shoulder and fell asleep. For a long time she lay awake. Did David only discuss the details of the tour with Duggie, how did Jessie know, she must have heard it from one of them. So why didn't David tell her – was he really going to tell her tonight? In the morning she would ask him how Jessie had come by the information. Finally, Ursula slept again. She woke with the dawn feeling exhausted and drained. Her emotional outburst had purged her of anger and hurt, she only felt sad and unloved. If it *was* only Duggie he had discussed it with, she reasoned, had she over-reacted? David woke and put his arms around her; he asked her forgiveness, he did not want to upset her, he had only discussed it with Duggie, he would always tell her everything in future, he loved her. He would love her forever. And she loved him didn't she? And so he poured balm on stormy emotions and she was relieved to be soothed.

For the next week David trained every day. Abe gave him a small retainer, but this, and Ursula's wage, were barely enough to pay the rent and buy provisions. Menus again made demands on her ability to make cheap ingredients appetizing. David no longer asked what they were having for supper, but ate his pickled *snoek* or vegetable curry, without comment. Ursula had enjoyed cooking for someone who enjoyed her meals and she worried that without a good diet David would not be able to fight. Added to this, she was worried about what they would have to celebrate their first Christmas together in their own home.

A money-making scheme occurred to Ursula; she packed two bags of her books and the pay day before Christmas took them to the theatre, leaving them piled on the counter while she did her work. To anyone who enquired about the books she mentioned that they were for sale. No one was surprised at her actions – everyone there was financially strained – but few had money for such things as books; any spare money they had was spent in the bars. Emma, who often came in to see Ursula when she arrived at the theatre, noticed the pile of novels and reference books.

"Are you selling all of them?" asked Emma, surprised.

"I am."

"That is a shame, you love your books."

"I don't need them anymore; I've read them after all and I can borrow them from the library if I want to read them again," said Ursula trying to sound casual. "I don't have much time now for reading anyway." She would miss her old friends.

"What do you have here? Oh, Dickens, I've not read this one, and Trollope, I've never read that. And this looks interesting, *The Myths of Greece and Rome*. I say, would you mind if I bought them all from you – most of my books are at home and I have so little here to read – would that be possible?"

Ursula looked at Emma closely, was she buying them out of pity. But Emma seemed genuinely interested, leafing through them one by one.

"Of course it would; it will be a comfort to know they've gone to someone I know."

"And you can always borrow one if you need," said Emma. "Would two pounds do?"

"That's far too much Emma."

"Not for these, they are in such pristine condition, they look new. I couldn't pay less."

"On the understanding that I can buy them back from you when you've read them and David has finished his tour, I accept," said Ursula, feeling less beholden.

"Of course."

That evening David was delighted when she served his supper.

"What's this – beef steak? Marvellous," he said and without waiting for a reply ate with relish, only stopping when he was nearly finished. "I wish it was pay day every day," he said pushing his plate away, "I haven't had such a good meal for weeks."

Ursula felt very pleased with herself and basked in his cheerful mood. She wouldn't tell David how she had achieved it – she would hate him to think she had made any sacrifice. During the evening they played dominoes and opened a bottle of berry wine Duggie's mother had made. That night David made love to her – not once, but twice – and Ursula did not regret the loss of her books.

It was after lunch the next day, Saturday, when she was getting

155

ready to go to the theatre, that David became aware there was something missing in the cottage.

"Can you pass me those cotton gloves on the shelf, please," she asked.

"Here you are. What used to be on this shelf?"

"My books," said Ursula, putting on her gloves.

"So they were; what happened to them?"

"Oh, I sold them," she said casually.

"Why?"

"We were buying such poor food."

"You sold your books to buy better food?" David asked, sounding annoyed.

Ursula nodded, "The butcher and the grocer refuse to take any more *good fors* from us till we settle up."

David did not look pleased. "But we were managing weren't we?" he asked accusingly.

"I thought it would help," she answered unsurely.

There was a heavy sinking feeling in her stomach – had she done something wrong. David scowled at her; she had not seen him look so angry since she had insulted him at the dance. Fearful of David's black looks, Ursula picked up her straw hat and walked quickly to the door, "I have to leave, I'll be late otherwise," she said. Looking around the door she asked apprehensively, "I'll see you tonight?"

But David turned his back to her and did not reply, and she shut the door behind her. Since the morning a mist had rolled down the mountainside and now a steady drizzle of rain forced Ursula to put up her umbrella. As she walked along, having to slow now and then to see her way, she worried about what had upset David so much; they had never parted before without a kiss. Perhaps by the time she got home he would have calmed down and would explain to her.

Half way through the evening performance a note was delivered to Ursula.

A Little Blue Jacket

I will be late. Alf will see you home. David

David always met her; was he still angry, where could he be going? Worried, Ursula put the note in her pocket.

Ten

Men, some to bus'ness, some to pleasure take;
But ev'ry woman is at heart a rake:
Men, some to quiet, some to public strife;
But ev'ry lady would be a Queen for life.

Epistles: To Lord Cobham (1734)
Alexander Pope 1688–1744

Jessie was quick to notice, "Anything interesting?" she asked.

"No, nothing exciting," Ursula replied. She would not tell Jessie, who was sure to make too much of it.

"Nothing exciting happens here anymore. All the famous foreign performers play at the Opera House and we only seem to have the home-grown variety lot or the ones who are past it."

Ursula was unsettled by David's note but was glad of a diversionary conversation. "That's not quite true Jessie. It was very exciting when the charmer thought he'd lost his snakes during the performance; I don't know how they kept it from the audience."

Jessie disagreed, "Bertie didn't think it was exciting when he found them in an empty beer crate."

"And the last musical group we had here said our acoustics were so good that they would be back when they had someone famous out from England," Ursula reminded her.

"No, still, there's not the same quality anymore. I hope there are more interesting things happening in the Durban theatre."

"Are you still thinking of going?"

"Well, Abe says I can work in his theatre for a few months and if I don't like it I can still have this job back."

Ursula was surprised, it was only since she had married and worked in the bar of the theatre that Jessie had even thought of a change of employment; she had not really expected Jessie's idea to come to anything.

"When will you leave?" she asked.

"When Duggie gets back here – he's in Johannesburg right now – I'll travel to Durban with him after Christmas."

"So you'll have Duggie's company in Durban?"

"I like to have a man all to myself," grinned Jessie.

"Jessie, really," said Ursula without her usual censorial conviction. So – she thought with relief – it probably was Duggie who told Jessie about the tour that time.

Ursula waited until Jessie left the theatre with some of the girls in the chorus before she looked for Alf. She found him talking to Joe, "Alf, David said you would walk me home, is that right?"

"Right enough. Are you ready then?"

She nodded and, as they left the theatre, she explained where she lived. Alf knew the area and explained how he knew every street in the town by the names of the saloons in them. But Ursula was pre-occupied wondering where David was and she soon interrupted him, "Alf, when did you see David?"

"Let me see now . . . oh yes, he was round tea-time – no it was later than that – looking for Petrus he was; only he'd gone home see an' he couldn't find Abe neither, so he said he'd have to do something or other like, I don't recollect what, but there was no way he'd have it sorted by this time, so could I walk you home like."

"And you don't know where he was going?"

"He wasn't his normal self; very tense like. I just said yes see, and he was off."

"It's very kind of you Alf, but I'm sure I can manage on my

own just for this once," said Ursula, who wanted time on her own to think.

"Oh no Miss, that will never do," said Alf. "He's the boss' boyo and not only that, but I've heard about his right hook, see. An undertaking is an undertaking Miss."

Ursula said goodbye and thanked Alf at the gate. When she reached the door it was not properly closed, David must be in, now perhaps he could put her mind at rest. But far from being reassured when she got in the cottage she was very perturbed. The drawer of the table was pulled out, the jar they kept coins in – although there had been hardly anything in it – was without its lid and the doors of the sideboard were open. She went directly into the bedroom and cried out in astonishment; someone had been going through her clothes, the drawers of her chest were open and clothes spilled out of them. She thought of any valuables that might be missing – everything she had was kept in the drawers. Feverishly she searched; her amethyst brooch and the pearl pin David had given her were missing and the small box David kept his best links in was lying open, and empty, on the top of his chest. Ursula sat down on the bed and covered her face with her hands.

Burgled! We've been burgled, she moaned, my lovely brooches, David's links. She remembered her brushes and, sitting up, was relieved to see them poking out from under a blouse. She leaned across and, picking them up, clutched them to her chest. I wish David was here, she thought, where can he be? She wondered if she might look for him but decided it was an impossible task. Duggie was away and he was the obvious contact – David could be anywhere. This is horrid, she thought, someone has robbed us, torn our home apart, and I can do nothing but wait.

After a while Ursula decided to straighten up the cottage to calm herself down; she thought it would pose less of a shock for David when he came in. She hated the thought that someone had rifled through all their personal items and defiled their home. She took all her clothes out of the drawers and, folding them neatly, methodically replaced them in tidy piles; she felt that she had reclaimed them as her own. In the sitting room she did the same with the contents of the cupboards and drawers. The house now looked tidier than when she had left it before work. She looked at her watch, it was nearly one o'clock. As David had not returned she turned off the lamp and went to bed. But her mind was overrun with tangled theories and wild conjecture and, unable to sleep, she got up and, finding her way by the light of the moon, sat at the dining table. Presently, exhausted, she folded her arms on the table and, resting her head on them, drifted into sleep.

A noise awoke her – rubbing her stiff neck she felt a breeze – the door must have opened.

"David . . . David?"

"Yes. It's me," his voice sounded miserable.

Ursula stood up and fumbling towards him in the dark she put out her arms and clasped him, "Oh David, thank goodness you're home. Where have you been? It's been horrible – we've been burgled."

David did not return her embrace and did not reply. Ursula stood back from him – she could not see his face clearly and he smelt strongly of tobacco, "David, what is it?"

"You better sit down."

"Why?"

"Just sit down," his voice was tired but his tone firm.

Worried, she complied silently. David remained standing.

"Shall I light the lamp?" she ventured.

"No, leave it. I've got something to tell you. We haven't been burgled. I took your brooches."

Ursula gasped audibly, "You did!"

"Yes."

"David! Oh, David, I don't understand?"

"I'll explain in the morning – I couldn't take a lecture now – I feel bad enough. We'll talk about it tomorrow."

"But David . . ."

"Not now. Go to bed. I'll sleep here on the couch."

"David," she pleaded, she wanted him to explain.

"Tomorrow," he said peremptorily.

Ursula slept fitfully. The idea that David had taken her brooches worried her more than if a burglar had; she was angry one minute, confused the next. It was such a strange thing to do. Knowing half an unpleasant truth was worse for Ursula than knowing the whole truth; her imagination completed the picture, until the proportions became grotesque. Through the hours of darkness that remained she imagined a gamut of possibilities: David had gone drinking in some rowdy bar, become embroiled with unsavoury sorts, been threatened and to extricate himself had paid them off with the jewellery. He had been accused of a crime, was being blackmailed and was forced to pay the demands; he was rejecting her, he no longer loved her and he had taken the brooches to give his lover! The morning dawned and, with the reassuring light, she knew how ridiculous her conjectures were. However, her wild imaginings were not wasted; they had prepared her for the worst.

Ursula lay in bed until she heard David moving around; she heard the kettle being put on the stove and thought it a good time to approach him. She dressed quickly – she would feel less vulnerable and better able to face bad news if she were clothed. David was sitting at the table drinking tea; he did not look up, but stared at the floor. Worried, Ursula took a deep breath and sat down opposite him.

"David, I haven't slept a wink," she said quietly, "please tell me what's going on."

David looked at her fleetingly, then resumed his study of the floor; when he spoke he sounded resigned, "I talked my way into a poker game."

"Oh," was Ursula's sole response. The evening before she would have been irritated by such news but now she felt almost relieved; none of her worst fears were true.

"Only it didn't go quite as I expected," he continued reluctantly. "A few of the men I won off last time were there. I had to borrow some money and when I lost they demanded I repay it immediately. They were very insistent. I couldn't get hold of enough ready cash and I had to have it right away. I had no alternative; I borrowed what I could and I pawned your brooches and my links to make it up."

"But why did you play?" she asked, her relief turning to anger.

"It's Christmas – I know it's important to you – and then I'm off to Durban soon. I didn't want to leave you without enough money."

"But I would have managed." Didn't he know that about her.

"Like you did on Friday?" He spoke harshly and looked at her accusingly, "My wife shouldn't have to sell her things to make ends meet."

The sharpness of his tone surprised her. Ursula felt her anger rise; he took my brooches, he pawned them, and he scared the living daylights out of me! But she paused – something had occurred to her – "sell her things to make ends meet". So that's it, she thought, I sold the books of my own volition and never thought to ask him; used to deciding things on my own, never considered for a moment that his pride might be hurt. Ridiculous, so utterly ridiculous – but perhaps men are all like that. After a moment she took a breath and said reasonably, "David, if the jewellery is pawned it can be reclaimed."

"It will cost us money to re-coup them so nothing's been achieved!" he said, shortly. "In fact we're worse off."

He sat forward, his elbows on the table, and laid his head in his hands.

Ursula remembered what an agonizing night it had been –

her worry, her confusion, her fears – and all caused by his actions; she never wanted to experience another night like it. But I must try and work this out, she thought, and be calmly logical for once. I didn't tell him about selling the books and he didn't tell me about his money-making scheme. I suppose we're both at fault – the difference is that his idea has gone horribly wrong. But fancy doing such a thing – what a terrible stumbling block a man's pride is. And as she looked at David hunched over and silent she felt pity and forgiveness; what a sorry sight he is with his clothes crumpled and his hair uncombed, she thought. We shall have to consider each other more, confide more. She touched his arm gently and said, "David, if I promise to ask your opinion before I sell things – or do anything that affects us – will you promise to tell me before you do anything rash like gamble again?"

David looked up at her and nodded. They looked gravely into each other's eyes and, after a few moments, he leant across, took her hands in his and kissed them, "I'm a bloody fool, aren't I?"

Ursula did not remark on the disastrous poker game during the week leading up to Christmas. David was penitent and so tender and charming – and she was so pleased they were in accord again – that she quite forgave him. Used to paying her way, with no experience or expectation of a man to rely on, she now thought it rather touching that he wanted to be the main provider. On Christmas Eve Abe gave David an advance that David proudly presented to Ursula, then promptly insisted they go into town and have a drink. The shops in Cape Town opened late on the night before Christmas and everyone – whatever their colour, whatever their class – enjoyed strolling about in the warm evening air. Last minute gifts and toys, flowers and ribbons, sweetmeats and fruits were purchased from the seasonally decorated shops and groups of happy people laughed and sang as they walked along, full of the Christmas spirit.

David and Ursula returned home late but happy. She arranged some of the delicacies they had bought on a large plate and he opened a bottle of Cape wine to accompany them. When they had nearly finished David produced a parcel from beneath the sideboard.

"This is for you," he said proudly, placing it in front of her on the table.

"Oh David. But I only have something very small for you."

"Never mind. Open it."

Ursula unwrapped the brown paper to reveal a fine cream material. She lifted it up; it was a soft shawl with long silken fringes.

"It's beautiful," she said with a smile, as she put it around her shoulders. "It's absolutely beautiful."

"You haven't finished – there's something else," he said, pointing to the paper.

Looking down Ursula saw a box, and opened it: on a bed of cotton wool lay her brooches. "Thank you, thank you," she said, remembering the unpleasant evening.

"They're not a present; they're more by way of an apology and a return to the rightful owner," he said, nevertheless looking very pleased.

"And this is for you," she said producing a small box from the drawer.

David took the lid off the box and took out a pair of silver links.

"These are splendid."

"They're not very valuable I'm afraid."

"Just as well perhaps," he said with a wry smile.

"And, David," she said putting her arms around him, "I bought them with what was left from the book money; I didn't use any more of it for housekeeping."

"Thank you, Funny Face."

The next day Ursula went to early morning mass at the cathedral and afterwards David and she strolled arm-in-arm under the overhanging oaks in Government Avenue, past the Houses of Parliament and *Tuynhuis*. Doves walked staccato style beside them as they passed along and a squirrel made them laugh as it ran backwards and forwards across their path, shooting straight up a tree trunk as a finale. At the end of the avenue they entered the Company's Gardens where Ursula admired the beds of full-blown roses. The sun shone brilliantly and as it was hot they sat on 'their' bench near the sundial, under the shade of the mimosa tree, and leisurely watched people go by.

Theatre life continued throughout Christmas with hardly a break. A few days after Christmas, at the end of the evening show, David and Ursula joined Jessie and some of the chorus and stage hands in the bar of the Crown. Whilst David chatted to the stage hands, and the girls from the chorus joined in with the songs around the piano, Ursula and Jessie sat and talked.

"Aren't the decorations in the shop windows lovely Jessie," said Ursula as soon as they had a drink. "Did you see the tree they put in the window of Stuttafords? There must have been a hundred candles on it on Christmas Eve."

"*Ag* man, I've had more than enough of decorations. I spent every free hour those last few days before Christmas helping the little ones make paper chains and *dingies* to hang on the tree."

"You obviously celebrated at home as usual then Jess?"

"I went to the morning service with Ma and the little ones and I had Christmas dinner with them all."

"I've never really had a family Christmas since Meg entered the convent," said Ursula wistfully, "there was only Nana and me. So I planned this one to be special and in the end it was really nice."

"I suppose mine was too but of course I had to work every evening. Still, I don't mind, I've not got long here now."

"So when are you off?" It was happening then.

"I thought Thursday, after New Year's all over. Might as well enjoy the festivities first."

"That soon!" said Ursula in surprise. "Is Duggie back?"

"He's back all right," said Jessie smugly.

"David's going on Wednesday."

"Is he?" said Jessie, surprised in her turn.

Ursula nodded, looking pensive, "I shall really miss him."

David came over with another drink for them.

"Do you know where Duggie will be tomorrow, Jess?" he asked as he put the glasses down. "I need to get a message to him."

"I'm seeing him *just now*, I'll take it for you," said Jessie eagerly.

"Thank you. Could you tell him I've decided to take the Durban train on Wednesday, and we can sort out things at the station."

"Yes, I'll do that."

"David, you'd better wish Jessie goodbye now, she's off to Durban already," said Ursula leaning towards him. "I'll see her before she leaves but you may not."

"Yes, of course. I hope it goes well, Jessie. I hope you find what you're looking for."

"I have every intention of doing that," said Jessie confidently, lowering her eyelids in her slow way. "I've planned it already."

Ursula was nervous about David's trip. She was increasingly conscious of the incident surrounding the poker game; David had not actually promised not to play again. If he was in Cape Town she was sure he would tell her if he was going to gamble. But in Durban, away from her, she was not so sure; he seemed to be easily led into any exciting sideline. During the days between Christmas and New Year she worried about the impending tour but, on the day after New Year, she made up her mind to forget her misgivings and enjoy the Cape Town celebrations with David.

The cottage they rented was close to the area where most Malays lived, with all the sights and sounds and smells that accompanied the district. The washer woman knocked early at their door to collect the laundry, hawkers going past on their rounds advertised their vegetables in sing-song voices, street vendors accosted passers by and boys on fish carts blew their trumpets. As David and Ursula passed *Bo Kaap* on their way to work the morning air was filled with the smell of laundry and earth closets, sawdust and glue, bread and fish; in the evening the aroma of spices and oil spitting on charcoal wafted across the streets that they crossed. They woke every morning to the sound of the *muezzin* calling the faithful to prayer and in the evening the last call of the *muezzin* reminded them once more that daily life for their neighbours was regulated by their faith.

For weeks Ursula had been aware of the preparations that residents of *Bo Kaap* and District Six were undertaking for their great New Year fancy dress parade that traditionally took place through the town. On doorsteps and behind stalls she noticed men and women – in their every spare moment – surreptitiously sowing feathers and ruffles, bright ribbons and beads, onto gaily coloured costumes. In the evenings, on street corners and in backyards, young men practised walking on stilts and keeping balls in the air; boys tried turning cartwheels. Mothers made batches of savouries – the smell of which invitingly filled the evening air – and wives made sweetmeats while sisters and daughters could be glimpsed through open doors, candying and dipping the offerings in sugar syrup. Finally, even the horses that pulled the hawkers carts were beautifully groomed and decked out in paper hats and jangling bells.

When David and Ursula heard the first strains of music they left the cottage to watch the parade. Groups of male singers and dancers dressed in fancy outfits tried to outdo each other as they played their *fluitjes* and banjos and performed acrobatics and juggling tricks, parading joyously through the streets on this, their annual holiday. From vendors at the roadside David bought *koesijsters* for Ursula and *mostbolletje* for himself and they took guilty pleasure in breaking the rules of etiquette by eating them as they wandered along, caught up in the informal atmosphere. As the parade progressed, chattering Malay women sat on steps and stood on roofs, whilst excited children ran up and down, every one of them enjoying the spectacle and the atmosphere of freedom and fun.

That night they made love as passionately as they had on their honeymoon and the next morning, Wednesday, there were many tender farewell embraces and kisses on both sides. Ursula was loath to leave David to go to work and so he offered to accompany her to the theatre. The frequent tablecloth of vapour lay over the mountain and prompted solicitous wifely remarks from Ursula as to his wardrobe and diet. And she begged that he did nothing as rash as gambling. He assured her that he would not; he would get thoroughly acclimatized and concentrate on his boxing, and nothing else. She asked him to be sure to write and, after giving him a chaste kiss, she disappeared into the theatre before she became too emotional.

Behind the bars of the auditorium and in the passages and offices of the theatre Ursula thought about David throughout the day. When she heard the sound of the midday gun – fired each day from *Schotsche Kloof* – she knew that he would be on the train. She was glad that she would be busy that night taking the cloaks and coats and have no time for moping. It was to be Jessie's last night, but as she was not there when Ursula got to the cloakroom she set about tidying up. Ellie arrived as she was brushing the floor of all the spent cloakroom tickets.

"Hello Ellie," she said, "are you helping in here now?"

169

"*Ja*, started today. Jessie left word she had to go earlier than expected."

Ursula stopped brushing the floor, "She never said; I was here all day."

"*Ne*, she never came in today. She took all her *dingies* last night. I did the matinée on my own."

"I don't understand it", said Ursula puzzled and uneasy, "she said she was going tomorrow."

"Jessie said that you would be on your own now and had nothing to rush home for," explained Ellie, "so she said that you'd be able to show me the ropes, and how to lock up any left property at the end of the evening. *Ja*, can you do that? Then I can show the *nonna* who's starting tomorrow."

"And Jessie never even told me who's to take over whilst she's away?"

"Miss Violet Brown."

"But I know that name," said Ursula, scowling.

"*Ja* man, she's the teacher lady going to marry Duggie McNair."

Ursula was very upset that Jessie had left earlier than expected without saying goodbye to her. During the first act she went to find Emma in the dressing room. The heat of the day had made the bowels of the theatre stuffier than usual; perching on a table Ursula fanned herself with a programme that was lying there as she questioned Emma, "Emma, were you here last night? Did Jessie say goodbye to you?"

"She did. She came down very excited, said her plans had changed, things were looking up."

"She didn't say goodbye to me, which is odd and very upsetting. Did she say anything more?"

"No, that's all she said."

"I don't understand why she went in such a hurry," said Ursula, still no clearer about Jessie's motives.

"I asked her when she'd be back. She said it all depended.

She didn't say on what but she gave one of those eyebrow raising look of hers – you know," said Emma mimicking Jessie, "like she does when she's suggesting something saucy – and she was off."

"Oh," said Ursula glumly. She felt hotter and more uneasy than ever; so Jessie was planning something she obviously didn't want me to know about, she thought. Had she timed her departure to coincide with Duggie's, or with David's, she wondered, and she fanned herself faster.

"Ursula, don't be sad, don't fret," Emma reassured. "I know we'll miss her, won't we, but Jessie needs to have something to look forward to – a challenge perhaps – and a change of scenery may be just the thing. She should meet some new and interesting companions there – she may even meet someone special."

Ursula was not sad, she was annoyed – upset and confused even – and she hoped Emma's remarks were nowhere near the truth. But she felt disinclined to admit her fears to someone as charitable as Emma.

"Emma, Emma, you always see the best in people and want the best for them," she said. "It's a very nice characteristic."

"Well, try and remember, you have David, don't you," replied Emma, softly.

Ursula walked home with Alf; she let him chatter on but was too deep in her own thoughts to contribute. Her mind was racing: why did Jessie leave early, without saying good bye? That was rotten, she thought, Jessie usually tells me everything in the greatest detail. Except about Duggie, she never really acknowledged how close her relationship with Duggie is. But to arrange for his fiancée to work at the theatre, why? So Duggie is free? Is Duggie a challenge, is Durban? Yes, that's it, Duggie's obviously changed his plans, she decided, and gone today and Jessie must have wanted to travel with him, yes that must be it, she remembered her saying she wanted to travel with him.

Nothing to do with David. Jessie obviously got her days mixed up, concluded Ursula, and had to go earlier because of that. But she should have left me a message.

"I'm sorry, Alf, what was that you were saying?" she asked, able to concentrate now she had rationalized her fears.

That night, late, there was a knock on her door. Ursula did not expect anyone and, afraid to open it, she called out, "Who's there?"

"It's Duggie."

She opened the door a crack, "Duggie, what are you doing here?"

He took his cap off, "Is David no here?"

"No, no he isn't," replied Ursula as she opened the door wider, "didn't Jessie give you his message to meet at the station?"

"I did'na get onie message – frae Jessie?"

"Yes, I thought she was travelling with you?" She felt as if something heavy was bearing down on her, compressing her.

"Nae, not me, I already told Jessie I wasne going Thursday. I'm here noo to tell David that."

"But he's gone," she said looking at Duggie with dismay.

"Tae Durban?"

"Yes."

"He's awfie early," said Duggie, raising his eyebrows. "Must want to train an awfie lot, must be worrit aboot the humidity. Och weel," he shrugged, "I'll see him next week."

"And Jessie's gone too," she said desperately.

"She has?" his eyebrows shot up again. "Weel I never, could'na wait," he said shaking his head and adding thoughtfully, "My, my."

Ursula, disconcerted and anxious, was loath to lose this only contact, "Duggie, I'm worried about David, I thought you'd be with him. Will you come and see me before you do go?"

Duggie smiled, "Aye lassie, that I will. Fare thee weel."

"Good night, *slaap gerust*, Duggie," she said in a whisper.

He replaced his cap on his ginger curls, gave her a nod and turned down the path.

When he had gone Ursula paced the floor and picked at her fingers. Nothing was quite as she had expected; this morning she had imagined David saying goodbye to Duggie at the station, sitting on the train on his own, finding his way alone to his boarding house, spending time with the boxing fraternity, meeting up with Duggie after a few days. This evening the image had changed – he was travelling with Duggie and Jessie. But now the whole picture was altered again; he was travelling with Jessie – only Jessie – he would have to see her to her digs. She loved David so much and, she assured herself, he loved her. Of course he loved her, and she trusted him, didn't she, of course she did. But Jessie – Jessie who had no scruples. No, she was being silly, Jessie was keen on Duggie – she knew that. But why didn't Jessie give Duggie David's message, was she worried Duggie would stop her going? Was she worried that she'd have no-one to travel with? Ursula's head was spinning.

Their bed seems very large this dark, stifling, starless night. Ursula feels like a solitary being, too hot to move, becalmed on an ocean of bed linen; deserted and rudderless. How she wishes David's comforting body was beside her, not far away from her, in a place she does not know; with company she has no knowledge of . . . or too much knowledge of. And she lies, eyes open wide, alone with fanciful imaginings and a strong feeling of disquietude.

The nursery
Johannesburg, February 13th, 1912

Sounds reached the room through the open windows; the distant clang of a tram, a car horn, horses' hooves on the road, the call of a vegetable seller, a bird chattering on a branch near the window. A slight smell of cooking still hung on the air, not quite removed by the breeze nor disguised by the smell of the eucalyptus soaked sachets that were hung on the cot. The nurse arrived and Ursula, resigned now to her being there, told Mrs Van Der Ploeg that she would see her in a few hours.

Ja, so much better for Madam to leave it to her.

Perhaps Mrs Van Der Ploeg would care for a little poached chicken in her sandwich today? No, it was no trouble at all; she had only cooked it this morning and she and her husband would be having a little of it themselves at supper time; Lizzie would prepare it for her.

As soon as Ursula had seen Mrs Van Der Ploeg off in the evening she went into the kitchen, then up to the nursery carrying a small tray with a bowl, covered in a cloth, and a tiny bone spoon.

So hard to stop him dribbling it everywhere these last few days but we'll see this time – the jelly's thicker now I've boiled it more. There we are Edward, this pillow will just keep your head up.

And where's the towel – here, let's pop that under your chin. Have just a tiny bit. Oh Edward, swallow. Swallow.

Wait a minute, when I have to give Sukey her pill, what did the veterinary surgeon say? That's it – use my finger to push the pill down or stroke her throat till she swallows it. Yes. If I hold his mouth shut with this hand – sorry, kleintjie *– and just with my finger, rythmically stroke, yes. Yes, I think it's working. This is better. And again Edward, come on, just a little bit more. This has got to work, it's got to.*

There – it doesn't look as if anything's happened – he's nice and clean. Sukey's eaten up all the left-overs. I think he looks pinker, I wonder if they'll notice tomorrow. But I have to do more – he's not getting enough nourishment. It needs to be more concentrated. That's it, I'll give him Brand's chicken essence neat – it's richer, stronger. But I'll have to push it down with my finger because it's more solid – sorry little one, I shall hate to do it but it's for your own good.

You can hear me can't you my beautiful Edward, I think you can hear me when I sing your favourite rhymes. Perhaps if the little one comes – she could talk to you. Will you recognize a little child's voice, her touch.

What a beautiful, little girl – a mop head of gold curls – such a delicious laugh.

See-saw Margery Daw
Johnny shall have a new master
He shall have but a penny a day
Because he can't work any faster

More, more – such pretty pleading – sapphire eyes wide open. No, no more.

It was very dark now within the room; Ursula covered Edward with a blanket and turned on the small electric lamp by the bed. The glow of the lamp cast shadows across the room that colluded to form monstrous spectres. Resting on the bed, she fell into a troubled sleep in which a large black bird was spreading its wings above her:

> *A lovely young child is holding her hand, a child two or three years old, angel's hair and dimpled cheeks. Together they walk up slopes covered with spring flowering bulbs and colourful fynbos, take off their shoes to cross the bubbling stream, pick a nosegay of wild flowers, chase a butterfly. In the fading light of early evening the heavy fragrance of belladonna lilies reaches them. But when they find them behind a koppie the stately blooms are completely smothered by moths. The little child is weary. They sit down under the shade of a boerboon tree, its scarlet flowers beginning to wilt, its leaves tinged with red. Bees are extracting the last of the nectar from the spent flowers. The child's head is on her lap, they fall into a deep, deep sleep. And the big black bird that had been soaring and sweeping through the skies above them as they walked, roosts on a branch above their heads and casts a deep purple shadow over them, chilling them.*

Ursula woke shivering – the little figure so full of life in her dream, so real to her awake. She felt her nose tingling, tears pricking her eyelids. *Did Edward stir?* Ursula was instantly back in the present, it was as if her thoughts had reached him – had he moved his head, his leg, his eyelids. There was no sign now, only the memory of movement, but it was a strong enough impression to give her hope. She closed the windows and re-fastened the screens. She must undress and get under the covers. In the morning, before the nurse arrived, she would feed him the essence.

This precious little baby would live.

Eleven

Twinkle, twinkle, little star,
How I wonder what you are!
Up above the world so high,
Like a diamond in the sky!

The Star
Jane Taylor 1783–1824

Hannah had married the week after she told Ursula of her intentions. She explained that Mr Essop would wait no longer and (not as secure financially as she had led Ursula to believe) she had agreed. On hearing the news Ursula felt heavy-hearted but tried to appear glad for Hannah's sake. Their old house had to be vacated; she had liked the thought of Hannah continuing to live there, but now the ties to her old home – her childhood and the only family she knew – would finally be severed. She arrived at the house earlier than arranged with Hannah – she wanted to be alone and look one last time at the home of her youth. She wanted to revel in her childhood experiences, to linger over fond memories, to wrap up and pack the items herself. I've my own home now, she told herself, David and I have each other. She took possession of the few belongings that had been her mother's and sold the remainder.

Whilst David was in Durban, Ursula suffered considerably from the summer heat. The theatre was airless and if she ventured out at midday to get some fresh air the sun gave her a headache. The lack of air made her feel faint and the constant heat caused her, and her colleagues, to be short-tempered. Even at night there was no respite as the corrugated zinc roof of the cottage absorbed the heat of the day and retained it. When she had lived with Hannah, on summer nights such as these, they had moved the old iron bedstead outside onto the *stoep,* where they had taken advantage of the night breeze. But such a thing was not possible in their cottage with its tiny cast-iron trimmed and trellised *stoep* so close to the road, and the atmosphere – even with every window wide open – was stifling. If Ursula woke in the depth of night the incessant, shrill sound of the crickets ensured that she would get no more sleep.

When David had been away for ten days he telegraphed that as everything was going well he was extending his tour to include Johannesburg. Ursula was disappointed and so miserable that she felt physically sick, her doubts and fears renewed. Automatically she felt need of the comfort that only Hannah could give. She left town secure in the knowledge that Hannah would be delighted to see her. But, as she drew closer to the *dorp,* she became apprehensive; how would she feel when she saw their old house, would she like Mr Essop in a husband's role, would he like her, would Nana act differently now she was married.

Mr Essop's house, in a small *dorp* about a mile further on from their own old home, was very similar to their old house – although a little larger – and Ursula found Hannah sitting on the *stoep* sewing as naturally as she had always done. Hannah did not rise and greet Ursula as she normally did but, turning her head towards the interior, called, "Mr Essop, my Ursula here!" encouraging Ursula, with flapping of hands, to go in and see him. Unfolding himself from his chair when Ursula entered, he towered over her – he wore a long *djibbah* which accentuated his height – and with great dignity bowed and welcomed her. Ursula excused herself as soon as she had exchanged pleasantries and returned to Hannah; it was unusual for Hannah not to be fussing about. "Nana, are you all right? You're not unwell with this heat are you?"

"*Ne*, I am well, man," she replied beaming. "Still, have to take a little care in my condition."

Ursula looked dumbly at her and sat lumpenly in the chair next to her. A slight frown formed on her brow and she opened her mouth once or twice as if about to speak but no words came out; surely Hannah could not mean what she thought she meant. But Hannah continued to smile broadly at her and laying her sewing in her lap – where Ursula's gaze now rested – she took one of Ursula's hand in hers and gently stroked it.

"A present from God," she said.

"But . . ." Ursula started, and stopped.

"Mr Essop is very proud," nodded Hannah.

"How . . ."

"He say if it is a girl we call her Miriam – after his mother – but if it is a boy we call him Muhammad."

"Still Nana, you're too old for . . . I mean, Mr Essop, he's . . . and you, you . . ." stammered Ursula. Surely her old nurse and Mr Essop, who was much older, did not indulge in anything physical.

"*Ne*, your mother forty-five years of age when you borned. I am forty-four. You her *laatlammetjie*, this," Hannah continued, patting her stomach, "is mine."

Nana and Mr Essop together in bed like herself and David; Nana to have a child. The news was a shock for Ursula, she mumbled congratulations but soon made excuses and started for home. She had expected to feel reassured as usual after visiting Hannah but the visit had quite the opposite effect; she had only just got used to the idea of Hannah having a husband, and now this! Ursula thought of all the women she knew who had children late and realized with surprise that Hannah – if she forgot who she was – did not look as old as many of them. She had only ever thought of her as Nana – comfortable, reliable Nana – and never as a woman, a wife, a mother. On the journey home Ursula became increasingly philosophical and resigned. Everything was changing, there were fewer certainties than ever, nothing was as she expected any more – she must rely on herself now.

Returning from his summer tour David was cheerful; he was so pleased to be home again, had missed his wife, had hated staying in boarding houses and third-rate hotels. He told her all about his tour in detail – not finally as successful as the previous one – and answered her every question willingly. And he displayed such passion and tenderness when they made love that Ursula could not doubt him. Her worst fears and deepest suspicions were allayed by his cheerful presence and as the unnatural heat wave passed, and more normal summer temperatures resumed, she regained her usual equable disposition.

Some weeks later a visit to the physician confirmed that Ursula was pregnant and both she and David were overjoyed. Ursula found David's pride and joyous anticipation of fatherhood touching but it was not for some time – when his savings were substantially depleted – that the full importance of what fatherhood entailed settled on him. The responsibility weighed heavily until he took Ursula's advice and had a long discussion with Abe. Reluctantly, David agreed with Abe that he had probably achieved all he was capable of in competitive boxing – married life was increasing his weight and had dulled his burning ambition – a fresh and reliable career was needed. They agreed that he should keep his hand in by training boxers and refereeing but he accepted Abe's invitation to join his diamond business as a permanent employee in the office.

That evening – the oil lamp dimmed and the windows open to

help the air circulate – David relayed to Ursula the details of their conversation and of his decisions, as they sat at the table after dinner.

"That's marvellous, David. I must admit I was a little worried about how we'd manage." Ursula was pleased for other reasons too – now there was no risk of injury and there would be no prolonged tours.

"I want to be involved in the acquisition and sales side too but, unfortunately, I'll also have to do some of the sort of bookwork I did in London," David said, adding solemnly, "Abe's offered me a very good salary though – I couldn't turn it down."

"No of course not," she smiled, reassuringly.

"And I'll earn a bit more with the training and refereeing."

"That's wonderful." But she thought he seemed a little downhearted, "Perhaps we should celebrate?" She knew David would respond cheerfully to such a suggestion.

"Yes, I'd like that," he said, smiling.

"We could go to the theatre and have a slap-up meal."

"Good idea, and as Duggie's back from Durban we could ask him and Violet to come with us; you wouldn't mind if they came too, would you?"

"Of course not. They seemed an oddly matched couple at first; I just couldn't imagine Violet with a risk taker like Duggie; she's so composed."

"Perhaps it's a case of opposites attract."

"I suppose so. I think Duggie's antics may be her outlet; she'd certainly never do anything rash or spontaneous herself. I've had weeks working with her – she never gets excited or raises her voice. And strangely she never scolds Duggie – doesn't try to dissuade him from doing hare-brained things and never loses her temper with him when he goes ahead and does them."

"I missed a chance there," said David, shaking his head. "She would have made an admirable wife for me."

"You horror!" Ursula remonstrated, giving David's hand a

playful slap. "You'd prefer me to be submissive and calm I suppose?"

"It has an appeal." He smiled and moved his chair to avoid another slap, leaving Ursula to fold her arms and frown.

After a moment's silence he again moved his chair close to hers, and putting both arms around her, said in a conciliatory tone, "No I wouldn't – I like it best when you get angry."

Ursula frowned harder for effect.

"You're my favourite Funny Face," David said, giving her a kiss and eliciting a wry smile.

She was secretly satisfied; teasing had reinstated his good humour.

David proved adept at his new business; as a youth he had spent his free time setting gems in his uncle's jewellery business, and had developed a good eye for precious stones. His easy manner and friendly disposition made him a natural salesman, his quick mind a natural dealer. After a few months he had earned several commissions that boosted their income substantially. And the more deals he struck the less he had to do tedious bookwork. Ursula was relieved and pleased with their new found solvency as she would have to give up working at the theatre when her condition became too obvious. They needed to find a larger house and, with three months until the baby was due, they began to look in earnest. South of the town centre, on the lower slopes of Table Mountain, the streets of *Oranjezicht* district were filled with attached and terraced houses, some of which had wonderful views of the bay or the mountain, or both.

The new houses in the district had been built at the end of the century for middle-class white families but with the depression that followed the Anglo-Boer war many were left unsold and respectable Malay and Indian families were able to rent or purchase them. As a result the district was affordable and David and Ursula thought it would suit them well. They found a two-storied house which, from the front window bays and the balcony above, had an awesome view of the mountain. And from the first floor balcony at the rear of the house the view of *Roggebaie*, and the park that stretched down the slope below the garden, was more wonderful than they could have hoped. They took the house straightaway.

However, the garden was much larger than they had expected. Their house stood near the end of the road and the small garden at the rear now incorporated part of an old garden from an enormous villa residence demolished – and not yet re-built – on the adjacent street. The unusually large plot meant that a gardener would be required, an expense and a responsibility that Ursula did not relish. Lizzie – a woman of indeterminate race – had lately come in on a daily basis to clean for them and was glad to accompany them to the new house and work for a single employer. She was doggedly thorough when there was any difficult job to be tackled in the kitchen and noticed everything, but rarely spoke. However, when Ursula interviewed a Bushman for the post of gardener Lizzie was bold enough to say to her afterwards, "Dose San no good for garden. *Rather* Lizzie find Khoikhoi for de *Oumissus*."

And she did, although Ursula suspected there was self-interest at heart; she was sure from their cordial relations that the Hottentot, Wellington, and Lizzie knew each other well.

David insisted they purchase new furniture for their drawing room but Ursula economized by buying a dining set from a house sale nearby. There was still ample space in the house for the furniture Ursula had inherited; she tried the pieces in various positions – moving them around with the help of Wellington and Lizzie – until she was satisfied with the result. Her mother's portrait was finally hung above the dressing chest in her bedroom, the small set of shelves – and the figurines that had previously stood on them – were hung in the small alcove of the drawing room. The handsome pair of upholstered chairs – her mother's and father's – were placed in the dining room, at the rear of the house. Here her books – bought back from Emma when finances allowed – were installed in the open shelves around the chimneypiece; at present she would use the room to read in if she were on her own.

Lizzie – her head covered by a *doek* – undertook the daily brushing that was necessary to rid the house of the moths and spiders and other dead *goggas* that built up in the rooms, and to guard against the cockroaches that might invade. The brushing complete, she dusted and polished the furniture and afterwards Ursula dusted and replaced the ornaments on freshly laundered, lace-edged mats. Lizzie 'did' a room thoroughly each day of the week and once a week she scrubbed every surface of the kitchen, polished the knives and pans, and cleaned the coal stove. On wash days Ursula helped her by turning the mangle handle (a new addition David was pleased to buy for them) and making soap. While Lizzie ironed the table and tray cloths, the bedsheets and nightdresses, shirts and petticoats, Ursula made preserves and experimented with cakes and biscuits for David, or anyone that called on her.

Resting in their new bedroom – stroking her swelling belly with pride and wonder – Ursula remembered with shame how she had reacted to the news of Hannah's pregnancy. Her earlier drive in the bus that morning to see Hannah and her newborn daughter – a perfectly formed, pale faced little girl with a shock of straight black hair and a nose like a button – had physically tired her. An unexpected wind from the north had brought pelting rain and an icy wind, and buffeted the bus on its way back to town. The experience had drained her emotionally too, adding to her torpor; Hannah had a child – a child as small and defenceless as she had been when Nana took charge of her. And soon she too would have a child: a tiny, totally dependent baby – a present from God.

"You are a wonderful cook now," observed Emma one afternoon, as she finished a slice of lemon sponge. "I've had a different cake every time I've been here, and each has been more delicious than the last. I'm afraid I couldn't bake a cake if I tried."

"You've probably never tried," laughed Ursula, "and I can't imagine you ever doing so."

"I shall never be any good at any practical household task; I never watched Cookie and, had I realized I may have to play the part of a parlour maid one day, I might have taken a little more notice of what our Sophie was doing."

"You're far more likely to be cast in the role of an aristocratic lady, Emma, so I don't think you need worry too much about that."

"But I do hope I get married one day, and that involves running a house. I want to have a whole pack of children," said Emma with an expansive gesture, "think of the fun."

"You're certainly not going to meet a suitable husband in the theatre, Emma," said Ursula seriously.

"Spare me, it's all I hear when I see mother and father. I've been given an ultimatum you know; if I've not made it by my next birthday father is either going to cut my allowance or marry me off to cousin Archie. That's an incentive to get my skates on because, dear that he is, he's not my idea of a dashing husband. I simply cannot see Archie as my Romeo."

Ursula thought of David with a surge of affection. He had been so understanding when she had explained to him that making love now she was so close to her confinement made her uncomfortable, and fearful.

185

"But you must have a partner in life that you love," she said earnestly. "Perhaps you should travel a bit. Couldn't you go around Europe or something; David says people are thrown together on boats and trains."

"But Ursula, you met David without leaving Cape Town."

"I was lucky, but I intend to travel one day. Wouldn't you like to travel and see the world? You'd be sure to meet someone then."

"No travel for me yet, first I have to get that lucky break. If I get offered something special, well, then I can travel. Indeed, I'd better be off now," Emma said as she gathered her handbag and gloves, and put on her winter coat, "or I'll be late at the theatre."

Ursula enjoyed being a homemaker – and had ample time to indulge her love of reading – but she missed the dramas and camaraderie of theatre life; the minor mishaps backstage, the sing-songs around the piano in the Crown bar, the gossip amongst the chorus. And she admitted to herself that she even missed Jessie's outlandish ways. The wintery weather did not encourage her to go out more than necessary and the highlight of her day was usually David's homecoming. Of late however, he had been less cheerful on returning from the office. That evening, after dinner, Ursula told David of Emma's unexpected but pleasant visit.

"I'm glad you had an enjoyable day."

"Yes, Emma's visit really cheered me up."

"Good, that is good," said David thoughtfully.

"Is there anything wrong David?" she asked, noting his suppressed mood.

"No, nothing wrong," he replied, "but, listen to me, Funny Face. I've got to go away for a week or so. You'll be all right on your own won't you?"

"Where have you got to go?" asked Ursula, alarmed.

"I need to visit the diamond mines; Abe says it's essential, and better sooner than later. There's not a lot on at the moment and I'm a bit bored – and I don't want to be away when the baby is born – so I think this is the best time."

"Are you bored? I thought you were enjoying the position."

"I was. But if I'm in the office it's the same every day," he said, despondently. "Bookwork and figures. There's no thrill – nothing to get worked up about. You understand don't you?"

Ursula did not reply immediately. Of course I understand, she thought, I miss the thrill of the theatre. But I don't want him to go away.

"Yes, I suppose so," she said shortly, unable to disguise her displeasure, "but you won't be away for very long, will you?"

"Of course not. I'll be back in plenty of time," said David brightening. "Perhaps you could ask Emma to stay with you?"

"Let me think about it," she said trying to be sensible, when in fact she was feeling upset and dreaded the thought of him going.

David said nothing but took her hand and squeezed it. Contact with him was always comforting and because he did not try and persuade her further Ursula began to persuade herself. How can I complain, she argued with herself, if he really needs to go, if it's necessary for his work. We need the money with an extra mouth to feed. And if it was Kimberley he might find out something about Jimmy.

"No, if you're not away long I shall manage," she said decisively.

"Of course you will," he said with a reassuring smile.

"And – I suppose it will be Kimberley – perhaps you could look up our old address for Jimmy? Would you do that, find out if anyone knows what happened to him, where he is?"

"Yes of course I could."

"That's not so bad then."

*

David left the following week – with Duggie for company on his journey – and with promises to write regularly and instructions for Ursula to telegraph him if there was any emergency. He kept his word and sent a stream of amusing and solicitous postcards which pleased Ursula and for several days she was content busying herself with further preparations for the layette. In the back dining room a set of French doors opened onto a wide *stoep* that framed a lawn where several small rose bushes lined a narrow gravel path. As spring set in the weather improved and Ursula enjoyed taking walks around the garden at intervals throughout the day; each day she noticed with interest how the leaves on the rose bushes had uncurled a little bit more. However, she did not linger here as the house threw shadow over the grass, but walked to the apparent end of the garden where three white pear trees stood on the top of a bank.

Below the bank the garden unexpectedly changed direction and ran at right angles to the house. This was the mature garden of the old house. Overgrown *saliehout* bushes straggled through a boundary hedge, their tapering mauve flowers – although beginning to fade – still wafted a strong scent along the worn path; bold clumps of handsome grasses punctuated the turf and large pincushion bushes – their bright yellow and brilliant orange flower heads shining like beacons – created islands. Nasturtiums rampaged over every inch of bare earth, their vibrant coloured flowers like flames licking the ground. In a central clearing a small ornamental pool was set, cool and calm in contrast to the riot of colour around it. Sword-like leaves of iris cut through the still water and furled pads of water lilies pushed their way up to open like plates afloat on the surface of the pool. And in one corner a solitary, stately arum lily stood proud – its chalice-like, simple white spathe ready for the Eucharist wine.

Nearby on the grass a simple wooden bench, split and stained with age, was placed to take advantage of the reflections in the water. Ursula was increasingly drawn to the pool; if the weather was warm enough she sat on the bench and embroidered the small jackets and caps, smocks and nightdresses that she was making for the baby as she listened to the scraping of the cricket's legs and the gulping of the frogs. Every now and then she would rise and walk about the grass to ease her back. Looking down as she stood near the edge of the pool she would examine the reflection of her rotund figure in the dark, cold-looking water. But the water lily leaves were proving rampant and without care the spreading leaves would smother the surface and conceal her reflection. She would ask Wellington to remove them.

During the evenings, with only her thoughts for company, Ursula would draw a woollen shawl around her shoulders and walk to the pool. Here, stroking her stomach with the flat of her palms she would commune with her unborn child, as she looked at the reflection of the moon – ghostly pale – in the pool. Looking up at it she traced the outline of the hare, was it running to give men the moon's message of death? She tried to remember the legend. And later, as she lay in her bed, the curtains drawn wide, she studied the still, deep sky with its countless pinprick stars suspended like diamonds, as the baby in her womb wrestled and made her back ache. She wondered if the baby was a boy and, fingering the medal that hung around her neck, she thought of David – where was he, what was he doing, whom was he with? Those long dark hours awake and alone produced images of David – and the company he might keep – so vivid she was sure they were real, and gave birth to doubts about her confinement so dire, they scared her.

When David had been away for over a week Violet paid Ursula a visit, bringing with her a selection of recent theatre programmes and illustrated weekly papers.

"Thank you, Violet, what a lovely surprise," said Ursula, "I've hardly had a soul to speak to for days. I only get to exchange pleasantries with the neighbours and acquaintances I see on my constitutionals to the park – the thought of taking the tram to see friends and walking back up the hill is too awful to contemplate, so I've been nowhere at all."

"I promised David before he left that I would call on you," Violet said in her precise voice, the Scottish accent barely discernible. "I'm sorry it has not been before now but my days are so full. I know you miss the theatre news."

"I really do. Has anything new or interesting happened? Is Ellie still helping you and are Bert and Alf still behind the scenes?"

"Och, you'd be surprised how little has changed; Ellie and Bert and Alf are just the same. You see Emma of course, and she can tell you all about her parts. The Opera House is rehearsing *Iolanthe* – which I believe is glorious although they will have to cut it to produce it here – but at the Tivoli they think they've eclipsed *Iolanthe* as Miss Lola Lee is booked."

"Oh!"

"Yes, she's going to perform her famous snake dances – she's transporting her snakes out on the ship from England – and she'll do her exotic eastern dances too."

"How exciting! Jessie will be green with envy when she hears you'll see her!"

"Have you heard anything from Jessie?" asked Violet searchingly.

"I had a note . . . three days ago."

"Did she say anything particular, mention any men friends?"

"No, just her normal prattle."

"I see," replied Violet, in a disapproving tone, her lips pursed. "Well, I wouldn't trust that girl further than I could throw her."

"What do you mean Violet?" asked Ursula, not sure to whom the remark applied.

"Och, she strikes me as devious, that's all. And before I forget, I have a message for you. Duggie was very insistent I came

190

right away to say that David is well and hopes to be with you soon."

"Thank you. Duggie's back already then?" Ursula was surprised, she had thought he would remain with David throughout their trip.

"Yesterday – I was not expecting him for quite a few days. But he arrived and immediately proposed a date for our wedding."

"Why, that's wonderful Violet." David had said Duggie had been dragging his feet, and Violet wouldn't wait forever.

"Indeed, he has made the decision at last. But soon enough he will be busy elsewhere, on some project or another."

"How do you remain so equable with a man who is so unpredictable and never stays still?"

"Duggie needs to be on the move – he enjoys a peripatetic life," replied Violet, in her measured way. "He could never work in a sedentary job – like David he would be bored – and then like him he would get up to even more mischief."

Ursula did not like the tone of Violet's remark – it brought her own doubts and fears to the fore – but she decided to ignore it; perhaps Violet thought that she had been critical.

"You're very philosophical about Duggie's adventures – I wish I could be as calm as you are," she said.

"I have had much practice with my younger brothers; the more I denied them the more they defied me. I eventually learnt that with a measured response I achieved moderate compliance; I considered that satisfactory. I have never liked Duggie visiting Durban but I never complained. This time he could have visited it and, quite of his own accord, he did not. And a few of Duggie's antics do cause me to smile – as do a few of the less bizarre events I encounter at the theatre."

"There's always someone causing a furore there or trying on some ruse or other," said Ursula with a wistful look. "I do miss the bustle of it."

191

"Och, you'll soon have all the bustle you can deal with. It would be wise to make the most of this quiet time," said Violet, looking more sombre than ever.

"You're very sensible, Violet. David thinks you'll be an admirable wife, and make a good solid home," said Ursula, smiling at her, "and that Duggie has made a good choice."

"Duggie is deep, and not always as dependable as I would wish, but he's a decent enough man for all that."

Violet's visit failed to cheer Ursula, indeed it worried her and over the following days a change came over her – a melancholy that spread like a mantle. She could not shake it off. She had not received any further letters from Jessie and, since Violet's visit, no postcard had arrived from David. Instead she read and re-read David's previous correspondence that she kept in the pocket of her pinafore. The first was from Kimberley – "Old De Beers Road" the caption read – but the buildings were large stone edifices that did not correspond with her memory of haphazard timber buildings and conical tents. However, a postcard of cattle, and those showing the mine workings and oxen carts waiting in the vast market square, brought memories flooding back to her but also the disappointing news that David had been unable to learn anything of her brother. Ursula had not reasonably expected David to be able to trace her brother after so many years and so many changes, but she had harboured a hope.

The next cards were from Johannesburg depicting different scenes of the town, with tall, stately buildings and wide avenues; further ones had smart automobiles parked in front of impressive offices. And then she received a postcard from Durban. Only one, with a photograph of the pier bandstand – and a few hurried words to say he had arrived there safely. Ursula could not remember him mentioning that Durban was on the itinerary.

Why was he there? Would he see Jessie? Distant memories wafted by like spectres, buried fears surfaced. Postcards are all very well, she thought, but I need to talk to him, I need to speak to him. How I wish he was home now.

Twelve

Let us, then, be up and doing,
With a heart for any fate;
Still achieving, still pursuing,
Learn to labour and to wait.

A Psalm of Life
Henry Wadsworth Longfellow 1807–1882

Over the next few nights Ursula was unable to sleep and her nightly fears began to ferment and fill her daytime reveries; previous suspicions became certainties, fiction became fact. During the day (if she was not sewing or busy with her hands) she picked nervously at her fingers and the circles that appeared under her eyes darkened to the colour of over-ripe plums. The change in her in such a short period was obvious enough for Lizzie – usually spare with her words and careful with her opinions – to risk a remark, "De *Oumissus* not look good. Need *boetatjie.*"

The thought of a healer struck a chord in Ursula and she immediately thought of Hannah; too uncomfortable now to drive in a bus, she wrote to ask Hannah to visit. She arrived two days later, her arms laden with bulging bags, a bunch of creamy yellow gladiolus tucked into one. "How beautiful these are, Nana," exclaimed Ursula whilst they were still in the porch, "but where's Miriam?"

"*Ag* man, I can only do so much," Hannah said, setting the bags down in the hall. "That little bundle on a bus, with bags,

194

bumps, I don't know what. More than Hannah can cope with. My strength not what it was, man, *rather* I come on my own."

"Nana, I'm sorry. I shouldn't have asked you."

"*Ne*, you still my *kleintjie*. I worry about you," she said returning Ursula's hug. "Mr Essop, he fuss over Miriam for today."

"Oh Nana, it's so good to see you," Ursula said with heartfelt relief. Hannah's familiar and friendly face was a comfort and joy and she wished she had written sooner. "You won't be able to stay then?" she continued, already less worried.

"*Ne*, I leave it all with Mrs Hendricks – she give Miriam what I leave. But if Hannah not there for long Mr Essop he fret more than any baby."

Ursula enjoyed showing the house off to Hannah – who ooh-ed and aah-ed over everything most satisfactorily – saving the nursery, with its trimmed bassinet and comfortable nursing chair, till last. With great pleasure they examined every item she had made for the baby's layette and Hannah admired the small, neat stitches of her needlework.

"I have the time, you see Nana. I don't rush it like before, and the clothes are so small I have to make the stitches tiny."

"*Ja*, good. But you look pale," said Hannah with concern. "Not good sitting sewing long times, *rather* walk, man."

"I walk to the park every day, Nana, and around the garden."

"*Is it?* You go to *kooi, slaap?*"

"I do lie down and rest," said Ursula. "But I can't sleep at night."

"You eat good?"

"Not so well as when David's here. Somehow it doesn't seem worth the bother."

"*Ag* man, I thought so," said Hannah slapping her knee. She stood up, "Come, I show you what I bring."

The watchful Lizzie had moved the bags and placed them on the kitchen table where Hannah unpacked the fresh, crisp vegetables she had brought from her yard and the carefully wrapped satin-smooth eggs from her chickens.

"There!" said Hanah proudly. "That put a little colour in those cheeks *just now.*"

"Nana, you are wonderful. I'll have eggs for tea, just like we did at home."

"And take some of these leaves. Make a pot of *tee* before you *gaan slaap*. It will help, man. You worry about something?"

"David's been away so much longer than I expected. He's in Durban now which I'd forgotten about ... I really can't remember him mentioning it ... I think I would have remembered because of Jessie ..." but she did not want alert Hannah to all her fears and continued, "and I worry about the baby of course – I mean what will happen and so on. As we've a spare bedroom the doctor suggested we employ a monthly nurse when I'm confined. I hope David agrees; it will at least reassure me a bit on that score."

"*Ja*, those first weeks difficult with no family to help. Wise man the doctor. Mrs Hendricks such a help to me. And she give me something ..." Hannah drew a small poke of paper out of her bag and unwrapped a withered stick that Ursula viewed with distaste.

"Put it in water and keep it safe. Be sure you keep the water up," Hannah emphasized, "must not let it die, man."

"What will it do?"

"It will bloom, protect you and baby," said Hannah. "It is Flower of Fatima. It belong to Mrs Hendricks' ancestors – but she only has sons. She had a good dream and give it to me."

Ursula took a glass from the cupboard, filled it with water and placed the stick in it, "Your little Miriam's perfect; so I hope it does the trick for me."

"*Ag* man, it is not *goëlery!*" Hannah, sounded shocked. "This is real *boetatjie* stuff. You have to believe, man. It will flower and your labour go well."

"Of course, thank you Nana." She knew Hannah had always believed in witchdoctors and healers and it had never done her any harm. And Ursula, thinking that she had flourished in Hannah's care, was superstitious enough now to believe in the token.

"You must put this someplace very safe," said Hannah, passing her another screwed up piece of oiled paper.

"What is it?" she asked, examining the small knob of fleshy root.

"*Ugobho*, river pumpkin. Use very little – tiniest bit – when you feel those pains get too bad. Too much is poison, man."

"Did you use it Nana?" asked Ursula, needing Hannah's reassurance that the judgement of the witchdoctor was sound.

"*Ja*, I did. Your Lizzie is right, man – the *boetatje* know these things."

The afternoon was warm enough to sit outside and, settling themselves by the pool, they hemmed bed linen for the unborn child whilst Hannah told Ursula all about Miriam.

"Miriam such a quiet child," concluded Hannah, "I am very lucky, man."

"Was I quiet Nana?" asked Ursula, wondering now about her own child.

"*Ne*. My goodness me you a handful. But I young – no experience, man. But Miriam, she never cry. Takes her milk good, *slaap* good."

"I'm glad it's worked out so well for you Nana."

"*Ja*, thank you," replied Hannah. "But Mister David, he be proud as Punch to be a *Pappa*."

"Do you really think so Nana?"

"*Ja*, you wait, see. Even more when the baby grow. How they grow – already Miriam too big for first bodice, man!"

"And does she sleep through the night, Nana?"

Hannah was happy to answer all Ursula's questions in the smallest detail and the rest of the afternoon passed very pleasantly. Ursula was sorry when Hannah had to leave; at the gate she was suddenly overcome with emotion and hugged Hannah as tight as her size would permit.

"Something else worry you?" Hannah asked, concerned.

"No Nana, not now. You were just what I needed," she replied. "Off you go, or Mr Essop will be worrying about you," and she waved from the gate until Hannah was out of sight around the corner.

Dear Nana, she thought, she always makes me feel better. I've been too much on my own. Miriam sounds wonderful – just lovely. I hope my little lump is just as good – he will be just as good. But now, she decided, with more conviction than she had shown of late, I shall have those eggs and make a pot of tea. And tonight I will sleep well, feel better, and stop worrying about silly imaginary things.

The next morning she received a postcard from David and whooped with happiness. He was on his way home.

"Are you pleased to have me home?" David asked, embracing Ursula for the second time.

"Of course I am," she said, thinking how handsome her husband was. "I've missed you dreadfully."

"Good. Now, let me look at you properly," he said standing at arms length. "By Jove, the little chap has certainly grown like Billy-O while I've been away."

"I think he's going to arrive before we have our wedding anniversary."

"We'll celebrate it early then."

"That would be lovely. I've hardly been out since you went away," said Ursula, hoping for sympathy.

"We could go to the Good Hope Bioscope or a recital at the Opera House if you'd prefer," suggested David.

"Something more lively, I think."

"The newspaper was advertising Wheeler's *The Blue Moon* – Alfred Woods and Maud Williamson are over from London to do it but I don't know if it's lively."

"It sounds grand but it's such a pity there's nothing that good on at the Tivoli so I can see everyone."

"Let me see if I can find anything out. If not we'll pop into the Tivoli then go to the Opera House."

"That will really be something to look forward to. Thank you. But come and sit down – I'm afraid I can't stand for very long now – and tell me all about your trip," said Ursula taking his hand and leading him to the sofa. "I want to hear everything you did."

"I told you in my postcards."

"But that's in short-hand – it's not the same, tell me what you found out about my brother first, then tell me what you thought of the cities"

"I'm sorry I couldn't find anything out about your brother" said David, taking her hand in his. "I followed up the address, asked around, but it's such a long time ago now, and the population there's always changing. It seems that the young men leave – the lack of marriageable women there is the reason apparently."

She sighed, "I knew it was unlikely; it was a long shot. I hope my brother's found a wife. Perhaps he has a child now; that's a nice thought."

David squeezed her hand, "You can't do anything more. And we'll have our own little lad soon, won't we?"

"Yes. Yes, I know. But come on, tell me what it was like," she said sitting up straighter, trying to forget about Jimmy.

"Let me see," David crossed his legs and leant back, "Kimberley was raw. But exhilarating too. I understand the process now, the difficulties, like the risks of flooding and rockfalls. De Beers – Rhodes' company – own most of the mines in the area. And the workers are segregated now which means it's very difficult to buy a diamond on the side. Not impossible, but very difficult."

"You've learned a great deal then?"

"A great deal."

"And what did you do in the evenings?" asked Ursula with interest, although she thought she knew.

"Duggie and I were staying in a very tatty hotel so we went out every night. There were plenty of bars so we had a bit of fun, billiards, a few card evenings – no wild gambling mind!"

He frowned and wagged his finger at her and made her laugh.

"And tell me about Johannesburg?" she said.

"Quite different – big and impressive but not as interesting – that's the business side of things. Lots of new money there; I made some good contacts. But, blimey, it's hot and dusty there already. And I saw some boxing with Duggie; a youngster Abe is interested in managing looks promising."

"Is that why Duggie went with you?"

"Yes. And to introduce me in Kimberley."

"So why didn't he go with you to Durban?"

"I wasn't due to go to Durban, Duggie was, but he changed his mind; when he was reminded he has responsibilities here."

"Oh," said Ursula, puzzled, "I don't understand."

"It was a personal thing – too complicated to explain. I said I would sort it out and deal with the business side of things for him there and follow up some leads of my own at the same time. And it gave me the perfect excuse to look up some of the boxing contacts I made on my last tour; offer myself for some refereeing."

"Did you see Jessie there?"

"Ah! I forgot to say. She's back – she was on the train – says she's going to call on you soon, tell you all her news."

"She didn't write and say she was coming back," said Ursula doubtfully.

"Well, you know Jessie – unreliable and unpredictable; I

thought she'd stay there. She was probably too busy having a final fling to have time to write. But don't talk about her," he said dismissively, firmly. "Come and show me the garden and the pond."

He stood up and pulled Ursula gently to her feet. Raising her hands to his lips he kissed them, "You know, I've missed doing things with my wife. Very much."

David was delighted with the burgeoning garden and diplomatically admired the changes that Ursula had made to the layette in his absence. Ursula basked in this approval. She was very relieved that he was back at home, and so obviously pleased to be so. Since Hannah's visit she had forced herself to focus upon her coming confinement and only consider facts not fancies. And her strategy seemed to be successful – she was calmer, happier. But to guard against her fancies taking flight again Ursula would not allow herself to question David too deeply about anything – in her advanced state she knew it was best to maintain her present equilibrium. Her anxiety about the coming birth diminished too when David readily agreed to a monthly nurse, who would be installed a week before the child was due.

Ursula had received regular animated, if short, letters from Jessie whilst she was in Durban imparting details of her latest conquests and achievements. Jessie now sent a note to say she would call and Ursula looked forward to catching up on her latest news, and the reason for her sudden return.

"Good gracious, Ursula," Jessie exclaimed when Ursula opened the door to her, "how you've grown."

"Thank you Jessie, I'd forgotten how direct you are," she said, momentarily deflated by the remark about her bulging figure. "Do come in."

"Sorry, I just wasn't expecting you to look so large," she said giving Ursula a kiss on the cheek. "I say this house is nice. And an upstairs!"

Ursula's sense of humour returned, "We're going up in the world," she said.

Jessie rolled her eyes to the ceiling and then gave Ursula a withering look.

"Very funny. I assumed you only had the ground floor, clever," she said craning her neck around the stairs and peering up at the landing. "How many bedrooms?"

"Three," replied Ursula proudly, "well, two and a box room actually. But come into the front room, there's a pot of tea ready. Oh, excuse me, I forgot to tell Lizzie I'd need another cup," and she called out towards the kitchen.

"I wondered that you hadn't a servant. Why didn't she answer the door?"

"She likes nothing better than to put on her white cap and apron if someone calls in the afternoon – but if I'm expecting a friend I prefer to answer the door myself; old habits die hard. But I couldn't manage without Lizzie; a servant full-time makes all the difference when you have a bigger house and a bump to carry around. Anyway, tell me about you," said Ursula, who knew Jessie was always happier talking about herself, "what are you going to do now?"

"Well, Violet says she'd be very pleased to give up the evening work; says she could earn as much tutoring some of her pupils after school – of course she doesn't get such good tips as I used to. So I can have my old job back if I want to. On the other hand, if she kept that evening job I could get a day job, and I'd be free in the evenings, she wouldn't. I could go out and about with my favourite old beau. And then again Abe's offered me bar work here, so I'll see."

"Did you enjoy the bar work in Durban?"

"Once I'd got the hang of it. The place is so busy – good houses every night – had to learn how to add up in my head really fast. And I was swamped with offers; could have had the pick of anyone I fancied there – men down from Johannesburg, up from Natal; still lots of soldiers about – had five Valentine cards and I'd only been there a few weeks!"

"Tell me about the shops," prompted Ursula, "David says I would love them."

"*Ag* man, excellent. Fanny – the girl I was in digs with – and I, we often spent our whole day off trying on the hats and frocks. Couldn't afford to buy anything much but we had such a hoot! Much more fashionable than here, the shops. At first I felt a bit *skaam* in some of the outfits I wore here, till I made them more up-to-date. One of the shops is all L'Art Nouveau, and so many Japanese things – all the rage – furnishings and kimonos and such."

"I've seen them in the magazines," said Ursula enthusiastically. "I could easily copy a kimono for myself."

"I'm not sure one would be quite the thing with a bump sticking out," replied Jessie with a questioning look at Ursula's girth. "The Japanese are very slight."

Ursula looked down at her large waist.

"No, perhaps not," she admitted. "I do miss wearing fitted things; I adore that little jacket you're wearing."

"Got it in a Bargain Sale. And Fanny flogged me this skirt because it goes so well with it; shows off my small waist. She's tiny you see, same size as me."

"So why did you come back, Jessie? It sounds so much more interesting than here, you were obviously having a good time," she said, just managing to keep a resentful tone from her voice.

"*Ag* man, too bloomin' hot already," said Jessie blowing out her cheeks, insensitive as usual to Ursula's feelings, "couldn't stand the thought of a whole summer of it. Didn't think I'd last when I first got there, so hot and sticky – but Abe had insisted I do a three-month stint and by that time it was getting cooler."

"And is that the only reason?" Ursula asked, wondering if Jessie had come to be near anyone.

"No, the place is crawling with *koelies* – squatting all over the place, pestering you to buy this and that, don't know why they don't stay in India; haven't got the energy in all that heat to brush them off – makes you appreciate this old place. Anyway, old sweethearts never visited as often as they promised to and I thought, *ag* well, perhaps I'll surprise them here. And it might just be nice to be back amongst family and old friends."

"I'll remind you that you missed this little place in a few months' time," replied Ursula wryly.

"Hmm," was Jessie's only retort.

"Another cup of tea, Jess?"

"Thank you, I've had enough. I'm dying for a cigarette though."

"Do you mind Jessie," pleaded Ursula, "at the moment I just can't bear the smell indoors."

Jessie sighed loudly.

"You could have one in the garden. Come and see it anyway, it's lovely." With her swaying gait Ursula led the way into the dining room.

"Very cosy," said Jessie walking past the table, which was pushed against the wall, and peering through the French doors. "Couldn't I just pull in this chair a bit closer to the doors and open them; we wouldn't get chilly then and I could blow the smoke outside."

"You could give it a try I suppose," said Ursula unenthusiastically, opening one of the doors. She did not want Jessie to sulk.

Jessie pulled the armchair closer to the open door and sat down. "Ursula, explain, why have you got a dead twig in that glass?" she said pointing to the glass on the mantelshelf.

"It's not a twig, it's a Flower of Fatima, if it blooms everything will go well at the birth but if it . . ." Ursula examined it closely. "Oh my goodness it is; it's dead Jessie!"

"Don't look so shocked, it's a daft idea. Anyway, probably not the real thing. I've never been keen on plants or gardens; don't know why people go on about them so much. I'd much rather have some nice silk blooms that don't need watering."

"You've always lived in the middle of town, I expect that's why," said Ursula trying not to dwell on the dead twig – and what terrible thing might happen – as she lowered herself into the remaining chair. "I love it here; the garden's very restful," she continued.

"Not as restful as staying indoors warm and cosy on a winter day or keeping out of the sun in the summer," said Jessie, taking a tin of cigarettes from her large bag.

"Those are different Jess," remarked Ursula, impressed with her cigarettes, "the box is really lovely."

The tin box was painted green, the edges decorated with classical columns between which a curvaceous woman, dressed in golden yellow, stood draped with sinuous snakes.

"*Ja,* this chap from London who works for Salmon and Gluckstein was rather stuck on me; he said the woman on the front reminded him of me," Jessie admired the figure as she lit her cigarette. "Said he could get me all the Snake Charmer cigarettes I wanted if I went out with him."

"He sounds a rather slithery charmer himself," said Ursula doubtfully.

"No, he really meant it; she is lovely don't you think?" replied Jessie, holding the tin up for Ursula to see the picture. "And they're jolly expensive; so I went for a drink or two with him. The cigarettes are Turkish – smell lovely but they taste too strong and so I didn't go out with him again. Put my own cigarettes in the tin now, stops them getting squashed; looks smart doesn't it?"

"Very. But tell me more about the acts at the theatre – I've been starved of entertainment."

Jessie launched into a lively exposé of theatre life in Durban; the more Ursula laughed at Jessie's stories, the more outrageous they became. When it was time for Jessie to catch her bus, Ursula showed her to the door and made her promise to call the following week.

"I've missed your tales, Jessie," she said. "I haven't laughed so much for months."

Full of gossip and innuendo, supposition and slapstick, Ursula appreciated that it was Jessie's rendition of the improbable stories as much as the subject matter that made them amusing.

"Well I'm back now," replied Jessie. "Soon perk you up and blow away all that mumbo jumbo stuff about dead twigs and . . ."

"Jessie, don't say it!" interrupted Ursula quickly. "I know it's nonsense, but . . . anyway, the nurse arrives next week and no doubt she'll tell me what rot it all is. Then the baby is due the week after and I suspect I'll have very little peace after that."

"*Ag* man, don't I know it. Screaming brats – I never slept right through a night for most of my childhood. The church bells are the only thing that wake me these days."

"Thank God for that Jessie," said Ursula with a mock reverential expression on her face.

Jessie looked at her sternly. "And I shall review the state of *your* humour in a few months' time," she said drily as she gave Ursula a quick peck on the cheek, and started up the path. "I better make it snappy, the mountain was covered in its tablecloth when I came and this wind will bring the rain," she said as she turned and shut the gate. "I think we're in for a bad patch of weather."

Ursula felt very tired after Jessie had left, with a dread she did not want to put into words. She wrapped a strip of muslin around the dead twig – and hid it in her sewing box next to the piece of *Ugobho* – so that she did not have to look at it.

*

The following week the nurse, Mrs Middleton, arrived. She was a plump, kindly widow and Ursula liked her immediately. Together they rearranged the nursery, where a bed for Mrs Middleton was assembled. Mrs Middleton checked the layette – complimenting Ursula on her handiwork – said she would oversee the laundry and made Ursula rest for two hours in the afternoon. She was such a practical and motherly figure that Ursula thought it best not to mention the dead Flower of Fatima to her, and her fears for the birth. She knew she would be told it was all nonsense.

A few days later David came home with the news that a famous Music Hall entertainer, Marie Lloyd, had arrived unexpectedly at the Tivoli and was causing a stir.

"Oh, that's such bad luck," wailed Ursula. "She's come to the Cape from London; she must have extended her Johannesburg tour. She's so famous – I would have so loved to see her."

"We could go tomorrow – Abe will let me have a couple of the seats he reserves."

"But I can't in this condition," she said, looking down at her ballooning midriff.

"Rubbish, of course you can," said David confidently. "It can do no harm can it, Mrs Middleton?" he asked a little less surely.

"As long as she ain't pushed and jostled about none," replied the practical woman.

"It would probably be a box," said David.

"Oh David – could we?"

"And you'd go by cab I suppose?" enquired Mrs Middleton. David nodded, "Of course, very slowly."

"Then I can't think of nothing more cheering," she beamed at Ursula, her double chins compressed like a feather cushion, her arms crossed on her ample bosom. "I worked and whistled till the day all mine was born and didn't do them or me not a bit of harm."

Between them, David and Mrs Middleton dismissed Ursula's

worries that she did not look respectable and, reassured, she set about disguising her appearance with the help of the nurse. A dark, capacious jacket belonging to Mrs Middleton was trimmed and, falling smock-like over a correspondingly full skirt, merely made Ursula look like a very large matron. She stuck a long, arching ostrich feather that Hannah had bought her in the Wool and Feather Market into her hat and hoped that eyes would be drawn towards that. Ursula was excited, she had not been to the theatre for months and this particular performer was a favourite of the Music Hall. When she was ready she came down for inspection; David was waiting in the front room reading the newspaper.

"What do you think, will I pass muster?" she asked shaking her head so that the feather quivered.

David got up and walked around her slowly, "You look very respectable Funny Face."

"I think that's a compliment – thank you," said Ursula raising her eyebrows.

"There's just one thing . . ."

"Oh?"

"It's very black, a bit dull, needs a little jewellery," he said screwing up his face.

"Look," she said parting her collar, "you didn't see my amethyst brooch."

"Not sparkling enough; it needs something that catches the light a bit."

"I haven't got anything sparkling, as you put it," she said frowning. She hoped he wasn't going to put a damper on her mood.

From his waistcoat pocket David took a small velvet pouch. Ursula was intrigued. Opening it he produced a narrow gold band set with a single diamond and held it out to her, "This might do the trick." She was speechless. "Do you like it?" he asked when she said nothing.

"David, it's beautiful. It's just beautiful."

"I couldn't afford one before my trip but I pulled something off; I thought it was time my wife had her just desserts."

"Oh David," said Ursula, wiping away a tear.

"It's meant to make you happy, not sad," he laughed.

"I am happy. It's just such a surprise, such a nice surprise."

David took her hand and tried it on her third finger; it was too small. He looked crestfallen.

"David, put it on my pinkie; my hands are swollen now but after the baby it'll fit. I must wear it tonight."

She held her hand up to admire it, "It is the most lovely present, thank you," she said. She put her arms around David's neck and kissed him, "What a kind husband I have."

David beamed with pride, "Good, now you're properly attired we can go to the theatre."

Ursula was enthralled by the show – the costumes, the songs, the repartee were superior to any she had seen before. A variety performer from Durban opened the show with songs made famous by Eugene Stratton – a contemporary of Miss Lloyd's. Dressed in a white frock coat and top hat he rendered 'Lily of Laguna' and 'Little Dolly Daydream' in the style of a true minstrel singer. Ursula's excitement dulled the pain she felt in her back – the seats were not wide and the arms constrained her. Unconsciously she took David's hand and squeezed it.

"Are you enjoying it?" he asked.

"Oh yes, I am," she answered.

In the interval Ursula said she would walk around and visit the powder room. Once there she was surprised that the jabbing pain in her back seemed to be worse.

"You look a little drawn," David said with concern, when she returned to the box. "Are you feeling unwell?"

"My back's aching that's all," she replied, "the seats are not as wide as those at home. But I can cope – don't want to forego Miss Marie Lloyd!"

Miss Lloyd opened after the interval to rapturous applause – the 'gods' and the stalls were equally enthusiastic. By the time she had finished her first two songs the audience was mesmerized. She left the stage and, within minutes, reappeared dressed in a frock of pale green and a large hat topped by pink and white roses. She sang two further songs with great verve – they verged on the saucy – and they received appreciative whistles and shouts of "Bravo, Our Marie."

For the finale Miss Lloyd changed her costume once more and her toilette this time was the most gorgeous: a gown and train of pale grey georgette was heavily embroidered with pearls and crystals and, in addition to her ropes of pearls, she wore a necklet of diamonds and a tiara of pearl droplets. Ursula committed to memory every detail of her dress. She now sang 'Oh Mr Porter' – for which she was justly famous – with charming naïvety, and 'The Boy I Love Sits Up in the Gallery'. This finale, rendered with great éclat, brought the house down; the audience was in raptures, and stood clapping and cheering. They were so exuberant that Ursula was very grateful to be in the safety of a box. She had been thrilled by the show and enraptured by Miss Lloyd's dresses but by the time the encores were over, and the curtain lowered for the final time, her state of elation had waned; the stabbing pains in her back were intense. Travelling back in the cab Ursula grasped David's arm more tightly at each bend or bump in the road.

"You're not in too much discomfort are you?" David asked.

"No, it's my back; the pain keeps jabbing away."

"We'll be home soon – Mrs Middleton offered to prepare a little supper for us – so you can lie down and rest until then. You did enjoy the show didn't you?"

"It was wonderful David; no wonder she's called 'The Queen of the Music Hall'. And so kind of Abe to let us have a box."

Mrs Middleton came as soon as she heard the door close.

"Hello Mrs Middleton", said David, "here we are, all in one piece."

"Except for my backache," said Ursula with a grimace.

"Backache? What sort of backache?" demanded Mrs Middleton.

Ursula explained and Mrs Middleton became brisk, "Oh deary me, that's no backache my girl – it's not the normal turn of events – we better be prepared for . . ."

David sprang to attention, "Shall I get the doctor?"

"No need for that just yet, but the midwife better be called. Off you go," said Mrs Middleton pointing to the door, "and when you get back put that copper on pretty damn sharp."

David kissed Ursula who was standing looking nonplussed.

"I shall be quick as a flash," he said.

"You do that," said Mrs Middleton firmly, adding softly to Ursula, "and you come with me my pet, up those stairs, carefully now, we don't want any accidents."

Thirteen

From quiet homes and first beginning,
Out to the undiscovered ends,
There's nothing worth the wear of winning,
But laughter and the love of friends.

Dedicatory Ode
Hilaire Belloc 1870–1953

It was dawn and the baby's cry was wonderful to Ursula. Within moments there was urgent knocking on the door, "Mrs Middleton, Mrs Middleton, is my wife all right?"

Mrs Middleton went to the door still holding the baby wrapped in a flannel blanket.

"She's tickety-boo Mr Lewis. You just let me and the midwife clean up a bit round here and then we'll be calling you."

Ursula could hear David going downstairs. It seemed only moments later – she realized that she must have dozed off – that David was standing next to the bed. He looked at her with concern and took her hand in his, "How are you Ursula?"

"I'm perfectly well," she smiled reassuringly. "Oh David, have you seen the baby yet?"

"No, I wanted to see you were well first; I've been so worried. You are quite well aren't you?"

"I'm only tired; very tired. But very happy."

"I see you had your talismans," said David touching the medal and cross that hung around her neck, now joined by the diamond ring.

"Yes," she replied, feeling the pendants herself, "and I put my ring on it too, I didn't want to lose it or hurt the baby. Mrs Middleton, do you think you can bring baby to David?"

Mrs Middleton left the room and returned with a little bundle of crocheted shawl and carefully laid it in David's arms; only a tiny, very pink, screwed-up face showed.

"There we are Mr Lewis, say good-day to your daughter."

David stared silently down at the miniature person asleep in his arms.

"So," asked Ursula after a minute, "what do you think of her?"

David looked up with incredulity, "Oh, Funny Face . . . she's the most beautiful child in the world. Our own Little Dolly Daydream."

"Lulu, Lulu, where are you? Come on out."

The small figure wriggled out on her hands and knees from under the overhanging branches of a flowering plumbago bush.

"Get up off the floor, your clothes will be full of mud," instructed Ursula and Lulu stood up with a scowl. "You must not hide from Mommy – I know it makes a lovely house but just look at your pinafore, all crumpled and dusty, and Nana and Miriam are coming to tea."

"Nice Nana?" asked Lulu.

"Yes, nice Nana. And you can play with Miriam. Now, would you like to carry some of these lovely flowers I've picked?"

Lulu's brow cleared and she nodded her head; Ursula placed a few blooms into the dimpled outstretched hands.

"Carefully, that's it, now we'll go in and find a vase for them and then we'll brush those curls and tie them up with ribbons again and make you look pretty for our visitors."

"Pretty Lulu."

Hannah had taken to visiting Ursula after she had been to the

213

Wool, Feather and Produce Market near Grand Parade and occasionally, if she did not intend to buy much, she brought Miriam with her. When she arrived Hannah gave Ursula a hug with her free arm, her other hand holding Miriam's hand. Bending forward Hannah spoke to the little girl standing next to Ursula, "Hello Louisa, you say hello to *Ouma*?"

The child stood quite still, mute. Ursula explained, "She won't answer to Louisa now Nana, if you don't call her Lulu she won't even look at you."

"*Is it?* Hello Lulu," said Hannah again.

"Nice Nana," responded Lulu giving Hannah a smile.

"And you say hello to Miriam, Lulu," prompted Ursula.

Miriam hid behind her mother with her face concealed in her skirt and Lulu, walking around the back of Hannah, pulled at Miriam's pinafore.

"Nicely, Lulu," warned her mother.

But neither child spoke.

"*Ag* well, leave them, man. They will be friends *just now*,"

"I suppose so, Nana," said Ursula taking her coat. "I thought we'd sit in here," she said leading the way to the back dining room, "it's cosier than the drawing room and the girls can sit at the table for their tea."

Ursula and Hannah settled themselves in the comfortable armchairs but Miriam continued to hold onto her mother's skirt. Lulu fetched a small wicker basket from behind her mother's chair and taking out some wooden animals made a line of them on the floor. After a while Miriam knelt down near her mother's feet and placed a small rag doll she was holding on the floor in front of Lulu; Lulu picked it up and examined it and Miriam timidly stroked one of the animals. Soon their two heads – one with neat black pigtails, one with unruly blond curls – were close together arranging and rearranging the animals on the leaves and flowers that decorated the rug.

"Tell me your news, Nana," said Ursula.

"*Ne, rather* I do my knitting," said Hannah, as she pulled a pair of knitting needles and a half finished waistcoat from her large cloth bag, "you tell me what been happening to you, man."

"Let me see ... you know David went with Abe to Bloemfontein in March?"

"*Is it?*"

"Oh, yes, they were supporting the African franchise up there. When the four colonies are united, it's planned that the Union *Volksraad* will be an all-white institution," said Ursula, adding for Hannah's benefit, "there's to be no vote for Africans in Natal, or Orange River Colony or Transvaal you know."

"*Ne,* Mr Essop votes, man," said Hannah.

"That's here in the Cape, Nana. The franchise is due to remain here, but Abe and his friends – a white lawyer and a black journalist among others – are worried that after Union the Africans and people like Mr Essop will inevitably, eventually, lose their right to vote here too."

"Mr Essop be very angry."

"A group of Abe's friends and an African delegation went to England and lobbied the British Government; they argued – let me see if I can remember the phrase – yes, 'that all South Africans should have full and equal rights, and that the colour bar would constitute an injustice'. We're hoping it will be successful but David says it's going to be an uphill battle trying to convince the powers that be."

"*Is it?* And Mister David, he go to Bloemfontein?"

"No, they can do no more at the moment. But Abe will need someone trustworthy and sympathetic to be a messenger again soon enough," said Ursula. "And I'm ashamed to admit that I don't like David going away."

"*Ag* well, we hope Mister David not go. We hope Mr Essop keep his vote," said Hannah in a resigned voice. "What about you, man, you been anywhere?"

"Yes, we had a day out last Sunday with Duggie and Violet;

they've been married two years now you know. We caught the train to Wynberg Station – we could have gone by bus but we thought Lulu would like the train – and then took a horse and carriage up to King Edward Park. I don't think it was quite Duggie's cup of tea, he hardly spoke to Violet. David and I mean to go back in the height of the summer because the Military Band give performances in the warm evenings then."

"*Is it?*" replied Hannah, smiling encouragingly.

"David takes us out nearly every Sunday, Nana," said Ursula with pleasure. "I think it's because Lulu is at such an interesting age – he's fascinated by her even when she's naughty and she thinks he's wonderful. He never reprimands her of course – he's too indulgent – and she plays to the gallery like a little prima ballerina."

"*Ag shame!* Mister David not see her so much, *is it?*"

"He spends plenty of time with her when he is here, Nana. But I love the outings too – the three of us together; our own little family. Being at home all day with Lulu can be very solitary."

"*Is it?* You join some ladies' circle, *ja?*" asked Hannah, counting the stitches under her breath.

"I have, and it's given me an outside interest. I've something to talk to David about apart from Lulu. And my bridge playing has come on leaps and bounds too; now I've cracked the bidding. It really keeps my mind busy."

"*Ja,* good. Mrs Mason – the lady I do mending for – she play bridge every afternoon. She have her ladies round, they play for a while. Then have a pot of *tee,* play a bit more."

"I do the same sort of thing with the ladies in our club off Burg Street," explained Ursula, "I hate to miss a session. And I'm organizing a charity Bridge Drive for the Soldiers Aid Society; they need every bit of help we can give. Like David says, it's not the soldiers who made the decisions about where and when and whom they fought; we agree they don't deserve to suffer more than they do. It was David's idea that I offer to organize it – he thinks it will give me something other than him to worry about if he's away."

"*Is it?* That is good."

"And, Nana, I've been nominated to make up the four to represent our club – it's quite an honour," said Ursula with pride.

"*Ja,* you always have a head on you, man," said Hannah casting off her knitting. "Who mind Louisa when you play bridge?"

"Mrs Middleton does, and she always takes care of her if we go to a dance or the theatre. Emma's looked after Lulu on the odd afternoon but generally David is opposed to anyone but Mrs Middleton. Lulu's very good for her, even though she's very inquisitive and gets up to all sorts of mischief with me. Does Mr Essop cope better now if you leave Miriam with him?"

"*Ag* well, I ask Mrs Hendricks if I go to the market, do my jobs. Mr Essop health not so good," said Hannah pulling a new skein of wool from her bag. "He never make *Hadji* now; his legs got no strength to get there."

"Does Miriam tire him?"

"*Ne.* Miriam not a busy child, but she talk non-stop to him. Chatter, chatter, chatter. Mr Essop, he listen, smile, answer all her question."

"Lulu doesn't chatter like that – pass it here Nana and I'll hold it for you to wind – she doesn't choose to speak much at all but, my goodness, she has a mind of her own," said Ursula, stretching the skein between both her hands to keep the wool taut. "She's a determined little character and if she wants to do something I have the devil's own job trying to talk her out of it."

"*Is it?*" replied Hannah, taking one end of the wool and starting to make it into a ball. "Some rule with a rod of iron, man."

"I know, but you never did with me Nana and I don't want to be a tyrant; she's not really being disobedient. She lives in her own little make-believe world – cooks imaginary meals, dresses-up, that sort of thing – and wants her own way, that's all. And she's fairly adventurous too."

"*Is it* – I wonder who she get all that from?" said Hannah smiling. Ursula laughed, "I suppose David and I can hardly expect a paragon of a child."

"*Ja;* I am very lucky, man," said Hannah, as she continued rolling the wool into a ball. "My little Miriam, she just play shop-shop in the corner, look at her picture books. Never stray from Mr Essop side, mine; do what she told. She is no trouble, no trouble at all, man."

This was borne out by the children's present behaviour: Miriam, singing quietly to herself, continued arranging animals in neat rows on the rug but Lulu had disappeared under the table. Hearing grunting noises, Ursula bent down and saw that she had pulled the clothes off the rag doll and was pushing the legs of the doll into the mechanism that extended the top.

"Lulu, Lulu, don't do that – that doll is Miriam's. Oh dear," she said getting up from her chair and passing the last few strands of unwound wool to Hannah, "can you manage that last bit of wool now Nana? You see what I mean, don't you? I think perhaps it's time for tea."

She left the room and returned with Lizzie, a tray apiece.

"Here we are," said Ursula placing the tray on the table. "Miriam, Lulu, please come and sit at the table; no Lulu leave that cushion on the chair for Miriam. You can leave the teapot, Lizzie. There's milk for the girls and, Nana, this is a seed cake I made this morning and some *soet koekies* for the girls."

"*Ag shame.*"

Ursula served the children and Hannah and sat down herself.

"This is *lekker,*" said Hannah appreciatively, after taking a bite of her cake.

"I'm glad you like it. After tea I thought we'd go out in the garden; there's plenty of room out there for the girls to play. I like to tire Lulu out before bedtime."

Lulu nodded, her mouth full of biscuit.

When David arrived home after work he called to Lulu as soon as he was through the door, "Where's my little Dolly? Lulu, Lulu."

Ursula came into the hallway and Lulu's small figure pushed past her skirt and ran along the passage, her arms open wide.

"*Pappa, Pappa*," she cried.

David scooped her up; Lulu put her small arms around his neck and pressed her cheek to his. David leant towards Ursula, the child still in his arms, and gave her a kiss on the cheek, "And how's my other girl?"

"Tired; Nana came today and brought Miriam. She's such a quiet little girl that I had to watch that our little treasure here didn't terrorize her."

"Lulu, were you a naughty girl to Miriam?" asked David.

Lulu shook her head, and tightened her arms around his neck.

"We took her animals outside for them to play with and, unknown to me, Lulu took Miriam's doll."

"Lulu," said David, with mock severity.

"When it was time for Nana and Miriam to leave, her doll was nowhere to be found. Fortunately we did find it; it was under the *saliehout* bush. I thought she was hiding in there but she was playing with the doll; it was covered up to its neck in leaves."

"Dolly bed," explained Lulu with a serious expression.

"Maybe, but it was Miriam's dolly not yours. You must ask before you borrow someone's toys. Anyway, now it's this little Dolly's bedtime; give your father a kiss and we'll go up."

A few weeks after Hannah's visit David came home in high spirits, "Listen Funny Face, how would you like to go to the races?"

"I'd love to. When?"

"Duggie wants me to go to the races with him next Saturday and I suggested making an outing of it with you girls; you've never been able to make it before and I'd love to show you the ropes. I wouldn't say he was enthused with the idea but I told him you'd be disappointed if you weren't invited."

"I think it's a wonderful idea – will we be gone all day?"

"Pretty well."

"I'll ask Mrs Middleton to look after Lulu. Is it a smart occasion?"

"No more than anything else – I shall wear my tweeds."

"Then I shall wear my wedding outfit. I'll go up now and get it out to air."

"Just a minute, I didn't suggest taking my wife to the races so that I could starve; let's get our priorities right – dinner first, dress later."

"Spoil sport!"

David bought Ursula and Violet small posies to pin on their lapels as their little party waited for one of the summer cars that ran regularly from the top of Adderley Street out to the racecourse at Green Point. The sky was azure, and with not a cloud in sight they could see the vast flat mountain top clearly. The bus arrived and they all climbed aboard looking forward to a lovely day; nearly everyone was headed for the races and there was a party atmosphere. Directly they reached the course David steered them towards the wooden grandstand from where he said Ursula and Violet could watch; he and Duggie would advise them which horses to back.

"What do you think of Maiden Voyage?" David conferred with Duggie. "Didn't do too well in the July Merchants."

"Terrible heavy going was a factor against her, but she's a canny mare," said Duggie thoughtfully.

"Let's go to the paddock and see," said David decisively. "Do you want to come girls?"

"Thank you, I think we'll stay here; better than getting tramped over don't you think Violet?" said Ursula looking at Violet for approval.

"Certainly."

"We're going to cast an eye before we commit ourselves then," said David. "Shall I explain the form to you so you can place a bet?"

"I think I'll just back what I fancy without any of your form," said Ursula, "it's incomprehensible to me anyway."

"But you need some sort of system if you're to place a bet," David said, leaning towards her to make his point.

"I'll choose the horses by the colour of their silks," she declared, confidently.

"There's a braw one carrying the black and white cap," said Duggie appreciatively.

"I'll stick with that then," said Ursula. "How about you Violet?"

"Och, I don't think I will, I shall simply be a spectator. Duggie will bet for me too, no doubt." replied Violet in a resigned voice.

David and Duggie did not return to the stand but Ursula caught sight of them down by the track.

"Look, Violet, there they are," she said, pointing them out as discreetly as she could, "they obviously want to be there in the thick of it."

"And as I imagine the language may get a little heated – Duggie can get very het up – it's possibly best if we are not too near."

"They're only just in time for the race; the jockeys are at the post." As the girls spoke starting orders were given. "They're off Violet. I don't suppose mine will be any good."

"I really cannot make out which horse is which."

"I think I can see the black and white. Yes," said Ursula, "just on the outside about three back. At least he's not last yet."

"Yes, I can see him now; he seems to be gaining," said Violet without a hint of anticipation.

"He is, isn't he; actually he seems to be coming up quite fast . . . my goodness he's racing ahead, look at him go."

"The jockey is whipping him on mercilessly."

"He's way ahead now; way, way out in front there. Oh my goodness gracious, I think he might win, Violet – I think he's going to win – Violet, he's won, he's won," cried Ursula, jumping up and down on the spot. "My horse has won!"

"Congratulations Ursula, that is very satisfactory," said Violet with a restrained smile.

"Satisfactory? It's sensational!" rejoined Ursula, waving furiously at David's returning figure.

"Perhaps not sensational," noted Violet, in her cool voice, "but you may find it thrilling."

"David, David, I won. I won," said Ursula as soon as David appeared.

"I know, well done," he said grinning widely.

"Beginner's luck I expect."

"It's a good start. Would you like to come to the paddock and see your winner."

"Oh yes. Shall we Violet?"

"As you wish."

"David, where's Duggie?" asked Ursula, not wanting Violet to feel left out.

"Probably already choosing his next animal."

"Perhaps we'll see him there then," said Ursula, looking at Violet reassuringly.

They pushed their way towards the paddock where horses were circling the parade ring, led by their operators. David leant against the rails and explained the proceedings to them.

"But when do I see my winner?" interrupted Ursula, who did not appreciate the details or the finer points of horse racing.

"In about five minutes. Do you want to stake your bit on one of these for the next race?"

"I think I'll stick to choosing by the colour of their silks. That blue and yellow looks jolly."

"Blue and yellow it is then. And what about you Violet?"

"Och, I think one gambler in the family is more than enough."

"Do you mind if I leave you here whilst I go and find Duggie?"

"Please do."

"Go ahead," said Ursula. "Oh, Violet, look over here, it's my winner coming." There was an announcement as a man with rolled-up shirtsleeves and jodhpurs led the horse in. "This is the first time I've been to the horse races, but I think winning is capital and I don't intend for it to be the only time."

"There is something seductive about winning, that's true. But losing can sober one very fast," said Violet grimly.

"We'll have to find our own way back to the grandstand now or we'll miss the next race. And then we'll soon see how likely it is that I'll be back."

The horse Ursula had chosen came in last and she decided not to bet on any of the forthcoming races. When they all met at the grandstand after the final race David reported that he had been successful three times out of five; he had won on the biggest race, the July Handicap, at long odds and was very cheerful. But Duggie was morose.

"Cigarette, Duggie?" David asked offering his packet.

"I hae mae aen," Duggie replied gruffly and, producing a tin from his pocket, he took a cigarette out, tapped it on the tin lid and lit it.

Ursula was fascinated; the green painted tin was decorated with classical columns and a golden-clad woman draped in sinuous snakes.

"That's a very unusual tin, Duggie," she said. "but I think I've seen one like it before."

"Aye, I hae a fair scunner agin squashed cigarettes; this keeps them fine," he said shortly, immediately replacing it in his pocket.

"Shall we be off then?" asked David.

Everyone agreed and David drew Ursula's arm through his as they turned to walk back towards the bus. Leaning close to her ear he said, "Best not to try and engage Duggie in any conversation; he's like a bear with a sore head if he's had a bad day at the track. He did very badly in the Handicap, wagered all he had. I think he generally prefers to do his losing in private. He certainly keeps Violet in the dark about his activities – she doesn't know what he's up to half the time."

Ursula looked at Duggie walking with his head down and his hands in his pockets. Violet walked beside him, looking straight ahead; they did not touch. Violet said losing can be very sobering, remembered Ursula, I wonder if Duggie is often this disgruntled. She decided that perhaps Violet was right to be unenthusiastic about racing and, from what David said, she was no doubt very long-suffering. Only Ursula and David talked on the bus back to Adderley Street. And throughout the evening Ursula kept wondering where she had seen Duggie's cigarette tin before; it was so unusual.

Fourteen

With spots quadrangular of di'mond form,
Ensanguin'd hearts, clubs typical of strife,
And spades, the emblem of untimely graves.

The Winter Evening
William Cowper 1731–1800

Both Emma and Jessie had stood as godmothers to Lulu and the day after her third birthday they arranged to come together and have tea with Ursula and Lulu. Lulu saw Emma regularly and seemed to accept that she and Ursula would talk together. Emma spoke quietly, including Lulu in her conversation when she was near. On these occasions Lulu usually sought Lizzie out soon after Emma arrived, and played happily in the kitchen whilst Lizzie got on with her work. Jessie, however, called infrequently and when she did her garrulous ways and frequent gesticulations over-excited the little girl. Jessie – inured to small children – rarely took any notice of Lulu and as a result, when Jessie came alone, Lulu was wont to behave abominably. Ursula wondered how Lulu would be with both godmothers present.

"Hello Lulu," said Emma leaning down and smiling at her.

"Hello Lulu," the child replied.

"Say 'Hello Emma', Lulu," tutored Ursula.

"Hello Memma," managed Lulu.

"Well done, what a clever girl," said Emma smiling.

"She's never called me anything, and I don't suppose she'll

ever manage Jessica," said Jessie, shaking her head. "Still, none of my little brats ever did; they only ever called me 'Siss'."

"Siss," repeated Lulu, clearly.

Ursula and Emma laughed aloud.

"There you are – what did I tell you?" said Jessie, unimpressed. "I suppose a respectful *Tannie* is out of the question. I'll probably be Siss forever now."

Lulu responded by smiling beatifically at Jessie.

"Siss," she said again, looking around for approval.

Jessie looked at her coolly and this time Ursula and Emma managed to stifle their laughter.

"Come, Lulu," said Ursula, taking her hand, "let's take Emma and Jess into the back room and you can show them what Nana gave you yesterday."

Lulu pulled her hand away and ran ahead of them.

"I've laid the tea things in here rather than in the front room; Lulu has a place for her favourite toys here and we can keep an eye on her if she goes out to play on the grass," explained Ursula.

They sat down and Lulu brought a gaily dressed rag doll with looped wool hair for Emma to inspect.

"Why, that's lovely," said Emma, taking the doll, "she has curls just like you. And does her pinafore come off?"

Lulu took the doll from Emma's hands and immediately pulled at the pinafore until it came off. Beneath it was a knitted bodice and pantaloons; she began to pull these off too.

"No Lulu, leave those," urged Ursula.

"Bath dolly."

"No Lulu, Mommy told you, you cannot bath a cotton doll."

"My little sisters used to bath theirs but I must say they made a terrible mess," said Jessie.

Lulu stamped her foot, "Bath dolly," she said louder, still pulling at the bodice.

"Lulu, Lulu – where's the present *Pappa* gave you?" said Ursula, redirecting Lulu's interest.

Lulu immediately dropped the doll that fell limply to the floor and plunged her hand into her large pinafore pocket; she drew it out, tightly clasping something small.

"If a man gives a child a present, ten to one it's a coin," said Jessie. "Is it a *tickey* Lulu?"

Lulu glared at her and, extending her arm towards Emma, she opened her fist.

"Oh, how charming," said Emma, gently lifting the small object, "a little lead rabbit, with a blue jacket on." She stood the small upright figure on the flat of her palm for Jessie to see.

"That's the only rabbit I've ever seen that can stand up straight," said Jessie.

"*Mister* Rabbit," corrected Lulu with perfect enunciation, holding out her hand for the toy.

"And I made her a little blue jacket the same as Mister Rabbit's," said Ursula, "with an especially deep pocket to keep him in."

Lulu smiled at her mother, wrinkling her nose and lifting her shoulders to her ears.

"Well, at least she can give that one a bath," said Jessica, "as long as it doesn't go down the plug hole."

Ursula offered them both a cup of tea and a scone.

"These look wonderful Ursula," said Emma, taking a bite, "delicious."

"Good," acknowledged Ursula with a smile, "it's my first attempt. We have a few animal biscuits too – you pushed the mix into the *speckolas* board didn't you Lulu – and some orange jelly left from yesterday, if you would care for some."

"A real birthday tea, how lovely," said Emma.

"Lulu, you'll have to sit at the table if you'd like your milk and scone now," said Ursula.

But Lulu immediately lay down on the floor and pulled the skirt of her tiny flower printed dress over her face.

Jessie laughed uproariously, "There's a Music Hall star in the making if ever I saw one – showing her *broekies* like that!"

"Lulu," admonished Ursula, scowling at Jessie to show she wanted no encouragement given to the errant child.

"Does she have to have her tea now?" asked Emma hesitantly.

"Not really, she'll have an egg before bedtime anyway."

"I only ask because I have a present for you too, Lulu," said Emma taking a flat packet from her bag. "If you get up, I'll help you open it."

Lulu sat up immediately and taking the proffered present insisted on opening it. It was a prettily decorated, slim book.

"Book," said Lulu, standing up and passing the book to her mother.

"It's called Mother Goose – what a beautiful present. Lulu, give Emma a kiss and say thank you," said Ursula. "We shall have great fun reading all these nursery rhymes," she continued as Lulu dutifully gave Emma a kiss, "and we love to do all the actions to them, don't we Lulu?"

Lulu nodded.

"And this is from *Tannie*," said Jessie, as she passed Lulu a large package wrapped in brown paper and string.

Lulu passed it to Ursula who undid the string and then Lulu pulled the paper off. There was a clatter as a tin bucket and small spade fell to the floor; Lulu picked them up and putting the spade in the bucket began stirring it round.

"Lulu, say thank you to Jessie for such a lovely present," prompted Ursula.

Lulu gave Jessie a kiss and continued stirring the spade in the bucket.

"I thought she could use it in the garden or on the beach," said Jessie.

"It was an inspired choice Jessie. In fact," continued Ursula, grimacing at the noise of the spade on the bucket, "she could go out with it now. Would you like to take it outside to play Lulu?"

Lulu nodded and Ursula opened the French windows. "Just on the grass here," she said.

"Can't she go to the end of the garden," said Jessie, putting her hands over her ears to block out the scraping noise.

"Not on her own because of the pond. I'll loosen a little soil for her here; then she'll have something to put in the bucket, and it won't be so noisy," said Ursula stepping out onto the grass.

Taking Lulu's spade she scraped a little soil from the side of a bed.

"Ursula, are those Clivias that you're digging next to?" asked Emma leaning out of the door and pointing at the row of green strap leaves that arched languidly along the edge of the path.

"Yes. I took out the roses – they always looked so bare – and we dug up large clumps of these bush lilies from over there where I couldn't see them, and put them here."

"You two sound like a couple of middle-aged matrons," said Jessie mockingly from the comfort of her seat.

"Well, I probably do," said Ursula coming inside whilst Emma strolled up the path. "Home and family are my little world now."

"Would you mind if I have a cigarette?" Jessie asked, taking a slim tortoiseshell case from her bag.

"Do, David smokes here; with the doors open the smell doesn't linger too much. It's strange, I even miss his smoking when he's away."

"He's not away now."

"Not till next week."

"Did Lulu's godfather come to see her yet?" asked Jessie, lighting her cigarette.

"You know Duggie – always got too many fingers in too many pies. He'll probably remember and call next week – at tea-time of course."

"Loves his tea nearly as much as he likes his beer," replied Jessie, blowing a puff of smoke towards the open windows. "But like most men, Duggie needs to be led by the nose."

Ursula suddenly remembered where she had seen Duggie's

cigarette tin before and was about to ask Jessie to explain when Emma came back inside and sat down.

"Talking of which, I'm awfully afraid *I* am about to be led to the slaughter," said Emma grimly. "I need a Prince Charming pretty quick. I've had one very narrow escape – fortunately for me Cousin Archie took a shine to a debutante when he was in London and was married last year. But in the light of me not taking the stage by storm I've been ordered back to camp before next season. I don't fancy being put on parade for any eligible chap that happens to be in thrall to father."

"Oh Emma, that is bad luck – Lulu mind you don't dig up those flowers," Ursula called. "But Emma couldn't you stay on here?"

"There are simply not enough roles for me Ursula; the Tivoli is mostly Music Hall now. The Opera House has every quality show: I auditioned for Stephen Black's play *Love and the Hyphen* – it's already been on at the Opera House so I thought I had a chance – but even for that there were too many professionals trying."

Lulu came in from the garden without the bucket and, taking advantage of the opportunity, Ursula immediately stood up and took her hand.

"We'll be back in a minute," she said walking swiftly out of the room. They soon returned – accompanied by the smell of coal tar soap – and Ursula sat Lulu up at the table, "Here's your milk, Lulu."

"Mister Rabbit," said Lulu breathlessly, taking the rabbit from her pocket and wriggling to get down from the table.

"No Lulu stay here, Mister Rabbit can have a wash after tea. You can even give him a bath then; when you've been a good girl and eaten your scone. Look, I've put Nana's special watermelon *konfyt* on it as a treat," she added by way of encouragement.

"I don't know how you have the patience," said Jessie. "My Ma just plonked us down and told us to do as we were told."

"It's not patience – it's compromise; it saves a lot of tantrums."

"Tantrums? But your Lulu is such a little angel," said Emma.

They all looked at Lulu, who immediately pushed the last piece of scone into her mouth.

"Lulu finish," she announced to them stoutly, her mouth full.

"Angel?" Ursula looked at Emma with amusement. "I don't think angels *skoff* their food and speak with their mouths full and wipe their jammy hands on their pinafores."

"Lulu finish," insisted Lulu.

"Nor do I think that angels are so demanding; yes, Lulu, you may get down then," said Ursula, rising to help her off her chair, brushing the crumbs off her face as she did so. "Would you like to play outdoors again?"

"Mister Rabbit bath," Lulu reminded her.

"Oh dear, I hoped you'd forgotten. Emma is that pot of water cool?"

"Quite cold, Ursula, but I've had more than enough tea."

"I'm sorry, I didn't mean it for the pot. I thought I might just pour some of it into the bucket for Lulu," and she took the pot outside and filled the bucket. "There you are Lulu," she said, "now you can bathe Mister Rabbit."

Lulu followed carrying the rabbit and immediately crouched down and put it in the bucket; she turned the rabbit over and over in the water, picked up a leaf and dried the toy, and then began again.

"There," said Ursula returning, "you see what I mean Jessie – compromise; she would have given me no peace otherwise. Once she gets an idea into her head she never gives up. Now we can have another half an hour of uninterrupted conversation."

"Hmm, well, the more we asked for something when we were little the more Ma ignored us – she just carried on doing what she had to do," said Jessie. "Still, she had a point, in the end we either gave up or did it ourselves."

*

The following week was Ursula and David's wedding anniversary.

"Do you have to go to Bloemfontein now," asked Ursula. She had hoped that any further trips would not be necessary and wanted them to spend the evening together. "Couldn't you put it off for a day or two?"

"I'm afraid not," replied David, "they're expecting the delegation to telegraph from England to let us know whether the British Government will amend the South Africa Bill at the last moment. Schriener and the deputation are doing their utmost in London to sway Parliamentarians; I have to telegraph on to Abe. We're all expecting the worst though."

"Oh dear," she said as sympathetically as she could; it did not sound as if he could postpone his trip.

"If they pass the Act next week as it is, without the amendments we want, it will be the death of equal rights and the African franchise" he said, closing his eyes and rubbing his forehead.

Ursula felt ashamed; she really must try harder to live up to such noble, selfless principles.

"It's important and I'm being selfish – of course you must go," she said, with as much conviction as she could.

David smiled at her indulgently, "We can have a family outing this Sunday to celebrate, how about that?"

"Yes, that would be very nice."

On Sunday morning Ursula attended early mass and Lulu – wearing the blue jacket Ursula had made her and carrying her bucket – was waiting for her with David when the service finished. Together they caught a tram to the railway station and took the train south, past Devil's Peak and Table Mountain, through the villages of Rosebank and Newlands, Claremont and Kenilworth, through leafy Wynberg and on down to False Bay.

On the journey Ursula and David reminisced about the happy days they had spent at Muizenberg.

As the train departed from the railway station there – following the shore of the bay past St James, and onwards south towards Kalk Bay – Ursula distracted Lulu's attention from the men cutting up a whale on the rocks, pointing out instead the cottages on the hillside, then the fishing boats in the harbour unloading their catch of *snoek*. The train passed through Clovelly and around Fish Hoek Bay where David identified the rocks they had sat on feeding the seals. It continued around the spectacular coastline – Ursula was sure she spotted a whale in the bay at Glencairn – to the end of the line at Simon's Town, the Martello Tower on the promontory testament to the strategic importance of the settlement.

They purchased a bottle of ginger beer at the general store opposite the station and climbed the grassy slope behind it. Laying a blanket on a small *koppie,* Ursula unpacked the *padkos* she had prepared. Simon's Town was a naval port and His Majesty's warships were moored in the bay, impressive in scale compared to the small fishing vessels that bobbed on the gentle swell. David pointed them out to Lulu and explained what the lighthouse at the harbour entrance was for as the family ate their pies, boiled eggs and fruit. When they had finished Lulu picked some *baviantjies* that grew on the grass beside them, and chased an early Christmas butterfly, but soon she became restless. They packed their *padkos* away and walked down the slope, across the road and the railway line and onto the beach. David and Ursula sat on a wooden groyne whilst Lulu explored; for some time she was content to fill and empty her bucket with sand.

When Lulu had exhausted that game she pulled at Ursula's hand and pointed towards the sea.

"Mister Rabbit bath," she demanded.

"The sea's too big for Mister Rabbit to have a bath, Lulu, you'll lose him," Ursula explained.

"I'll take her down, Ursula, she can take her shoes and stockings off and we'll get some water in her bucket."

"All right. Sit down, Lulu, and I'll undo the buttons on your shoes."

"I'll have to roll my trousers up," said David, sounding as if he was looking forward to the experience. "D'you know, I haven't done this since I went to Southend years ago; I hope the sea's warmer than it was there."

"Yes, and I'd better tuck Lulu's dress into her *broekies*."

David stood up and took Lulu's hand, "Bring your bucket Lulu, we're going for a paddle."

Ursula followed them down to the water's edge and watched as David showed Lulu how to lay the bucket on its side and let the water flow into it. He did it a few times, and helped Lulu do the same, then he carried the bucket full of water and placed it on the firm sand for her; crouching onto her heels Lulu placed the toy rabbit in the bucket and dunked him up and down. A larger wave than hitherto came close and surprised her. Jumping to her feet, she knocked the bucket over, spilling the toy rabbit onto the wet swirling sand.

"Mister Rabbit, Mister Rabbit," she cried out in dismay, looking up at David.

David quickly snatched the toy from the eddy, "There, put him safe in your pocket now," he said firmly.

Unused to her father's tone, Lulu immediately took the rabbit, and carefully put it in her jacket.

"Mind out," warned Ursula, "here comes another wave Lulu."

Lulu looked round and ran back from the wave; from a safe distance she watched as it receded, and then followed it back to the shore line. Lulu had discovered an exciting new game; with squeals of delight she ran backwards and forwards escaping and chasing the waves in turn. David and Ursula laughed with her; it was infectious.

When Lulu grew tired of her game Ursula took her hand and

they walked slowly along the beach collecting seashells and small pieces of mother-of-pearl. The bucket was soon full and (after David had dried Lulu's feet with his large cotton handkerchief) Ursula put Lulu's stockings and shoes on her, and they left the beach and walked along to the town and onto the jetty. Bold gulls came strutting up to them and, undoing their picnic hamper, Ursula took out the scraps of pastry. Protecting Lulu with her skirt, she helped her throw the scraps to the gulls who greedily snatched at them. When they had used up all the scraps, David picked Lulu up – to escape the menacing beaks – and they stood and watched the fishing boats and smaller sailing craft in the bay.

At the British Hotel they treated themselves to tea – bread and butter and cakes – in the dark panelled dining room. Afterwards, in the general dealers, Ursula allowed Lulu to choose some *tamaletjies* for herself from the array of sweets in glass jars and David bought some snuff in a small paper wrapper and they explored the shops that lined the main road. Finally they turned to walk back to the station, David carrying the tired child who was soon asleep on his shoulder. To the north Table Mountain brooded black, and the sun, setting behind it, infused the sky with a deep orange flame, casting an eerie glow over the calm bay as they boarded the waiting train for Cape Town.

"What a lovely day that was," said David.

"It was a perfect day," said Ursula, sitting down next to him and laying her head on his shoulder. "It was such fun to visit those places again and Lulu loved the beach. It was the nicest way to mark our wedding anniversary."

"And we can have our final celebration when we get home to bed," David whispered, putting his free arm around her, and giving her a squeeze.

"David, shh!" said Ursula in embarrassment, looking round to see if anyone had heard.

He left the next morning for Bloemfontein.

*

Ursula had organized the Bridge Drive for Thursday. Unfortunately, almost immediately after David left for Bloemfontein, Mrs Middleton sent a note to say that she would not be able to look after Lulu for a week or two as her daughter had started to go into labour. Ursula decided to contact Emma immediately and ask if she could come and look after Lulu instead. She and Lulu caught the tram to the centre of town and bought a few choice fruits at the market – those that were not readily available at the small *winkel* close to them. When they were finished they called at the theatre and Ursula asked to see Emma.

"She's not in Miss," Joe informed her. "So this is the little 'un is it?"

"Yes Joe, this is Lulu."

She sat Lulu on Joe's counter and Joe immediately took out his watch and dangled it for her. Ursula was surprised that Lulu seemed quite at ease with him and had taken hold of the shiny silver case.

"Can I leave her for a moment Joe – I need to leave a message for Emma with Jessie."

"She's safe with me," nodded Joe.

Ursula found Jessie counting tickets in the cloakroom.

"What are you doing here?" said Jessie in surprise.

"Hello Jess. I can't stop – Lulu's upstairs with Joe," she said hurriedly.

"Wonders will never cease!"

"I need to give Emma a message, Jess, but she's not here."

"What's the message, I'll give it to her," said Jessie putting her tickets away.

"Could she please come on Thursday afternoon – about one o'clock – and look after Lulu for me. I wouldn't ask her but it's very important. Lizzie will be able to give her some tea before she goes at four but I won't be back till well after five," explained Ursula.

"I'll make sure she gets it," said Jessie. "I might even come with her, there isn't a matinée on a Thursday."

"You're most welcome to Jess. I must dash, see you on Thursday perhaps. Goodbye."

When Ursula reached the foyer she found Lulu inside Joe's cubbyhole moving her toy rabbit from pigeonhole to pigeonhole. Joe seemed quite unperturbed.

"She don't take no for an answer, do she?" he said, picking Lulu up and depositing her like a large parcel on the counter again.

"She doesn't," laughed Ursula, as she lifted Lulu down. "Thank you Joe, you've been very kind."

"Well, I got a dozen of me own see – grandchilder that is; one little 'un like that don't pose no problems so it don't."

"All the same, we won't impose on you again," she said taking Lulu's hand and walking to the door. "Goodbye Joe, and thank you."

"Bye Miss, bye little 'un."

Turning her head Lulu gave Joe a sparkling smile and held up her rabbit as a parting gesture.

Ursula already had her jacket and hat on when the doorbell rang.

"Hello Jessie, come in. Where's Emma?" she asked, peering up the path.

"*Ag* well, I saw her yesterday and she said she'd just organized a singing lesson for today. So I thought – no point in making her feel guilty – I'd just come instead."

"Oh I see," said Ursula, looking concerned.

"Well, let's face it, I've looked after little ones more often than she's had hot teas," shrugged Jessie.

"I suppose so."

"And you said your Lizzie would be here till four; then I've only an hour or so on my own."

"Of course, I'm sorry Jessie, it's just that you haven't looked after Lulu on your own before."

"Still, I might not be on my own at all, someone might pop in for tea – I mean, Emma might come unannounced after her lesson – people do call in sometimes don't they?"

"Yes, they do sometimes Jess," said Ursula diffidently.

"Well there you are, worrying about nothing," replied Jessie firmly.

"I'm going to be late for the Bridge Drive if I don't go soon Jess, so you better come into the back room," Ursula said leading the way, "and I'll show you everything."

Lulu was sitting at the table with a colouring book, her toy rabbit stood on the table beside it.

"Lulu, Jessie's here; she's come to look after you."

Lulu put down her crayon and wriggled off the chair. Going to the glazed doors she pointed out to the bucket and spade that were lying on the grass. Jessie followed her and looked out.

"Oh, so you play with them then," said Jessie.

"She plays with the bucket constantly," replied Ursula, "it's a real favourite; that and Mister Rabbit."

Lulu returned to the table and reached for the rabbit, "Mister Rabbit bath."

"Not now Lulu. Jessie will put some water in the bucket for you later – first I have to explain a few things. Jess, all Lulu's toys are here so I thought it would be easier for you here than in the front room. You can go out for a walk with her if you want, or she can go into the garden, but not on her own obviously," said Ursula checking that she had her key and gloves.

"No, we'll stay in, we won't go out. You know how I like my home comforts."

"Lizzie will bring you tea before she goes. I should be back shortly after five."

"No rush, it doesn't matter if you're later than that; I know how to cope with a three-year-old."

"If you're sure . . ." she said, walking back into the hallway.

"Quite sure," said Jessie firmly.

"Lulu, you will be a good girl for Jessie won't you, and do what she tells you?" Ursula said, turning around as she opened the front door.

Lulu nodded.

"Good. Now give Mommy a kiss goodbye," and she bent down to Lulu's level in the open doorway.

Lulu put her arms around Ursula's neck and gave her a kiss. Through the cloud of curls that smelled of rosemary, Ursula found the small cheek and kissed it. Lulu released her and held the rabbit out.

"Mister Rabbit kiss," she said.

"Goodbye Mister Rabbit," Ursula said, and gave the toy rabbit a kiss. "Now I must dash, I'm going to be late," she said, straightening up and pulling on her gloves. "Thank you Jessie, goodbye. Goodbye, Lulu."

At the gate Ursula paused and looked back; Lulu did indeed look like a little angel to her today – her smocked white pinafore unusually clean, blue eyes wide, curls a froth of gold. She looked so small, encased in the porch, partially concealed by the black-skirted figure of Jessie.

"Goodbye Ursula, you don't want to be late," urged Jessie, waving. "Have a good afternoon."

Lulu, smiling, held up Mister Rabbit and waved him. Ursula waved back and blew a farewell kiss.

Ursula caught the tram back from the Bridge Drive and as she did so congratulated herself that the afternoon had gone well: they had made a fair amount for the Soldiers Aid Society and made most of their rubbers too. She did not have her umbrella and as she alighted she noticed that a cloud as black as a judge's cap loomed over the mountain ahead of her. Soon the heavens will open, she thought, and I shall be drowned. The road from the tram stop was steep and Ursula talked to herself under her breath as she forced herself to hurry. She went over in her mind all the hands she had and what mistakes she had made. 'No point in crying over spilt milk, must just learn by my mistakes,' she told herself, 'was worrying about Jessie and Lulu and not concentrating; silly'. As she reached the front door she heard a crack of thunder; thank goodness, just in time, she thought. Entering the hall she heard voices – adult voices. Emma must have come then, she decided, and I was worrying unnecessarily. She closed the door and called out, "Jessie."

Standing at the small hall table she pulled off her gloves and put them in the drawer.

"Jessie, I'm back," she called again.

She could hear movement within the back room and, looking in the mirror, she removed her hat and smoothed her hair. As she did so the dining room door opened behind her and she saw the reflection of a man. Ursula gasped and turned. Duggie closed the door behind him.

"Hello Ursula," he said, turning his cap in his hands.

"Oh, hello Duggie. I'm sorry, I didn't expect to see you," she said apologetically, "I thought you were Emma."

"Do I look like a lassie?" he asked, raising his eyebrows.

"No of course not Duggie, it's simply that I was expecting . . ." she paused, what was Duggie doing here? "Is everything well?" she asked.

"Aye, fine. But I must be aff noo," he said, glancing unsurely at the closed door behind him, looking sheepish.

Ursula was instictively alert, "Very well Duggie, but I must talk to Jessie before I see you out."

"She's gone oot to find the wean," he said, almost apologetically.

"To find Lulu?" asked Ursula, opening the door to the dining room. "Where is she?"

240

"Just skiddling with her bucket in the garden," he replied following her.

Ursula walks over to the open doors. At that moment Jessie's voice comes clearly, calling, "Lulu, Lulu where are you?"

Fear strikes Ursula.

"Was she out on her own?" she asks urgently, grabbing Duggie's arm.

"Aye," he says, questioning.

She does not answer but steps out into the garden. The sky is dark and it is beginning to rain.

"Jessie, Lulu," she calls, taking deep breaths through her open mouth, her chest beginning to tighten.

She can see Jessie walking through the trees.

"Jessie," Ursula calls, panic in her voice, "where's Lulu? Where's Lulu?"

Jessie turns towards her, arms spread in a shrug. It seems to her that Jessie moves in slow motion, speaks a strange language. And she begins to run, and does not understand the words Jessie uses. Runs past her through the trees, down the bank.

"Lulu, Lulu."

Runs on around the pincushion bushes. Hope strengthens her legs; fear constricts her throat and stifles her breath.

"Lulu."

The pumping of her heart batters her chest; blood beats in her ears, drumming like a ship's engine. By the pool she stops dead.

"LULU!"

Later, as Ursula lies on the floor, curled in a tight ball in the corner of the room, she grasps the crucifix and medal that hangs around her neck. With unusual strength she wrenches the chain that holds them till it breaks, and flings them across the room.

And later still, through the fog in her mind, she hears the doctor say, "Mrs Lewis, your daughter was holding this little lead rabbit."

"*Mister* Rabbit" corrects Ursula, sharply, holding out her hand for the toy.

PART III

The nursery
Johannesburg, February 18th, 1912

Ursula was tired; tired from lack of sleep, from clandestinely feeding Edward and tired of being optimistic. Tired of being tired. Her concentration had dissipated and – in spite of wanting to keep her mind busy – she could not read, was unable to write, was far too exhausted to sew. Normal everyday activities jarred on her nerves: the noise of the dustcart passing by, the rattle of tin buckets and pails being stacked in the morning by Lizzie, the door knocker banging when the milkman called in his cart, Sukey barking at the birds in the garden at evening time. When Mrs Van Der Ploeg came to look after Edward, Ursula lay on her bed and immediately dropped into a deep and dreamless sleep, from which she awoke a few hours later feeling as tired as when she had lain down.

Ursula felt locked in an unreal world; a small and solitary world. Friends – unable to keep up the words of encouragement, incapable of practical assistance – no longer called to enquire after Edward's progress. Afraid of what they might hear, fearful what they may see, they sent notes instead of visiting. Her husband and she exchanged only the most essential news; both so tense and tired that they could not comfort each other with anything more than platitudes.

Today the doctor would call. He no longer called daily, for which Ursula was thankful. Since she had embarked on her own campaign to save Edward she wanted no interference. Deciding to feed Edward had taken all her courage, if challenged she would not have the confidence to argue her case – she would have to capitulate. Her husband had wanted to take his turn in sitting up with the child – and did so during the early morning hours – but he too was unaware that Ursula was feeding their baby.

Doctor's coming today. Before Mrs Van Der Ploeg I hope. Can't cope with two sour faces; two heads shaking. Please let him say something hopeful – just this once. One little ray of hope so that I can keep going. There we are, the bell. My thoughts are getting through to him. I only hope they are getting through to you my little prince.

No doctor. He is much the same. Do you not think he looks a little more flushed, a little more healthy?

The Doctor looked closely at the sleeping child. Lifted his eyelids, one by one, and closed them. Picked up each small arm in turn and let it drop.

I notice a change for the worse, respiration pulse . . . should have recovered by now if he was going to . . . unlikely to now . . . surprised he's held on so long . . . most unusual in such cases, my dear, most unusual . . . must have had quite a reserve of strength there . . . time is running out, running out . . . won't be long, best brace yourself.

"Just in case there is something that can be done even at this late stage, my husband and I should like the opinion of a consulting physician."

"So I understand. Professor Michaels is a prominent man, in similar cases he has injected strychnine into the heart with some small success."

"Strychnine? You are suggesting injecting poison into my baby, poisoning our baby?"

"*In extremis,* Mrs Lewis, *in extremis.* It may work; there is a very slight possibility that it might give his system the sort of shock that will bring him out of his coma. The Professor has to carry out the procedure. We cannot let this state of affairs go on much longer; we may have to make this life-or-death decision."

"Doctor, I shall be praying that Edward will recover before you call next. I will not give up hope. It's what keeps me going. Good day Doctor."

Horrid, miserable, depressing man. Poison my baby! Inject poison into Edward's heart! Murderer.
But I can't keep Edward alive forever. I need help.
Here I am God – looking for you, praying to you.
So tired, so very tired. I don't know how much longer I can keep all this up. Hoping against hope. Whistling in the wind.
If it all goes wrong, if the worst happens, this time I will . . .

Ursula opened the sewing box that stood on the table beside her and searched for the small twist of paper hidden in the base; the paper that held the small knob of *Ugobho* that Nana had given her all those years ago. She found it and turned it over a few times between her fingers. She closed her eyes and could only imagine blackness, a never ending tunnel, a deep dark pit. Quickly she replaced it in the base of the box.

Oh God, forgive me!

Fifteen

But, O the heavy change, now thou art gone,
Now thou art gone, and never must return!

Lycidas (1637)
John Milton 1608–1674

The pond had been drained, the furthest area of the garden fenced off. Ursula spent her days in Lulu's bedroom. Burying her face in clean cotton nightdresses she inhaled the innocent smell of dusting powder – a poignant reminder of bath times. Yet again she arranged and rearranged the tiny tucked bodices in the lavender strewn shelves, remembered soft feet as she unpaired and paired the small stockings in the drawer, knotted tresses as she unrolled and rolled the hair ribbons: saved the hair from the hairbrush. Afterwards she would lie in Lulu's bed and, pulling the coverlet over her head, she would fall into a deep and dreamless sleep. At other times she sat silently and stared into space or, starting a task, would pause half way through completing it, forgetful of the purpose.

David and Ursula had not discussed the sequence of events that had occurred on the day of Lulu's death. Ursula was aware that others had given David the details; she was so distraught that David – devastated himself – had not questioned her but had comforted and cared for her. In her catatonic state Ursula was incapable of focusing on how David felt; she would not talk of the fateful day. In an effort to communicate David eventually broached the subject; Ursula broke into hysterics and he did not do so again.

One day she started to cry, not racking sobs, but slow steady rivulets that coursed down her cheeks and which she could not halt. Despair engulfed her – it was an effort to rise in the morning, an effort to go to bed at night – life held no promise. She did not notice the weather, she did not taste the food that Lizzie prepared; she did not care if she lived or died. The doctor prescribed a plain diet, plenty of exercise and occasional doses of castor oil. Most importantly he urged that an amusement, or some event to look forward to, should be encouraged. David thought a change of scenery would help; Hannah suggested a retreat at the convent that Meg had entered.

Ursula agreed to the latter and slowly during the next weeks, still deep in grief and consumed by her own anger and guilt, she began woodenly to perform essential tasks. David had written to the convent and received an affirmative reply; he explained the arrangements to Ursula. In hopeful expectation of seeing Meg, Ursula began to show more interest in events than she had evinced since the accident.

The white painted convent, built in the Cape Dutch style, was both simple and elegant in design. The walls were thick as mahogany trunks, the thatched roof steeply sloped and the shaped gable that rose above the body of the house stood up as proud as a bishop's hat. The heavy wooden door with its carved fanlight above was answered by a lay Sister who took the baggage from David and admitted Ursula. The Sister asked her to wait whilst she went to inform Mother that Ursula had arrived. The reception room in which she stood was spacious, with several tall windows and a high beamed ceiling. The furniture was sparse but large and handsome, and the vinegar and oils that had been applied to it over the centuries until it had acquired a pleasing patina, permeated the room with a wholesome smell. A large door swung open and a nun entered. Mother Agnes Connell was not striking in physical appearance but she had an air of authority, a serenity that impressed Ursula as she came forward to greet her. A younger nun, dressed in a simple white habit with a black veil, walked in her wake, head bowed.

"Welcome, Mrs Lewis," said Mother Agnes Connell as she inclined her head to Ursula. "We will do what we can to comfort and heal you. I trust that after some time here you will feel stronger in body and mind. You may spend your days in contemplation and prayer and rest all you need," she continued in well modulated tones. "You will join us for meals of course and benefit from our community care and prayer. And now," she concluded with a patient smile, "I will leave Sister Margaret to explain our regime and show you to your room."

"Thank you," said Ursula, dropping a small curtsy as she had in school days.

Mother Agnes Connell bowed her head and Ursula watched, as with a measured walk and upright posture, she appeared to glide across the yellowwood floor of the hallway and through the door she had entered by. The remaining nun had followed her and now, softly closing the door behind her superior, she turned. Dark eyebrows, like the outstretched wings of a bird, stark on a porcelain skin. Ursula exclaimed: it was Meg.

She had expected to see Meg during her stay but this sudden confrontation was unexpected. Meg smiled at her and Ursula, unable to control her emotions, called, "Meg, Meg, it's you!"

She thrust her arms out but looking over the robed and distant figure seemed at a loss what she would do. Meg had not moved. Could Ursula hug her as she would Nana? Could she kiss her? It had been so many years since she had seen her. The figure in white, her smile as demure but her eyes more alive, seemed to understand and removing a hand from the wide sleeve of her habit held it out to Ursula. Ursula grabbed it, squeezed and pumped it in both of hers.

"Oh Meg, Meg," she said, tears streaming down her face.

Meg removed her hand.

"It is good to see you Ursula. You have grown taller," she said quietly, slightly raising her eyebrows.

"Oh Meg," said Ursula, pleading, again putting out her hand towards her sister.

Meg smiled indulgently but her hands remained folded in front of her. Inclining her head towards an open door that led into a corridor she picked up the portmanteau that stood on the ground beside Ursula and asked, "And is Hannah in good health?"

"Yes, yes she is. She . . ."

But Meg had turned and begun to walk towards the door. Ursula, unable to continue with her response, followed automatically. As she caught her up Meg spoke again, "We are all sad to hear of your loss and your suffering. Very sad. The Sisters will do what they can to comfort you. Prayer is very important to us and we do this together. We hope you will join our daily Eucharist, where your intentions will be remembered. Repose and quiet will do the rest."

Ursula, torn between joy and sorrow, wiped the tears from her cheeks with the palms of her hands and accompanied Meg – silently like a stranger.

They passed through the corridor scented with incense and out across a courtyard, through further passages and by closed doors, until Meg opened a door onto a darkened room. Entering it she lifted the window and pushed open the shutters; she returned to the doorway and invited Ursula to enter. The room was small and painted white, the window uncurtained, the floor uncovered. There was a wrought iron bedstead, a high backed chair, plain wooden table, a washstand with bowl and jug, and a small cupboard for possessions. The only decoration was a simple wooden cross on the wall above the bed and a coloured print of Jesus ministering to the sick. Ursula could see the garden through the window – the bright flowers and asymmetrical form of the trees seemed to compensate for the plainness of the room.

"Sister Rose will show you the way to the refectory in the main building at midday," said Meg, her hand on the door handle, the smile on her lips as tranquil as before, "and Sister Catherine and Sister Mary will collect you for prayers in the chapel."

"Oh. Th . . . thank you," stuttered Ursula, realizing with consternation that Meg was about to leave. She wanted Meg to stay; she wanted Meg to talk to her, to comfort her. Ursula wanted to tell her about Lulu, about David. And to ask her what life was like in the convent. She had an idea and suddenly threw up her arms.

"Meg wait, wait," she said and she stooped and undid the clasp of her portmanteau. From under her nightdress she removed her silver-backed hairbrush and standing up, held it out towards her sister.

"Look. Mother's brush," she said, her eyes wide – this was sure to bring to mind their former close relationship, fond memories, shared experiences – "our brush."

Meg's smile widened a little but she did not move.

"Indeed. God bless you and keep you," she said evenly, before she pulled the door to behind her.

Ursula slumped onto the bed and burst into tears.

Sister Rose, her back humped with age, small wisps of grey hair escaping from her veil, led Ursula slowly to the refectory where a very long table was arranged in the middle of the room. She was shown to a chair at the side of the table; the nuns stood waiting behind their chairs for the signal for grace. Ursula felt confused, disorientated – was this déjà vu, something she had dreamed, was she really here? She looked around at the tall sash windows divided into many small panes of glass; up at the high beamed ceiling lined in strips of yellowwood; at the large painting of the Last Supper in its gilded frame that filled most of the wall above the table. Memories of school flooded over her. Bless us, Oh Lord, and these Thy gifts which we are about to receive from Thy bountiful hands, through Christ our Lord.

"Amen."

Like the buzz of bees, voices surrounded her and Ursula realized that she had not imagined the words but that they had been intoned, because a bell tinkled and the nuns drew out their chairs and sat down to eat. Ursula ate without noticing; the practical enquiries about the meal and gentle and quiet tone of the Sister's voices helped to soothe the turmoil that gripped her.

After they had eaten, Sister Rose motioned to Ursula to join her.

"Would you care to rest in the garden," she asked in her soft Irish brogue.

"I'd like to, yes."

"The garden is a healing place to be sure, 'come apart and rest awhile' said Mark," Sister Rose continued, slowly leading the way.

With difficulty she opened a large door onto a wide terrace where a flight of steps led down to a pair of palm trees, standing like sentinels, and a vast lawn that stretched out beyond to meet shrub and flower filled borders. Behind these the turf continued in an informal way with rhododendron bushes dotted here and there, some large Norfolk pines and a striking monkey puzzle tree.

"It is beautiful," remarked Ursula in a subdued voice, "and very peaceful."

"To be sure, the perfect place for a retreat."

The day was warm and Sister Rose falteringly led the way to a spot under a wide, spreading banyan tree.

"We find our visitors are usually more tired than they think," she said, indicating a reclining chair with some cushions and a homespun rug folded on it. "It's warm but if you drift off to sleep, you may catch a chill; it would be wise to keep the rug over your legs."

Ursula lifted one of the rugs, beneath which was a small black bound bible.

"If you are in need of spiritual comfort," said Sister Rose by way of explanation.

"Thank you. I'm very tired – I think I'll simply rest."

"Bless you," Sister Rose smiled. "We will bring you a cup of tea at four."

Deliberately placing one foot in front of the other, she carefully retraced her steps.

Ursula lay under the banyan tree looking at the sky through the branches. The large clusters of green leaves with their lustrous sheen looked healthy and rich. The pattern of the branches, some twisted, some straight, made her think of a map. A map of her life perhaps. Muttering to herself she traced the pattern. It began strong and straight, upwards, onwards – my life as a child, she thought, following where I was led, obeying the rules, decisions made for me, cared for and catered for. The tree then split into two branches; and that branch on the left is when Meg brought me to Cape Town and Jimmy took the other branch, went his own way. She traced the left branch that had limbs in all directions. But still there was no choice, she continued, there was no Meg to guide me anymore. I had to take the widest path, follow the strongest branch, take the job I was offered. And there, right there – she thought, looking at a smooth strong side branch – that's where I decided to work at the theatre, where I met David, where I chose a life with him. And that pretty cluster of flowers so clearly silhouetted against the sky, so vibrant and bright with the sun shining on them, was our Lulu. Ah. And then, yes there, an impossible bend, a gnarled knotty branch whose end is lost in a thicket of leaves. And where will that lead? Nowhere; it's come to an end. No sun can penetrate those leaves.

Ursula lay for a long time, her legs stretched out on the rattan chair, pillows supporting her arms and neck, as a gentle wind played upon the leaves causing them to flutter like bunting. And the hole inside her felt huge. Even after seeing Meg: Meg whom she remembered so well, had imagined so often, had missed so much. She reminded herself that her sister had been a nun for many years but would surely be more natural when next she saw her. I'm sure everyone's right, she counselled herself, the sanctuary and solitude of the convent will help me heal. I've never really been a *proper* Catholic – at school I let it all wash over me, didn't absorb it as I should – but now I'll try. Try and find some answers. And Meg will help me understand – make sense of it all. Ursula, desperate for comfort in this strange place, imagined Meg consoling her.

But Ursula grew tired of expecting Meg, who did not come. Over the ensuing days her soliloquies under the tree were repeated and gradually, as her sense of abandonment increased, became even less hopeful. Now each branch of the banyan tree appeared misshapen and mutilated, every one terminated in a withered and leafless stump, or a clump of leaves of blackest green. Alone in her room every evening with nothing to occupy her, the state of her mind deteriorated further. Imaginative and questioning at the best of times, she was wont to dwell on events. As her pessimism increased so too did her bitterness.

And during the nights she suffered a recurring dream:

She calls – where's Lulu? Jessie, dressed in black, shrugs. She runs past her through the trees. But there are many trees. She bumps into them. She cannot see her way. She will not get there; she will not get there in time. And now she is on the grass. Running. But she moves in slow motion. Lulu, Lulu, she calls. But her voice is silent. She cannot call a warning. Fear constricts her throat and stifles her breath;

255

Lulu. She runs but she does not move. The pumping of her heart batters her chest. Blood beats in her ears, drumming like a ship's engine. And then there is water, far out of her reach she sees a billowing white, like the sail of a capsized dinghy. LULU!

And, shouting her child's name, she would wake from her nightmare.

Ursula did not see Meg again until she had been at the convent for four days, when Meg knocked on the door of her room after breakfast and asked, "Good morning, Ursula. Did you sleep well?"

"Very well," she replied, mechanically.

"May I enter?"

"Of course," said Ursula. She got up from the bed but as Meg did not come towards her, sat down again.

"Mother has given me permission to spend a little time with you," said Meg.

"How long?"

"Long enough."

"Does she know I haven't seen you for years?"

"May I sit down?" asked Meg, resting her hand on the back of the upright wooded chair.

Ursula nodded.

"We lead a regulated life here, Ursula, we are contemplatives and some of us are teachers," said Meg as she took her seat, her tone verging on the censorious.

"Is that where you've been these last few days?" asked Ursula, ignoring the tone.

"Yes, we have a school for deaf children; I visit there to teach a few days each week."

"But Meg . . ."

"Sister Margaret," corrected Meg.

"Must I call you Sister Margaret?"

"That is my name."

Ursula had forgotten how pedantic Meg could be. "But I don't think I'll be able to keep it up. It won't feel like I'm talking to you," she said plaintively.

"This is my life now, Ursula. I am a daughter of the Church."

"But you are still *my* sister, my Meg," pleaded Ursula.

"These are exceptional circumstances," said Meg, softening, "perhaps Mother would not be askance if it were only this once, whilst we're alone."

"Good. I feel all alone here – no, no, I know," she said, responding to the shake of Meg's head, "the Sisters have been here, and Sister Mary and Sister Catherine and Sister Rose have been kindness itself but – Meg, it's you I've needed to talk to."

Meg's composed expression remained unchanged, "If you prayed with the Sisters, God, Our Father heard your prayer," she said calmly, coolly.

"No, I only wanted you," said Ursula impatiently, "there is no Father."

"Ursula, you must not say so," said Meg, raising her dark eyebrows, her face showing the first signs of animation Ursula had noticed.

"There was no saviour when I needed one, Meg; no kind and caring God."

"Ursula, you are suffering," said Meg with a pained expression. "He is here; He is here for you."

But it did not seem to Ursula that Meg was trying to reassure; she thought she was being didactic.

"No He's not, you don't understand," she replied with feeling. "You haven't lost the person you care for most in the world."

"I did lose two such persons," replied Meg quietly, with a solemn expression.

"I'm sorry, I forget; I was hardly there. But that was different; father and mother were at least adults."

"We are all His children," replied Meg firmly. "And when I was at my most low, God was there for me. God gave me hope."

Ursula could not decide whether the tone was sententious or self-righteous, but neither pleased her. Vague recollections, vignettes, of similar tones in situations long past drifted like mist through her mind.

"But that's you," she said in a frustrated voice, "please don't feed me homilies. Have you never questioned any of this Meg?"

"I have never questioned, Ursula, for I have never doubted," was the reply.

Self-righteous, definitely, Ursula decided.

"But I doubt," she replied, a challenging edge to her voice.

"Ursula, come to the Chapel with me," said Meg more softly, "pray with me; perhaps you will feel His presence more keenly there."

Ursula knew that Meg genuinely wanted to strengthen her faith but she was annoyed with what she considered a colloquy of clichés; hurt too by Meg's lack of personal attention and show of affection, she spoke more forcefully than she intended.

"I went there yesterday evening. And I looked long and hard at the paintings of Our Lady and Our Lord. And I concentrated on the crucifix, the idea that God sent his Son to die for us. They used to mean something Meg but, Meg, now I see they're just images, images and stories – they're not real. They're not telling me anything, Meg, they're a lie!" she finished, a look of pain on her face, hurt betrayal in her voice.

"Ursula, do not blaspheme," said Meg, her smooth face shocked. "May God forgive you my sister. Christ was sent to die for us, to save us Ursula. You must not relinquish that faith."

And she closed her eyes and moved her lips in silent prayer; or apology.

Ursula felt the tightness in her chest increase – how it hurt – as she watched Meg pray and tried to understand her sister's cold reaction. She obviously hears but she doesn't listen, Ursula decided, it's as if she's lacking in some way; she seems incapable of digging deeper, coming closer. Meg's intelligence and faultless memory meant she had excelled at her lessons and devotions, and everyone who knew her praised her common sense and capable application. The inclination to mild hysteria and melancholy that Ursula had sometimes been aware of were blamed on her sensitivity and the painful loss of her parents. But Ursula, with jaundiced eyes now, saw things from a different perspective. Meg's never shown a natural, spontaneous warmth, she decided, her enquiries about others have always been factual, impersonal; to her now pity and forgiveness don't seem to be true sensibilities but cerebral ideals to feed her soul. Perhaps the academic study and strict regime of the convent calms and organizes her mind. And maybe the actual images and energy of the scriptures – the wonder ascribed to the Creation itself – supply the colour and joy that her life lacks. Yes, all of this must be why Meg's embraced her faith with such fervour, she concluded, her own emotions calmed and cooled by this severe analysis.

Meg opened her eyes, "Pray with me, Ursula, pray to our Lord God. God who sent his Son to save us . . ."

"No Meg," she interrupted, cynicism having supplanted her disappointment in Meg's glib responses, "that is dogma, it's all dogma – there's no thought to it. There are no questionings and now, now when I need it most, there are no answers."

"Ursula, you must pray; pray to accept the will of God," urged Meg.

"So, was it God's will to set man against man in this land? And is it God's will to let little children die?" challenged Ursula, unintentionally passionate once more.

"God is outside the aspect of such physical events, Ursula. But now, in the aftermath of this sad event, He hears you," said Meg, slowly, as if speaking to a child who does not understand. "If you open your heart to him He will comfort you."

"Meg, I have tried, honestly," she said, softening her tone in the hope that Meg would respond differently. "I have prayed with the Sisters – they are kind and they mean well – but I can't get things out of my head."

"God is here for you Ursula."

Ursula sighed deeply, the same old thing, "No Meg, don't sermonize, he is *not* here for me, or he wouldn't have let such a terrible thing happen to us," she said, resignation in her voice. "And Jesus wasn't keeping watch, looking after the little children. It's all boloney," she finished emphatically.

Meg looked with sad eyes at Ursula and shook her head, "I will pray for you Ursula. The sisters will pray. We will all pray together, pray that the broken relationship be restored between God and yourself."

She sank to her knees and, making the sign of the cross, muttered her prayers with bowed head. Ursula watched, dolefully.

Friday

Dear David,

I have made a mistake. This place is not the answer. Do you remember when we first met and you asked me if I had ambitions, if I wanted to be famous? It was as if you had somehow seen inside my head, had opened Pandora's box, and let all my silliest, flighty, impossible dreams escape. I could not catch them and put them back then. Indeed I did not want them. There were different dreams after that. Well this is the same, but sadder.

I wish I had left Meg wrapped in cotton wool, tucked just beneath my heart, protected and preserved. But she is

unwrapped and I cannot put the old Meg back. She belongs
here in the convent now. She is a different person to the one
I remember. But then, I suppose, I am changed too.

Please come and collect me. I should like to come home as
soon as possible.

With love, Ursula

David was solicitous and kind as usual when he came to collect
Ursula and he put his arm around her as they travelled home. But
once over the threshold everything that had happened there
seemed to be waiting for them. She felt that the very walls she
brushed past, each door that she opened, every piece of furniture
she touched was imbued with a spirit, heavy with a message,
redolent of a memory. And soon depressed, she became as
despondent as before. Between David and herself an emotional
chasm had opened; in that void were words best not spoken,
thoughts too painful to be given substance – a mire of guilt and
blame too dangerous to cross. And this chasm had a physical
element too – David and Ursula had not slept in the same bed
since Lulu's death. Ursula chose to sleep in Lulu's narrow, iron
nursery bed with its patchwork cover that had been hers as a
child. Here she felt spiritually nearer to her dead child and here,
by denying herself the comfort of her husband's arms, she sought
to punish herself.

"Ursula, we have to do something about our situation," David
gently began one evening.

"What situation?" asked Ursula, her shoulders drooping,
afraid the subject might be their separate sleeping arrangements
that she knew he disliked.

"Let me see," he said, taking a deep breath, "well, to start
with – the house."

"What about the house?" she replied, slightly relieved.

"I think it's dragging us down," he said, looking grave.

"What do you mean?" she asked, knowing exactly what he meant but apprehensive.

"Everything here reminds us so much of what's happened. I spoke to the doctor when you were at the convent . . ."

"Why did you do that?" interrupted Ursula, defensively.

"Because I was worried about you," he replied, patiently.

"And?" she asked, subdued.

"He said that very often the house holds too many memories and it's better for one's health to move."

"To leave here?" asked Ursula, with disbelief and panic in her voice. "Where we were all together?"

David nodded. Silent tears ran down her cheeks and David, moving to sit next to her, put his arm around her shoulders. Stroking and patting her arm, he said, "I know, I know."

And every week David took Ursula to the cemetery, where he, never religious, hung his head and swayed in prayer whilst she, arranging the *chinkerinchee* blooms on the grave, cried silently.

David found an attached, single storey house in the *Vredehoek* area which was not too far for him to walk to work, which he liked to do to keep himself fit. After much coaxing, Ursula finally viewed it with him and reluctantly agreed that it would do. Narrow residential streets rose up the slope that looked down over the town and bay; the tiny front garden was neat and bright red bouganvillia climbed up the pillars that supported the roof above the *stoep*. Beneath this the front door opened onto a small vestibule, which in turn led through a pillared opening onto the *voorkamer*. It had a window to the front, a polished wooden floor and a high panelled ceiling and, with a small brick chimney piece across one corner, was intended to be used as a sitting room. The other rooms opened off the *voorkamer* and, after storing the largest articles of their furniture, there was room for their favourite pieces. The garden – which had an apple tree, an orange tree and several small bushes – was small and enclosed, which pleased them. Ursula finally busied herself with the move and as a result had more energy than before. Soon she and Lizzie had everything neat, curtains hung, furniture arranged and Ursula took over from David the responsibility for household tasks she had ceased to perform.

Hannah had visited the new house soon after they moved in but she had not brought Miriam. Before long however, with renewed strength, Ursula wanted to see Miriam and to hug her – to feel small arms around her neck, the weight of a little child upon her lap. On a particularly dull day, when a dark cloud, heavy with moisture, lay like a black dog over the mountain, the desire became unbearable. She took her umbrella and walked to Adderley Street – her first time into the centre of town – and caught the bus out towards Sea Point. The drive in the bus was a welcome diversion, the scenery beautiful, the salt-laden air invigorating. By the time she had climbed to the *dorp* the outline of the mountain and Lion's Head were visible again. Children were playing cricket on the green while older folk rested against the trunk of the Cape Beech tree, just as they had done since her childhood; she waved to them but kept walking. Getting closer she felt a sudden nervousness – she hoped that seeing Miriam would not be upsetting.

Sixteen

Skill'd to retire, and in retiring draw
Hearts after them tangled in amorous nets.

Paradise Regained (1671)
John Milton 1608–1674

Finally, she could see Hannah's house – whitewashed walls and zinc roof. A figure in a fez, obviously Mr Essop, sat on the *stoep*.

"Hello Mr Essop," Ursula called, as she neared the intent figure.

Mr Essop started, "Miss Ursula!" he exclaimed, looking up from his newspaper. "Mercy me, where you come from?"

"I'm not expected – I've come to see Nana."

"I am sorry Miss Ursula, Hannah is not here" he replied, folding his newspaper and rising with difficulty; the wide *sambalbroek* he wore did not conceal the thinness of his legs. "She has gone to do her mending work and she take Miriam with her."

"Oh dear, I should have written," she said regretfully. "Please will you tell her I came, Mr Essop."

"*Ja,* of course, Miss Ursula. But Hannah will return *just now* – you must stay for a pot of *tee*."

"Thank you," she said quietly, "I'll come another time."

"Miss Ursula, excuse me, but Hannah not forgive me if you leave with not a thing to sustain you. Will you not have a pot of *tee*?"

Ursula considered for a moment, she did not want to appear

ungrateful, "You're very kind, Mr Essop, I think perhaps a little tea will revive me."

"*Ja*, I too find *tee* refreshing. Please take a seat," he said gesturing to one of the wide rattan chairs on the *stoep*, "I will bring some."

Ursula sank into the chair and felt a wave of tiredness. It was pleasant to sit and look around at such familiar surroundings but it made her nostalgic.

Mr Essop returned, walking stiffly, carrying a pot of tea on a tray with great care. "Here we are, Miss Ursula," he said, depositing it on a small box between them.

"Thank you Mr Essop, but really, you must call me Ursula."

"When I courting Hannah I refer to you as Miss Ursula," he replied, taking his weight on his arms as he lowered himself into his chair. "To call you anything else will not feel right. But you must call me Ebrahiem."

She laughed, "Ever since I learnt you'd been courting Hannah I've thought of you, and I know you, as Mr Essop. So, thank you, I think I like to call you Mr Essop."

"*Ag* well, in that case we are both satisfied," replied Mr Essop, nodding his head and smiling.

They sat for a while in companionable silence, sipping their *rooibostee*. Then Mr Essop leant forward, "May I offer you my commiseration for the loss of your sweet child, Miss Ursula, it sadden us most particularly."

While acquaintances spoke in euphemisms and made trite comments of sympathy, Ursula could remain composed. But unexpectedly kind gestures, or words that displayed true feelings of regret, were likely to reduce her to tears. Touched by Mr Essop's sincerity, she struggled to control her feelings.

"I appreciate your kind thoughts, Mr Essop," she eventually replied, eyes cast down.

After a few more minutes silence she turned her chair a little towards him, "But you too have suffered loss, Mr Essop."

"*Ja*, indeed – my dear wife."

"Were you very angry afterwards Mr Essop?" asked Ursula, to her own surprise.

"Angry, *ja*, indeed every emotion take hold of me – bother me night and day, man. But eventually it all subside and I accept it," he sighed, "I accept it."

"But didn't you think it was unfair?"

"*Ag* well. Life is not fair. Life is life – it carry on whatever, Miss Ursula. It is like a river – sometime swift, sometime slow. Raging it wrest thing away, gently flowing it give back. If I had not lost my dear wife – I never wanted another when I have her – I not have the good fortune to marry Hannah; the great blessing of a daughter that bring. I am content," he concluded, with a benign smile.

"I don't think I'll ever be content, Mr Essop. And I don't think I'll ever believe in God again," she said forcefully. "Did you still believe in your God Mr Essop?"

"There is only one God, Miss Ursula. Myself, yourself, your husband – we are all of a different persuasion," said Mr Essop gently, "but we have the same God, Miss Ursula, we share the same God."

"Yes, of course we do, Mr Essop, you're quite right. I only meant that you might think of him differently. When I was a schoolgirl my classmates and I always thought that our religion had the one true God. After all, the nuns that were teaching us were bringing God's word to Africa and India, so we were convinced at the time. We never studied other religions and no one ever pointed out at the convent that we shared the same God with anyone but Christians."

"*Ja*, there you are Miss Ursula; that go to show that education is not always a good thing," he replied, sagely shaking his steel grey head, "if it teach how to build barriers not how to build bridges."

For a few minutes they both sat, deep in thought, until Ursula resumed the conversation, "What do you understand by God, Mr Essop. I mean, do you believe He's omnipotent in heaven on high or is He all around us, here, now?"

Mr Essop nodded, and answered without any hesitation, "I believe He is within us, Miss Ursula, in all of us; in our heart and in our head."

"I don't think He's within me – not now anyway," said Ursula, "and probably never was."

"*Ne*, to think that is to believe that you are bad, Miss Ursula," said Mr Essop earnestly, leaning forward as if to emphasize his words. "And you are not bad – I know this from Hannah – you have love in your heart and you strive to do what is right."

Ursula did not reply, but frowned in concentration. After a few seconds silence she said, "So you still believe in God, Mr Essop, even after your wife passed away?"

"*Ja*, I do."

"Well I cannot believe in a God who lets a beautiful, innocent little child like Lulu, die." Her face crumpled and she drew out her pocket handkerchief and blew her nose.

"*Ag*, Miss Ursula; God does not *make* terrible thing happen," he said looking at her with a kind expression on his deeply fissured face, "he does not *let* them happen, man. They do happen. In every place unfortunate event occur – flood, fire, famine. We cannot blame these thing on God."

Ursula looked at Mr Essop: he sat very still – the flat of his hands on his thighs, his long fingers spread out like a palm leaf, a calm expression on his sallow face. What a thoughtful man he is, she decided, an educated man. I can see now why Nana holds him in such regard. But I don't know if I understand him; I don't think I can agree with him. Tired, she drew on her gloves and straightened her hat.

"I've been bothering you with too many questions, Mr Essop," she said rising. "I think perhaps I'd better be off. Thank you for making me tea."

He rose too, slowly, gave a small bow and said, "It a pleasure, Miss Ursula."

"Goodbye Mr Essop, and thank you. Thank you for talking to me."

"Goodbye, Miss Ursula."

Ursula walked back down towards the bus deep in thought, turning over in her mind everything she and Mr Essop had talked about. When she reached the children she stopped for a minute to watch them play and hear them laugh, regret and sorrow washing over her. Mr Essop is right about some things, she thought, life carries on whatever. Here, for these children, nothing has changed – today is like yesterday, tomorrow will be the same.

December came and with it the burning sun, long summer days and short-sleeved blouses. The ancient apple tree in the small garden had wept pale blossom and campanulas had hung their heads, silent bells, in tune with Ursula's mood. But, as if to mock her melancholy, the hydrangea bushes concealed in the shade produced monstrous blue heads on Christmas Eve. Christmas passed – a cheerless festival for David and Ursula – and they did not turn out to watch the noisy New Year celebrations as they had always done previously. And so the year began with no expectation of happiness for Ursula although, since she had visited Mr Essop, she felt the beginnings of a more positive attitude.

She could not forgive Jessie, nor cease blaming herself, but these emotions were no longer so destructive. Her concentration improved, her depressions decreased in intensity, and Ursula began to feel that she had judged Meg harshly. In encouraging Ursula to embrace her faith she was surely sincere. After all, Meg's belief in God had to be strong enough to compensate for the privations she must endure. And perhaps Meg had felt torn, reasoned Ursula, had found it difficult to commiserate with her at the same time as fulfilling her loving commitment to God. In solitary introspective moments Ursula questioned her own actions – had she been intractable and demanding at the convent? No longer able to remember their actual words, she began once more to think of Meg as someone to admire and emulate: it was a more comforting thought, a more comfortable memory.

As Ursula slowly became more aware of others, she noticed a change in David; it seemed to her that the patience he had shown her grew brittle, his sympathy for her less. Had his pity dissipated, she wondered, his love for her evaporated; had blame consumed them? He increasingly came home late, the smell of whisky or ale on his breath. She could not talk to him about it – dared not open the invisible sluice gate that held their feelings in check – for fear it might release a river of blame, a torrent of emotion. Was she more afraid of his accusations, she wondered, or her reactions.

Emma had always called at regular intervals to see Ursula, usually for tea at four but if David was away she sometimes joined her for luncheon or supper. Ursula had come to rely on her company. One afternoon she called with unexpected news.

"I'm going home, Ursula," Emma said as soon as they sat down with their cups of tea in the shade cast by the orange tree.

"Home – to your parents?"

"Yes, I'm afraid so, I can't fool them or myself anymore; the Tivoli is struggling – its closure is imminent."

"It's such a shame Emma and you have such talent. Couldn't you try at the Opera House?" she suggested, hoping that Emma would stay.

"I have enough talent for the Tivoli, Ursula, but not enough to compete with professional actors," shrugged Emma.

"You've always been too modest, Emma," said Ursula, wishing her friend were more pushy.

"With the hope of success one can do most things but my wonderful web of fantasy is only made of gossamer," said Emma simply, "it's worn awfully thin Ursula and it could rip apart – and then what would I be left with? And I'm fighting the battle on two fronts – father and the lack of work. I think it's best to choose to make a change in one's life before one is forced to, don't you think?" she finished.

"That's very wise of you Emma, and very decisive. You're so marvellously more sure of yourself than when I first met you."

"I think I am," agreed Emma. "It's probably because I've had to stand on my own two feet these last few seasons – have the courage of my convictions – ever since father has been a bit cool and reduced my allowance."

"He and your mother will be pleased to have you home."

"I shall miss the theatre dreadfully," replied Emma.

And I shall miss you, thought Ursula, her spirits sinking.

"You'll find something else," she said with forced conviction. "But, are you quite sure that the Tivoli might close?"

"The new Gaiety Theatre is giving it a run for its money and Abe is talking of selling up, or changing it to a bioscope, so it seems very likely. I expect David's told you all about it."

Ursula was perplexed, "David hasn't mentioned it, Emma. He hasn't said a thing about it."

"Perhaps it won't affect him," said Emma, giving Ursula's hand a reassuring pat, "or maybe he doesn't want to worry you."

"I don't know," replied Ursula, frowning. "Emma?"

"What is it?"

"David's changed, Emma – I can't say exactly how – he seems preoccupied," she said, relieved to put her fears into words. "He's often out drinking."

"The boys at the theatre mentioned they've seen him out and about in the bars."

"Do they say with whom?"

"No, no, it was general chatter that's all. They've seen him down at the harbour and thereabouts."

"But those are such shady bars, Emma. I've heard that deals are done there and there's betting and brawls." What was David doing, was he involved in something untoward, was he planning something. If only they talked as they used to, she'd know about it.

"David is probably doing business," said Emma smiling confidently, "I'm sure if you ask him he'll explain."

"Of course," replied Ursula, not wanting to admit to her changed relationship with David and their lack of communication. "I only meant that it's the sort of place with the kind of company that would appeal to him – the army scouts drink there and tell tall stories and bet on the most unbelievable things."

"David is an honourable man, Ursula, and a devoted husband. I only hope I find one as fine."

"I shall miss you dreadfully, Emma," she said taking Emma's hand, grateful to her for her unfaltering benevolence.

"And I shall miss you, Ursula dear. You must come and visit me. Please do, perhaps when David's away on one of his trips. Mother and my sisters would love to meet you and I know you'll take to my young brother. He's such a breath of fresh air – the apple of father's eye."

"I should love to meet your family, Emma, it must be such fun to be surrounded by brothers and sisters, and to have parents to advise and guide you. I'll be delighted to visit you all one day."

Ursula's conversation with Emma had not quelled her misgivings about David. She naturally turned to Hannah and wrote asking to see her – and Miriam too – suggesting they meet half way, to save Hannah such a long journey on a hot bus with Miriam. The following week, on market day, Ursula met the Sea Point bus in Adderley Street and, after the sudden pain in her chest and the initial feeling of panic at seeing the child had passed, she was able to embrace them both calmly. The three of them walked to the Company's Gardens – Miriam between them holding their hands – where they strolled around the paths for a while. They admired the beds of full-blown roses, the profusion of tall, flame-coloured watsonia spikes and the dense, dusky blue umbels of the agapanthus plants that had spread uninvited in quiet corners. On a bench in the shade Ursula unpacked the picnic she had taken and they ate the *samoosas* and gherkins, the *naartjies* and bananas on their laps and talked of domestic things. When they had finished, and Miriam searched on the ground around them for *goggas* or tumble bugs and pretty shaped leaves, their talk became less general and Hannah asked how Ursula was feeling.

"I think I'm more composed – resigned maybe a better word – but you know Nana," she replied, "the sadness is so close, it never goes away."

"*Ne*, it never go away but it get better *just now*, man" said Hannah sympathetically, immediately adding, "How is Mister David?"

"David?" Ursula had hoped to speak of David but did not expect Hannah to broach the subject.

"*Ja*, he take it very bad," replied Hannah.

Ursula hesitated before admitting sheepishly, "I'm afraid I don't really know how he is now."

"*Is it?* You don't talk, man?"

"Nana . . . I thought – no, I knew – that he was grieving too but I dared not ask him. I was desperate; it was all I could do to keep control of my own feelings, to function at all. I simply couldn't have coped with his pain too," she said, a suggestion of panic and hurt in her voice. "I think I would have drowned if his pain and mine were put together – I would never have come to the surface again."

"*Ag* well, time will help," Nana comforted, patting Ursula's leg. "Time will help."

Miriam looked up and catching Ursula's tone, brought a tiny flower bud and offered it to her with a shy smile.

"For you," she said, with her head on one side.

"Thank you Miriam," said Ursula taking it gently. Miriam smiled sweetly. "I shall take great care of it," she added, placing the small flower bud in her pocket, as Miriam returned to her hunt. "I've only just begun to realize what David's suffering might have been all this time, Nana," she continued. "He's always been so quiet about it. I suppose you think I'm very selfish."

"*Ne, ne.*"

"But I do realize it now. That he was looking after me. And as I'm beginning to understand it, he's changed," said Ursula with a look of consternation.

"*Is it?* How changed?"

"Well, he regularly comes home late."

"Mister David work hard, man."

"No, I don't think it's work – although Emma tells me that Abe is reorganizing his business. He often comes home smelling of alcohol, he goes out . . . drinking," said Ursula. She knew that Hannah did not approve of drinking but needed to unburden herself.

"*Is it?*" said Hannah frowning. "You ask him about it?"

"How can I ask him, Nana? How can I ask anything of him when he has done so much for me?" And might accuse me of so much, she thought to herself.

"Men, they keep so many feeling to themself, *rather* it come out somewhere else."

"That may be so, Nana, but I must be as patient with him as he was with me – he's never said a word of blame to me and I shall not say a word to criticize him," she said, determined to be fair; equally scared of recriminations.

"*Passop!*" warned Hannah with a shake of her head and a waggle of her finger. "You maybe stop talking about thing altogether, man. Become a habit if you not careful."

Ursula felt the truth of this and determined to be more communicative with David on subjects that were not contentious.

They packed up the remains of the picnic lunch and decided to walk to the market. There were often bargains at the market after midday and Hannah could stock up on goods to take home with her. The market was still bustling when they reached it and Ursula picked Miriam up in her arms, so that Hannah was free to make her purchases and Miriam was not tramped over. She was not a heavy child and Ursula experienced the bitter-sweet pleasure of small arms around her neck. Mats and baskets spread on the ground spilled over with vegetables and fruits; any type of these could be purchased – some locally grown, the more exotic shipped in from Port Elizabeth or Durban. Armoured fruit in weird and wonderful shapes – multi-faceted custard apples, spiky pineapples and bumpy *grenadillas* – were made into pyramids. Delicate papery-clad Cape gooseberries were piled in pans, bunches of grapes reclined on leaves, whilst enormous amputated limbs of green bananas stuck out from underneath tables. Long dull white roots, orange roots, shiny crimson *rissies*, glossy purple eggplants, bunches of fresh green leaves – all were piled high with precision to tempt buyers drunk on the surfeit of shape and colour.

When they found the tall young Indian trader with a wide, white smile that Hannah liked to buy her fruit from they stopped.

"Good day Sammy, dozen peaches please," said Hannah, opening her bag for him to place them in.

"Two pounds of apples," piped up Miriam, in a high clear voice.

"*Ja*, quite right, two pounds of apples," repeated Hannah.

The friendly young man smiled broadly at Ursula and, nodding at Miriam, said, "She quite a helper, that little *pickin* of yours."

Ursula felt a sharp pang as if she had been stabbed – and closed her eyes tight – she did not trust herself to speak. Her little *pickin*. Her little *pickin* was no more. As soon as Hannah had paid for her purchases and they had moved away from the crowd she put Miriam gently back down on the ground.

"Nana, I have to be off now," she said falteringly, as a feeling of nausea overcame her.

"*Is it?*" said Hannah looking at her with concern. "*Ja. Ag* well, I understand."

Ursula gave Hannah a quick embrace and bending down, gave Miriam a kiss and as cheerful a 'Goodbye' as she could manage. Turning rapidly she walked away in the direction of her home, wondering at the fragility of her composure, and if she would ever be master of it again.

That night David came home on time but seemed deep in his own thoughts. During their dinner – so often taken silently now – he asked her if she would like a pet.

"What sort of pet?" she asked, puzzled at such an unexpected suggestion.

She had never had a rabbit or a guinea pig as many of the girls at school had, and was sure that she would not be tempted by the offer of a parrot or a monkey that some adults she knew took such delight in.

"A chap I've been . . . seeing – cultured sort – was saying that he had just bought his mother a kitten, and there were more where it came from."

"Oh, a kitten," she said, with more interest. "I suppose that might be nice. What's it like?"

"Like the one the Polish woman next door to us had."

"A Siamese cat?" she asked, aghast. "Oh David, no. The eerie noise they make – it's like the plaintive sound of a baby crying. Please, please don't buy me one of those."

"It's all right, it was only an idea," he shrugged. "I thought it would be company for you."

"Thank you, it's a very kind thought, but that cry . . ." she said, and shivered.

David looked deflated, or was it melancholy Ursula wondered, and said nothing. Remembering her conversation with Hannah, and Emma's news, she made an effort to communicate, "David?"

"Yes?"

"There's nothing new wrong is there? Nothing wrong . . . at work . . . or anything?" she ventured.

"No. I may ask Abe for some time off, that's all. Why do you ask?"

"Emma said the Tivoli was struggling. I wondered if Abe has financial difficulties."

"There may be some changes, but Abe doesn't have any money worries as far as I know."

"That's reassuring." This was going all right, he seemed relaxed, she felt braver, "Emma says the lads have seen you in some of the bars."

"Maybe, but I only drink there when I have to. I've had enough of the company and I'm pretty tired of being insulted and called names."

"Names?" There was so much she didn't know about.

"Many and various – they're trying to rile me, to get me to give something away – *kafferboetie* is the latest," said David, as if he was talking to himself. "I put on a show of being offended, denied it of course, but I was just laughing to myself at that one. They're not to know I don't find it insulting. I'd prefer to think of myself as on the side of the native, than on theirs."

"It sounds like trouble, why do you drink there?"

"Sometimes it's the only place to get important information," replied David shortly. "And I can walk away from trouble if I need to – I don't need to prove I can fight."

"But who are these people," she asked, her worry making her bold.

David face became rigid, expressionless, apparently on his guard.

"No one you'd like," he said curtly.

His tone warned she should say nothing more; Ursula could see that he regretted talking about it. She must tread warily – she had meant to encourage him to talk but had only succeeded in making him annoyed – she would change course.

"I forgot to tell you, I met Nana today, she asked after you," she said as brightly as she could.

"Good old Hannah. Was she well?"

"Quite well, yes."

Ursula thought of Miriam but did not mention her – she felt a natural disinclination to – and he did not mention the little girl either. And as they lapsed into silence she realized that their previous easy conversations would be difficult to revive.

For the next few nights there was little opportunity for conversation – beyond normal practical enquiries – as David went out after their supper and came home late. When he came home she noticed a strong smell of tobacco on his clothes but no smell of beer on his breath. She hoped that after their conversation he may have stopped drinking in disreputable bars. Perhaps the next day she could ask – without appearing critical again – where else he went late into the evening. However, the next day David came home earlier than usual, with a very large basket and a bundle covered up with a rug.

"What have you got there," Ursula asked, as she opened the door.

"A surprise, let me come in. There," he said, gently putting the basket on the floor, "come over and take a look."

Ursula bent down and lifted a corner of the blanket, "Oh, my goodness!" she exclaimed as she uncovered a small ball of feathery fur; a little Buddha. "Where did he come from?"

"I had to see Abe and when I was waiting for him at his house I sat with Rhoda. She's got a little Pekinese dog – I've seen her with it before, she never stopped speaking to it and fondling it – that's had puppies. She couldn't find a home for this one – although she says they're wonderful company, and very affectionate – so I brought it for you."

"He's adorable – thank you so much. Look at his sooty black nose, so squashed, as if he's been at the window too long!" she said with pleasure, as she gathered the puppy into her arms. "Has he a name? We could call him Sooty."

"I think you'll find that he is a her," said David, smiling wryly.

"Then she is adorable. She can be Sukey. Hello Sukey, aren't you a funny little thing?"

"I'm glad you like her," he said, looking pleased.

"I do. Thank you, David, thank you so much," said Ursula giving him a kiss on the cheek – her first spontaneous step towards an outward show of affection, towards intimacy.

"I hope she'll be company for you," he replied, "but she may not be properly house trained yet so you must be prepared for puddles. My mother used to put newspaper on the floor of the scullery at night when she had a new puppy."

"How long will it take?"

"She should be house trained within weeks but after that you'll have to teach her to sit, and to stay and so on."

"And how long will that take?" she asked, putting the little dog on the floor.

"I reckon that if I didn't see her for three months, she'd be a reasonably well trained little dog when I did. Do you think you could manage that?"

"I'll have a go," replied Ursula with conviction. "And I'll get a book from the library on training. Yes, definitely. What do you think Sukey – shall we impress him?"

The little dog barked and jumped up against her legs. David looked relieved.

Ursula was thrilled with her new pet and more cheerful than she had been for months. Later that evening as she was settling Sukey in the scullery for the night she heard a banging noise.

"What's happening David?" she called.

"Nothing," he called back.

Ursula shut the scullery door and saw that the small bedroom door was open. They used the room for storage and David was bent over an old wooden trunk there.

"What are you looking for?" she asked.

"My heavy boots – you haven't seen them have you?"

"Not since we moved. They wouldn't be in that old kit bag of your uncle's there, would they?"

"Maybe."

"Why do you want them?"

"Ah! Here we are," he said pulling out a pair of thick leather boots, their long laces trailing, from the top of the kit bag. "They were always very comfortable. Have you put your little dog to bed?"

"Yes, but I can hear her whining. She wants to come to me."

"You mustn't take any notice of that. She'll do it for a few days but if you ignore it she'll soon stop, once she knows you're not going to come. You'll have to be firm."

"I suppose so," said Ursula wrinkling up her nose.

"Look, you go on to bed. I'll sort these things out, I shan't be long."

Lulu had been the result of David and Ursula's union – but their daughter was no more. Now that they shared a bed again Ursula – not wanting to accept David's advances, equally fearful of rejecting them and dreading explanations or recriminations – had evolved a pattern around their bedtime. If David went to bed first, she manufactured some household task and crept into bed when she was sure he was asleep. If David came to bed late and Ursula was awake, she feigned sleep and pretended not to hear the softly spoken "Ursula" or feel his touch. That night Ursula woke when David got into the bed but she pretended to sleep and did not respond to his whisper in the dark, "Ursula?"

She lay quite still.

"Ursula ... Ursula?" he whispered louder. He shook her gently but she did not move.

Was there something in the way he said her name, she wondered – an insistence, an urgency even – that had not been there before. She dismissed the thought as fanciful. He removed his hand and she heard him sigh. But yes, there had been a crack in his voice when he said her name and it might mean something more. She felt him turn on his side, away from her. It might be that he only wanted to talk, to tell her about the dog, or where he'd been going in the evenings.

"David," she finally whispered in reply.

"Never mind," he replied, in a voice inured to defeat. "Go to sleep."

She was annoyed with herself – too many minutes had passed and with it the chance to share a confidence. She would try harder next time. Soon she heard his breaths come deep and rhythmical – the sound of sleep.

When Ursula awoke in the morning she was alone in the bed and, remembering the puppy, immediately got up.

"David," she called.

He must be in the kitchen, she thought, his suit is still on his valet stand. She went to the kitchen. David was not there. In the scullery Sukey was overjoyed to see her, and she let the puppy out into the garden.

"David," she called again.

She looked about her – the shelf on which he stored his shaving kit was empty. Perplexed, she looked into the small bedroom – his uncle's kit bag was gone, the thick boots too.

"David," she said as she went to the bedroom with a feeling of heaviness, no longer expecting an answer.

In the bedroom she looked around. It looked normal. But on

the top of David's chest of drawers a thick envelope was propped against the box that held his links; "Ursula" was written on the outside. Ursula undid the flap and pulled out a small chamois leather pouch. Opening the heavy little bag, she gasped: it was full of golden sovereigns. She peered into the envelope and shook it – something jingled. Upending it, her silver chain – beautifully repaired – the small crucifix and the enamelled medal David had entrusted to her, fell into her palm. She smoothed the medal between her fingers and, as she did so, words from long ago came back to her, "If I leave again I'll take what's precious with me." Intuitively she opened the lid of his links box – the safe depository for Mister Rabbit – the small lead toy was not there. She sat on the bed, stunned.

David had gone.

Seventeen

Look into my face; my name is Might-have-been;
I am also called No more, Too late, Farewell.

A Superscription
Dante Gabriel Rossetti 1828 –1882

Ursula could not believe that David had left her. Too surprised and worried by his disappearance to do anything constructive, she went over in her mind all the possibilities as she played with her small dog throughout the day.

"He'll come home tonight as usual, Sukey, won't he. He's probably just gone on a hike or he may have gone to do a job for Abe, and forgotten to mention it. He took the boots and that's a clue. We'll stay in and wait for him shall we?"

But David had not come home by late evening. Ursula went to bed, more anxious than she wanted to admit.

She runs but she does not move. The pumping of her heart batters her chest. Blood beats in her ears, drumming like a ship's engine. And then there is water, far out of her reach she sees a billowing white, like the sail of a capsized dinghy 'LULU'

And waking in panic in the early hours, the space next to her was as empty as it had been the night before.

"Where is he – I don't understand," she moaned to Sukey, as she ate her breakfast, "he must have gone on a spree with

Duggie, or else why didn't he say? Why hasn't he left me a note – and that money, where did it come from?"

But she could think of no logical reason for such a sudden and silent disappearance and was confused and hurt, and very anxious. She took Sukey on the lead and they called in at the *winkel* on the corner where they bought their everyday provisions, but the shopkeeper said David had not been in for a few days. They walked on into town, passing all the places he might stop, the people he normally purchased his newspaper and cigarettes from, the hotels he might have called to drink in. She walked to the theatre but the doors were locked and no one was about: "Closed For Refurbishment" a notice said. She visited David's office but it too was locked up, deserted. On the third day, lack of sleep and the strain of uncertainty were causing Ursula to imagine accidents and actions too awful to contemplate for long.

She decided to visit Abe as the person most likely to know David's whereabouts. Putting on stout shoes (no bus or tram travelled in the direction she wanted) she set out to walk to Abe's house. It was over three miles across town and Ursula had only visited it once before. Determined to find it she took several wrong turns until, at last, she came upon it by chance. Tired from the search and drained with fantastic imaginings of the possible explanations, she sighed with relief. As Ursula rang the bell she noticed that the window blinds were all closed, which gave the house a blank look. The door opened only a crack and the black face of the servant that peeped around it was difficult to see in the dim interior. She held out her calling card and, leaning close, enquired if Abe was home.

"*Baas* not home, *missus*," said the servant, taking the card and reducing the crack still further.

"Do you know where he is? Could you tell me when he'll return?" asked Ursula.

"Dey is gone to Johannesburg; not know when," the servant said by way of explanation, and immediately closed the door.

Ursula, disappointed, sat on the low wall outside the wide-fronted house, her head bowed. After a few minutes she sat up. Without an address I can't write to Abe in a place as large as Johannesburg, she reasoned with herself, and if he's in Johannesburg he's not likely to know what's happened to David. No, I must try something else, that's all there is to it; I must be resolute, I won't let this beat me. She stood up and started back. Sukey, shut in the scullery by Lizzie for the duration of Ursula's outing, was delighted to see her when she returned thirsty and tired, and jumped up, yapping, against her legs. Ursula, bending down to pat the small dog – who licked her hands with pleasure – was warmed by the small dog's affection.

"I was too optimistic Sukey; I'll have to ask elsewhere tomorrow. But I'm so angry with him – fancy going away without telling me, he must know I'd be frantic – why did he do it?"

Later, as she lay alone in bed too worried to sleep, she tried to push the fear that an accident had befallen David to the back of her mind. If it was an accident someone would have come to tell me, it's not that, of course it's not. I shall have to see Duggie and I was hoping not to involve him, she decided grudgingly; still, there's nothing for it, I shall have to face him and all those associations I want to forget. But if David's gone away on work or on a gambling spree – or goodness knows what – I must know; I'm going mad with worry. She slept fitfully, and dreamt her anxious dreams.

Ursula had not heard from nor spoken of Duggie since that fateful day. Except for a neatly written letter of sympathy from Violet there had been no contact. She steeled herself for the visit in the hope that they knew something of David. She would call in the evening when Violet would be there. At seven o'clock – when they would have finished their supper – Ursula arrived at their flat.

"Ursula!" Violet exclaimed, opening the door to her, "what a surprise. Please come in, come in."

"Thank you, Violet."

"Would you care for a cup of tea?" she asked leading the way into their sitting room.

"Thank you, I had some not long ago," replied Ursula, still unsure of how she would react on seeing Duggie.

"I am about to have one myself," said Violet indicating the teapot on the stand, "do join me."

She's pleased I've come, thought Ursula, and there's only one cup, so Duggie can't be here.

"If it's no trouble then, that would be nice, thank you."

"I shall fetch another cup. Please sit down, I'll be back directly."

Ursula looked around the room – the walls were plain, decorated with a solitary picture and a few china plaques, the furnishings heavy, the chairs over-stuffed. Books were placed in tidy piles on the polished table, neatly folded mending in a basket upon the floor. The room spoke of order, but not of joy.

Violet helped her guest and herself to tea and, sitting down opposite her, asked, "And how are you Ursula, are you well?"

"Yes, I'm well Violet, it's kind of you to ask," replied Ursula. "But, I've really come to enquire if you know anything of David?"

"Of David?"

"I wondered if Duggie had seen him?" There, she'd said his name.

"Duggie has been away since . . . well, since your sad loss."

"Away?"

"He joined up," said Violet, a hint of resentment in her voice.

"Joined up?"

"They've never stopped recruiting, Ursula – in spite of the coming Union," she said, as if she were speaking to one of her pupils. "There are still skirmishes and always the possibility that the peace will be threatened before the Union's formalized; so the Cape regiments are still active."

285

"I didn't know," said Ursula, thoughtfully. She noticed Violet's raised eyebrows and added, "I mean, I didn't know that Duggie wasn't here."

David and she had never discussed Duggie's complicity that awful afternoon – they simply did not refer to him at all. Had Duggie joined up out of guilt, she wondered, to deny himself, punish himself. Perhaps Violet had no idea about Jessie and Duggie's relationship. She would think about it later, now she needed to concentrate on David.

"He took it into his head – quite unaccountably – that he must have a change, get away. But that's Duggie, never explains." Violet shrugged and continued, "You asked where David was."

"Do you know?"

"No. Has he gone away?"

"Yes, without a word," Ursula answered, and it struck her again how unbelievable it was. To leave after an argument, after angry words was understandable. But to leave without a word.

"What strange behaviour. Do you think he might have joined up too?"

"It never occurred to me, but, no, David's never been a supporter of war."

"I see," said Violet, her raised eyebrows now exchanged for pursed lips.

Ursula tried to interpret the look – Violet possibly thought David was a lily-livered objectioner.

"David's no coward," she said robustly. "He wouldn't fight but . . . he might do something else."

"Ah, one reads now and then of intelligence reports, or of scouts," said Violet thoughtfully, "and of troubles still going on in the other colonies . . ."

Violet's words were an inspiration to Ursula and she interrupted, "Of course . . . how silly of me; I'd better make other enquiries. I'm sorry, I shouldn't have bothered you." It would be just like David to volunteer as a scout; there had been his visits to the bars they frequented. "Thank you for the tea, I'm afraid I haven't time to finish it."

Violet looked annoyed, "Och, well, I trust that someone is able to furnish you with news of David," she replied, her tone now crisp, as she followed Ursula to the door. "Like Duggie, he was always one for adventure and pleasure."

Ursula wished she had not admitted that David had gone without a word and resented Violet's implication. She knew in that moment that it was not for any hedonistic reason that David had disappeared. David's character is wholesome, she reassured herself, even if his enthusiasm for causes and his willingness to take risks for excitement sometimes lead to actions not always as circumspect as they should be.

"That may be your interpretation, but it's not mine," she said. "Thank you for the tea, Violet. Goodbye."

She thinks I'm snubbing her, thought Ursula, as she hurried away, but I've got to get home and think. David may have left me but he's taken Mister Rabbit; that means he's doing something serious, something honourable.

Ursula – worried now that David may have become involved in intelligence gathering – tried to recall all the conversations she had had with him regarding his visit to Bloemfontein and Abe's friends. She remembered the first time David had been called a *kafferboetie*; it wasn't that he loved the African more than the European, he had explained to her long ago, he simply worried that a Union parliament might not safeguard natives' rights. And they had rights if anyone did. But he also insisted that Union was the only way forward. Could there be something happening to threaten the forthcoming Union as Violet had hinted. How she wished she had paid more attention in the past, taken note of his contacts.

And then again, if it was not something purely political, Ursula knew that he and Abe also discussed military actions. Just lately there had been more fighting in Namaland between the native tribes and Germans – and the Germans were winning. It was only recently in a bar that David had been called a *kafferboetie* again but she couldn't remember exactly what he had said to her. Perhaps he had criticized someone of German descent, although the insult could equally come from an Afrikaner or even an Englishman. She could not possibly figure it out; she was surmising, guessing, possibly inventing. She would have to search out the bars he frequented and enquire among the men that drank there if they had seen him – such actions would be frowned on by any who knew her and were far from pleasant, but it had to be done.

The very next day she dressed as smartly as she could and – pulling a veil down over her face to leave no one in doubt that she was a lady – went out, taking Sukey on a lead, for company not protection. At each bar she gathered her courage and forced herself to ignore the strong, stale smell of ale that emanated from the doorway. Once inside, the unwanted attention of the drinking men upset her, lascivious comments insulted her, lack of information depressed her. At each she showed David's photographic portrait and asked the same questions – do you know, have you seen? And with no success she left, as quickly as she could.

On the third day of her quest a barman recognized the photograph of David and suggested she tried a small establishment in a street not far from the dock. She found the bar in question but, receiving no help and even more lurid comments than previously, she hurried out, her face burning with indignation. She slowed to a normal pace but when she felt the presence of someone following her, she scooped Sukey up into her arms and increased her pace once more. The faster she walked, the faster the footsteps that followed her came. Finally, rounding the corner and coming on a busy street – where she felt safer – she halted and turned. She would confront whoever was following her.

A man turned the corner and halted.

"Do you want to talk to me?" she asked, standing as tall as she could – outwardly bold, inwardly trembling.

The man, tall and slim, looked over his shoulder, and then directly at her, and removed his hat.

"I know something of your husband," he said in a cultured voice that belied his working man's dress.

"Oh." Ursula was taken aback.

"Here," the stranger said, pointing with his hat to a nearby bench between the trees that lined the road, "please sit, I'll stand. Don't look at me, don't talk."

Ursula, her heart beating fast, did as he asked. The man leant against the tree beside her, looking away along the street, and lit a cigarette. The silence was torture for Ursula.

"What do you know?" she asked urgently, leaning forward, unable to wait.

"Very little – don't speak. I only tell you this because such bars are no place for a lady . . . and you'll make trouble asking around," he said, pushing his wavy sand-coloured hair back from his forehead. "You must never repeat what I say, nor refer to it with any person." He spoke severely.

"I shan't say anything," replied Ursula, "I promise."

The man turned to look at her closely. She had never before seen such cold grey eyes.

"Do you understand," he said, narrowing his eyes, "no one, no one must hear of this."

"I do understand, I shan't say anything to anybody," she assured him, desperate to hear something and fearful of what it might be.

"I can only tell you that if your husband – I say *if* – your husband returns he will either be a rich man or . . ." he hesitated.

"Or?"

"Or he will be in a box," the man finished brutally, looking away.

Ursula gasped.

"Only a brave or foolish man would agree to undertake what he has," he continued, turning to look at her intently, accusingly. "A man who has everything to gain or . . . perhaps nothing to lose?" he added with a sneer.

Ursula noticed a small scar above his eye, which became more livid as he stared at her, baiting her. She drew in her breath, his contemptuous manner made her bristle and she felt her face warm. Nothing to lose; how terrible. Had David said the accident was her fault, that she was nothing to him now, that he had lost everything dear to him. But desperate to hear more she forced herself to concentrate and ignore his insulting tone and after a minute of silence – during which the man resumed his indifferent stance – she addressed him evenly, "Do you know where he is?"

She could hear her heart beating – *tell me, tell me.*

"Travelling," he said abruptly. "There are certain factions that already suspect something's going on. And there are some that wouldn't hesitate to commit treachery if they gain any information and track him down."

The sound of revellers reached them and, furtively glancing over his shoulder, he spoke quickly, authoritatively, his insolent tone gone, "Take my advice, if you want to protect him, keep your mouth shut and go away for a while."

A group of men, their arms about each other, rounded the corner. The stranger straightened up, threw his cigarette down, ground it beneath his foot, replaced his hat and crossed the road before the group reached him. When the rowdy men had passed in front of her, Ursula glimpsed the stranger as he slipped away down a side street.

She sat for a long while with Sukey on her lap, unable to rouse herself. She knew now for certain that David was not on any spree. However, what he was involved in was not at all clear to Ursula and the address of the stranger – his ominous warnings, his threats, his sudden disappearance – all chilled her. His insinuations saddened her. What could she do; whatever she did she must not do anything to endanger David. Her anger at his unaccountable disappearance was now replaced with fear. The light began to fade and, as a gas light flickered in a nearby window, Ursula remembered that she did not know the area well. She got up and, carrying Sukey, began to retrace her steps. As the gloom deepened and gentle rain fell she stumbled and faltered in the unlit streets, progressing slowly, until she was confident of her route. But her mind raced. She tried to fathom what David was doing; confused and scared she imagined every possible – and many impossible – explanations.

That night Ursula went out into the garden and gazed at the stars. Leaves had fallen on the path and the dying flowers had faded, further bowed by the evening rain, but the air was fresh and the sky clear. Above her the arrow shape of Orion glimmered and she remembered that it was called the Bushman's compass because it always pointed north. Was David looking at the Milky Way, was he steering by the stars? She could not know. From her pocket she took a small packet of cigarettes and a box of matches that she had found in a drawer; I shall try one, she decided, and perhaps many miles away David will think of me as I think of him. She might will him back. She lit it as she had seen him do, and took tentative puffs. She did not enjoy the sensation, but as she watched the smoke waft upwards in the night sky, she prayed to the stars that Mister Rabbit would protect him and bring him back to her.

After a sleepless night Ursula wrote to Emma and asked if she could visit. She would go away for a while as the stranger suggested and do nothing to jeopardize David's safety – whatever he was doing, wherever he was. She threaded David's medal onto the chain, hung it around her neck and waited for Emma's reply.

*

And Ursula went to the cemetery as usual and as she quietly wept she hoped that Lulu, somewhere, high in the heavens above her, was watching over David, guiding him home.

When Ursula received Emma's letter inviting her to come, she took two golden sovereigns from their hiding place under the floorboards and left her forwarding address with Lizzie, in the event that David might return in her absence. Putting Sukey in a basket, with Lizzie to help her with her luggage, they went into town where she caught the train to Stellenbosch. Ursula intended to be away for a month by which time she hoped that anyone interested would have ceased to enquire after David's whereabouts. Emma came in her mother's buggy to meet her from the station – her father drove the car, she explained, and it was for only for high days and holidays.

"But I think this is lovely, Emma, we'll go slower and I'll be able to see more," said Ursula, as the driver helped them into the buggy.

Stellenbosch – originally built by the Dutch – was a small elegant town nestled in a verdant valley. Abundant trees provided pleasing shade and everywhere gardens, separated by hedges, added a green lushness. Amongst the greenery, partially concealed villas were glimpsed, their blinds drawn, blossoming shrubs in pots by the green painted front doors. Everywhere there were freshly painted fences and pristine white walls, well-tended shrubs and neatly edged beds that reflected the residents' love of order and the pride they took in their homes.

Their route followed the Eerste River and Ursula looked down into the pebble lined stream, low after lack of summer rain. On the opposite bank she noticed a small boy fishing and thought how perfectly he completed the bucolic picture. They crossed the stone bridge over the river towards Somerset West and, as the Hottentots Holland Mountains gradually came into view, she could see manicured rows of vines, like the teeth of a comb, following the curved scalp of the hills that surrounded her.

"I expect you'll meet everyone straight off at tea-time," explained Emma, as they drove along towards the farm. "Bunty, she's sixteen, short and plump like father, except she's a very jovial character. And Juliet, she's twenty and a bit of a blue stocking – or would be if she were allowed – is tall and willowy and as quiet as Bunty is noisy, so you'll know them straight off. Then there's Freddie. Generally Freddie is just Freddie; at twelve he's a law to himself. He's the only boy I know not to be schooled in England but his time is up, I'm afraid, he's to go next year; father fears he's turning native. Up to now, I think father was so pleased to finally have a son and heir that he let him get away with things we . . . anyway, you'll see for yourself," she finished.

"Is there anything else I should know, Emma, I mean about house rules or anything?"

"No, no. I'll show you everything."

"And Sukey?" asked Ursula, steadying the basket that held her little dog.

"Mother adores lap dogs; she'll be quite happy for Sukey to sleep in your room – it's not as if she's a hunting dog, father doesn't allow them in the house. But there is one thing," said Emma looking at Ursula apologetically, "it's probably best to agree with what father says at first – he is a funny old thing, a bit old-fashioned, thinks women should, well, you know . . ."

"Don't worry Emma, I shan't do anything to frighten the horses," she replied, intrigued to meet this old gentleman.

The house stood alone – a handsome and imposing whitewashed building in the Cape Dutch style – surrounded by a wide gravel carriage drive, flanked by a coach house and stables; large barns and small cottages ranged beyond, where several young native children played in the dirt. As the buggy drew up,

Mrs Gibson and her daughters came out and invited Ursula into their home.

Stepping into the enormous hallway she drew in her breath, impressed with the unexpected simple grandeur of it. The room was sparsely furnished, the superior quality of the pieces obvious. A handsome teak screen divided this room into *voorkamer* and *agterkamer*. Looking through the pair of double doors in the centre of the screen, Ursula could see a door corresponding to the front door at the farther end of the room. The upper half of the door was open and framed an idyllic country scene.

That evening Mr Gibson was dining out, and so the rest of the family ate in the dining room – the *agterkamer* – without him. During the meal Ursula noticed that Mrs Gibson displayed the innocence and sweet sparkle that Emma sometimes did, as she recalled the gay time she had as a girl in Wynberg. She decided that in her youth Mrs Gibson must have looked like Emma but now it seemed that someone had taken an India rubber and blurred her fragile outline, dulled her delicate colour. Mrs Gibson's daughters encouraged her – quite obviously not for the first time – to recount how her father had thought her first ball dress too daring. They begged her to tell them all the details of the parties and balls she had attended; which flowers she had chosen for her hair, what ribbons for her gowns.

After dinner, as they had a cup of tea in the drawing room, Emma played childhood favourites on the piano. Later, the eldest among them played bezique – whilst Bunty and Freddie watched and advised – and Mrs Gibson served sweet Constantia wine from her father's cellar. Ursula basked in the *bonhomie* of colonial, upper-class family life.

The following day, Sunday, a very large luncheon was served; it was the first time Ursula had met Mr Gibson, but as he ate steadily and heartily they did not have an opportunity to get acquainted. He excused himself from the table as soon as he had finished, and Freddie soon followed suit, so Mrs Gibson suggested those remaining retire to the drawing room. The drawing room opened off the dining room and was generous in proportion, the ceiling high, the windows many and tall, the chimney piece wide. But the furnishings – cluttered by contrast with the hall and dining room – gave it a comfortable air.

The women immediately took up their pursuits: embroidery from the work table, cards from the games table, a book from a pocket and a scrapbook from a drawer of the bureau. Ursula noticed that everyone seemed to have a chair that was habitually theirs and a unique method of approaching their recreation; Mrs Gibson was tentative, Bunty ebullient, Juliet pensive, Emma calm and organized – the scissors and paste she needed placed carefully by her side on the bureau. Ursula took a book – chosen for its binding of springbok skin as much as for its title – from one of a pair of handsome bookshelves that stood on either side of the chimney piece and sat with it on an upright chair near one of the windows. These looked out onto a broad tiled *stoep* shaded by a pergola of vines and, as the day was unseasonably warm, the windows were fully open to let in any breeze there might be. As Mrs Gibson sewed she talked steadily to her daughters, and asked polite questions of Ursula. She thought that their life was a blissful one and wondered if all such families were as united and benignant as this.

However, instead of reading, Ursula admired the garden where a wild almond tree stood on the lawn, most of its pale petals now covering the ground from the wind of the night before. The garden – with its edged beds, clipped shrubs and colourful bedding – looked like a page from a picture book to her. Ruminating, she wondered how often it was that the tree with truly delicate flowers had the sharpest thorns, the sweetest scented bush the most poisonous berries; how perfection and beauty in anything could hide pain and ugliness. Sadness washed over her as she thought of their garden in *Oranjezicht* and how a calm and green garden had concealed a cruel and black danger.

And as Ursula, in melancholy mood, absorbed the tranquillity and beauty of the scene she saw a small black boy creep around the side of some outhouses and poke gingerly in the borders there. He then ventured onto the blossom strewn lawn disturbing the white surface with his feet, parting the petals with his hands, desperately casting about – a fly caught in a jug of milk. The nearer he came to the *stoep* the more nervous he appeared. Ursula started as somebody bellowed and the boy, more startled still, jumped to attention.

"Hey! Boy! What on earth do you think you're up to?"

Mr Gibson burst out from some shrubs and came striding across the lawn towards the house, scattering petals like fluttering confetti, his white cotton jacket showing signs of his exertion. The boy, who looked no more than ten or eleven years old, stood still and put secret pink palms together in an attitude of prayer.

"Well?" continued Mr Gibson, stepping up onto the *stoep* and turning to face the boy. "I've been following you creeping about and this is where you lead me," he said, clasping his hands behind his back. "What are you doing here, boy?"

The boy wore no hat, his shirt was washed of all colour, his shorts patched. He lowered his plum pudding head and looked at his feet; he was *kaalvoet* but, ingrained with pale dust to well above his ankles, his feet gave the impression of being clad in a pair of boots.

"Answer me. Or shall I have to whip it out of you?" Mr Gibson continued brusquely. "Look at me boy, what are you doing here?"

The boy lifted his head and rolled his huge eyes upwards until they looked liked hard boiled eggs. He lowered his arms to his sides, and held them rigidly, but still he did not speak.

Ursula found the scene very discomfiting; Mr Gibson was bullying the boy, who was obviously too scared to talk. She stood up and put her head out of the window.

"I think he was looking for something, Mr Gibson," she ventured.

Mr Gibson turned and glared at Ursula.

"Excuse me?" he said shortly.

"I, I said, I think he's looking for something," said Ursula, surprised at Mr Gibson's tone. "I don't think he was doing anything wicked."

Mr Gibson fixed Ursula with a stony stare.

"I will thank you not to interfere," he replied curtly.

Ursula, embarrassed, felt her cheeks warm; as a guest had she overstepped the mark, she wondered. Resuming her seat she looked around at the now silent women in the room and was relieved that no one was looking at her accusingly. Mrs Gibson had physically shrunk in her seat, her eyes down, her needle forcefully piercing the shawl she embroidered. Emma, concentrating closely on the scrap book she was filling, jabbed hard at the decoupage flower she was sticking. Bunty – a half finished game of patience laid out on the table before her – rapidly shuffled and reshuffled the cards in her lap, her nose wrinkled up and her eyes screwed tightly shut. Juliet, who sat on the chair next to Ursula, had shut her book and with her eyes closed and head laid back on the antimacassar appeared to be asleep except for a slight movement of her jaw – as if she ground her teeth.

Again Ursula was distracted by Mr Gibson's strident tones.

"Well boy?" Mr Gibson leant forward with his hands on his hips, his face red, chin stuck out, moustache quivering. "You have to the count of three and then if you've not answered we'll go over to the sheds and beat it out of you; *donder* you, do you understand that lingo perhaps? One . . . two . . ."

The child, his eyes stilled rolled up, opened his mouth, "*Umnumzana*, me . . ."

"What was that? Spit it out."

"Me . . . me . . . ," he stuttered.

Ursula, plucking up courage, was wondering what she could say to help the boy when the door to the drawing room burst open and admitted Freddie, out of breath and panting.

"Hello Mother," he blurted out, as the door slammed behind him, "have you . . ."

"Freddie?" Mr Gibson's voice rang out, interrupting him.

"Oh hello Father, I didn't see you out there," he said as he reached the open window. "Jacob – there you are; I've been waiting by the sheds for you to find my *schietertji* and bring it down."

"What is going on, Freddie?" demanded his father, scowling.

"I asked Jacob to find my catapult for me," said Freddie, climbing out of the window. "I was in such a rush this morning, with so much to carry down before church, I dropped it and didn't have time to come back for it."

"You told him – him – to come up to the house for it?"

"*Ja*, we're off shooting; Jacob uses the catapult and I use the gun," Freddie answered, looking at his father with wide-eyed innocence.

"Well, you've caused quite a palaver, you and this damned little blighter, digging about all over the place," said Mr Gibson, looking thwarted. "If he'd answered me I'd have known the score."

"Yes Father. You probably gave him a *schrik* that's all," said Freddie in an off-hand way, shrugging his shoulders. "Jacob's a bit *doormekaar* sometimes but he's a good *ou*, really he is."

Mr Gibson glowered.

"Better cut along sharp before I change my mind," he said, between clenched teeth.

"Righto Father," said Freddie airily.

"And don't dare tell him to come up to the house again, do you hear me? Not on any account whatsoever," finished Mr Gibson with a warning wag of his finger.

"No Father." Freddie winked at Jacob and grabbed his arm, "Come along Jacob, we'll find the *schietertjie* on the way."

Mr Gibson watched them run across the grass.

"Boy doesn't even speak proper English any more," he grumbled.

After a further minute he tore his glance away from them and, scowling fiercely in Ursula's direction, turned along the *stoep* and soon appeared in the drawing room, swearing bitterly.

"Bloody mission school blacks!" he said forcefully, looking at Mrs Gibson.

"Samuel says he's very willing, dear," said Mrs Gibson, in a conciliatory tone, sitting up a little straighter now.

"Willing! Willing to make mischief more like," he said vehemently, stomping out of the room and banging the door.

There was an almost audible sigh as the women were left alone again – no one mentioned the incident with Jacob – and resumed their pursuits. Ursula opened her own book as she was not yet ready for conversation, but neither could she concentrate on the text in front of her. She assumed that such outbursts must be common, and wondered how the women managed to tolerate Mr Gibson's boorish and unfair behaviour; and why none of them had come to aid her.

Soon Ursula and Emma made their excuses and went up to Emma's room, where they settled themselves on the *chaise-longue* to talk of personal things.

"Now, it's about time you told me what's happened with David, Ursula, it's all very intriguing," Emma said.

"There's not much to tell; he's gone away without a word and I don't know why. It's very upsetting, Emma, and such a terrible strain. If I tell you my thoughts you won't mention it to anyone, will you?" she begged.

"I won't tell a soul, dear, but you must talk about it if it helps."

"I've gone over all the possibilities in my mind until I'm dizzy with them, Emma. And still I really have no firm idea. He may have gone on a mission – I've no proof of course. But why else would he leave without a word? It could be something political to do with the Union – although he usually told me about that. Or I'm wondering if it's anything military; from the newspapers David leaves at home I keep up with the news and I know there's been trouble in Namaland – the Germans are trying to seize the chiefs' lands. David mutters about the reports when he's reading them but does that mean anything?"

"My poor dear, you must try and forget about all that while you're here," said Emma sympathetically. "He's probably working on some secret scheme or other for Abe and will be home safe and sound in no time. Military and political life's a closed book to me I'm afraid, so I can't hazard a guess what he could be involved in, although it's sure to be worthwhile. I'm very impressed that you know so much about such a weighty subject as politics."

"I don't Emma; I didn't care anything about government or politics till I met David. And I didn't know much about military matters and nothing at all about sport. One's naturally curious about one's husband's interests – I've simply picked up the rudiments of such things as politics from David. But you couldn't say I know much," said Ursula shrugging.

"And I'm sure he's learnt things from you too, dear."

"I suppose so. He certainly never went to a concert or a museum before he met me."

"You've learnt from each other then," said Emma with an encouraging smile.

"I'm now thinking and realizing all sorts of things about us I never thought of before Emma. Like you say, how we have different interests but somehow we want to learn from each other. How dissimilar we are, how we're responsible for different things, yet how much we consider ourselves equal. Isn't that the silliest thing, when it's no earthly use to me," said Ursula, shaking her head, "Now that it's too late, much too late," she finish abjectly.

"Come, try not to get too downhearted," replied Emma as she put her arm through Ursula's, "It's never too late. Appreciating what you have will be of use to you one day and it will all work out, I'm quite sure of it."

"I do hope you're right," replied Ursula, unconvinced.

"I'm much more sure of things since I've been back, Ursula. I've begun to see my life more clearly – because I've started to question things, look for reasons, solutions, that sort of thing. I may have no future in the theatre but I can't go on living here like this either; if I don't escape I shall only ever be a daughter," said Emma, looking defeated, "do you know what I mean? Father is so forceful that eventually I'll end up completely under his thumb."

"So what will you do?"

"It's time I thought about marriage – don't you think – I'm quite sure that's the answer."

"Have you someone in mind?"

"No . . . *there's the rub!* Stellenbosch is so small there are no candidates whatsoever."

Ursula had always believed that being fatherless was a disadvantage, yet now it occurred to her that no father of class would have allowed his daughter to marry a man like David; a man with no money, no prospects and of a different religion. To be thwarted in her own choice of husband would have been anathema to her. Ah, but how I'd love to thwart Mr Gibson, she thought. I must help Emma to come up with something practical.

"Let's think of a course," she said. "You need a large metropolis where there are excellent theatres and concerts . . ."

"Yes, somewhere where there are numerous handsome men who love the stage and music as much as I do," interrupted Emma with a clap of her hands. "And they must enjoy literature and be capable of taking care of me and standing up to father."

"An essential requirement. You should travel, Emma." Ursula liked the idea of Emma escaping, "Go to Paris!"

"I hear the theatres are a bit risqué there. What about New York?"

"No, they've simply transported their morals and manners from the old world; they're just like us – copying and learning it all from somewhere else," said Ursula, shaking her head. "What you want is tradition, culture – you must go to the root of it; it will have to be London."

"London it is then. Now the only problem is . . ." said Emma in a confidential whisper leaning closer to Ursula, "how to convince father."

"We shall have to be subtle; have you any relatives there?"

"Bags of them."

"That's it then – out with your writing case, it's time to forge links."

Eighteen

*No passion so effectually robs the mind of all its
powers of acting and reasoning as fear.*

On the Sublime and Beautiful (1756)
Edmund Burke 1729–1797

Bunty had offered to share a bedroom with Juliet – they had done so as children – in order that Ursula could use hers. Ursula had never before stayed in a bedroom so large or so pleasant and was happy to spend most of her mornings there. A mahogany four poster bed was hung with sprigged cotton curtains, the bed covered with a white crocheted spread, the window dressed with white muslin. Leaning on the windowsill, she would try to spot the houdihou bird as it searched for food between the ferns and nerines that grew under the shade of the shrubs in the beds below. From her vantage point, Ursula could see the *mossies* flutter down in a crowd to steal grain from the chickens. She watched the servant cleaning the copper pans on the *stoep,* rubbing them until they shone; the cook test the medlars to see if they were soft, and pluck the ripe figs that grew against the wall of the chicken yard. And she observed the experienced *volkies* as they moved up the rows of vines in the clear early autumn air, carefully inspecting the grapes – bunch by bunch – that grew in neat parallel lines on the bare stony slope below the house.

Sometimes, the sight of everything so peaceful and perfect depressed Ursula. The horror of Lulu's death, the pain of her loss, the anxiety of David's disappearance overwhelmed her and

303

on such days – after the servant had done her room – she would crawl back under the coverlet and stay there, hibernating, until she heard the bell for lunch. Generally, however, to avoid this downward spiral she tried to keep her mind busy. She penned letters and wrote up her diary seated at the small table and, as she did so, shared her thoughts and fears with Sukey, the patient and sympathetic companion at her feet. Resting on the day bed, Sukey on her lap, she immersed herself in novels to blot out unpleasant thoughts. Emma leant her *Middlemarch* which she found thought provoking and *Mansfield Park* which she thoroughly enjoyed. Juliet leant her *The Iliad of Homer* which – flattered by Juliet's opinion of her ability, and vain enough to try to live up to it – she valiantly struggled on with. At luncheon she agreed to take part in any activity the family arranged for the afternoon – whether croquet or badminton, rambles or drives.

Over a week passed which Ursula found pleasant when Mr Gibson was absent but strained when he was present. After one particularly difficult dinner conversation, when Mr Gibson rudely told Ursula that she did not know what she was talking about, Emma apologized to her. "It seems that the more successful father's become, the more he expects to be obeyed – he wants his own way and he thinks he has a right. The fact is that correspondingly, he's less inclined to be forgiving,

'And earthly power doth then show likest God's
when mercy seasons justice.'

– sadly this redeeming quality is not alive in father."

Ursula, unconsciously smoothing the medal that hung around her neck between her fingers, thought of the men that had worked so hard trying to achieve African enfranchisement – successful men who had used their power to others' advantage – and she felt a glow of pride that David had helped them, no matter how modestly.

"It's sad that your father's success hasn't improved his character," she said thoughtfully.

"No, it hasn't in the least I'm afraid."

"And success – wealth – is power, isn't it?"

"I suppose it is," admitted Emma. "And we've all – all except Freddie – got rather into the habit of doing as father bids. It's simply been easier and less painful."

"But the easy way isn't always the right way, is it?" suggested Ursula tentatively, remembering Emma's lack of support and her own feeble efforts to aspire to David's principles.

"No. One shouldn't let bullies win. In future when I hear father picking on someone I'll try my best to be more courageous Ursula, I will, really. But, unfortunately, I've always been aware that if I challenge him about decisions that affect myself it would be poor mother that would suffer. She can't escape like us girls."

"Poor Emma," said Ursula, putting her arm around her friend's shoulder, "dear Emma."

Emma had not led the charmed life that she had always imagined; her father was a dictatorial and unpleasant man. She remembered what a close shave Jacob had at his hands and hoped that Freddie would continue to protect him, just as Emma protected her mother. Ursula knew that Emma was not as strong as herself but thought that she was admirably more selfless.

Throughout her visit, the presence of Lulu never left Ursula – in dazzling sunshine, in deepest shade, in convivial company or quiet solitude; Lulu was her shadow, part of her, invisibly attached, always there when she paused. As conventional family life – a revelation to Ursula and no longer held in such reverence – began to pall, she started to long for home. Walking together one afternoon Juliet suggested Ursula read the book she had just completed herself, *The Story of an African Farm*; she felt that the issues in the novel would interest Ursula as much as they did herself.

But it was the author's name that caught Ursula's attention – it was familiar: Schreiner. She couldn't concentrate on what Juliet was saying. Her mind having so recently dwelt on David's associates she remembered the names of Abe's friends with sudden clarity – Schreiner and Jabavu, the lawyer and the journalist. Could they be the clue to his whereabouts, she wondered, was this her chance to trace David? She picked up Sukey and carried her in order that they could make their way back to the house faster than was normal. At last she could do something positive; although she had intended to stay for a month, Ursula was now determined to return home immediately. On reaching the house she explained to Emma that David might return and she wanted to be waiting. They agreed that Ursula should catch the train the following morning.

The next day Ursula – assuming a reserved, polite smile – thanked Mr Gibson for his hospitality.

"I should be delighted if any of your family care to call on me when they're in Cape Town," she added.

"I do not think that likely, Mrs Lewis, we are very satisfied with Stellenbosch," Mr Gibson replied shortly. "If you will excuse me, I have matters to attend to," and without waiting for a reply he turned towards his study.

"And thank you, Mrs Gibson, for all your kindness," said Ursula, with a genuinely wide and warm smile. "I hope you give lots of parties for the girls and perhaps have the chance to dance a little yourself."

"Yes Ursula, that is indeed a charming thought. We have so enjoyed your visit, you will come again I hope and wake us sleepy heads up."

"Of course she will Mother," interjected Emma, "or we shall visit her. Come Ursula," she continued, picking up Sukey's basket from where it had been placed near the door, "I'm driving to the station with you."

"Goodbye Ursula," chorused the women.

"Goodbye everybody," Ursula kissed all three, "and please say goodbye to Freddie for me. Goodbye!"

She was happy to be leaving, and hopeful.

Ursula was relieved to reach home; Lizzie seemed pleased that she was back and Sukey snuffled around the furniture, and wagged her tail. But that night, alone in their bed again, her nightmare recurred.

She calls 'Where's Lulu?' Jessie, dressed in black, shrugs. She runs past her through the trees. But there are many trees. She bumps into them. She cannot see her way. She will not get there. She will not get there in time. And now she is on the grass. Running. But she moves in slow motion. 'Lulu Lulu' she calls. 'David, David.' But her voice is silent. She cannot find them. Fear constricts her throat and stifles her breath.

And choking, she woke and felt the empty space beside her. How she missed the comfort of David's arms close around her, his body to embrace. She pulled the bolster down in front of her and slept with it, clutched to her, close.

With Abe far away Ursula would have to find out what she could about his friends without his help. She would ask at the newspaper offices, they would be most likely to know the movements of such well-known figures. But it took only a morning to discover that William P. Schreiner was still in England and John Tengo Jabavu was in Natal; the first she could not contact, the second she dared not. Her enquiries could not be confidential at such a distance and might endanger David. Bitterly disappointed, she knew that if David was in Natal she had no option but to patiently wait.

However, over the following few weeks, unable to do anything practical to find David, Ursula's behaviour became more erratic. Without an obvious trigger, uncontrollable anger would erupt and when it did so she slammed doors and banged books down hard on the table; just as quickly, her anger at Lulu's death and David's disappearance abated. In its place she picked at her fingers or plucked at her clothes, devastated by the loss of her child and racked by anxiety for David's safety. One day – after screaming uncontrollably at Lizzie for some minor mistake and obsessively pulling at Sukey's ears until she yelped – Ursula realized that her emotional reactions were affecting her ability to function normally and act rationally. There was no-one now to shield her, no-one to help her – she must take herself in hand; she needed purpose and regulation. Aware that there were insufficient duties to fill her time, she decided to find work that would not only keep her occupied and get her out of the house, but also provide an income. Ursula did not want to use the sovereigns – she did not know where they were from – and she preferred to keep them for an emergency; she did not put into words what such an emergency might be.

Ursula and Bernard had kept in touch over the years and she wrote to him and arranged to visit his office. He had been promoted to manager and was delighted to see her and demonstrate his elevated position. She was delighted to be amongst old friends.

"So, you're after some occupation while David's away, Ursula," he said when she explained that she was looking for employment.

"If possible Bernard; it's so boring sitting at home, twiddling my thumbs."

"How long will this business trip of David's keep him away?"

"A month or so, I think. It may be longer," she said, groaning inwardly; it was all too true.

"Well we have an awful rush on at the moment," he said thoughtfully. "It would certainly get me out of a fix if you could step into the breach, even for a little while."

"Of course I can, thank you Bernard. May I start immediately?" asked Ursula, relieved to have found an occupation.

"Absolutely; tomorrow if you like – all the sort of stuff you did formerly. And perhaps as David's away you might like to go to the odd concert with me," he said hopefully, "what do you think?"

"Bernard, isn't it time you found a sweetheart to go to such things with?" She really did not feel like attending events.

"They're slippery things, Ursula; you think you've got one, then before you know it they've wriggled away – taken up with some rich or clever cove."

"Perhaps you've walked out with the wrong sort in the past, Bernard. I must tell you – a few weeks ago I went to Stellenbosch to visit Emma."

"By Jove, she's gone already has she?" said Bernard, sounding shocked. "I meant to see her before she sloped off. See what I mean Ursula, they all desert me, even old friends."

"I only mention it because Emma may come down and visit and if she does perhaps I can persuade her to bring her sisters. If there are enough nice girls about perhaps you'll catch one."

"The very next time I think I've a chance with a girl, I'll come to you and David for advice on how to keep her keen," he said, smiling.

"Bernard, I really don't think we can be considered experts on the subject," replied Ursula wryly.

The next morning she left Sukey to be cared for by Lizzie and started at the office. Bernard's gentle and simple character and the repetition of undemanding tasks soothed her frayed nerves. Whilst there was still warmth in the late summer sun she walked to work and caught a tram only if it was raining. After work – by the time she had reached home, walked Sukey, and cooked her supper – she was weary enough to fall asleep immediately. But instant sleep is no guarantee of uninterrupted sleep and Ursula, often waking up in the early hours, or as the day dawned, would feel a soft breath play on the nape of her neck, a warm dry palm stroke her. On these occasions she would rise and in the chest of drawers find the familiar crumpled shirt and pressing it to her face, inhale it: his smell, him. Returning to bed she would sleep again, her cheek resting on David's shirt.

Emma wrote to say that her mother was planning her annual visit to the Rosebank Agricultural Show. Mr Gibson had arranged a shooting trip for Freddie and was unable to accompany her; Mrs Gibson, Bunty and Emma would therefore come by train and Emma wondered if Ursula might like to join their party when they changed trains at Cape Town. Ursula wrote to accept – relieved that she would not see Mr Gibson – and asked if she could invite Bernard to accompany them. Emma replied that it was an excellent idea, the arrangements were agreed and on the intended day the weather co-operated with no cloud in the sky.

Ursula and Bernard waited at the train station for Emma and her family to arrive and when they did – after warm greetings and introductions – they all boarded the train for Rosebank. A woman with a small boy in a blue smock sat beside Ursula in the carriage and a moment of sheer panic took possession of her – a little blue jacket with a pocket – and she had to take deep breaths to control her emotion; she was glad that nobody noticed. The conversations around her were animated and Bunty, a naturally open and friendly girl, soon had Bernard deep in conversation.

"Mother, Mr Atkins intends to go onto Rondebosch whilst we're at the show," Bunty said, "he's going to see Mr Rhodes' old house and the animals on the farm there. He's invited me to join him."

"I had thought you wanted to see the entries at the show, Bunty, and all our old friends," replied Mrs Gibson incredulously.

"But I've seen them every year, Mother, and I've never been to *Groote Schuur*," pleaded Bunty.

"I really don't know if it is a good idea Bunty," Mrs Gibson replied unsurely, looking from Bunty to Emma.

"Mother," said Emma, placing her hand on Mrs Gibson's arm, "do you remember how you enjoyed this part of the country when you were Bunty's age? It would be wonderful for her to see it when she has one of Ursula's oldest and most dependable friends to escort her."

"If you put it like that dear I am sure it will be quite all right," said Mrs Gibson without further thought. "We're nearly at Rosebank Station, so goodbye Bunty, goodbye Mr Atkins. We will see you back here at tea-time, in the refreshment tent at four," she finished, collecting up her parasol.

Goodbyes were exchanged all round and Bernard jumped down onto the platform and handed each one of them out of the carriage.

"The refreshment tent at four, then," Mrs Gibson repeated as she disembarked.

Bernard nodded, "I shall take good care of your daughter, Mrs Gibson."

Mrs Gibson and the girls climbed the hill from the station and passed through the turnstiles into the packed Show Grounds of the Agricultural Society. Whilst taking a light luncheon in the large marquee they discussed their preferences with the help of a programme of events. Mrs Gibson – observing from experience that one would have no energy for anything but tea once one had tackled the rest of the show – suggested that they visit the indoor exhibits first. Several tents were filled with tables covered in well-starched linen cloths displaying a variety of top-class vegetables and fruits, preserves and pickles, plants and flowers. Sheds of various sizes had bulbs and packets of seeds, tools and labels for sale. All were briefly visited in turn.

But it soon became clear to Ursula that this part of the proceedings was first and foremost a social event for the likes of Mrs Gibson, and probably the last one of the summer season. All the ladies they met were dressed to impress – the frilliest muslin dresses, the largest of hats, the prettiest parasols; some of the gentlemen wore boaters to complement their light cotton suits, others Panamas and dark suits – their watch chains swinging, their moustaches rigid. And here and there a military officer proudly displayed his spotless uniform, a woman rather tastelessly her sparkling stones. Mrs Gibson greeted old friends and acquaintances with undisguised pleasure and dedicated more time to exchanging news than to viewing the entries and exhibitions. Whilst the Governor and his lady judged the produce entries, Mrs Gibson reluctantly agreed to have a turn around the remainder of the show deriving courage from the rousing rendition issuing from the bandstand.

Between the tents and sheds, in small livestock enclosures, were enormous sows, their squirming piglets attached like limpets. In others, indifferent thick-coated sheep stood by as their spindly- legged lambs pushed their heads between the rails and tried to nibble ladies' skirts or children's fingers. In a central enclosure a large bull led by a proud breeder strutted and lumbered around the ring whilst the spectators, awed by the size and menace of such a large animal, ooohed as the spectacle passed them by. Bushmen and Hottentots, down for the day with their masters, did what they could to tend their livestock – squeezing between the crowd distributing bales of hay and straw where it was needed, and much of it where it was not. With so many feet, clouds of dust rose off the bare earth and covered ladies' hems and everyone's shoes with a thin red brown film; the strong, earthy smell of the animals pervaded everything and the noise and crush of the crowds made conversation impossible.

Exhausted, Mrs Gibson and the girls made their way to the refreshment tent where cucumber sandwiches and small cakes were ordered, arriving only minutes before Bunty and Bernard.

"Mother!"

"There you are Bunty, hello Mr Atkins," said Mrs Gibson with a sweet smile. "Here, sit next to me, dear – Mr Atkins there's just room for you between Ursula and Emma – and tell me all about it."

"We had a lovely time, Mother," said Bunty enthusiastically. "There are antelope and zebra on Mr Rhodes' farm and one can walk among them. And there's a zoo with lions in cages and ostriches in compounds. And all sorts of other animals and birds; Freddie would have been in his element. And we met the nicest couple, Mother, didn't we, Bernard, who gave us a drive in their smart motor up to The Woolsack – Mr Kipling's summer residence – and then back here."

"I almost wish I had come with you, dear," said Mrs Gibson without conviction, "but I've met so many old friends here that I hardly had time to view all the entries as it was."

"Mother," said Emma, leaning forward and speaking quietly to Mrs Gibson, "I think this is another one coming towards us – Mrs Collins, with her son, I think."

"Ah!" said Mrs Gibson beaming, and turning around.

A young officer accompanied a large middle-aged matron to their table.

"Cecile, how lovely to see you," the lady exclaimed. "You have met my son, Captain Collins, have you not," she continued, placing a proprietorial hand on his arm.

The officer removed his helmet; his wavy sandy hair stuck to his forehead, drawing attention to a small scar above his eye.

"Of course Georgina, although not for many many years. Allow me to introduce everyone here to you" said Mrs Gibson. "This is Emma my eldest daughter whom I'm sure you have met before, Bunty my youngest, and this is Emma's friend, Mrs Lewis, and her friend, Mr Atkins. Mrs Collins, Captain Collins."

Mrs Collins bowed, as did her son, and Bernard (who had risen when Mrs Collins approached the table) and the girls bowed or inclined their heads in return and everyone murmured their delight at the meeting. But Ursula, under the stony stare of the Captain, immediately shrank back in her seat, her face warm. Whilst Mrs Collins and Mrs Gibson exchanged family news, Ursula turned to Emma, "If you don't mind I think I'll just take another look at the exhibits."

Bernard pulled out her chair for her, "Would you like me to accompany you?" he asked politely, if not enthusiastically.

"Thank you, I don't want company," she said firmly, aware of the Captain's disapproving look. "You stay with Bunty and Emma, whilst I view the produce and flowers," she added more loudly. "Excuse me."

Ursula hurried out of the refreshment tent and into the crowd. She was mortified to meet the Captain – her anonymous informer – under such circumstances. But perhaps he had some news for her. She wandered into the produce tent and there walked up and down the aisles staring at the vegetables now proudly displaying the silver, gilt and gold encrusted certificates. "A man with nothing to lose" – he may now think she and Bernard were more than friends! Elongated tapering pods of okra lay adulterously side by side with firm fleshy pimentos; yams, like bewhiskered old men's faces, rested cheek by jowl with rotund breadfruit. She needed a more calming sight and escaped to the floral marquee. Surrounded by handsome chrysanthemums and bold dahlias, delicate criniums and beautiful roses, she wondered what part Captain Collins had played in David's disappearance.

Ursula stayed for some time in the marquee; if Captain Collins had a message for her he would know where to find her. She hoped that by her reticence in the refreshment tent she had demonstrated to the Captain that she was discreet. But he did not search her out; he obviously had no news for her. Eventually she made her way back to the family but as she entered Mrs Collins and the Captain were walking towards her; Ursula had no alternative but to stop and say farewell to the complacent mother, the sour-faced son. As they passed she heard Captain Collins murmur something to his mother and he turned back towards her. Bowing his head slightly he said, shortly, "Not good news, I'm afraid."

"What have you heard?" she asked in terror.

"Not a word; nothing. Fear the worst. Excuse me," he finished with a nod, and returned to his waiting mother.

Ursula felt that he had purposely given her no chance to converse with him or to question him, and no opportunity to tell him that she had kept his confidence. Nor to tell him how difficult it had been not to share his information with anyone – to have no relief, to have no comfort – and to have no chance to defend herself. And finally he had peremptorily left after ominous and negative words.

Mrs Gibson had been able to procure seats on the wooden benches of the small grandstand, so after tea the whole party took their places to watch the extensive programme of events that were due to take place in the ring. Beautiful *schimmelblauw* horses went through their paces and energetic dogs rounded up flocks of sheep; knights put on a medieval display of tilting and jousting and a falcon expertly caught his prey. These events all drew an appreciative response from the crowds that jostled for space around the ring but it was the competition between the teams of mules pulling the wagons with such gusto, that received

315

the most applause; the crowd clapped and shouted, cheered and whistled. But the pleasure of the day out had been spoilt for Ursula by the appearance of Captain Collins; she was numbed by his information and fretted dreadfully whilst the family, oblivious, wholeheartedly enjoyed the boisterous events.

"Oh Sukey, Sukey, you're my only consolation," she said that evening as she fondled the small dog, who lay on her lap and looked up with adoring eyes. "David went away once before you know, a hundred years ago, and I thought it was the end of the world – if only everything was that simple now. My beautiful baby's gone – the light of my life, our lives – and now David goodness knows where, alive or . . . if I didn't have you to look after Sukey . . ." She paused, and took a deep breath. "Still, I mustn't feel sorry for myself – I have to guard against falling into that trap again. And things can only get better, David will come back safe, yes Sukey, he will, and then we'll be as we were. Nearly, as we were," she said more firmly. "Off you get now, we'll have a quick walk, just up the road and back, and then I'll have a cigarette in the garden and we'll blow these beastly thoughts away."

But in the void of the lonely night all seemed doubtful again: the memory of Lulu was heavy to bear, though borne in loving remembrance, but David had *chosen* to leave, and that was unbearable. Ursula smothered the thought and repeated over and over to herself that all would be well, David's disappearance was unavoidable, he would return; Captain Collins was at best ill-informed, at worst an evil man. And in this way she talked herself through the darkest hours until her mind had had enough of consciousness and, as reason departed, treasured experiences were remembered.

Petals, curving back, over and back to reveal delicate stamens. Daisies opening wider in the warmth of the sunlight. Dappled light. Flickering through leaves. Softest moss. Bubbling stream, moving, flowing. The sunbird

thrusting deep, deep into the soft sweetness of the protea,
transported in pleasure.

She woke. David was not there and yet his presence was tangible; cloaked in the darkness of the room, his hands, his mouth, his body were beside her. And in the enveloping dark another physical memory came to her – a sensation she had not had since nursing Lulu – her breasts ached, her nipples hardened. Through her nightdress she cupped her breasts in her hands and squeezed the firm flesh until her fingers hurt, and the ache for him lessened.

But Ursula's fear that David would be killed grew steadily as the weeks passed, in spite of all her efforts to convince herself otherwise. And as it did so her desire for him increased. Unfulfilled, the physical desire she felt soon turned to frustration; frustration to helplessness and dejection. Devising a strategy to guard against such disturbing nights and the cycle of emotion that ensued, Ursula took longer and more arduous walks from home. The autumnal days were clear and the bracing wind, cutting her cheeks like glass, tired her. At work she took on the job of two and drove herself hard; seldom did she have a break – she was the first to arrive in the morning, the last to leave at night.

"I say, Ursula, you shouldn't work so hard," Bernard said one evening as he accompanied her out of the office. "I mean, I'm the manager here and you put me to shame."

"I prefer to be busy," she replied firmly.

"Busy is one thing, but there's a limit old thing."

"I thought you'd be pleased to get up to date with everything, Bernard?"

"Actually, we are up to date now Ursula," said Bernard, looking embarrassed.

"Ah," said Ursula, nonplussed.

"You're doing half of Elsie's job and half of Teddy's too; they were cock-a-hoop at first but now they're worried they may no longer be required."

"I hadn't realized," she said, worried now. "Do you – do they – want me to leave?"

"I wouldn't put it that strongly, but perhaps you could just ease off a bit," he suggested.

"I will, Bernard," Ursula agreed wholeheartedly, grateful that he had not terminated their arrangement.

"And how about coming to a concert with me? I haven't seen you smile or heard you talk about anything but work for the last month."

"No, I must admit, since the agricultural show I've been keeping my nose to the grindstone."

"Here, look," he said, indicating the tea room above where they were standing, "come and have a cup of tea with me now, before we catch our trams."

"Thank you, but I should get back." She had got into the habit of concentrating on what was strictly necessary; efficiency was an effective curb to her imagination and fears for David, her desperate grief for Lulu.

"There you go again – there are some of us who'd welcome a little company," he replied dejectedly.

"I'm sorry Bernard," she said kindly, realizing suddenly that she had been too absorbed in her own troubles to notice others, "of course, I'll be pleased to take tea with you."

They sat at a small table in the window looking down on people passing below and ordered bread and butter and tea. When they were served Ursula asked, "Tell me, Bernard, have you heard from Bunty since our day out?"

"Yes, we've corresponded. She's quite a girl you know, Ursula; bit young perhaps but so jolly, laughs a lot. Didn't seem to notice my mistakes – you know, clumsiness and so on – when we went to Rondebosch."

"And are you going to see her again?"

"Yes, we're trying to arrange something. She seems to think it will be better to meet here than in Stellenbosch," he said looking surprised.

"I think she's probably right, Bernard," replied Ursula with conviction.

"And you know, Ursula, I can actually imagine myself with Bunty," he said, looking at her in amazement. "I mean, some girls are so particular that I seem to be more awkward than ever with them. But she was the easiest person, I just talked about any old thing that came into my head. And she didn't seem to mind making the decisions – which way we should go, if we should go to the The Woolsack, all that – she just said, come on, let's do it. That's what it's all about isn't it? Being with someone you can laugh with and feel comfortable with."

"Yes Bernard, that's what it's all about."

"And love of course."

"Yes, love of course."

Ursula knew too well that in sleep the mind forgets to do what it is bid in daylight hours. Slipping into that nebulous state between sleep and wakefulness Bernard's words come uninvited; then fond memories come alive, anaesthetized emotions awake, the past and the future merge.

David whirls her around a cavernous ballroom, music surrounds them, chandeliers glisten in incandescent light, taffeta trains brush against silk skirts – but nothing impinges on her consciousness – nothing except the warm words softly spoken in her ear. And she is with Lulu, picking up shells. In turn they hold one to their ear and hear the sound of another world – deep and dark and pulsating. And now, the three of them are on the burnt brown grass –

herself, Lulu, David – holding hands. Round and round they skip. Happy, laughing.

'Ring a ring of roses, a pocketful of posies, atishoo atishoo we all fall down.'

And they fall to the ground, arms and legs askew. Motionless.

And she stands aloof, watching the train as it draws into the station – David, with Lulu in his arms, waiting on the platform. He opens the door of the carriage, they board, he closes the door. Bang – it clangs shut. She can see them in the carriage, Lulu still in David's arms. And she thinks . . . I should catch the train. The steam from the engine fills the platform. She thinks . . . I should catch the train now or they will leave without me. The whistle blows, the train begins to move. She calls . . . David, Lulu, wait for me . . . don't leave me . . . and she runs, but she does not move. She can see David with Lulu. The train gathers speed. It is nearly at the end of the platform. She must run faster, run faster. Don't leave . . . but she can no longer see the carriage. The steam disperses, Lulu and David hang their heads out of the train window. They look towards her. A photographic image in sepia hues – a still moment caught in time – etched on her mind. And Lulu the only bright flash of colour – a little blue jacket. Then David raises his arm and waves goodbye and Lulu, smiling, holds up Mister Rabbit and waves him as a parting gesture. They are gone.

Nineteen

Not in the clamour of the crowded street,
Not in the shouts and plaudits of the throng,
But in ourselves, are triumph and defeat.

The Poets
Henry Wadsworth Longfellow 1807–1882

Autumn weather sent gusts of winds – hot off the desert – that dried the leaves, rendering them crumpled and brittle. Ripe oranges fell from the tree, whilst the flowers and foliage of summer lay tired and spent. The end of another season: spent life. Lulu never left Ursula's thoughts and memories of David often punctuated them. For months she had kept her fear in check, had desired David and missed him, had hoped that he would return fit and well; had railed at him – had blamed herself. Now she no longer expected his return with any confidence. The clerical work that Ursula had helped Bernard with was completed and he could not continue to employ her. Then the first real rains of winter came, filling her days with their melancholic drip, drip, dripping. The despair into which she had sunk after Lulu's death appropriated her nights once more and beleaguered her days. Only the practical necessity of having to feed and exercise Sukey helped Ursula keep her sanity. Sukey was her only companion, her confidante.

But for the general population of Cape Town the impending Union Day Pageant gave them something pleasant to look forward to; in every store and at every tram stop arrangements were discussed. The women that Ursula had played bridge with – like all the women of society in Cape Town – expended all the artistic energy at their command in creating pretty but practical items to sell at the celebration Bazaar. She politely declined an invitation to join their sewing circle but agreed to collect small gifts for the bridge club bran dip, hoping to fill some of her lonely hours. Various festive activities were planned for the great day and, for those wanting a lasting keepsake, all sorts of commemorative items were produced. Men balancing on tall ladders were already hanging the bunting and flags on the Town Hall. But all this failed to inspire or excite Ursula.

Emma wrote that the family would be coming to the celebrations but that she might come a few days early and stay with Ursula; she had some exciting news to share. Ursula was pleased, she could busy herself with baking and making marmalade and look forward to some company. She wrote by return to press Emma to visit. They met at the railway station and Emma, bubbling with her news, explained to Ursula as they caught the tram home.

"Juliet's gained a scholarship and is going to read English at Oxford!"

"Oxford!" Ursula exclaimed. "Oxford University in England?"

"Yes, yes," said Emma, her eyes open wide at the wonder of it. "We none of us knew anything of it. We knew she was clever but it seems she's even more brainy than we realized. She secretly took Greek – when mother thought she was improving her French – and worked up her mathematics and Latin. Father is beside himself – furious – but Juliet didn't tell him anything about it until she had a letter from Aunt Maud inviting her to stay with them in London, and then the country, before she goes up. And after that father had a letter from Lord M – our uncle – congratulating him on being such an enlightened father!"

"That's not a word I associate with your father," said Ursula, drily.

"Father can't be seen to disagree or disapprove too much without seeming very parochial. As I'd already corresponded with my aunt I'm invited to accompany Juliet. What do you think of that!"

"It's amazing and absolutely wonderful news, Emma. And your father, will he allow you to accompany Juliet without any bother?"

"He's not giving in gracefully. He doesn't want Juliet to go, of course, but she's twenty-one soon and is determined to go with or without his approval and father says she cannot travel alone. Bunty's too young to accompany her and so I'm the obvious choice."

When they reached the house, and after depositing Emma's baggage, they settled in the sitting room to discuss the impending trip.

"When does Juliet have to be in England?" Ursula asked, hoping it was not imminent.

"She actually goes up in September, October maybe, but she has to have a *viva voce* – apparently it's only a formality – and so Aunt Maud suggested we come for the summer season. Father will find it difficult to refuse – Aunt Maud never misses an opportunity to remind him he didn't give us a London season for coming out."

"This will be your entrée into polite society. If you're to accompany Juliet you'll be off in a month or so, then." So soon – she tried not to think about it.

"Yes. Just think of the theatres in London, Ursula: plays, concerts, musical evenings – it will be marvellous. But I'll need to update my wardrobe and I think I've hit on the very thing. Look," she said opening the copy of Tatler she had bought for her train journey. She showed Ursula a glossy photograph of a society lady, "Do you see the skirt she's wearing, shorter and narrower. It's more practical than these gathered ones don't you think? And here, this photograph of suffragettes, the younger ones are wearing the same sort of skirts and little jackets to match. They're quite obviously thoroughly modern women so I think I'll adopt their style."

"I'm all for suffragettes, stylish or not."

"Don't whatever you do mention suffragettes to father," said Emma suddenly grave. "Juliet believes fervently in their campaign of course – she even joined the Women's Enfranchisement League here – but the very thought of them makes his blood boil."

"Well I hope Juliet comes back here with tips from the British suffragettes for us; if Africans lose the franchise here what hope will there be for us women getting the vote?"

"Gosh you sound like Juliet – she says you're my most 'aware' friend – I suppose we do have even less chance of voting than women in England do."

"Nothing is easy, is it," sighed Ursula, adding dolefully. "Everything's a hurdle."

But Ursula was not worrying about anything as worthy or egalitarian as the vote for women or Africans; everything was unimportant now compared with her present circumstances. She was feeling thoroughly forlorn; Jimmy, Meg, Nana, my beautiful beautiful Lulu, David – and now Emma – everyone's deserting me, she thought, I can't bear the thought of it. Emma, my only friend, leaving; whom will I talk to, where will I turn?

"You do seem depressed, dear, have you still not heard of David?" asked Emma, with concern.

"No. I've wandered down past the bars, and been to the Telegraph Office but haven't seen or heard anything of him. I've almost lost all hope, Emma. I've left the back door unlocked every night – in the vain hope he might walk in – but of course it's a silly idea, a futile gesture. But, until I actually have confirmation that he is . . . you know . . . not coming back . . . I can't talk to anyone about it. And I can't let go – you know what I mean?"

"I think so. But, is there no one you can ask?"

"I tried to see Abe again but he's gone to run his theatres in Durban and Johannesburg. The Tivoli is being turned into a bioscope – you were quite right – and only Joe is there now. Duggie's joined up. So I have no contacts, no."

"But what about the mysterious man who told you what David was doing?" asked Emma encouragingly.

"I thought of that; I know his name and sent a note to his . . . where he's meant to be staying. He replied, explaining he was involved because he is one of only a few who speak native languages, but couldn't tell me anything new and was rejoining . . . I mean returning, to Pietermaritzburg. No, no I mean Port Elizabeth," she added hastily.

Oh dear, I hope I haven't given him away, she thought – Pietermaritzburg is where the Captain's regiment is stationed. Fortunately, Emma looked at her with nothing but sympathy.

"What bad luck. You poor love," she said.

Ursula sighed – it was a strain keeping it all to herself – and the now the thought of isolation depressed her further.

"So what can I do but sit and wait, Emma, and go mad in the process. 'If only' dogs my days. If only my lovely Lulu was here, if only the accident hadn't happened, if only I'd shared my grief with David, if only I'd not been afraid to ask him how he was coping; if only, if only, if only," she said, covering her face with her hands.

"Don't fret so, Ursula," comforted Emma, putting her arm around her. "You mustn't feel guilty."

"I don't feel guilty, Emma – I'm guilty of far worse as you know. I pushed him away Emma; I didn't want him close, I didn't want him to blame me – it's regret I feel."

"You shouldn't feel either."

"But I do. I keep asking myself if it's all my fault David left

and it will be no more than I deserve if he doesn't come back."
She had told herself this over and over again.

"Remember, you were in such pain yourself," said Emma
gently.

"Still, my life is quite, quite empty now. I always dreamed of
a real family – had my own little family – and look what I did
with it. Now the only person left to me has gone too. And I've
come to realize how much I relied on David to be here – to talk
to if I needed, to make me laugh, everything. And I've come to
see all over again how much I love him," she said as she shook
her head in her hands.

"Don't underestimate your contribution, Ursula, you were a
constant companion and good wife to David."

Ursula looked up at Emma and continued, "There's much,
much more to loving someone than simply being with them and
caring for them, you know."

"Of course there is. You shared so many things."

"It's much more than that. He made my world bigger, Emma,
he made it so much larger."

Ursula enjoyed visiting the dress shops and Emma's company
was a comfort to her. But, with fittings and visits to the milliner,
the days passed quickly. When it was time for Emma to join her
family at the Royal she asked Ursula to accompany her. Ursula
immediately noticed the changes in the hotel since she had first
been there – the foyer and public rooms were now lit by
electricity, with a Telephone Office off the vestibule, and smart
new fittings in the lobby – but she was unprepared for the effect
the venue had on her. Emma's parents had not yet arrived – they
were motoring down in Mr Gibson's Wolseley-Siddely – and so
Emma suggested they order tea in the lounge bar which was
quiet at this time of day.

Just as an unexpected word, a scene, a smell so often took

Ursula unawares with memories of Lulu, so too the interior of the lounge bar stirred memories of David. Every detail of the room was exactly as it had been when he had first taken her and Jessie there for a drink; when she had celebrated with the theatre crowd and seen him with Duggie's sister. And when they had come on subsequent occasions for various anniversaries or treats.

"Do you mind if we sit somewhere else Emma?" Ursula asked, taking Emma's arm.

"No, of course not," replied Emma, concerned. "Are you all right? You look very pale."

"I'll be perfectly fine in a minute."

"Let's go to the main lounge then; that is where they usually serve tea."

Mrs Gibson and the girls arrived unexpectedly as the tea was being laid out. More was ordered and after they had greeted each other – Bunty with vim, Juliet with reserve, Mrs Gibson twittering between them all – they sat down together.

"Mother, where is father?" Emma asked.

"Your father is organizing the garaging of the car and the distribution of the luggage, dear, and is likely to be some time. He said we should have tea without him, which we shall do because then you and Ursula can tell us what you've been doing here."

"I've ordered two new outfits Mother – Ursula helped me choose the cloths from the new stock," began Emma enthusiastically. "You'll approve I'm sure, and you can come for the final fitting with me tomorrow. I should like to wear one of them to the celebrations, and the other is a travelling costume – it's very tailored in a plain serge; perfect for London."

"We will take your sister – don't make a face Juliet – as she'll need a new white voile for Henley and something for Ascot," replied Mrs Gibson, hardly drawing breath. "And tennis gowns! Write that down Emma or I'll forget again, tennis shoes too. And we'd better order you a floral muslin for garden parties and for Juliet a dark blue linen frock for everyday."

"What about me, Mother?" asked Bunty, plaintively.

"You are not going dear and so you can wait until the old stock is cleared at sacrificing prices. We must economize somewhere or your father will dig his heels in more than ever."

"That's so unfair," said Bunty with feeling.

"Bunty, you can come and visit me when your sisters go away," said Ursula, "and we'll go to the sales together."

"Thank you, Ursula, I should like that," she replied, cheering up. "I take every opportunity I can to come to Town."

"Of course, we shall have to re-examine your evening wear girls," continued Mrs Gibson with relish. "One or two new formal dinner frocks each – with lower bodices than you've been used to I think – and maybe some high-necked chiffon blouses for dinner on the boat, with new chemises to wear under them . . . or perhaps high-necked silk gowns would be better? And new gloves of course, several pairs each. Ball gowns! Have we got time? You'll want to be the height of fashion. Gauze for you Emma, tulle for Juliet . . ."

As Ursula listened she felt herself shrink – blend into the background, become insignificant in her chair. And there she hid from unwanted enquiry whilst the conversation dwelled on costumes and college, travelled from south-west London and back to Stellenbosch. She did not want to stay – an outsider looking in – but she did not want to go, back to an empty house and solitude. Finally, during a lull in the conversation, afraid that the talk might turn to her, or that Mr Gibson might arrive, she roused herself and took her leave.

"And will we see you at the celebrations, Ursula?" Mrs Gibson asked as Ursula said goodbye.

"I'm not sure Mrs Gibson," she replied despondently.

"But your husband, will he not want to take part in the festivities?"

"It's not likely that he'll be able to, I'm afraid. Please excuse me, Mrs Gibson, but I really must be off."

"Must you dear?" she asked, looking genuinely disappointed.

An expedient excuse occurred to Ursula, "Sukey – you remember my little dog – has been left all alone."

Mrs Gibson clearly understood this completely, "Of course, my dear. Poor little Sukey. You must not stay a moment longer."

Ursula could see that Emma thought her excuse a bit thin but she said nothing as she gave her a warm embrace and Ursula hurried away before she was asked any more questions.

But Ursula did not go straight home, where no family awaited her. She decided to walk about town for a while – surround herself with people, with life. She walked down past the Town Hall to the railway station, but the sight of the red, white and blue banners and bunting, the lavish swags and golden fringes that now festooned them, only depressed her. From every direction she felt bombarded by noise and activity. On Adderley Street flowersellers called and held out bright bunches for her to admire, Indian traders clamoured and pushed baskets of colourful fruits in front of her; as she crossed the road bicycle bells rang and trams clanged. In St Georges Street animated groups of girls clustered around dress shop windows and men greeted each other with hearty slaps on the back and jovial words.

With a heavy heart, Ursula soon started towards home. It seemed to her that the whole noisy, busy town was ready to celebrate the end of strife, the promise of stability. And she, alone and lonely, could feel only pain and an endless nothingness – a vast empty landscape – stretching out before her to a never-ending horizon. Lulu was dead; there was only David left. And if he did not return soon – the thought had occurred to her often in the days after Lulu's death – she would walk the high coastal cliffs. And if she slipped – if she slipped – she would fall into glorious oblivion.

But that night Ursula left Sukey on sentry duty as usual and in addition secured the back door. For days the newspapers had warned residents to take precautions; they reported that the streets were full of undesirable figures intent on taking advantage during the Union celebrations. Why should I care, she asked herself as she pushed the bolt firmly in place, what have I to fear, I've lost everything important to me. But still she did it. As a prelude to sleep Ursula evoked her cherished memories of Lulu to ward off unpleasant dreams; Lulu playing houses under the bushes, snuggled up close to her looking at picture books, Lulu sitting next to her on the grass as they made daisy chains together. But in spite of these precautions when Ursula finally slept her nightmare returned.

She calls 'Where's Lulu, where's David?' Jessie, dressed in black, shrugs. She runs past her through the trees. But there are many trees. She bumps into them. She cannot see her way. She cannot find them. 'Lulu, David' she calls. But her voice is silent. Fear constricts her throat and stifles her breath. 'David, where are you.' She runs but she does not move. The pumping of her heart batters her chest. Blood beats in her ears, drumming like a spear on a native shield. The ground around her reverberates with victorious stamping feet. She stumbles on a figure; prostrate, bloody. 'David!'

And she woke, her heart pounding and her head aching.

The following morning – the day before Union Day – as she unbolted the door, Ursula gave herself a strict talking to. She must do something positive to keep herself from sinking so low again; she must take herself in hand, she must soldier on. Wistfully she wrapped each gift she had collected for the bran dip. She could visualize the joyful face of a small boy or girl as – drawing a parcel from the depths of the tub and tearing off the

330

crêpe paper – a cardboard horn or a small wooden top, a bag of marbles or tiny carved horse, fell to the ground. How she would have liked to see Lulu's face light up, to see David smile. By mid afternoon Ursula had completed her task and, piling the gifts in the large basket on wheels she had been supplied with, she delivered them to the hall. She did not linger there; organizers complained that banners had yet to be hung on the stage and flags draped as backcloths. Helpers moaned of their aching feet, the pain in their backs from setting up amusements, moving tables, placing chairs. But all were flushed with importance, puffed with pride, eager for their work to be appreciated and admired on the great day. Ursula felt none of their self-righteous anticipation, no sanguine expectation.

She stepped out into the darkening evening and made her way up the hill, homeward. A scruffy native – the worse for homemade spirits – sang loudly as she passed, his alcoholic breath enveloping her. Holding her gloved hand over her nose, she quickly crossed the road and hurried on. Lost in her thoughts, Ursula took no notice of the small boys still playing with their football in the gloom, of the women chattering in the doorways, of the silent, tattered vagrant sitting upon a low wall. But as she passed the tramp, he made an indistinguishable guttural noise and tried to grab her arm. Remembering the warnings, she walked faster, increasing her distance from the unsavoury figure. Ursula was relieved to reach home and, patting Sukey, made a fuss of her.

"I should have taken you, shouldn't I, Sukey? But I couldn't with that enormous trolley to handle. You would have protected me from horrid men, wouldn't you my brave little dog, my dear little friend – at least you'd have made a noise. I'll take this hat off, and hang up my coat – there – then I'll prepare some dinner for you."

She fed Sukey and was about to warm some soup for her own supper when there was a rap on the door. Telling Sukey to curb her barking, she opened it a crack.

Ursula gasped in shock and distaste; the dirty unkempt tramp was leaning on the door frame, his hat battered, his bearded face smeared and dirty. Her heart pounding, she quickly shut the door on him but he had placed his filthy hand, the nails broken, on the door jamb and pushed his foot across the threshold.

"Go away, go away!" she demanded, desperately. "I haven't any food, I haven't any money."

She continued pushing the door with all her strength until his fingers lost their grip, and his hand slid down and away, and she heard his body slump to the ground. Only his boot, now twisted on its side, the foot inside it immobile, remained in the crack of the door: a thick leather boot, worn through on the sole. Peering through the crack she could see the tramp lying on the step; she would have to open the door and push his foot away. Then she would be able to fasten the door shut. Cautiously she opened the door and, kneeling down, tried to lift his boot. He groaned, his eyes closed, and she watched his face intently in case he rallied. He might become violent once more. His hat had fallen from his head and the light from the hallway illuminated his face. It was a face that was not unfamiliar, under the beard and the dirt, a face that reminded her of someone.

"David!"

He ate the soup slumped at the kitchen table, his arms hardly able to lift the spoon to his lips, while Ursula lit the copper and heated water for the zinc bath that she had placed by the fire. When there was enough hot water she undressed him, and was shocked at how thin he was. With his arm around her shoulders she helped him to step into the bath and sit down. Pouring jugs of water over him, she knelt and washed his back, feeling each of his ribs as the bar of soap jerked over them like a wheel rim over cobbles.

"Would you like a shave?" she asked, when she had finished.

"Not now. I need to sleep. Just sleep," he replied wearily.

She helped him to bed and when he was comfortable, his eyes closed, she turned to go.

"Stay with me," he said, suddenly opening his eyes, "lie down. Keep me warm. And some more soup perhaps, later."

Ursula was pleased to be wanted and lay next to him fully clothed; he slept immediately. Later he woke and she fetched more soup for him and watched while he drank, sometimes with his eyes open, sometimes with them shut. Finally he finished.

"Thank you, Funny Face. I'll be better tomorrow," he said, and was asleep within seconds.

He called her Funny Face! His affectionate nickname for her; she had always hated it when he used it in place of her name but missed it when he did not. She could wait for explanations.

Ursula returned to the kitchen and gathered up the tattered rags of his clothes. When she had the noxious pile in her arms something fell on the ground; a small, hard sound. She looked around: there, at her feet, lay Mister Rabbit. She froze for a few moments, transported back in time, until dropping the clothes she stooped and picked the small lead animal up. She had been so upset with David for leaving her without any word of explanation, for causing her such worry and fear, for compounding her loneliness. Controlling her anger, stifling her fears, had cost her much. But now, holding Mister Rabbit, overcome with memories of Lulu and their love for her, her tears flowed freely. And the anger that had kept her strong, melted away; an enormous sense of relief replaced it – in spite of everything he was back, safe, that was all that mattered. Drying her eyes, Ursula went into the scullery where she washed the small toy under the tap until its little blue jacket was bright again.

"Thank you for bringing him back to me, Mister Rabbit," she said aloud.

She carried the small lead toy to the bedroom; walking softly she stood it carefully on the cupboard by their bed, next to her silver-backed hairbrush.

"There you are, Mister Rabbit, you won't be hidden away any longer," she said under her breath. "You're here with us now, out in the open, where you belong."

David slept deeply; he did not move. Ursula, beside him, woke early and lay watching him. His beard was thick and, what should have been dark brown, was faded to a reddish wheat; skin deeply coloured, burnt from the sun. His face was altered – more lines around his eyes and deepened furrows between his brows – and as she watched the dilating of his nostrils and the parting of his lips, she thought how a well-worn face was more than merely features; awake it was a barometer, asleep it was a history. And she wondered what had happened to him. However, the study of David's face confirmed something: this was the face she wanted to kiss goodnight every night, to wake to every morning. David stirred as the dawn brightened and turning his head towards her, he smiled; she smiled. He held his arm out and she moved to lie in the crook of it, her head resting on his chest. She heard his breath come slow and deep again and, with relief and contentment, she slept too.

Much later they woke, Ursula curled around his back. Putting her arm around him she spoke softly into his neck, "I'm so glad you're back safe. I was so worried about you, David."

"Mmm."

His eyes could not silence her, she could safely say more, "I didn't know where you were, if you were alive or dead . . ."

He interrupted her, "Ursula, I'm too tired to tell you all I have to say, too tired for questions," he said taking her hand, "let's just enjoy being here, together and safe."

"But David . . ."

"Tomorrow's time enough for explanations," he said, turning around and kissing her forehead.

She knew she could only press him so far. And she had better enjoy his company now – she might not like to hear what he had to say.

"Ooh – your beard scratches," she said, laughing.

"I could have a shave now if we had a razor here."

"I'll get one from the corner *winkel*, it will be open this morning. But not this afternoon, it's Union Day."

"This afternoon – I made it then!"

"There's lots going on in town," explained Ursula, "they've planned a three-day pageant."

"I could do with a haircut," he said, running his hand over his hair that came down over his ears, "do you think you could make me look presentable?"

"I'll give it a try."

"And what about some food – have you anything? I'm starving," he said, more animated now.

"I've got eggs and yams," she replied, pleased to be in demand, "that should be enough for a hearty meal. And we've plenty of oranges which will help you get strong again."

"Good. I could do with a cigarette too."

"I've got some," she said, smiling.

"Cigarettes?"

"Yes, I bought some. I've been having one now and then – they calmed me a bit."

"Well I never – we'll have one together then," he said with satisfaction. "And do you have any of the sovereigns left?"

"Of course," she replied, stoutly.

"Then we'll go to the celebrations, just for a little while. I've not run myself ragged to miss what pleasure there is to be had from it."

David and Ursula bought the *Cape Times* in which was published a commemorative supplement patriotically coloured

red, white and blue. Stopping to rest on the way to town, they poured over the programme of events printed inside it. Archery competitions were to be staged for the young ladies, polo for energetic young men, and roller skating – the latest fashion craze from England – would be demonstrated for everyone's amusement. Races for men and children were organized for the holiday and the final evening was due to end with bonfires and barons of beef roasted whole, whilst dances and songs were performed. They agreed it was an impressive programme.

With other couples and families they wandered down Adderly Street marvelling at the enormous wooden arches that had been erected to symbolize each of the provinces. There was a carnival spirit and everyone was out to treat themselves: at the Bazaar ladies purchased artistic souvenir cards that were carefully placed in handbags and little girls hugged their new dolls to their chests. On the steps outside, men stood about smoking large *serootjie* as boys practised imaginary shots with shiny new cricket bats. When they finally reached the railway station at the bottom of the street, people were issuing from it in great waves.

"David, it's such a crush now, we'll never get a seat to watch the pageant and you're much too tired to stand," worried Ursula. "Shall we have tea and ices on White's balcony instead – we can watch what's going on from there."

"That's a good idea but the crowds are really too much for me, so many people. And you deserve a real treat," he said, smiling at her, "so how about we take a cab and go up to the Mount Nelson for tea?"

"Oh, yes, please," said Ursula, eagerly.

The Malay cab driver, high on his perch, had decorated the reed *toering* that covered his fez with a tricolor rosette; his horse with red, white and blue ribbons, the handle of his long whip with bells. His eager face glowed – teeth gleaming in a smile, *kaaprings* shining in his ears – reflecting the happiness that everyone felt that day. But as David and Ursula sat side by side in the hansom cab – glad to be together – they were pleased to leave the crowds behind.

"I haven't had my wife on my arm for so long," said David, smiling at Ursula, "and haven't had any luxury for even longer, that today I'm going to enjoy both in style."

Ursula beamed. How long it was since she had felt this way.

At the hotel they sat in comfortable armchairs and listened to the chatter of the guests and the pianist playing. They watched with interest as important personages and dignitaries staying at the hotel gathered together before leaving in patriotically decorated landaus and spiders for their seats at the pageant. Once rested they ordered tea and David, devouring sandwhiches and savouries, cakes and scones, patted Ursula's hand, "Good English grub – it's wonderful to be back."

"Is that because of the food or because of me?" Ursula asked, smiling.

"The food of course," David grinned.

"You're still a horrible tease."

"Funny Face," he said, smiling, "it's a pleasure, amongst many, that I've missed," and he took her hand and kissed it.

She gave him a wry smile, she had even missed his wicked humour.

They returned home in a cab and David, exhausted from the day, said he would sleep for a while. Ursula put her hand on his arm to delay him, "And David, you know how worried I've been; I need to know why you went, where you were," she said. "Later, will you to tell me everything that happened?"

"When I wake up, I'll tell you everything."

"Promise?"

"Promise."

Ursula was proud of herself for being so patient. Lizzie had been given the day off and, whilst David slept, Ursula cleared up and took Sukey for a short walk. When she returned she undid her hair so it tumbled down her back, undressed to her underclothes and crept into the bed with David; his body was warm, and lying close to him, she waited for him to wake.

Twenty

So we grew together,
Like to a double cherry, seeming parted,
But yet an union in partition;
Two lovely berries moulded on one stem;
So, with two seeming bodies, but one heart.

A Midsummer Night's Dream
William Shakespeare 1564–1616

David lay on his back, his arm around Ursula's shoulders, and addressed the ceiling, "It was too good an opportunity to miss – the reward was so large because it was secret and dangerous. It couldn't be a military man; if anyone associated with the army was caught then the British Government would be implicated. So I was on my honour not to tell a soul; one whisper could have put too much in jeopardy – British lives, African lives."

"But you could have given me a clue that you were leaving," Ursula said, trying hard to keep the annoyance from her voice.

"When I was told where and when to meet I didn't realize I wouldn't be given the chance to pop back and see you. It was lucky I'd left you the envelope. Once they had kitted us out and given us our instructions they were adamant – go now, no farewells. I'm sorry, I had no choice." He looked at her, shrugged apologetically, and continued, "The journey was easy at first. There were three of us and we had mules to carry the guns and our supplies." David caught Ursula's eye and warned her, "You must never utter a word of this." Ursula shook her head, and he continued. "The terrain wasn't hard at first –

through vineyards, some cotton fields. But it was a long way to the Orange River, and it steadily became more difficult, arduous. At the crossing we made the rendezvous with our Bushman tracker, Rooi. It wasn't easy following the river, where it ran fast, but at least we could cool ourselves and drink. And, Ursula, in the eddies and slow sections we picked up stones . . ."

"Like the ones I played with in the rivers of Kimberley?" she asked eagerly.

"Probably the very same. And we took handfuls. Later when we were desperate – when we could hardly pull ourselves along – we ditched them. I threw away your tiara," he said, with a shake of his head and a rueful smile.

"I'd rather have my husband," replied Ursula, giving him a squeeze.

He tightened his arm around her and then carried on, "When we got right up into South-West Africa, close to their eastern border, it must have been well over a hundred degrees, a hundred and thirty, a hundred and forty perhaps in the day. We had to travel at night to avoid the Germans of course – they'd have made mincemeat out of us. Then there was semi-desert; we had to take what cover we could in *spitskoppe* or sparse bush, wherever we could. I've never been so hot, never been so dependent on another man; without Rooi we wouldn't have found our way, wouldn't have known the tricks of survival. No wonder they promised to pay us well – probably never expected us to return. Lucky I started a fit man; it's an inhospitable land. Even for the native tribes."

"Did all three of you get back?" asked Ursula, awed by David's tale.

"No, Jack died; he wandered off, soon after we'd made contact with the Nama chief and handed over the guns. When we found him he'd lost his hat, his water, the heat got to him, the birds . . . Oh God, the state of him!" David screwed his face up, tightened his hand on her arm and grasped it firmly.

340

"Don't think about it, don't think about it," urged Ursula, concerned to see David so upset, "think of something else. Tell me about Rooi, about the Nama, the Herero."

He took a deep breath and continued, "For the Herero it's too late: they lost what pastoral land they had to the Settlers several years ago – about the same time a rinderpest epidemic nearly wiped out their herds – and now they've lost more land to the railway companies. Traders have taken what's left of their herds. If the Herero and Nama had united earlier they could have beaten the Germans without our help," he said impatiently. "They're skilled guerrilla fighters in desert country, the Nama; their leaders have all been educated men. If Witbooi had lived, or Morenga – he was half-Nama, half-Herero – they would have successfully resisted the Germans sooner. South-West Africa wouldn't have been at such risk of German control." He sounded despairing and his voice trailed off.

Ursula turned her face to him, "But David, was it just for the money that you went, nothing else?"

"No, not just the money; I believed in the mission – the army and I would both like the Nama to retain control of their own lands – even if our reasons for doing so are different," he said firmly. "If the British want to deter the Germans for military reasons, so much the better; the more help they give the Nama, the more chance the Nama have of survival. These people have been pushed further and further north, they have a right – they need – to hold on to what they have now. And the mission was fortuitous – I needed to get away. In the state I was in I might have said things I'd later regret. I wanted to escape."

"Oh dear; David," Ursula said imploringly. *Mea culpa*; I pushed him away; I was afraid of what he would say.

"No, not you: everything. Not boxing any more for a start. And I'd begun to hate my work – you know how I like a challenge, something to pit my wits against, something exciting – well, everything I was doing was so dull, not what I came here

341

for. Money would allow me to do something I wanted. But, more than anything . . . above all . . . the overriding reason . . ." he faltered.

"The overriding reason?" prompted Ursula. She wanted him to say it, to tell her how he felt, even to blame her outright. Nothing could be as bad as everything she had already been through.

David looked away and stretched his free arm out across the cupboard that stood beside the bed.

"I never realized . . ." he said quietly, as his hand reached out for the small lead figure and he gently rolled the toy between his fingers, "Dear Mister Rabbit . . ." he whispered.

Ursula groaned, "I'm so sorry," she said contritely, tightening her arm around his chest. If only she hadn't played bridge that day. If only.

David gave a loud sniff and shook his head, "What are you sorry for? It wasn't your fault, it was an accident," he said gruffly. Staring at the ceiling again he continued robustly, "When they put the proposition to me the time was right that's all. We'd lost . . ." he turned Mister Rabbit round in his fingers once more and then, carefully placing the toy next to Ursula's hairbrush, he took Ursula's hand. "Anyway, I was sure you'd be all right. I knew you'd overcome loss before and I expected the fearless, independent woman I married to return – once you were on your own again."

Ursula was too surprised to comment; independent and fearless – was that how she'd been, how he had seen her. Had she changed so much as a wife, as a mother. She would think about it later when she could concentrate, could examine and tease the words and the meaning out; could it have been true.

"So I calculated the odds of the task and I was in a state of mind to welcome the risks," he continued. "I thought I was. But on the return journey we ran out of food; there was no game, even the biltong we relied on to chew when we had little else was finished; hardly any water. Then the mules died, we had to leave them and carry on; couldn't even wait to butcher them or the Germans might have butchered us. I really thought we'd never make it back. It makes you look at things differently, you know. If it hadn't been for Rooi we'd be dead."

"What did he do?"

"Found us something to keep us alive. Searched and found a clump of *xhoba* growing – even though the ground was so dry and barren – and we pulled off the thorns and ate it, just like that. It was so bitter – revolting – but it staved off the hunger and thirst. The next time he cooked it over a fire which was better – it gave us enough strength to carry on."

"It sounds like a cactus."

"Sort of – he also called it *hoodia* – it enabled us to make it back to the Orange River which took days. It was such a relief. And Ursula," David turned to look at her, "have you ever lain and watched the stars and thought about things, ideas, you never had before?"

"Yes. Yes, I have," she said, remembering lonely nights.

"Well, I don't know if it was because I'd been so close to death – or whether death has come so close to you and me – but lying there, cast away from everything familiar, with the hope of coming back so tenuous, I began to see things more clearly," he said, looking up at the ceiling once more.

"Like what?" asked Ursula, more fearful than curious.

"What is important. What's not. That forgiveness can be liberating, that blame can be destructive. And ... Ursula ... lying on my back, looking up into that great firmament I saw a tiny sparkling star; forever beautiful, there for all eternity. And I felt that after all Lulu is still with us – part of us."

Ursula felt as if someone had gripped her heart, had grabbed and wrung it out; she lay, hardly able to breathe.

After a minute he continued slowly, "I felt such overwhelming peace surrounded by that vast sky – what can only be described as beauteous infinity. And I knew then that there's something more, something bigger than all of us, something inexplicable."

David lay quite still, staring at the ceiling, his face in complete repose. Never before had she heard him speak in such a way, heard him lay his soul so bare. Ursula closed her eyes; she could not trust herself to speak, to break the spell.

"And then," he continued, "under that neverending sky, I realized . . ." he paused.

"Realized what?" she whispered, looking at him. Realized what.

He turned his face to look at her, his dark brown eyes moist, "That my love for you is the only thing on this earth, the only thing I have now, to equal that feeling."

Guilt and fear – like a leaden cloak bearing down on her shoulders – was lifted from her. Relief engulfed her.

"Oh David," she said, and pressed her face close to his cheek, "I love you too. I do. So much."

They lay, David's arm clasping her tightly, for several minutes until Ursula wriggled apart from him. She needed to explain.

"David, my life's been so dreary and colourless since Lulu died, and then when you left I thought it was pointless altogether. Even my dreams have been monochrome; I thought life would be drab for evermore."

He smiled and kissed her on the forehead. "Our life will change," he said with conviction, "we'll start again."

"I thought it was all spoiled," said Ursula sadly, looking up at him. "I thought we'd never be together again, happy again."

"You know what Funny Face – you think too much."

"I know," she said solemnly, "I *think* that's the trouble."

David raised his eyebrows at her remark and grinned; that mocking, mischievous smile she remembered so well.

"Oh you!" she retorted and laughed with relief and pleasure.

"Come here," David said, turning onto his side and embracing her with both arms, "let's see if this absent-minded beggar can put a little colour into those cheeks."

A Little Blue Jacket

When Lulu was born, Ursula – overcome with wonder at their small miracle – for many months felt sure that any act of desire that could lead to the conception of a child so perfect and pure, should also be exquisite and gentle; beautiful, never bestial. When Lulu died that feeling resurfaced in a different guise: Ursula could not reconcile the grief she felt at the death of their child with an act of corporeal desire, a lusty act that celebrated life itself. The continuous cycle of birth and death had been too cruelly reduced in her experience. Death and sexual desire – just as birth and sexual desire had been – were incompatible in her mind. But now, enfolded in David's arms – arms she had lately feared would never welcome nor comfort her again – and aroused by his kisses, love and physical desire were paramount.

The feel of it. Skin. Pink skin, sun-browned skin. Smooth, rough. Soft, now firm. The colour! The feel of it! Sliding through shimmering silk – ice blue, cool blue – slippery smooth satin. Like Alice – down, down, no control – a well of wonder, disappearing into the darkest sea, the deepest night. Out of space, without time. Indigo – richer than lapiz – darker than midnight. Down, down into soft brushed velvet – palms caress the plush pile – feel the colour. Cobalt blue – Stygian. Falling, falling, into eternity.

She had never experienced colour like it.

"Tomorrow, I must present myself at the Bank of Africa and collect my reward," David informed Ursula, as they faced each other across the dinner table a few days later. "We'll have enough to start afresh. The Union will safeguard the Colonies and provide economic stability – fewer benefits for the African I'm afraid – but it means any business I start has more chance of surviving, and thriving."

"What sort of business?"

"I've a hankering to breed racehorses and I could do it in Johannesburg. There are opportunities there," he said confidently.

"Johannesburg?" She was alarmed.

"Yes. We could make a clean break."

"I see," said Ursula, fearful, ambivalent. To leave Cape Town, her home, where Lulu was born, where Lulu . . . She looked at him hesitantly. He smiled.

"Start again. Find a house," he said, putting out his hand to take hers. "What do you say?"

"Well . . ." she faltered. She did not want to leave what she knew, everything she loved. But I *can* do it, of course I can do it; I only have to say. I've made mistakes but I've managed to survive everything so far; I've been brave when I've had to, so I'll not stop now. I must do it. She took a deep breath and, feeling her stomach churn, gave herself no further time to think, "Yes, all right, I'm ready."

"Well done. And you'll love the town, it's so large and impressive," he said enthusiastically. "You wait till you see the shops in Pritchard Street – the smartest I've seen anywhere – and grand hotels, and places like the Balcony Tea Rooms to show off your latest hat. And on Sunday evenings everyone walks up and down, eyeing each other's outfits – although they pretend they're looking at the fancy goods in the shop windows – and there are clubs, and societies and the theatre and . . ."

But the descriptions of the elegant life there only made Ursula feel sad for everything she would leave behind.

"Stop, stop, you've convinced me," she said, removing her hand from his and holding it up halt him. She forced a smile and added, "It all sounds very exciting."

"But I can't wait till then to get some clothes that fit," added David, looking down at the suit that hung from his thinner frame. "After I've been to the bank I shall go straight to Fletcher and Cartwrights and invest four guineas in a new suit, and a couple of pairs of flannel trousers."

Ursula remembered how close to starving he had been, how near she had been to losing him too. "And maybe you could buy a couple of their fancy waistcoats as well," she said, wanting him to celebrate, trying to share in his optimism.

"Why not – splash out. And what about you – how about a new hat and gloves to start with?"

"That would be lovely." And in that instant she made a decision: I can be the person he married. I will show him and everyone how determined I am to make a new beginning, a new life together.

"And I'll put away my mourning black, how about that? Mourning will be in my memory, not in black crêpe; it's six months after all, which is quite conventional," she added, to justify her decision. "I'll buy one of the new skirts that I saw with Emma – a decent grey or dark mauve of course – but I want to make it obvious that I'm ready for our new start."

"Are you sure?" he asked, his eyebrows raised, a hint of admiration in his voice.

"Yes, I need to do it," she said firmly.

"Very well. Then we'll have tea on the balcony afterwards as a little treat – we can afford it after all," he said, looking at her with undisguised pleasure.

She smiled, a genuine smile. She was pleased with her resolute words; pleased with his approval. "And I must go and see Nana and tell her all about everything."

David and Ursula, visiting the cemetery together, knelt by the grave and David peeled the oranges they had brought: Lulu's favourite fruit. She had loved to watch him peel an orange with his penknife, removing the peel in one long magical spring. And when they had eaten the fruit they pushed the pips into the ground around the edge of the grave and placed the whorls of orange peel in a pattern by the headstone. The fresh tangy scent of orange oil filled the air.

Ursula wrote to Hannah that she would visit the following week. On the bus drive out of town she enjoyed the feel of the wooden seats, ridged and uncomfortable as they were; with each bump in the road a journey remembered. Winds off the Atlantic had denuded the crowns of the wild chestnut trees that lined the road, revealing small warty fruits that hung like tiny lanterns from the bare branches. The smooth grey trunks of the chestnuts looked beautiful next to the shimmering leaves of the silver trees that fluttered merrily in the wind. Salt laden air filled the bus as it passed the coast and ocean waves raced up and slapped the low wall. As usual, when Ursula reached the *dorp* small boys were playing on the green, the bow ties on the tails of their homemade paper kites weaving wondrous arcs through the air. She waved to them and, walking on some way, she finally picked out Hannah's house so similar in style to their own old home.

"Nana," she called out, when she was close. "Nana, I'm here!"

And out of the door, onto the *stoep* and down the steps, scuttled the familiar figure of Hannah, Miriam holding her skirt, now able to outrun her, pulling her forward.

"Ursula! *Ag shame*, it been so long, man."

They embraced and Ursula bent down and lifted Miriam up into her arms. "Hello Miriam. Do you remember me?"

Miriam nodded.

"*Ja*, of course she remember you. We talk about you all the time, man. Mr Essop, Mr Essop," Hannah called as they reached the door and entered, "my Ursula is here."

Ursula put Miriam down and looked around for Mr Essop.

He was sitting in his chair, a rug over his legs; he raised his arm in greeting but did not rise. Miriam ran to him and leant her elbows on his lap.

"Good afternoon, Miss Ursula. Please excuse me," he said, putting his hand on his heart, "but these old legs feel the damp. Sometime they refuse to do as I ask."

Ursula went to him, "I'm sorry to hear that Mr Essop. Still, you're well?"

"*Ja*, Miss Ursula, I am well," he replied smiling, "I have Hannah and my little Miriam, between the two of them I am not allowed to feel sorry for myself. Hannah tell me there is nothing wrong with me and Miriam prove it – she run and fetch everything I want!"

"Now, Mr Essop," said his wife, as if chiding a child.

"I suspect you're more mollycoddled than you all let on, Mr Essop," said Ursula with a smile.

He gave a wide grin, "*Is it*? What about you Miss Ursula?"

"Well, I've come to tell you all," she said, taking Hannah's hand in her own, "that David is home now, and we've decided to move to Johannesburg. To start anew in Johannesburg."

"Johannesburg! *Ag kleintjie!*" said Hannah, squeezing Ursula's hand tightly, her other hand clapped over her mouth.

"I'll come and visit, Nana, I promise," she said, putting her free arm around her old nurse's shoulders.

"*You* come to *Kaapstad* to visit, *is it*?" asked Hannah, shaking her head. "*Ag* no man, Johannesburg is far far away to visit."

"David needs a change – we need a change – for all sorts of reasons," said Ursula slowly and reasonably. "It's for the best."

"Still, Miss Ursula," said Mr Essop, "you seem happier than when I see you last. Does she not Hannah?"

"*Ja*, Mr Essop," replied Hannah, giving a sniff and wiping a tear away. "Happier."

"And this is what you have chosen, Miss Ursula," Mr Essop asked, "to go on with your life in Johannesburg?"

She nodded and smiled at Hannah.

"Then you have made a brave sensible decision. Has she not Hannah?"

"*Ja*, you are right of course, Mr Essop," said Hannah, nodding her head. "She have."

"I'll write and tell you all about the town, and where we live," said Ursula reassuringly. "And Lizzie's going to follow us there so we'll have someone to keep us in order."

"*Ag shame*. Mr Essop will send you our news – *ja* Mr Essop?" said Hannah looking at her husband for approval. "Hannah and Miriam can chatter ten to the dozen and Mr Essop can write. He understand what we mean even when we not understand ourself, *ja*, Mr Essop?"

Mr Essop smiled, and Miriam stretched up and planted a kiss on his cheek.

"And Miriam, will you make a drawing for me," asked Ursula, kneeling down near the little girl, "a drawing of your house?"

"My house," nodded Miriam. "I got a green door."

"Yes. And when I look at the picture of your house I shall think of you all," said Ursula and stood up. In a tremulous voice she said, "And Nana, would you . . . ." She faltered and with tears in her eyes, continued, "Would you visit Lulu's . . ."

"*Ja, ja*, of course I go," interrupted Hannah, "every week, man."

"Thank you Nana, that's such a comfort," she said, wiping the tears away and giving Hannah a hug.

"*Ag* well, we have a pot of honeybush *tee*, man. You try my *soet koekies*. We talk of other things *rather*," said Hannah sensibly, nodding and smiling at Ursula. "You tell us about this business trip Mister David been on when Mirian go to *kooi*. What he is going to do *just now*, all your plans."

"A cup of tea and some of your biscuits would be lovely," replied Ursula, "then I'll tell you about it."

Ursula wrote to Emma that David had returned and that she would like to see Emma before she left for England. Emma replied that she was coming to town at the end of the week, and if Ursula met her under the clock at the railway station at eleven they could lunch together. Ursula arrived early and took a seat on one of the benches inside the main entrance. She sat watching people go to and fro, one or two overburdened with parcels nearly as large as themselves, others with only their hands in their pockets; some buying tickets for their impending journey, a few like herself waiting for an arrival. A tall gangly young man waiting at the gate to one of the platforms caught her eye. As he turned and looked about she recognized Bernard; jumping up from her seat she hurried forward.

"Bernard," she called as she neared him, "it's me, Ursula."

"Ursula – what are you doing here?" he said with his arms thrown wide.

"I could ask you the same thing."

"I suppose you could," he nodded, goodnaturedly.

"Do you think it might be a good idea if one of us was to say?"

"I suppose it would," he agreed seriously.

Ursula smiled, the same old Bernard.

"I'll take the lead," she said, "I'm here to meet Emma."

"And I'm here to meet Bunty," he said, surprised.

"I didn't know she was coming too," said Ursula, surprised in turn.

"I only got her letter this morning. She said we could have lunch together."

"Snap."

"Oh, you're having lunch with her too," said Bernard, sounding disappointed.

351

"No, I'm having lunch with Emma," she said, laughing.

"Oh, that's all right then," he replied, bluntly.

"Bernard – that didn't sound very gallant," said Ursula with mock severity.

"Sorry, I meant, you know . . ." he said, looking uncomfortable.

"I'm teasing again Bernard. I wouldn't dream of spoiling your tête-à-tête. And I don't think for one minute you'd like to listen to all our chit chat."

"Righto."

"By the way, David got back and we've decided to move to Johannesburg."

"Johannesburg? And Emma off to England. And Jessie in Durban – oh, oh I'm sorry," said Bernard looking embarrassed, "I didn't mean to mention . . ."

"It's all right Bernard," interrupted Ursula quite calmly.

"I only meant, well, there'll only be me left here at this rate."

"No Bernard, Bunty will still be here. You better stick tight and make sure she doesn't get away."

"I'm not very good at that," he said diffidently.

"She likes you Bernard. You're kind and quiet – the opposite of her Papa – and Bunty is kind and jolly. You're very well suited."

"We met over the Union holiday, you know, and we got on like a house on fire," he said enthusiastically. "But I'm not sure how to make sure she stays keen on me."

"Just be your own sweet self, and let her make the arrangements – Bunty knows what she wants – and everything will take care of itself," replied Ursula with a reassuring smile.

"You make it all sound so easy, Ursula," said Bernard with admiration.

"It is when you let it – ah, here's the train – and Bernard, before you rush off . . ."

"Yes?"

"'If thou dost love, pronounce it faithfully'"

"Who said that?"

"A wise friend."

When they had packed their belongings, and sent their furniture to store, David took Ursula to the cemetery where they stood together – his arm around her waist – as she explained to Lulu.

David and Ursula travelled to Johannesburg in the luxury of a sleeping car, with room for Sukey to move around. Ursula had never been far from Cape Town since she had first arrived and her excitement at the journey, and what lay ahead for them, partly overcame her apprehension at leaving her home and Hannah behind. She had written one more time to the address in Kimberley where her brother had lived and mentioned the train she would be on; she would look out for him if he could be on the platform.

"This is strange, David, me passing through Kimberley after all these years."

"I suppose it must be."

"It's almost as if I am travelling back but, at the same time, going on," said Ursula philosophically.

"Yes, I suppose so," replied David, not sounding convinced.

"Kimberley will have changed considerably. I'm sure I won't like it. Of course if my brother did come . . ."

"You really mustn't expect anything," warned David.

"No, I know it's unlikely – he's probably living miles away by now. But Johannesburg, I hope I like that," she said, uncertainly.

"Of course you will – it's quite different from Kimberley – it's a busy, vibrant town," he replied confidently. "I told you, its growing all the time – mining wealth – you should see the enormous office buildings in the business district. It looks different every time I visit."

At the stations there was time for them to get out and stretch their legs and give Sukey a much needed run. But when they changed trains at Kimberley they had a little more time and Ursula and David covered the entire platform looking for any man who did not board the train; eventually however, Ursula had to give up hope. There had been no one waiting, no recognizable faces there. She was despondent for some time until she finally succumbed to one of David's jokes and responded to everything new he was pointing out to her. There was some spectacular scenery to be enjoyed from the train. The journey took them through beautiful country, from undulating hills to snow-capped mountain peaks, past thundering waterfalls and still rivers, dramatic canyons and the wide spaces of the lowveld and, eventually, on to the highveld with its silvery grass and forests of blue-gum trees. As they neared Johannesburg the gold mines became more frequent – tall shaft heads and smokestacks punctuated the skyline, miners' lodgings spread haphazardly on the barren ground. By the time they arrived in Park Station, Ursula was eager to disembark and see the town.

"We'll see what there is on the property front tomorrow," said David, as they booked into the North Western Hotel. "And I shall telephone the people I met in the racing business. But now, I'm taking you for a guided tour."

"Shall we walk? Sukey could do with it."

"Yes, if you like. You won't be able to in the summer; it's definitely only early morning or sundown you'd choose to be out in. But you'll need to keep your coat on today."

Although the winters could be bitter, the air at present was clear and cool. In the summer, Ursula was to learn, the scorching sun melted the tar on the metalled roads and wilted the inhabitants. Then the heat accounted for precise walks and protracted lunchtime naps – long cooling drinks and short tempers. Now, as they walked, the town seemed enormous to Ursula compared with Cape Town: monolithic buildings towered above her, electric lights illuminated every public place, pavements bordered every street. Black faces outnumbered white, automobiles outnumbered horses.

"It's so different David. I wonder if I'll ever get to know it," said Ursula, awed.

"When we have a house, then you will. Let's acquaint ourselves more intimately with some of it now," he said cheerfully, "we can either have tea in The Princess Tearoom or a drink at the Carlton Hotel, which shall it be?"

"Let's plump for the drink," replied Ursula, smiling. She knew which David wanted her to choose.

"Jolly good – we'll take a cab – when we get there shall I order you a whisky and soda? Good, I'll have the same. We'll drink a toast to our new start."

During the next few weeks David contacted all the people he had met on his visits to Johannesburg; through introductions he bought into a racehorse syndicate and made further enquiries regarding horse studs. Between times they searched for somewhere to live; they viewed large sandstone apartments, small detached houses; they looked in the centre of the town, they tried the new suburbs, they visited the outskirts. But finally, unexpectedly, they were introduced to a gentleman who was selling a newly-built house. On the edge of town, it was a solid two-storied construction that stood on one of the new avenues, the gate flanked by two karoo trees. The house had been designed for someone who was due to work for a mining company but now he was posted to England. He had insisted on high quality fittings and commissioned handsome hardwood features. The modest back garden was filled with neatly edged paths and beds, and a large acacia tree that would give welcome shade when it was in leaf. And there was a small room off the kitchen for Lizzie. Both Ursula and David were delighted with it and they put down a payment on the property.

Whilst they waited for their furniture to arrive Ursula visited the department stores. There was as yet no telephone connected to the house but it was fully wired for electricity. With this convenience in mind Ursula methodically purchased – encouraged by David – the latest labour-saving devices and appliances. A modern icebox, a sewing machine and an electric kettle were among her first choices. Then a complete suite of dining room furniture was reserved and a small wind-up gramophone taken immediately, so they could dance to gramophone records in their hotel room.

On the day they moved into the house – when Lizzie had made the beds and polished the furniture until it shone – Ursula and David inspected the ground floor rooms together. They were impressed with the shutters and high ceilings that would keep them cool in summer; with the well-designed fireplaces, to keep them warm in the cold highveld winters. Thrilled with the small architectural details and modern fixtures over which no expense had been spared – the silver-plated electric light fittings and servant bells, the fashionable design of the bronze window stays and handles – they examined them closely. And they were delighted with the ultimate luxury of a water closet downstairs, with its throne-like convenience and overhead cistern, shining copper piping and gleaming brass taps.

Ursula disappears upstairs and shortly, no longer able to contain her excitement, leans over the landing rail and calls down to

356

David whom she can hear explaining to Lizzie how to use the kettle, "David, save that for tomorrow. Come up here – I've something to show you."

She watches as he comes slowly up the stairs, polishing the banister with the palm of his hand, fingering the turned spindles that support it. "The workmanship here is excellent," he says, reaching the top.

"Yes, yes," says Ursula, gesticulating impatiently, "but, come on."

"What is it?"

"I want to show you which rooms will be which."

"Go ahead," he says good humouredly, putting his hands in his pockets, as if willing to be enlightened at length.

Ursula pushes a door open to reveal a dressing table – reflected in the mirror stands the small lead figure of Mr Rabbit in his little blue jacket – and a large, gleaming mahogany bed covered with a snowy white linen coverlet.

"This is ours – obviously – but here, this one . . ." she says, walking into the room next to it, empty except for a dressing chest.

"My dressing room?" asks David.

"No, I think it's wasted as a dressing room. After all, it's not essential to have such a large room for that. The teak screens in here are exquisite – even prettier than the ones in our room – and it has such a lovely view of the garden, and a hand basin . . ."

"What then?" he queries.

"Don't you think it would make the most perfect nursery?" she asks.

"Hold on a minute," he frowns and takes his hands from his pockets, "nursery?"

"Yes, nursery. Baby's nursery."

"Are you telling me . . . ?" he asks slowly, his eyes widening, a smile dawning.

Ursula beams at him and, nodding enthusiastically, claps her hands, "I am, David. I am!"

Life would begin again.

The nursery
Johannesburg, February 22nd, 1912

This was the day the Professor was due. Ursula had not slept but had dressed and crept into the nursery when David was sitting up with Edward. She slipped her hand into his and they sat watching over him, side-by-side, neither of them speaking. When the sun was finally up David squeezed her hand and rose.

They must be brave, they must take the Professor's advice. Meningitis was his specialty. It was their only hope now.

But she does not want the nurse there. Refuses.

Very well. He would send word to Mrs Van Der Ploeg. He would bathe and dress and send Lizzie up with a cup of tea and a slice of bread and butter for her.

My poor baby. My poor baby . But I won't give up on you. I know it will be all right. I'll say it over and over again. And it will be true. But I'll go mad if I sit here doing nothing till the Professor comes. I'll write to Nana; ask her to bring the little one here whatever happens; just to hear a little child's voice, her touch. And Emma, of course, and Bernard. And Jessie; I'll write to Jessie, I must be as forgiving to her as David was to me. Wipe the slate clean.

Ursula wrote her letters hunched over the small table that acted as her desk, every few minutes looking over at Edward and sighing. She wrote to Hannah as she had intended. She wrote to

Emma in Venice, and thanked her for the postcard from Paris, and asked when she and her new husband were due back in London. She scribbled a note to Bernard to enquire if he had proposed to Bunty on her eighteenth birthday as he said he would. And she wrote to Jessie – wording the letter with care – and was humble and generous in her forgiveness. When she had finished she left the letters on the landing chest and went into her bedroom. Swiftly collecting all of Edward's favourite playthings that she had rescued from the drawers where Mrs Van Der Ploeg had incarcerated them, she piled them now on the chair next to Edward's cot.

There we are my darling boy. Here's your rattle, your drum, and look – your furry monkey. And our best nursery rhyme book, the one with all the actions you love. Now we're all ready.

The bell rang and Ursula's heart began to beat a tattoo; the noise of her heartbeat filled her ears, it stopped her breath. Holding herself still she heard David tell Lizzie that he would get the door. She heard the Professor's voice, David questioning, the Professor reassuring. She heard them coming up the stairs.

"Ursula, Professor Michaels is here."

She must acknowledge him; try to be gracious.

Would she like to wait downstairs?

No. She would stay. She would not disturb him.

Ursula could not watch. She went over and opened one casement as wide as it would allow. She leant on the sill, leaning as far out of the window as she could so that she could not hear what they said, what they did. She did not care about the dust, ignored the insects. Nothing was important any more, except what happened in the room behind her. A storm cloud loomed – when the rain fell it would come in sheets, it would flatten the flowers, turn the garden to thick mud. But what did that matter. Everyday activities were still taking place below.

Joseph was tidying the beds in the still garden. Now Lizzie propped the wet floor mop to keep the fly-wire door of the kitchen open. She started to empty murky water from metal pails onto the plants. Sukey raced backwards and forwards at her heels. When Lizzie had finished she piled the pails on the doorstep to dry and, after exchanging a few words with Joseph, went indoors. Joseph continued with his task with the same slow deliberate action as if there had been no disturbance. Ursula shut her eyes tight.

How can such a momentous, such a terrifying event be taking place in this very room behind me, and still the world continues to turn – people following their routines, carrying on with their work – oblivious? And all this time the Professor doing horrible things to my baby.
Dare not look; must not speak. But I have to be near.

And, as she shut her ears to everything going on behind her, David's words came to mind: "the fearless and independent woman I married."

Is that what I've been to feed Edward against all advice?
Independent, yes, but of course I had to be, I'm the only mother he had . . . has . . . a mother's instinct dictated my actions; no one would listen to me, no one would help me.
And fearless – I don't know. I was so afraid of losing Edward, surely I was fearful – yes, I was certainly scared, really scared. How can anyone think it was easy to act against expert advice, to bear the responsibility alone.
But to have done nothing . . . to have waited for the worst to happen . . . I had to believe in myself . . . I had to take my courage in both hands to do what I could . . . I had to have faith . . .
I understand it a little better now, Mr Essop. And I have forgiven. But will I ever forgive myself if . . . And if I have done the wrong

thing will I be vilified when they learn the truth? Yes, I'm sure to be; blamed and damned.

But can it be wrong, so wrong, to want to save a little life, my darling baby, so passionately that the risk is worth taking; to hope against all odds . . .

Yes, yes, of course – there is still hope!

Please God, he's an innocent baby and his life's so precious.

Please God, please, make him better.

There's still time.

Ursula, Ursula, do you hear me? It's done. No, no, leave the window open now.

And Ursula knows. She moves and slowly opens the other casement too; as wide as it will allow, not bothering with the stay. Her conscious action spurred by unconscious thought: to set the spirits of the nursery free. She turns. The Professor is washing his hands in the basin. He wipes them on the fresh linen hand towel. David stands with his head bowed. Ursula walks over to the cot. Edward lies as still as before.

"Ursula, Professor Michaels is leaving."

Ursula leads the way downstairs in a dream-like trance. She cannot utter polite phrases as she waits for the Professor at the foot of the stairs but looks away from him towards the kitchen. Pink nails, brown fingers appear round the edge of the kitchen door, which opens stealthily. Ursula sees the edge of a black skirt, a bare foot; Lizzie is eavesdropping. She does not care. Through the fly-wire screen and the open back door of the kitchen, over the buckets piled on the step, Ursula can see the garden. Bright flowers cascade over the rims of their pots; the sight of them is meaningless, colourless. Even Sukey fast asleep on her bed, eyes screwed shut, a small sooty nose poking out, does not elicit any change in her countenance; she feels no affection, only emptiness. Ursula hears the Professor speak her name and turns towards him.

"I am so sorry Mrs Lewis . . . there was a slight chance . . . but it was only a slight chance."

Ursula walks with leaden feet to the front door and, opening it to speed his departure, bows her head and holds tight to it as the Professor passes through.

Can't look at him, can't speak to him.

David follows him to the front gate, where his carriage waits. Ursula watches through the crack of the door as she grips the edge of it. Her fingers shine white, pressing hard. Mentally she imagines it disintegrating between her fingers – her anger barely held in check. David turns, withdraws his handkerchief from his pocket, wipes his eyes. Replacing the handkerchief, shaking his head, he walks up the path.

Hurry up, hurry up David; if you don't come soon I'll break this door, smash this door . . .

David walks into the hallway and immediately Ursula steps backwards drawing the door fully back on its hinges and, with every force in her body, slams it shut. Like the crack of a coconut, the wood that holds the hinges splits; the big brass lock shudders, the small glass panes in their delicate lead bindings shake and rattle. Instantaneously the rear door of the kitchen slams with a sharp clap, the metal pails clatter noisily on the brick steps, and Sukey runs into the hall yapping and jumping up at David. David grasps the newel post of the stair in surprise and Ursula slumps to the ground with a distraught and terrifying cry.

Lizzie scurries out of the kitchen to retrieve the excited dog and David bends to help Ursula to her feet.

"David, David," she sobs, clasping the lapel of his jacket.

"Ursula."

"David, I can't . . ."

"Be quiet! . . . listen . . . what was that noise?"

"Noise?" asks Ursula, confused.

"It's like a cat crying . . . listen."

"A cat?"

"Listen . . . there it is again," said David as he moves to the foot of the stairs, straining to hear.

Ursula stares at him.

"Just like the cry of a Siamese cat," he says, with disbelief in his voice.

Ursula remembers the cry of a Siamese cat and what it reminded her of.

"It is!" she answers, incredulous.

And, as David turns and starts up the stairs three steps at a time, Ursula gathers her skirt above her knees – and pulling hard on the blackwood banister to help her – follows him as fast as she can.

Glossary

Ag frequent guttural exclamation often expressing exasperation

Is it? Really? Is that so?

just now in a little while, later

kleintjie little one

nou nou immediately, right away

rather sentence adverb used as equivalent of 'instead'

shame exclamation of sympathy or warmth towards something endearing

Notes and terminology

Boer: an Afrikaner or early Dutch inhabitant of the Cape. The Dutch settled at the Cape in 1652 and the British captured it in 1795. The second Anglo-Boer War 1899–1902 is sometimes referred to as the South African War. The peace led to the Union of South Africa in May 1910 which united the four colonies – Cape Colony, Orange Free State, Natal and Transvaal – as one country.

Hottentot and Bushman: early settler terms for members of the Khoikhoi and San tribes respectively. These indigenous herders and hunters of the Western Cape became known as Khoisan, as is their language, although the term Bushman has survived.

Malay: a term that referred to those inhabitants of the Western Cape, mainly of Indonesian extraction, speaking Afrikaans or English.

Acknowledgements

I should like to thank those who have encouraged, helped and supported me. However, ultimate thanks must go to my parents who answered all my requests for family stories over the years (some true, others apocryphal); none of us suspecting at the time that these might one day inspire a novel.

Many publications, as well as contemporaneous materials, were used when researching the background for this novel. However, for specific botanical, cultural, historical and social facts a number of books proved particularly useful. They include:

A Cape Childhood, Norah Henshilwood (David Philip Publishers, Cape Town, 1972)

Afrikanderisms (Longmans, Green & Co, London, 1913)

Curtain Up, The Story of the Cape Theatre, Olga Racster (Juta & Co, Ltd, CT & J'burg, 1951)

Etiquette for Women (C. Arthur Pearson Ltd, London, 1902)

Illustrated History of South Africa (Readers Digest Assoc. of South Africa (Pty.) Ltd, 1988)

South African Shrubs & Trees, U. Van der Spuy (Hugh Kaertland Publishers, Johannesburg, 1971)

Southern Africa since 1800, Donald Denoon (Longman, 1972)

The British in Africa, R. Lewis & Y. Foy (Weidenfield & Nicolson, 1971)

The Story of Theatre in South Africa, Gill Fletcher (Vlaeberg Publishers, Cape Town, 1994)

Victorian Buildings in South Africa, D. Picton-Seymour (A.A. Balkema, Cape Town, 1977)

Wild Flowers of the Cape, A. Handel Hamer (Maskew Miller, Ltd, Standard Press, CT, circa 1930)